mental notes

Elle Ann Brown

This is a work of fiction. Names, characters, corporations, institutions, organizations, events, or locales in the novel are either the product of the author's imagination, or real used fictitiously. The resemblance of any character to actual persons, living or dead, is entirely coincidental.

No part of this publication may be produced, stored in a retrieval system, or transmitted in any form or by any means, electronic, mechanical, photocopying, recording, or otherwise, without the permission of the publisher. All rights reserved.
Published by Brown Creative LLC

Cover design: joshandrewbrown.com
Author Photo: Hargrove Studios

ISBN: 978-1981304110

Copyright © 2018 Elle Ann Brown

to S.M. Smith
- for opening my
 eyes to a whole
 other world!

I still remember the first time I saw him. Forever ingrained in my memory, it plays like a movie in my mind as soon as I walk into a coffee shop. The smell, so strong and promising, triggers the start button. Every. Time. The brain is truly astounding, powerful enough to attach those mental movie reels to a simple smell. I've replayed that day so many times, every detail, every moment, that if the memory were an actual old-timey film strip, I'd fear it close to wearing out. It was the day that changed the course of my life as I knew it.

~ 1 ~

I walked into Kristoph's Coffees, the small, locally-owned coffee shop in town, on Thursday evening. The glorious aroma assaulted my senses, but I didn't mind—it was one of my favorite smells in the whole world. I came for the open mic night but was mostly looking forward to some downtime. My co-worker was a mutual friend of the girl playing her acoustic guitar and singing tonight. She was inviting everyone she knew, even the cashier at the grocery store.

The female musician who didn't appear too far from my age was still setting everything up when I walked in. I didn't really know what to expect, but this girl just looked like any of the other people sitting in the coffee house. Nice, pleasant, friendly, stylish. She looked up and smiled at me, coming off a bit nervous before returning to unwinding her cables and getting everything set up just right.

I made my way over to the short line and pondered what to order. I'd never been affected much by caffeine at night, so I wasn't worried about drinking coffee after eight p.m. Still, nothing sounded particularly tasty at the moment.

"What can I get started for you this evening?" the overly friendly male barista asked, snapping me out of my glossed over stare at the menu board.

"Oh, um, sorry. I was having a hard time deciding. I guess I'll just have a caramel dulcé, please." A total creature of habit, I don't even know why I looked at the menu board as if I'd order anything other than my usual, but that was just what you were supposed to do while you stood in line at a coffee shop. *Right?*

After the awkward interaction with the barista, I scanned the room for a table. A few people were sitting in groups, but there were also a couple of people sitting alone at big tables. I hoped they were saving the seats for friends because I always hated it when you had a big group and couldn't find a table due to someone sitting alone at a large table. *Why do they do that? Ugh!* Were they trying to draw attention to the fact that they were all alone? I, on the other hand, liked to blend in. Only I wasn't doing such a good job at blending in thus far and hoped more people who didn't appear to own stock in Instagram would show up soon.

Not sure if my co-worker would want to sit with me or if she was coming with someone else, I made my way to an empty two-top table. Trying to escape from my negative train of thought, which I had to do often these days, I began aimlessly looking through my phone since the musician still hadn't started.

I scrolled through Twitter until I noticed a post I had already seen, then closed that out and went over to Facebook to see what other people were up to tonight. Again, I hit things I recognized and closed the app out as well. Checking to see what other people were doing via social media was what I could be found doing most nights since I didn't have much of a life of my own.

As I switched to my calendar app to check what I had in the next few days—work-related only, of course—the overly friendly barista called my name.

"Maddison, your caramel dulcé is ready at the bar."

I headed to the counter, leaving my things at the table so no one would take my seat since the room was filling up, beyond ready to partake in the marvelous drink. My week hadn't been an easy one at work, and with just a few sips, I could start unwinding.

"Maddison?"

I turned around to find an old friend I hadn't seen in ages at the table just in front of the bar, almost spilling the latte.

"Ethan! Oh my goodness, how are you?"

No doubt, my face revealed honest shock because I wasn't always great at controlling my facial expressions. Make that never.

He rose from his seat and walked toward me, arms open for a hug. Someone was sitting with him, but they kept their back to me, so I didn't pay much attention. "I'm doing great, what about you?" he asked over my shoulder as we embraced. "Look at you. You haven't changed a bit! I mean, what has it been, two years?"

"Thanks. Has it really been that long? The last time would've been that spring break trip the old gang took together, right? Wow, it was two years ago. Crazy. Have you kept up with anyone?"

We had a pretty large and fun group of friends back in college. You know the ones that get way too loud laughing through the night in a restaurant until the other patrons start complaining. Life slowly started pulling us apart as some went to grad school out of state, some got married, and others began their full-time jobs that all those years of college were supposed to prepare us for. That's why we took a trip to celebrate our last spring break together before everyone started going in different directions. It registered then I hadn't talked to anyone from the gang since graduation.

Wow, how sad. How did I go from that lively group to the loner table? Oh yeah—

"Only Billy," Ethan said, interrupting my thought like I should've known better before asking.

"Oh, of course. You two were joined at the hip. What's Billy up to now?"

"Still in grad school. He's basically a professional student. He wants to become a college math professor. Nerd," he huffed.

"That sounds about right from what I remember. And what about you? What are you up to?" The smile on my face had to be huge, and not the slightest bit fake. I had been so caught up in the day-to-day, cross-it-off-the-calendar mode that I forgot just how much I needed days of hanging out and laughing with friends through life.

"I'm still working for my dad. He's pretty much grooming me to take over in the next few years so he can play golf twice a week," he said sarcastically, confirming he hadn't changed a bit. "He still wants to make guitars, I doubt that'll ever go away, but he needs a stress outlet."

Ethan's dad started a business back when we were still in high school, repairing any and every kind of stringed instrument in our small town. He was good at it too. Eventually, he became a luthier and moved to the metroplex to open a shop. He made the most beautiful guitars. People came from all over the state to have a one hundred percent custom-made guitar by the one and only Simon Wilson.

Ethan wasn't much of a musician himself, not without many failed attempts by his father to teach him. Still, he worked for Simon, keeping everyone on schedule. His primary role was keeping track of the books. Simon was a complete musician, down to the artsy right brain that left the business side of the business, well, a mess. Thankfully, Ethan was all left brain with logic and numbers to keep his dad in line. Ethan was already working for his dad while getting his Business Management degree. He was so lucky to already have a job secured before graduating, unlike me.

"But I guess that's the nature of a family run business. We've hired some guys to help with the actual building, so really, my day-to-day won't change much. I couldn't do what they do, even if I wanted to."

I couldn't tell if he was happy or sad about having a more significant role in the company by his tone, so I didn't know how to respond. When looking down out of insecurity, I realized I hadn't even taken one sip of my latte yet.

"What about you, Maddy? What keeps you busy these days?" he asked as I tried to keep my eyes from rolling into the back of my head at the savory goodness of my drink.

Mid-swallow, I chuckled and wiped my mouth before attempting to answer him. "I took a position at an advertising agency because I got tired of sitting on a degree that wasn't bringing in a career. The job has grown on me, but I'm not sure how long I'll stay there career-wise. My co-worker is actually the one that invited me tonight, but she hasn't made it yet. She knows this musician chick." I pointed over at the young artist who still hadn't begun.

"Really? She knows Stacy? Small world!"

"Oh, you know her too?" So that was her name. Stacy.

I glanced up as Stacy was getting situated on her stool and noticed the SW on the headstock of her acoustic guitar. All of a sudden, my brain started firing on all cylinders.

"Yes, I do. You could call her my girlfriend," he bragged as he winked at me. "She was a frequent visitor to the shop, and I finally got the nerve to ask her out several months ago."

"Good for you, Ethan. I'm glad working for your dad paid off somehow," I said, reaching out and jabbing his stomach like I always used to. Only it didn't feel right. Even though I'd done that hundreds of times when we were younger, I regretted it the second I made contact.

"What about you? Are you in a relationship these days?"

Touchy subject. Which he should've known. I dated one of the guys in our group, Garrett, off and on over the years. We were the only couple, making it awkward at times. As time passed, we were more off than on until it fizzled altogether. Looking back now, I wondered why I wasted so much time trying to make our relationship work. Being with Garrett wouldn't have been so hard if it was meant to be, only I didn't realize that when it would've been more helpful because I kept believing the lie that he was *the one*.

"Nope. Just me and my betta, Sea-bass." I started willing him in my mind not to press any further. *Drop it, Ethan. Move along.*

It was then that the other person sitting with him turned around and cleared his throat.

"Oh man, sorry. Where are my manners? Maddison, this is my friend Aaron."

He was the most beautiful man I'd ever seen. I felt everything around me stop as I looked at him. His smile was radiant over his perfect teeth. His light brown hair was reflecting the overhead lights, complementing his shining eyes. He was dressed perfectly for a night at the coffee shop with a gray beanie hanging off his head, hiding exactly how long his hair was, a plaid button-up shirt with dark blue jeans, and brown laced boots. I honestly wasn't sure if I had a type in the past, but at that very moment, *this* was it.

"He works for my dad. I guess you could call him the protégé. He helped build that guitar," Ethan said, pointing over to Stacy, who was finally testing her mic. Of course, he built her guitar. This perfect man made that perfect guitar—both exquisite to the fine details. My mind went blank for a minute. I stood there and hadn't acknowledged the fact that I was now supposed to say something or do something to reciprocate the introduction.

Naturally, I was a hugger, but since Aaron was still sitting down, I wasn't sure what to do and prayed my brain would kick into auto-pilot while I tried to come out of the haze. But it didn't.

That's when I curtsied.

I began returning from the fog just in time to hear Aaron chuckle at me, greeting him like royalty.

"Well, I'm not that important," he said, his laugh lingering, "but thank you for the honor."

How in the world was I supposed to play that off? *Thanks a lot, brain. When did I become so awkward?*

"Anyone with such an impressive skill as Simon Wilson deserves as much," I said with copious amounts of wit and sarcasm, hoping I wouldn't have to run back to my table and wait for my co-worker in shame.

When Ethan laughed, I knew I'd managed to not make a complete fool of myself with my winning comeback.

"It's nice to meet you, Aaron. I bet working with Simon and Ethan is an entertaining job." *I have got to make this guy see that I'm not a complete nut.*

"Oh, it keeps the laughs coming, that's for sure. Simon is usually trying to explain to Ethan how and why he's doing what he is doing, stressing why he needs more expensive parts. Ethan typically stares back at him completely oblivious to the difference, reminding his father how important the new budget is. I just enjoy working on guitars. Can't imagine doing anything else. So if putting up with the Wilsons is part of the job, then it's just a sacrifice I'll have to make."

I was pretty sure he was exaggerating, trying to poke fun at Ethan. His personality was hard to read, so I let out an awkward chuckle and took another drink from my latte. "I bet it's more entertaining than it sounds." *What?! Why did I say that?* How rude did that sound? Why couldn't I just be normal right now? "I mean, I bet it's very interesting." *Lame recovery Maddison, you need to just back away.*

"Anyway," Ethan said, changing the subject from him and his dad being total opposites, "we're here to support Stacy. She's still kind of new to these open mic nights, but she is really good."

"That's great. I can't recall how my co-worker knows her, but Vicki wouldn't stop talking about tonight for days until I agreed to come. I realized it'd been a while since I had something to do other than work or binge Netflix, so I probably needed to take the invite and crawl out of my cave."

Cave? Really Maddison? Do you want this beautiful man to think you're a recluse, workaholic monster with no social life? What are you doing? Get it together.

"I can't believe Vicki isn't here yet, actually." *And she really needs to hurry up and get here because I'm making a complete fool of myself and don't know how to get out of this conversation.* I didn't say that out loud, although it was deafening in my head. "Isn't she about to start?"

Reaching for my back pocket to check the time on my phone, I realized I'd left it at the table. "Oh, my stuff is over at the table. I should probably go back over there before it goes missing. Vicki has probably sent a text or tried to call me. It was so good to see you, Ethan, and it was very nice meeting you, Aaron."

I quickly walked back to my table before the conversation could continue, undoubtedly looking like the hunchback of Notre Dame. That had to be one of *the* worst first impressions I'd ever made. And I'd made a ton.

I picked up my phone like I was checking, and then answering a text from my co-worker, but all I was really doing was fumbling around and trying not to look like an even bigger weirdo than I already let on. I didn't dare look up and see if the guys were looking my way or laughing at my awkwardness, so I kept pretending like my phone was being used for phone-like reasons.

"Thank you all for coming out tonight. My name is Stacy Jenson, and I have a few songs I wanted to play for everyone, a few originals, and a few covers. I hope you enjoy them." The slightest bit of nerves were still audible in her voice.

I was optimistic the music was exactly what I needed to get my focus off of all that had transpired over the last several minutes.

She started playing a song I hadn't heard since I was a teenager as I took another sip of my latte and instantly felt the tension in my Quasimodo shoulder dissipate. My older brother swore I owed him for my excellent taste in music. I listened to a good portion of his favorites for years after they were considered new.

I adored this song, especially the simple guitar picking part currently resounding in the small coffee shop. I started looking around again to see if Vicki was indeed there. Some people watched Stacy with smiles on their faces, swaying back and forth, or tapping their hand along to the rhythm. Others who probably didn't even realize they were coming to the coffee place on open mic night continued along with conversations, click-clacking on their laptops, or nose deep in novels.

Kristoph's was a place where people could come together or stay isolated, and both seem to be accepted. In fact, I felt both of those social statuses warring inside of me. *Which group did I fit into now?* Surely my old group of loud friends would've driven book-boy over there crazy, no doubt he was reading some kind of sci-fi.

After a full scan of just about every person in the place, there was still no sign of Vicki. I looked down and placed my hands around the paper cup and hummed along with Stacy. I couldn't remember the name of the song or all the words—which I was commonly guilty of—but pieces of the tune began to come back to me.

When she got to the chorus, everything rushed back to me like muscle memory. "You Were Meant For Me" by, what was her name? Jewel. How many times had I sung this song as a teenager? A dozen times after each breakup, at least.

She really did have a phenomenal voice. I saw her grinning in Ethan's direction as she sang the last few lines of the song—which was technically a love song though it was full of sad, post-breakup emotions—and looked back at the guys for the first time after heading back to my table. Ethan was sitting there with the proudest, most goofy, little-boy-with-a-crush smile I'd ever seen on his face, and it made me so happy for him. Ethan was a great guy who deserved a great girl. The thoughts running through my head caused a smile of my own to sprawl across my face, although I was almost positive it wasn't as huge or cheesy as Ethan's.

In mid-thought, my eyes panned over just the slightest to Aaron, and I realized he was looking at me. When our eyes locked, he smiled at me, smiling at Ethan, smiling because of Stacy. At least that's why I thought he was smiling. Still not fully recovered from the embarrassment I put myself through, I looked back down at my table despite his friendly face.

As Stacy finished the song, some people clapped, while others snapped—fitting to the scene. Then there were the few that still sat there pretending like she wasn't even playing exceptionally great live music. Not that I wasn't appreciative, but I gave a small clap while looking down, too afraid to look up again and catch a glance from Aaron.

"What was that?" Vicki asked, pulling my eyes up.

"What was what?" I was a little lost and asked for clarity.

"I was standing by the door and saw a goofy grin on your face, followed by a mortified look. Then you clammed up and stared at your drink like it was all that was connecting you to the earth."

Oh man, was it really that bad? "Great, that's the icing on the cake."

"Rough night, huh?"

"You could say that. I ran into an old friend who just so happens to be Stacy's boyfriend and friend slash co-worker to Mr. Dreamy over there." I gave my head a slight nod in the direction of their table, hoping she'd catch the subtleness of the situation.

"Which one?" She was half standing, not possessing a single nonchalant bone in her body.

"Well, this just keeps getting better," I mumbled.

"I'm sorry," she said, sitting back down. "It's Mr. Gray Beanie, isn't it?"

"That would be him. And to say I torpedoed the first impression would be an understatement."

"I'm sure it wasn't as bad as you think."

"I curtsied. *Then,* I made it sound like he had the most boring and lame job in the world. I went on to make it seem like I had absolutely no social life, and people should be hunting me down with pitchforks. There was no recovering. I was praying you would walk in and rescue me. Why are you so late, anyway?"

"Traffic. There was an accident on thirty-five. Honestly, I kind of wish I would've been here to see Miss Professional List Maker have a moment where she actually went off the script."

"Really?!" I poked her arm. Lists were the only thing that helped me learn at work—or function in life for that matter. Design and computer programs came from a totally different world than I grew up in.

Another song had started, but it was most likely an original because I didn't recognize it.

"You were right; she is good. I'm mostly glad I came," I whispered.

"You're welcome. Sorry I left you out to swim with the sharks, but I'm sure you're overreacting."

I looked at her with the most sarcastic face I could manage and flailed around like I experienced a shark attack, losing part of my arm. She laughed, a bit too loud, drawing some unwanted attention our way, and away from Stacy.

Oops.

We continued to talk between songs for the rest of the night, and I snuck out while the guys went to help Stacy teardown, so I didn't have the opportunity to embarrass myself any farther. I *was* mostly glad that I came, and maybe one day I would look back on this and laugh.

No, probably not. Worst first impression, ever.

~ 2 ~

Thankfully the next day was Friday, and I only had a few ads to finish before the weekend—I helped manage the magazine ads for our company. All I had left for the day was a going-out-of-business sale ad for the local sporting goods store and another for a Christian dating website. I'd like to say I had a natural eye for design and balance even though my degree was a major in Counseling with a minor in Psychology. After barely over a year of working in the industry, I saw improvement in my skill. Mark a win for the arts electives I chose, which made me feel like some of my schooling was actually being utilized.

Creating an ad for Freeman's Sports Emporium going out of business made me sad. I was never the overly sporty type, but it reminded me of the place back home we frequented growing up—Al's Locker. Both of my older brothers played whatever sport was in season all through school, which led to me knowing the layout of the store like the back of my hand.

I became quite the cheerleader, from the stands only, missing less than a handful of games throughout their overlapping school years. My oldest brother was five years older than me, so we never attended high school at the same time, but my middle brother was a junior when I was a freshman. I enjoyed being "Christopher's younger sister" around campus. The fact that most upperclassmen didn't know my real name didn't bother me much.

But other than cheering on my brothers, I wasn't into the school spirit thing much. I was more involved in theater. Barely.

I wasn't like a major theater geek or anything, but we had to pick an elective, and that seemed like the easiest one for me to slide through gracefully with a passing grade. It made some priceless memories. And that was where I first met Ethan; he needed an elective too, he said, but he was a natural. We mostly hung out in the back and never auditioned for anything that required something extra of us until our senior year when he finally auditioned for the lead role and surprised us all. I think he secretly loved the theatrics.

Then we both came to the metroplex for college. Being the only other familiar face around campus, on top of growing up in a small town, we stayed close through most of college and eventually became part of the larger group of friends.

Focus. Back on track, Maddison.

I typed out "Everything Must Go" followed by a large "70% OFF" in the center of the ad. My mind slowly started to wander again as I chose my font and graphic to complete the ad. I looked over at the time, wondering how much longer until I was free to live on my couch for forty-eight hours in a baggy T-shirt and yoga pants. Three forty-five. *I can make it*. Finishing the sports store ad didn't take much longer once I focused. I submitted my design for approval and closed it out before opening a new blank template for the last task of the day.

ChristiansConnecting.org wanted to run a spring ad. I typed out according to their request, "Don't spend another Valentine's Day alone! Try 3 months free, and you could find your mate by summer."

That easy, huh?

I'd never really thought about joining a dating website, but they seemed to be getting more and more popular, and increasingly accepted. I could still remember not too long ago when people were embarrassed to say they "met" someone online, but it was almost the norm nowadays. I heard someone in the lunchroom say there was even an app version on the phone that he used.

Maybe I should create a profile for myself. It sure would be nice to have a "mate by summer." I did fit the criteria: single and Christian. Well, I was raised Christian, and I still believed all of it, but it had been entirely too long since I went to church. It seemed that adulthood had made me a couch potato on Sundays. I needed to get better about that.

Mental Note: *Go to church.*

I filed that sticky note in the back of my mind, along with the thought of creating a dating profile, and honed in on the job at hand. Spring meant bright colors and symbols of newness. *Hmm, what graphic would best fit here. Birds? Butterflies? Flowers?* Perhaps those were all a bit too feminine.

I decided on a cherry blossom tree and zoomed in, showing only a part of the tree with crisp detail of several bright, newly blossomed pink flowers with a washed-out blue sky background. Pleased with my progress, I placed the words just right and made sure there was an even balance to the design. I stared at my screen for a minute, tipping my head to the left and then to the right making sure I loved it and not just liked it. I decided I loved it.

Getting lost in the image for a minute, I pictured myself under a beautiful cherry blossom tree, leaning against the trunk, gazing up at the thousands of delicate flowers. I felt something on my hand, which caused me to look back down and realize I wasn't alone. Our hands were interlaced, and my heart was full of glee. Who was the handsome man next to me, perhaps the new beau I met on the dating website? As my eyes scrolled up, I saw the perfect teeth of none other than Aaron, and as quickly as my daydream began, it was over with a shake of my head. *Where did that come from?*

"Mind already on the weekend?" Vicki asked as she walked past my desk.

"Huh? Oh, no. Just got distracted for a minute. Back to work," I responded, embarrassed.

"Any plans for this evening?"

"Yep. Pretty sure my couch missed me last night, and I need to make it up to him. I'll probably end up picking up some Chinese takeout on the way home and watch the gushiest chick-flick I can find on Netflix. It's going to be a fabulous evening. You?"

"Nothing, really. I promised my mom I'd come by sometime this weekend, though. Haven't seen her in a few weeks."

Sparked by her words, I made a mental note to call my mother, trying to remember the last time we spoke. When it didn't come to mind, I knew it had been way longer than I should've allowed and added two exclamation points to the mental reminder.

"That should be fun. I need to do the same, but my mom is a couple of hours away. I've probably been spending too much time alone in my apartment in recent months. Made evident last night as I acted like a complete weirdo in front of Mr. Gray Beanie."

"You are still hung up on that? Seriously, you need to stop beating yourself up over last night!"

"Probably so, but I can't seem to stop playing it over in my mind like a horrible video loop. Anyway, seeing Ethan made me realize I've let my friendships take a backseat to work life. Just because I'm a full-time working adult these days doesn't mean I shouldn't still be having ridiculous laughter sessions and enjoying life with friends."

"I couldn't agree more and wouldn't mind being one of those friends you laugh with outside of the office."

I'd known Vicki pretty much the entire time I worked for our company. She started a year or so before me and gave me the rundown of who to avoid, who to impress, and exactly how the unspoken lunchroom rules worked. This was my first real job post-college after trying a few temp agency placements, which were mostly disasters. I didn't want to mess it up over something trivial, so I was extremely thankful for her in the early days. As the months passed, our relationship developed naturally and easily. But when I thought about it, the open mic night was the first time we hung out outside of the office. Not that we never talked about our personal lives on the clock, because we did to some extent, that was just the first time it didn't occur from eight to five. I really needed to make more effort to build some genuine friendships.

"Deal."

Exactly what I need, and it just fell into my lap.

I glanced at the clock again and realized it was almost time to leave. Returning to my screen, I saw I hadn't saved or submitted my last ad of the day—hopefully, Jerry liked my work. Our boss was sending back way fewer ads for revision than he did in the beginning, further proof I was improving my skills.

A few clicks later, I was shutting everything down for the weekend. I put my laptop into my leather bag and made sure I wasn't leaving anything I'd need over the weekend. I had a bad habit of leaving my cell phone charger behind at both the apartment and the office. Not that my phone was buzzing with notifications anyway. But I definitely didn't want to forget anything at the office all weekend and be unable to retrieve it. I should probably buy a backup charger to keep on my desk.

"You out?" Vicki asked from her desk, still working.

"Yes, ma'am. My couch awaits."

"All right. Maybe we can get together and laugh this weekend."

"I'd like that! I'll text you." I only had her number because we swapped digits months back in case one of us was running late for work. I'd probably text her less than three complete sentences since, but it was something I planned on doing more since we were growing closer.

While walking out of the office, I tried to leave work back on my desk. Sometimes my brain didn't shut work mode down like I asked it to. Especially in the beginning when I was still getting the hang of the advertising design world. I watched tutorial videos online until all hours of the night and my entire weekends off, trying to better my skill. Actually, just trying to figure it all out period. I put on a front that I knew what was going on, but inside my head, I was screaming. Thus the hundreds of notes that caused Vicki to think I was organized.

I made a few commitments to myself as I navigated the parking lot. *Don't think about work this weekend. Hang out with Vicki. And laugh.* I got into my car and flung my bag onto the passenger seat, feeling quite positive this was going to be a good weekend.

If there was anything I needed to make sure and balance in my diet—well, two things—it would be carbs and sugar. Those items together made for many good weekends over the past year. I wouldn't say I could become a vegetarian though because I loved burgers, like *loved* them, but there sure wasn't meat in every meal I ate.

I pulled up to the drive-thru where I was a recognized patron. As usual, the speaker was way too loud, but once again, I forgot to leave my window mostly up to shield my poor ears. One would think as often as I ordered there, I would've remembered by now. I reassured myself that once I was home eating my delicious lo mein noodles, curled up on my couch, my ears would no longer be ringing.

I ate out more than I probably should. I never really enjoyed cooking much, and making a meal for one felt depressing, but I was spending way more of my paycheck on food than I needed to. The idea to get on my

PinBoard if I wasn't too tired after my movie and search for "Easy Recipes for One" seemed wise.

Mental Note: *Eat at home more.*

I was quite positive if one could actually see inside my brain, it would be a collection of different colored sticky notes reminding me of all the things I wanted or intended to do, which would probably be overwhelming to most people. The signs didn't always get taken down either. Sometimes new notes of the same colored genre got placed on top of the old ones, and it would take a considerable amount of brainpower to remember just what all I had put up there. That was why I made some reminders on a physical calendar, so things of highest importance didn't get lost in my mind's genuine intention.

The woman at the window passed me the white bag containing my dinner with a smile. "I put extra cookie for you. Two fortune better than one."

"Thank you." The cookies I would eat. The fortune I didn't put any stock in.

My car instantly filled with the fabulous fragrance of saucy noodles and veggies. Well, you couldn't actually smell the veggies. You didn't even taste them really, but it made me feel better they were in there, and I was at least eating *some* vegetables. The drive home seemed faster than usual as I tried to sort through the rainbow of most recent sticky notes in my brain.

It was safe to say that my post work home routine was down packed. Before I even realized it, I was on my couch in my favorite yoga pants, my old youth group shirt that thankfully still fit after years of carbs—a top wasn't really comfortable until it was adequately aged, anyway—a messy bun, the remote in my hand, and my food in my lap. I already inhaled two bites before I came out of auto-pilot long enough to pick a movie. I pondered the commitment I made to myself for the weekend and decided to forgo the initial plan of a chick-flick and pick a comedy.

As I opened the menu for comedies, I passed several titles that were too old or obviously a never-heard-of, straight-to-tv movie. I landed on *Clueless* and felt a nostalgic pull back to my pre-teen years, maybe thanks to my shirt. I started the movie and continued to devour my noodles.

I quoted countless lines along with the tv, remembering how I acted out this movie with my two best girlfriends growing up. I never wanted to

Mental Notes

be Dionne because she had a little too much going on with Murray, and I didn't want to be Tai because she cussed too much—and we *had* to recite the entire movie. I usually wanted to be Cher even though she was the main character, but I didn't really convey her either because I wasn't a fashionista or the center of attention. I almost always ended up as Tai and left out the curse words—my mother might've died otherwise. If there was a fourth friend, I was confident it would've been someone like me. Well, maybe. I never fit into any easily described label and was always a bit of a floater that could find something in common with almost anyone.

I shoved too much food into my mouth but managed to catch the falling noodles in the takeout box. A perk of living alone: no one could watch how sloppy I ate. I blamed my brothers. I looked around for a napkin but hadn't brought one with me, a common occurrence, and set my food down on the coffee table to get one from the kitchen. The melody for a text message rang out from the living room just louder than the movie. The notification was most likely Vicki—wondering if we were going to hang out—but I hurried anyway.

Wrong. I didn't recognize the number, and the text simply said:
Maddison??

Not too sure I wanted to answer, I reluctantly responded
Yes??
and anxiously waited for the reply. *Who had my number without me having theirs saved into my phone?* I instantly regretted replying and had the worst case, scary movie scenario in my brain.

Mental Note: *Watch less scary movies.*

I stared at my phone like it was going to come alive, and after what seemed like an eternity, a new text popped up.
Hey, it's Ethan. I wasn't sure if
you still had the same number!

Oh, thank God. *See brain, nothing scary.*

Hey! Yup, Same number. I don't have
this number for you, though.

Sorry. I got a new number a while
back and never gave it to you,
 apparently.
I'm so glad I ran into you last night.

> *Me too. It made me realize I haven't been getting out enough.*

Well the reason I was texting you was to make sure I still had the correct number and also to make sure you were okay if I gave your number out.
Aaron was asking for it.

My mouth hung open as I read the text. Like jaw to the floor. I re-read the text. Then a third time: Aaron was asking for my number.

Ethan already knew me pretty well. He was my closest guy friend—friend period—before I became an anti-social adult, so there was no need to pretend.

> *Are you kidding me right now?! I made a complete fool of myself last night. Does he want my number to have a personal jester?*

Haha. Stop. He asked me a few questions about you after you went back to your table. Then today at work, if I had your number or a way of getting back in contact with you. I figured I'd try your number before Facebook.

I was pretty sure the room was spinning.

> *Uh, yeah you can give him my number.*

That's all I had.

Okay. Let's get together soon. I'd love for you to get to know Stacy.

> *Sounds great.*

I lost all interest in the movie with my mind racing as if in a marathon.
He wants my number.

Feeling hopeful, I opened my two fortune cookies. *"The fortune you seek is in another cookie."* What in the world? Did I get one from the sarcastic bag or something? I didn't have much hope for the second one

after that. These things were a joke anyway. *"Love, because it's the only true adventure."* Boy did I know that, with twists and turns and heartbreak.
No thanks.
But that was obviously the still wounded Maddison talking.

~ 3 ~

In typical guy fashion, the whole weekend passed, and Aaron never messaged me. Perhaps it wasn't for anything personal. Maybe he wanted to run an ad or something, so he was waiting until Monday. Or maybe Ethan hadn't even given him my number yet. Their conversation was probably way less detailed than the four or five scenarios I played out in my mind, typical guy fashion. Guys seemed to lead less complicated lives. Not fair. Or maybe us women made it harder on ourselves than need be. *Life is hard,* I thought as I let out a sigh.

When Vicki passed by my desk, it registered I hadn't fulfilled all of my commitments to myself this weekend. I was able to not think about work thanks to the text I read over and over while waiting for a new text from a number I didn't have saved in my phone. Also, I laughed before my mind was off of the movie. And I definitely laughed when I decided to make a profile on Christians Connecting to have something to do while killing time, hoping to chat via text message with a certain cute boy. But I didn't hang out with Vicki. I gave my best intentionally-forced smile and said, "Sorry I didn't text you this weekend. I got a little distracted."

The smile on her face communicated I was still good. However, I needed to be careful not to make a pattern of this, or I might not only lose an off-the-clock friend, but I'd also lose the only friendship I had at work as well.

"It's okay. I ended up spending most of the weekend with my family. What had you so distracted?"

"Oh, you know. Just a text from my friend Ethan asking if he could give my number to Mr. Gray Beanie because Mr. Gray Beanie asked for it." I spoke nonchalantly while looking at my computer screen before turning for a peep to see her expression.

Her eyes were bulging with surprise, and her smile grew to her eyes. "See! I told you your first impression wasn't as bad as you thought. What'd he say?"

"Nothing. He hasn't text me yet." I tried not to let annoyance appear on my face but was unsuccessful.

"Oh."

"So I spent the rest of the weekend at my apartment awaiting a text that never came while keeping my schedule open by surfing PinBoard and making a profile on Christians Connecting." I was somewhat embarrassed to admit that last part, so I threw in, "It was the last ad I did on Friday. I still had work on the brain. They were offering three months free."

"Oh, did you now?" she asked, amused. "That could keep us laughing for a while. Maybe I should make one too." So she considers herself to fit into those categories as well. Something I hadn't known before.

I was glad she didn't make me feel any more awkward than I already did for making the profile. "You totally should. I've laughed quite a bit already."

"Good. I think it's great you're putting yourself out there. And don't worry about Mr. Gray Beanie. His loss if he doesn't text you," she said as she made her way to her desk.

"Thanks." Vicki gave me way more credit than I probably deserved. "I wondered earlier if he might've wanted my number for work-related things, and that's why he didn't message me during the weekend. I'm trying pretty hard not to think about it, but you know me."

Did she know me? Had I opened up enough to her during our short work conversations to have the right to say that?

Mental Note: *Stop being so guarded and get closer to Vicki.* The sticky note was purple, my favorite color. All of the most important notes were purple.

"Oh, for sure."

So she did think she knew me well enough to agree. Maybe our relationship wasn't as shallow as I thought.

"Just go into work mode like you do," *wow, she really does know me,* "and I'm sure he'll text you soon. Again, if he doesn't, his loss."

I managed to nail out four ads before noon as I put the pedal to the metal, trying not to think about Mr. Gray Beanie. Aaron. I probably needed to stop referring to him with Vicki's nickname before it stuck. Knowing my luck, I'd most likely embarrass myself by calling him that to his face.

Mondays always contained a heavier workload than any other day because of all the requests we received over the weekend were waiting for us. Thanks to a full inbox, the second half of the day went even faster, and my day was already wrapping up. I was planning on trying one of the new recipes I pinned over the weekend, but I didn't have it in me to go to the store and cook since I accidentally skipped lunch. All of that helped me decide to grab something on the way home. Maybe I'd go to the store tomorrow. I knew my routine: more takeout, more Netflix.

I was on the couch, eating my dinner in record time and decided to watch some cooking shows to possibly spark my interest in trying the new recipes I recently acquired. While searching, I found a show called *Kid Vs Chef* and thought it would be entertaining to see what kind of food kids would make. *PB&J,* I huffed to myself. I thought the show would make me feel better about my lack of knowledge and spirit of adventure in the kitchen. Wrong. Those kids were using terms I didn't know and making foods I'd never even tried, let alone heard of—chalk one up to the kids.

I was pretty sure I could feel myself leaning over the edge and falling into a pity party, so I picked up my phone to text Vicki.

Still no text from Mr. Gray Beanie.
Unsuccessfully not thinking about it.

I put my phone back down and decided to watch something else that wouldn't make me feel like I was failing at life. Maybe I needed to watch that documentary about fast food to further motivate myself to eat at home more. *Nah. Don't need that negativity in my life.*

My phone chimed. I was pretty sure it was Vicki telling me "his loss" again, so I didn't give much thought to what else it could be when I saw it wasn't a reply from Vicki. A tiny "1" was on the top left corner of my phone.

OMG! Just got a text!

What did he say?

I don't know I just got the notification
I'm afraid to check.

Oh stop. Check it already. I don't want a reply for at least five mins! GO!

I stared at my phone for a minute before realizing how silly I was acting, looking at a notification bubble that might not even be from Aaron. I pushed on the blue number and saw the new text was from a number I didn't know. I closed my eyes before reading anything and then opened them again. *Okay, Maddison, this is a bit dramatic.* Thankfully no one was watching me.

Hey there, it's Aaron. Ethan gave me your number. I hope that's okay.

Stay calm. Stay calm. I waited just a few more seconds before starting my reply. I didn't want him to think I had absolutely nothing else going on, although it was absolutely true. I mentally sang my ABCs—because that was what I always did when I was timing something—and started typing.

Hey, Aaron, the guy from the coffee house, right?

Click click click click sounded as I erased the text. I didn't want Aaron to think I didn't remember him.

Oh! Hey, Aaron, you mean I didn't scare you off?

Click click click click. That was even worse.

Hey Aaron.

My reply was short, so I quickly added:

How are you?

I'm good, thanks for asking. How about you?

Doing great. Just finished dinner, busy day at work.

You had a case of the Mondays too, huh? Ethan and Simon had some intense conversations about the most recent order Simon made that was over budget.

Haha, I can imagine. I'm not sure I'd be able to work around that constantly.

Just part of it. I usually put in my earbuds and drowned them out.

Smart.

I felt like our chat was going pretty well, but with that one-word reply, I was afraid he was going to think I wasn't interested or was being short. While thinking of something else to type, he responded.

Anyway, I wanted to invite you back to Kristoph's on Thursday. I'm playing this week for open mic night.

Of course, he was. Why would he make guitars if he couldn't play one? That wasn't perfect enough. I bet he was phenomenal.

Oh, awesome. I'd love to go. I really enjoyed it last week. Stacy was great.

Yes, she is. Cool. I'll see you then!

I'll be there!

I flipped back over to Vicki's text, checked and rechecked I was on the right text feed before typing:

OMG OMG OMG!

What happened?

He invited me to the coffee house this week because he is playing at the open mic night! Ugh... why does it have to be so far away!

That is awesome! I told you he would text you.

Well I guess I need to start listening to you a bit more often!

Agreed! Would you like a wingman on Thursday?

Of course. I didn't do so good on my own the first go-around.

* * * *

Mental Notes

After work the next day, I went to the store and got enough groceries for the four different meals I pinned over the weekend. Unfortunately, I was too tired to try a recipe after going to the store, so I ordered a pizza. I could probably eat pizza every day and never get tired of it. At least I accomplished step one, and the food was at my house now. Next meal, I'd be able to eat something from my kitchen. Hopefully.

Wednesday was a bit slower, but I finally cooked. Me, cooking. I felt like a real adult. Not that it took much talent to make crockpot chicken tacos. I set the slow cooker up before work and came home to a house that smelled delicious. Still, I was quite proud of myself, and it tasted as good as it smelled — one point for me.

I spent the rest of the evening trying on almost everything in my closet, knowing I was probably overthinking. Aaron had already seen me in an outfit I hadn't put much thought into. However, this time around, I had hours and insecurities eating away at me.

I was about ready to give up and tackle the mountain of clothes on my bed when I decided on an outfit that pretty much perfectly explained me as a whole. Slightly plain, but not dull. Never the most popular girl in high school, but people knew who I was. I didn't get lost in the crowd, but I wasn't the leader of any packs.

As I looked in my floor-length mirror, I began overanalyzing my reflection. My long, aged-penny colored hair was getting a bit straggly.

Mental Note: *Make an appointment with Lily for a trim.*

And I'd have to put on more makeup tomorrow than I did today because setting up that crockpot took more of my morning than I planned for. I called this the "simple look" with just the basic makeup covering my flaws and accentuating my good areas. Tomorrow, I planned to do the "total look" that added a few more layers of makeup, and a higher level of blending was required.

I should probably do the total look more often, but I just didn't like spending that much time getting ready every day. I was pretty happy with my black v-neck and floral kimono I settled on and was glad I went with my size six jeans. I could squeeze into some size fours, but it showed off my muffin top I let get too big.

Mental Note: *More water, less sugar.*

The note was pink like all the others I needed to do but probably wouldn't actually accomplish.

I had on one gold flat and one short black boot with a bit of a heel and stood there in flamingo pose switching from my right to left foot trying to decide which look I liked better. Considering that I'd most likely be sitting the majority of the night, I went with the boots.

The outfit was a pretty cute look for me and made me wonder if I should start putting more effort into my appearance. I wasn't ashamed to be somewhat of a "Plain Jane," but I felt better about myself when I put more effort into my image.

Now to take tomorrow's outfit off, get comfortable, and put back almost my entire wardrobe that was now Mt. Everest on my bed. Before I changed, I remembered to take a mirror selfie to send to Vicki for some reassurance. There was no way I'd risk wearing this to work because I would inevitably spill something on it at lunch and wouldn't have enough time to pick something else to wear.

As I put everything away on the correct hanger and in the proper place in the closet, my mind started drifting. I realized the last date I could remember was with Garrett. The super awkward final date where we came to a mutual agreement: no matter what feelings might arise in the future, we needed to end our relationship. We were never "on again." I wanted him to be my future husband so bad, I convinced myself it would be different every time we were back on. Honestly, I never even knew what I was doing for it to be off in the first place—at the time, at least. *Forget the past, Maddison. Nothing good lives there.*

I wasn't really sure if tomorrow night was considered a date, though. Technically, Vicki invited me to do the same thing last week, and that was not a date, so I scaled my brain back as not to put any false hopes in the evening.

Returning to my phone on my bed, I saw that Vicki had replied with two thumbs up.

Thanks! I'm excited and just a bit nervous.

We are gonna have a good night! See you tomorrow.

I wasn't wound down enough for bed, so I went back out to the kitchen to do some cleaning and planning for tomorrow's dinner. Unsure of how much time I'd have between rush hour traffic on my way home and getting to the coffee house by eight, I decided another crockpot meal would be best. I really liked the simplicity of coming home and dinner being ready anyway. Not to mention, it didn't take much talent to throw everything in and set a timer. Cooking this way might just be the ease into working in my kitchen and eating at home that I needed. All of a sudden, I was super thankful for the crockpot my grandma got me for my house—well apartment—warming present. It only took me a few years to use the appliance.

With the kitchen cleaned and the ingredients for cheesy chicken and rice neatly lined up on the counter—sans the chicken, of course—I didn't have anything else to stay up for. Even though it was earlier than my usual bedtime, I retired to my bedroom. All the work in the kitchen helped me to tire out. I was so excited for tomorrow, and the only thing that would bring it faster was sleep. When I completed my pre-sleep routine of brushing my teeth and moisturizing, I crawled into bed with the last bit of energy I had. Before I knew it, as usual, I was no longer praying but dreaming.

~ 4 ~

As I feared, I tossed and turned all night, too excited for the open mic night. Thankfully, excitement took over when my alarm went off, and I jumped out of bed elated to get the day rolling. My eyes were darker than their normal hazel glow. I added extra concealer and decided to hurry with my morning routine so I'd have enough time to get a double-shot latte on the way to work. Knowing I'd consume more caffeine tonight made me question if three shots of espresso in one day was good for me? *Eh, I'll be fine*.

I threw everything into the crockpot and made it out the door with enough time to get my latte and arrive at work three minutes early. Today was going to be a great day; I could feel it. Like a scene from a movie, I got out of my car with "I Gotta Feeling" by The Black Eyed Peas playing in my mind. I didn't realize I was singing along out loud as I walked to my desk, and of course, Vicki heard me.

"Yeah, it is!" If it was possible, she seemed even more excited than me.

"What?"

"A good night. You were singing again."

I often sang or hummed without even realizing it, but I never intended to do so around an audience.

"Oh my gosh, how embarrassing. I *hope* it will be a good night."

All I had to do was get through the next few hours of work without being too distracted, go home to eat dinner and change, and then the moment I'd been waiting four days for would finally happen.

Mental Notes

The ad for the dating site I submitted Friday was back on my to-do-pile for the day. The notes requested some spacing and font adjustments, so thankfully, it didn't need to be overhauled. I laughed as I worked on the ad, thinking about how I made a profile out of pure boredom and would probably never log in again.

My job was growing on me, even though it had nothing to do with what I went to school for. Add me to the ever-expanding list of people who weren't working in their degree field. I even started noticing how some aspects of psychology made sense in the advertising realm as well. Like balance and proportion and emphasis. At least relating them in my mind made me feel better about the hard-earned knowledge I wasn't using. Some days my job felt like busywork to pay the bills—like today—but I was glad to hustle through my stack and be on my way.

"So, are we just meeting there?" I asked Vicki as I passed her desk at the end of the day, all of my things in tow.

"Yes. I'm not quite finished yet, and I don't want to make you late. I'll text you when I'm on my way." Vicki did go to school for graphic design, easily the best employee here. I was genuinely grateful for all she did to help me hone my skill.

"Okay, I'll see you soon." I shook my keys like a pom-pom, pretty sure it was obvious how excited I was—even to a stranger.

"You're too cute. Remember: have fun tonight. Don't put any fake pressure on yourself."

"Right. Fun. No pressure. Okay, bye."

I didn't want to feel rushed because that always left me in a frazzled state, and I started doing strange things when frazzled. My mission was to remain cool, calm, and collected, so I reminded myself, "Fun, no pressure." Also afraid the butterflies fluttering around inside my stomach would force my dinner back up, I decided not to eat too much and saved the rest for lunches. This new meal plan would save me tons of money if I ate at home for dinner *and* had leftovers for lunch.

Not wanting to risk getting dirty moments before leaving, I made sure to clean my dinner mess before changing clothes. But even after eating, cleaning, and changing, I was ready earlier than I expected. I looked up a few more slow cooker recipes, stalling to not arrive at the coffee shop too early. My recent routine was growing on me. I added chili, lasagna soup, and sesame chicken to my board.

Remembering the meal I ate contained a heavy dose of garlic, I brushed my teeth to freshen my breath, rechecked my makeup, and grabbed my favorite lip gloss to take with me. With no other ways to stall left, I sat on the corner of my couch and drummed my fingers on the end table.

After growing tired of sitting there waiting, I sprung from the couch, swiped my keys off the bar, and bound down the stairs, not caring if it wasn't time to leave.

On the way there, I repeated my "fun, no pressure" mantra until I felt confident and in control of my nerves. I arrived five minutes early but figured that wasn't early enough to show that I had been eagerly awaiting this for days, though I had. I sent a quick text to Vicki, letting her know I arrived and reminded her to let me know when she was on her way, then ran my clammy hands down the front of my jeans before heading in.

When I walked into the coffee shop—after my senses processed the glory—I realized nowhere near as many people filled the space as last week. The emptiness caused me to notice things I hadn't seen last time, like the large world map on the wall full of pins indicating where the coffee in this shop came from. I'd heard something about this place being a non-profit, but I didn't know much other than that. A huge corkboard overflowed with business cards and flyers for upcoming local events. I decided to check that out later. With new, healthier patterns in my life, being home alone less was another thing I should develop. I never realized how amazing this place was since I usually only saw it from the drive-thru window.

"Hey, Maddison." There he was. He looked even better than I remembered. And tall. In all the times I replayed the night we met, I forgot he never stood up.

"Hey, Aaron. You all ready for tonight?"

"Almost. I just have a few more cords to run."

"I don't really know much about that, but I'm a quick learner if you need help."

He chuckled. "It's fine, but thanks. I'll remember for next time, though." *Next time, huh?* Sounded promising.

"Is Ethan coming? And, oh man, remind me her na—"

"Stacy." He didn't let me finish. "They said they were, but he just text me a few minutes ago letting me know traffic was bad. I guess that's why this place is so empty. An accident—"

"On thirty-five." This time I didn't let him finished.

"Yeah." We both laughed. "Thirty-five is the worst," he said. When wasn't there an accident on I-thirty-five?

"Okay. Well, I'll go order a drink then since you don't need my mad helping skills."

"Oh, just go tell the barista your name, and he'll get it started. I already ordered for you. A caramel dulcé, right? Unless you want something different, then let him know."

"How did you know my order?" I was kind of in shock for a second and had to fight the urge to let my mouth hang open.

"Last week. 'Maddison, your caramel dulcé is ready at the bar,'" he repeated the overly friendly barista in a rather impressive impersonation.

"Wow, that's a pretty good memory you have." *And I am pretty blown away with you right now!*

"Why thank you," he said, as he curtsied.

"Too good." I laughed, trying not to let my cheeks turn red. "Okay, finish up. I don't want you to be running behind on my account."

I couldn't believe what was happening as I walked over to the bar and let them know I was Maddison and indeed wanted the drink Aaron ordered for me, then pulled out my phone to let Vicki in on the night's events thus far.

> *OMG!*
> *He remembered what I drank last week*
> *and already ordered my drink for me.*
> *I got a feeling....*

Yes!!! I love it. It IS gonna be a good night. I should be there by about 8:20, but it seems like you are doing just fine on your own.

I didn't want to be on my phone all night, so I put it in my back pocket and walked over to the map on the wall while waiting for my drink. I read the poster explaining how this shop bought coffee directly from farmers who ran orphanages in all the pinned locations on the map. I felt even better about almost single-handedly keeping this place in business for a few years. Maybe that was a bit of a stretch, but the small-town-girl still alive and well inside locked me in as a customer over the larger coffee chain in town. And this newfound information further sealed the deal. I scanned over the sweet, innocent faces of the children in the photos and felt good about contributing to their lives simply by being a loyal patron. When I turned back around, my eyes locked with Aaron's. He just so happened to be smiling as he watched me.

"Maddison, your caramel dulcé is ready at the bar." With our gaze locked, he motioned for me like a butler to retrieve my drink. I thanked the young barista, which wasn't the overly friendly guy from last week, and found a table closest to the small stage set up for nights like this.

"Thank you for my drink." I raised my cup to Aaron as I sat down.

"You're quite welcome." He climbed onto the stool, dwarfing it in size, and spoke into the microphone. "It appears that no one wanted to come tonight or everyone is running behind, but I'm going to go ahead and get started. My name is Aaron Walker, and I am the entertainment for the evening."

Yeah, you are!

"Feel free to sing along, or you can simply listen. Either way, I hope you enjoy it."

Oh, I'm going to enjoy it!

He started by playing a song I didn't recognize, even better than I imagined. Aaron played with such eloquence and ease, I felt confident he'd played for a long time. I couldn't help but be intrigued by this man sitting in front of me.

As I listened to him play the song without words, I found myself looking over his features. He wasn't wearing a beanie tonight, so I could see his glowing light brown hair was longer on the top with a faint wavy texture that laid down on the side of his closely trimmed head. I couldn't tell what color his eyes were, but they were light—lighter than mine. I resolved they were blue. He had some stubble on his jawline, but it was pretty blonde. If he hadn't been sitting under the stage lights, I probably wouldn't even have noticed. He wore a deep red v-neck and a gray hoodie with jeans, but I was pretty sure those were the same boots he had on last week. He looked amazing and very much in his element.

I must've been analyzing him for a while because people started clapping. The noise pulled me back to paying attention to what Aaron was doing and not just taking in his comely appearance. Under the warmth of the stage lights, he pushed up the sleeves on his hoodie between songs. That's when I noticed a portion of a tattoo on his right inner forearm. I tried to make it out, but couldn't tell how much more of the tattoo was covered up.

He started playing another song, but abruptly stopped and leaned into the mic.

"I consider myself more of a musician than a singer, so bear with me on this next one." When he embarked on the same song, it sounded familiar, but nothing registered in my head. By the time he got to the middle of the song, I'd figured it out.

It was "The Time of Your Life" by that grunge band my brother liked, but something about Aaron's rendition was different.

"It's called 'Good Riddance,' Maddy," Hank, my oldest brother, corrected me.

"But that sounds mean. I'll call it what I want."

The flashback made me homesick, but only for a fraction of a moment because he was never particularly kind to me—for lack of better words. I blamed the five-year age gap.

The song was a lot slower than I remembered, granted it had been close to a decade since I heard it ring out hundreds of times from my brother's bedroom when we both still lived at home. The last time I listened to the tune was probably when it played at the end of my brother's graduation. Hank was quite convincing with the ladies back then and practically rigged the vote so his favorite song would win the slot of the final anthem. He had his persuasive ways, just not with me.

I liked the arrangement Aaron played even more than the original.

Most of my drink remained in the cup, so I took a big sip before the whole thing turned cold. Just as my hand lowered back to the table, Vicki slipped into the open seat beside me.

"Wow, he is good." She spoke softly.

"Yes, he is. Easy on the eyes *and* the ears." We giggled like a couple of school girls.

"Sorry, I'm so late. I had to finish up at work while I was in the zone." Vicki swore her work was exponentially better when she was able to get into one of her zones. I'd never experienced such creativity, so I thought she was exaggerating. *No wait, exaggerating was probably more accurate at describing me.*

"It's fine. I'm actually kinda glad I was able to have a few minutes with Aaron earlier. I mean...." I lifted the coffee cup and gave her an elated grin.

"So sweet. I couldn't be more excited for you."

"I know, me too, but I'm trying not to get ahead of myself. I don't want to get my hopes up just to be let down again." She gave me a bit of a puzzled look. "Ugh, long story. Another day." Her glance was further proof I needed to continue opening up to Vicki, even with the painful parts of my history.

I looked back up at Aaron just in case he glanced my way, I didn't want him to think I wasn't paying attention. He played another song I didn't recognize, and I figured maybe he wrote it or changed it up from the original again.

Out of the corner of my eye, I saw Ethan and Stacy sitting down a couple of tables over. Ethan saw me looking and waved.

The night continued with me in awe of Aaron and noticing more and more about him as he had my full attention. Like how he moved his mouth when he held out the longer notes, or the gorgeous guitar he most likely made.

"Thank you all for coming out." Aaron waved and stood up from his stool. Everyone clapped, but I wasn't ready for the night to be over. I waited at my table just a minute because I wasn't foolish enough to think I was the only person he invited tonight. Ethan and Stacy made their way up to the stage. The guys did a one-hand-clap-handshake-pull-into-a-hug thing guys do sometimes, followed by Stacy getting up on her tiptoes to hug him. So I didn't imagine it. He was tall.

"Aren't you going to go up there?" Vicki questioned me with her eyebrows raised.

"I'm waiting for just a minute. I don't want to be one of those annoying groupies who ask him to sign my forehead."

"Oh my gosh, you're something else. I'm gonna get, I'm beat. See you tomorrow."

"Sure thing. Thanks for coming."

"Hopefully you'll have something to share with me, and if it's really good, you better text me tonight."

"Deal." I stood up to hug her and used the transition to head toward the others fangirling over Aaron.

"So what did you think, Maddy? Just okay, right?" Ethan was heavy on the mockery.

"Yeah, I'd say somewhere in between average and mediocre." I joined in on the obvious sarcasm.

"Wow." Aaron looked down and pulled his hand through his hair, and I knew I needed to reassure him in case he couldn't tell I was only playing along with Ethan.

"No really, I was very impressed. You were great, Aaron."

"Thank you."

"Of course, he was." Stacy defended her fellow musician while issuing a hairy eyeball at her boyfriend.

"I appreciate you all coming. I'll take you up on that fast learner offer, Maddison, if you don't mind hanging around a little longer to help me tear down."

"Oh, sure." I turned to throw my empty cup away to free my hands and get the cheesy grin off my face.

"We can help too." Ethan offered himself and Stacy—who actually knew the gear.

"It's okay. Maddison and I got it." Aaron denied the other's help.

I thought I saw Aaron nudge his head to Ethan like he was trying to spend some time with me but pretended I didn't notice.

"Sure, we'll see you guys soon then." Ethan replied in an I-catch-your-drift manner.

I waved to the couple as they left and realized I still didn't officially meet Stacy since I was kind of distracted by Mr. Gray Beanie—well, hoodie tonight.

"First things first," Aaron turned to me with a long black cord in his hand, "you always want to gently roll the cord into a loop and not just wrap it around your elbow like a rope."

"Gentle loop. Got it." Only my cord was not cooperating for me the way his did.

He made it look so easy and chuckled as he grabbed a second cord to roll up next to me in demonstration.

"Slide for slack, then loop."

I could watch him roll cords and be just as entertained as when he performed.

"Got it. I'll be the best cord roller in no time."

He headed back and grabbed his guitar from the stand.

"Did you make that one yourself?"

"No, this one was my dad's. It's my favorite because his big hands wore it in just right." He noted as he ran his hand across the neck of the guitar.

Briefly, I wondered if I would ever meet his dad. "I can see how that makes it even more special." I commented after learning his story as a smile illuminated my face.

"That's a good look for you."

"What look?"

"When you were looking at the map earlier, and again just now. Your smile is dazzling when you don't realize you are doing it."

"Oh, thank you." I looked down because I was pretty sure my cheeks were redder than his shirt. When I built up the courage to look back up, he pushed his stretched out hoodie sleeves even higher than before, and I could see more of his tattoo.

I walked back toward him with my one cord I rolled while he managed to do three, and ran my finger across his arm without even thinking about it —our first physical contact. Why did my brain continually betray me?

Nervous about how he would respond, I blurted out, "What does this mean?" In my closer view, I made out his tattoo was some sort of symbol or roman numerals.

"That," he paused, "is my reminder."

"Ah. And what does it remind you of?"

"That I'm just an ordinary guy with flaws like everyone else. That I can't let my pride or dreams make me think I am somebody I am not. That there is more to this life than just me."

How do I respond now?

Failing to come up with a decent reply, all that escaped my lips was a breathy, "Oh."

I was fascinated by his answer and how humbly he told me but equally sure there was a longer story that went along with it. I hoped one day he would trust me with the full narrative.

He closed his guitar case and put the rest of the cords in his well-aged backpack before slinging it over his shoulder and grabbing his guitar.

"Thanks for staying to help." He broke the silence with his warm voice.

I felt a smile spread all the way to my eyes. "My pleasure. My current goal is to try new things to bring some positive change to my routine. So technically, *you* helped me. Now I can add another achievement to my branching out list—roadie."

He grinned as he glanced toward the door, packed up and ready to leave.

Disappointed the night was coming to an end, I leaned back down and grabbed my purse from the table. We walked in hesitant silence, and even though he only had one free hand, he surprised me by stepping ahead to open the door for me.

What a gentleman.

The night was beautiful with spring on the cusp of coming to life, with only a small chill in the air, causing me to shiver.

"I guess I should've brought a thicker cover."

"Let's get you to your car. Which one are you?"

Though I couldn't really see since darkness settled in, I pointed in the direction of where I parked. "The black Nissan." We walked toward my car, him with his massive guitar case in his left hand, and me with my arms wrapped tightly around my chest. A few steps later, I eased my grip in order to retrieve the keys from my purse.

As I was digging, we both started talking at the same time.

"Go ahead." I gushed with a laugh.

"Do you have anything going on this weekend?"

Please be asking me on a date. "Not yet."

"Maybe we can do something on Saturday night?"

Yes! "I'd like that."

"Great. I'll text you later then. Goodnight, Maddison." He leaned in and hugged me, but only with the one arm not holding his instrument.

I got on my tiptoes and delighted in our embrace—and our plans for this weekend.

"Goodnight, Aaron."

I drove home with a massive smile on my face that wasn't going anywhere.

~ 5 ~

This was my first weekend to have plans, any plans, let alone with a hot guy in I can't even remember how long. Aaron sent me a text on Friday to solidify our Saturday schedule. We decided on the Movie Lounge because they offered dinner and a movie, then agreed on the new comedy, even though I reassured him I liked action films. He offered to pick me up, but I suggested we meet there because I wasn't sure I was ready for him to see my place yet. I knew I liked him, but my apartment was my bubble. My escape.

When the time came, I arrived early once again, too eager to wait around at my apartment.

Let me know when you get here.
I'll be looking for you in the lobby.

Elated he was early too, I wanted to get inside with him as soon as possible.

About to head in.

I checked my makeup one more time in the visor mirror and added another layer of lip gloss. Not that I needed more, the habit was my M.O. Never really a lipstick person, I had enough lip glosses to consider an official collection. With a fresh coat of shiny confidence, I flipped the visor back up and made sure I had everything I might need in my purse—debit card, keys, backup gloss.

When I got out of the vehicle, I examined my somewhat distorted reflection in the side of my car. Tonight I went with a long, maroon shirt and my black tights—the type that were acceptable as pants— complemented by my brown rider boots, my most worn pair of shoes from

November to March. With a deep breath and a flip of my hair, I made my way toward the theater.

I saw him as soon as the door opened. He smiled and waved, already holding the movie tickets.

He leaned in for a hug. "You look very nice tonight." His words made me feel like a giddy little girl, although I tried to remain composed.

"Thank you, so do you."

He was wearing that iconic gray beanie again. In the brightly lit lobby, I could now see that his eyes were undeniably blue. He paired his black v-neck with some simple but well-fit, jeans, and a new-looking pair of Vans. V-necks were a good look for him. An astounding look for him.

I needed to clear my head before my face gave me away, as it always did.

"We can head to our seats now and order some food if you are ready."

"Sounds good."

As Aaron showed our tickets at the check-in barrier, I continued to check him out subtly. *Man, he is good-looking*. The attendant pointed us to theater nine on the right in a full monotone demeanor.

Our seats were the type with a small table for every two chairs, causing me to suddenly get really nervous to eat in front of him. Since junior high, eating in front of a boy I liked was an issue for me. All thanks to Patrick Lewis, who embarrassed me in front of the entire seventh-grade class for having nacho cheese smeared on my chin. Crush over. I healed as the years passed, but I still felt a fraction self-conscious around food and boys simultaneously

I looked over the menu to figure out the least awkward—and messy—thing to eat and wasn't confident in any of my options. "What are you going to get?" I asked Aaron to try and see if that could help me make a decision.

"I'm thinking a burger sounds like it will hit the spot. You?"

"I love burgers, but that's what I usually order, so I'm just making sure nothing else jumps out." Not to mention, burgers could get sloppy and sometimes un-ladylike to eat. I could ask for plasticware and eat my burger by cutting it into little bite-sized squares, but that would be far more than misleading of my traits on our first date. "However, I do love fries just as much if not more than burgers, and if there is bacon involved?" My taste buds salivated. "Yup, I'm getting the burger."

He laughed. "Sounds like you have good taste."

I looked at him in all of his splendor and replied, "I agree. How has your weekend been so far?"

"Very relaxing, which I needed. In fact, this is the only thing on my calendar." He waved his hands over our shared table. "I took the weekend off."

"Oh, I didn't realize you worked weekends for Simon."

"I don't. I play guitar at my church. I'm up there most weeks but have the week off."

"That's awesome."

"Yeah?" His tone was full of surprise.

"Yeah. I was involved in church as a teenager. I sang with the youth worship team."

"Really?"

"Yep. I sang in theater and choir too, all through high school." I chuckled, remembering the awkward years.

"Well then, I'm going to need to hear this voice of yours."

"Deal, but some other time," I spoke over the booming speakers, saved by the waiter who came to take our order just as the previews started.

Aaron ordered for both of us. I gave a giddy grin when he looked at me to confirm my portion was correct.

"So you aren't involved now?" He picked our conversation back up despite the running previews, but I had trouble recalling.

"I'm sorry?"

"In church? You said in youth, do you not participate anymore?"

"No, but it's on my to-do list. Once I moved away for college, I tried a few churches but never settled on one I liked. Before I knew it, months had passed, and I hadn't gone at all. Then I threw myself into a job I knew nothing about, along with some other issues." *Issues* was a gross understatement of the downward spiral of my life, but I wasn't going to give up all that information and scare him away this early on. "And I just never went back. Unfortunately, I created a routine I'm in the process of changing.

"I've kinda made my apartment a bubble. I'm sure I've spent more time there alone than I should. Pretty much from Friday at six p.m. to Monday at eight a.m."

Before I spilled too much and ruined our chances at a second date—if I hadn't already—I decided to stop prior to admitting something I would regret. "Anyways, maybe I need to go next week when you are playing again. Groupie in tow." I gave a wink as I pretended to roll a cord in the air.

"I'd like that. Although I hope you aren't just coming for me."

"No, I promise. It's been on my mind lately. I already made a commitment to myself before this conversation."

"Okay. Good."

As the next preview started, I let it be a natural transition to end our conversation. Being in such close proximity to him, even though we weren't talking, was amazing. I could smell the spicy scent of his cologne—a new fragrance to me—and once again couldn't believe I was really on a date with this striking man. This handsome musician. This drop-dead gorgeous Christian musician. It was as if God put a bow on him and said, "Here you go."

Thank you.

I wasn't extremely old-fashioned, but I'd made mistakes in previous relationships. Clingy would've been an appropriate definition and a harsh lesson learned. Tonight, I was going to let Aaron make all the moves, although it would be a lot nicer watching this movie with my arm linked in his and my head on his shoulder.

We'd get there, hopefully. I reminded myself to stay in the moment and not rush things again as I'd done in most—all—of my previous relationships.

Take it slow, Maddison.

My last lame relationship, if you could call it that, was the first guy after the saga that was Garrett and Maddison. I'd mentally closed the college-life chapter and wanted to jump into the find-a-husband chapter—though I always somehow skipped ahead to the find-a-husband chapter. I thought the guy was as into me as I was him, but when I started bringing up conversations about the future, he split. I'd planned so many things in my mind it was almost like a death occurred, forcing me to grieve through the loss of a future I already outlined. It took me way too long to

Mental Notes

understand just because a guy asked me on *a* date, did not mean he would ask me to marry him.

So this time, I would sit back, enjoy every moment of each day, and not worry too much about what might or might not happen in the future. Or at least try really hard to.

Aaron laughed, and I realized the movie already started while I was lost in my head, for who knows how long. He must've sensed me looking and glanced at me, so I smiled because I didn't want him to think I had no sense of humor even though I didn't know what he was laughing at. I think I pulled it off.

Our waiter came in clutch again with our food, taking the attention off of me. We thanked him and dove into the hearty spread in front of us. Mercifully, I wasn't as nervous to eat in front of Aaron thanks to the dark theater, and the fact we were paying more attention to the flick. Well, he was. I mostly watched him.

We continued to laugh through the film, only I knew what I was laughing at most of the time. The movie ended sooner than I was ready to stop having Aaron so close to me, but I was pretty confident we'd have another date. If nothing else, I planned on going to his church next weekend. Hopefully, I wouldn't be considered a stalker if he didn't think our time together went as well as I did.

"Good movie," I said as the credits started rolling.

"Agreed." He took one last sip of his drink and stood up. "Shall we?" He offered his hand to help me stand.

I gladly took it but wasn't sure if he would let go right away and tried to keep cool on the outside as my insides were jumping with excitement.

"Are you a dessert person?" he asked, still not dropping my hand.

"I most definitely am."

"I saw an ice cream place across the parking lot. Would you like to walk over there and get some?"

"It would be the only thing that could make this night even better."

The movie theater was a part of a vast shopping and entertainment district I frequented many times, so I confident I knew which place we were headed to. We still walked hand-in-hand as we exited the theater and started down the sidewalk. I gave a shiver as the breeze hit me.

"Is it too cold for ice cream?" he asked.

"Never."

He laughed and switched his grip so that our fingers were now interlaced. I was beside myself as the simple movement of his hand made my heart beat faster.

The walk wasn't far at all, and we made it into the ice cream shop quickly. The bells hanging on the door jingled and clanked as Aaron opened it with his free hand, then rang out again as the door closed behind us.

We were in one of those self-serve, add-as-many-toppings-as you-want and pay-by-the-ounce places. I could eat an insane amount of ice cream, but I wasn't about to show off that skill on a first date.

He dropped my hand and passed me an empty cup, then grabbed one for himself. "What is your vice?"

"This one." I walked over to the cheesecake sign and pulled the handle down, filling my cup in swirling perfection. "I usually go for chocolate in most desserts, but I love this cheesecake with fresh strawberries. You?"

"Oooh, that sounds good. I usually get chocolate and top it with the cookie dough bites or peanut butter cups. Or both."

"I love that combo too. Peanut butter cups. Why don't you get that and we can share. Uh, if you want. I'm not a germaphobe." I didn't know if suggesting to share ice cream was a good idea. Feeling my cheeks redden, I wished I hadn't.

"Great idea." He gave me a satisfied grin, and I was relieved he didn't freak out.

We leisurely filled our cups with toppings before heading to the scale at the register. I reached for my wallet, wanting to pay for the ice cream since he paid for the dinner and the movie, but he wasn't having it.

"Put that away. This was my idea."

"I don't mind."

"Neither do I," he said as he swiped his card before I could protest any farther.

I wasn't sure which emotion in me was the strongest: feeling bad at the fact he probably dropped close to a hundred dollars on our first date or allowing myself to be swept off my feet by a guy willing to do so for me. With both thought clouds looming in my head, I decided to be positive for a change. *Wow, he wants to do this. I finally found a winner.*

But there I was again, jumping to conclusions. Old habits die hard.

I shook my head ever so slightly to erase any future plans of me in a wedding dress from forming as we made our way to the sleek white leather sofa in the back corner.

"Thank you for the ice cream. And the burger. And the movie." I ate a scoop of my dessert with a fresh strawberry slice on top. "Mmmmm. This is the best," I said with the cold bite still in my mouth, then chuckled.

"You're welcome. I'm glad we did this. Thank you for being my date tonight." He smiled before taking a bite from his bowl. I hadn't called it a date out loud yet, not wanting to freak him out, but I was sure over the moon when he did.

"Anytime." I smiled and offered my bowl for him to get a bite. "Make sure you get a strawberry, it doesn't taste nearly as good without it." He took a scoop from my cup, then offered me his.

"Mmm, that is good," he said.

"I'm telling you, it's the strawberries that make it."

After a few more bites, he was done with his dessert and placed his empty cup on the small table. When he picked up his phone, I feared he checked out. He held the phone up in front of his face like he was looking at something, but I heard the little ding, letting me know he was recording a video.

"Tell me something about yourself, Miss Maddison. Something that will make me smile."

I smiled from his prompt alone. Finishing my last bite, I pondered his question, vaguely nervous he was recording.

A tiny laugh escaped. "Make you smile? Um, my favorite color is purple," I said more like a question.

"Noted, but not really smile-worthy."

"Oh, the pressure." I joked. Or was I flirting?

He already smiled, watching me squirm as I tried to figure this out.

"I don't know." For a minute, I looked down in silence as I swirled my spoon around the bottom of the empty cup. "I'm happy to be here now, at this moment," I paused before admitting, "with you." Never having the courage to look up. When I finally did raise my head, he was, in fact, smiling.

"Me too. Thank you."

I ran my hand through my hair before looking away. He was still recording when I looked back, the smile on my face then joined by rose cheeks.

"You ready to brave the cold?" Ending the video and returning his phone to his pocket, he offered his hand out again. This time our fingers naturally interlaced.

"Only if you're with me." My words made him smile again.

The loud clanging song of the bells rang one last time as the door opened and closed behind us. We walked back the couple hundred yards toward my car, hand-in-hand, and I didn't seem to shiver this time even with a stomach full of frozen dessert. Probably thanks to the hunk pulled in close on my right.

Tonight was the best first date I ever had, no doubt. I started to think about when our next one would be but quickly pulled myself back to the moment as we arrived at my car sooner than I wanted to say goodbye.

"Here I am." I dropped his hand and dug for my keys.

"Thanks again for coming with me tonight. I had a great time."

"So did I. I hope to do it again soon."

"For sure."

I smiled as I leaned in to hug him. This time he didn't have one hand preoccupied and wrapped both arms tightly around my torso. My arms were trapped, so I put them both up under his arms going up his back and wrapping my hands over the top of his shoulders, my face pressed up against his.

"Your cheek is cold." He released the hug, rubbed his hands up and down my arms to warm me up, then leaned back in and gently kissed my cheek. Maybe for warmth. Maybe for affection.

I liked it either way, which caused my smile to double in size.

"There's that smile again."

My cheeks felt full of warmth then.

"I'll text you later. Goodnight, Maddison."

"Goodnight, Aaron."

I turned to unlock my door as he walked to his vehicle and looked back up. He turned around, our eyes locked with matching grins taking over our faces.

Finally. I finally got those flutters in my stomach and the thump of my heart for a good guy. The right kind of guy. As I got into my car, I couldn't have been more pleased with the night.

When I got home, I started to text Vicki but realized how tired I was since I hadn't been out so late in ages. Unsure if I had it in me to stay up another hour texting, I changed into some comfy PJs and put my hair up before retrieving my phone from my purse.

A notification bubble sat on the text app. I assumed Vicki wanted the scoop, but when I opened the app, a huge smile stretched my face again.

BTW you didn't just look nice tonight. You looked beautiful.

~ 6 ~

If I was still teenage Maddison, every inch of paper on my desk would be covered in hearts and multiple combinations of mine and Aaron's names—first and last. But I was an adult now, which meant the doodles were all in my head, safe from anyone's discovery. More than one mental note had a heart—or four—added to it.

I still beamed at work Monday morning, and Vicki wasn't the only one to notice. I promised to give her all the details in person because I didn't want to diminish the wonder of my night by trying to explain it all with emotionless words on a screen. I messaged her Saturday night before crashing the date was "so GOOD," and I'd give her the play-by-play Monday over lunch. Another addition to my new routine—have lunch with co-workers more often. And by co-workers, I only meant Vicki, but whatever.

It was somewhat common for me to accidentally work through lunch and leave earlier than five p.m. It was also common—especially in the earlier days—to sit in my car alone and cry over fast food. Neither of which good for me. I'd come so far and was genuinely pleased with the recently upgraded, and still loading, Maddison 2.0.

Vicki picked the salad buffet place and started as soon as the passenger door shut. "Okay. Spill it. I haven't had a date in months, and I'm totally, and unashamedly," she held up her finger, "going to vicariously live through you for the next hour. Leave *nothing* out."

I was grateful for my deepening friendship with Vicki. I needed a girl in my life for years, growing up with two brothers, and my closest friend being Ethan through high school and most of college. There were girls in our big group back at the university, but I still considered Ethan my go-to person. Then add in the fact I was either hanging onto or dramatically avoiding Garrett, left me with little time to get close enough to any of the girls in our group. I never felt like anything was wrong with having closer relationships with guy friends, but I saw now the value of a friendship where the other person equally processed things the way you did on an emotional side. I tried to picture Ethan saying the sentence Vicki just spoke and had to refrain from laughing, took a deep breath, and started from the very beginning.

"I got there early and waited in my car, but then he text me he was already in the lobby. I practically ran in. He looked as dreamy as ever in his gray beanie already holding our tickets. After we ordered our dinner, there was some small talk."

"Nuh-uh. Details. What small talk?"

"Um." I had to think back for a minute. "Oh, I found out he plays guitar at his church." I looked over at her with humored, sarcastic eyes. "Of course he does. I told him I would go next weekend to hear him and attend the service. Then it came out that I used to sing at my church back home, and he seemed pretty excited to hear me sing."

"That makes two of us." She held out her hand in front of my face like she was holding a microphone. Without hesitation, I leaned in and started singing along with the radio for a couple of lines. Vicki heard me sing around the office more than I intended. Someone even complained about it once after I first started working there. It seemed Vicki was having fun by playing along—I was too.

I continued dishing out the details of the date as we walked around the bar, filling our plates with a veggie-heavy lunch. I meticulously loaded my plate, evenly spreading the various ingredients around as I went. Vicki went for the scoop of this and scoop of that and tossed it all up with two forks back at the table—another thing I discovered we did differently.

"We didn't really talk much during the movie because I wasn't sure if that was okay with him. I'm a movie talker, but my brothers always hated if I interrupted. When it was over, he offered me his hand—which you know I took—and didn't let go while he asked if I wanted to get ice cream across the street. About halfway there, he switched his grip from this to *this*." I demonstrated with my own two hands, slowly switching from a clasped position to an interlaced position, trying to add the electric significance of how it made me feel.

"Yes. So cute." Vicki beamed for me.

I looked at her while chewing and wondered why it was she was still single. She was probably several years older than me, although we'd never discussed age. She commented once about trying to decide if she was going to attend her upcoming ten-year high school reunion, and mine was still a few years out.

Her textured blonde hair not quite to her shoulders complemented her breathtaking light blue eyes, and perfect matching dimples decorated her full-lipped smile. Vicki always dressed extremely fashionable, especially compared to me, and wore things I never thought I could pull off. Perhaps she had more confidence than me. She was also highly competent and a hard worker. The more I knew about her, the more I appreciated and respected her as a person, not just a colleague.

Mental Note: *Have a girls' day with Vicki ASAP!* The note was bright yellow.

"Hey, how about a girls' day Saturday? I could use a pedi. My feet need to look cute in case I wear open-toed shoes to church Sunday."

"I'd love that, but keep going. So you were holding hands like this." She held her hands interlaced in front of her face as she mimicked my dramatic motions. "And then?"

"We got to the ice cream place, frozen yogurt place whatever, discussed our favorites, and decided to get our usual and share. We didn't feed each other or anything; we just tasted each other's favorite. That's when he held up his phone and started recording me."

Vicki's face looked like mine probably did in that video on his phone —shocked yet full of intrigue.

"He told me to tell him something that would make him smile. I kinda froze and said my favorite color was purple, but that wasn't what he had in mind. So after a pause, I told him I was glad to be in that moment with him. It worked. He smiled."

"Oh my goodness, that's adorable. I'm *totally* jealous right now." She went back to her salad, then chewing a mouthful, waved her hand in the air for me to continue.

"Then we left and held hands again on the way back like this." I pantomimed my hands in front of my face once again, poking fun at her poking fun at me, only this time my fork was sticking out to the side. "We laughed about the movie as he walked me back to my car. He felt that my cheek was cold when we hugged, so he rubbed my arms and kissed me on the cheek. I told him I hoped to do this again, he said he did too, and told me he would text me." I let out an airy breath, trying to find words to adequately convey my overall assessment of the night. "It was perfect. Everything about it. And you already know about the text he sent me at the end of the night."

Vicki let out a big swooning sigh. "I'm so happy for you. It does sound perfect. Has he text you again since?"

"Yeah, Sunday." I stabbed around my plate and took a bite of my lunch.

"You mean he didn't wait several days leaving you to squirm?"

"Nope. Nothing about him seems to result in what I expect him to do, and it makes me even more into him. My exes were always predictable, down to the lame disappearing act leading up to the breakups. I keep having to stop my mind from going there because I'm very good at dwelling in the past and not focusing on the moment. I don't want to project anything on him then act out of fear for what he might, but most likely won't, do."

"That's smart. Good advice, Maddy. I need to remember that tidbit when I finally get a date of my own. Hopefully soon. So what was the conversation on Sunday?"

"Around noon or so, he text me asking me what I was doing. I told him I was deepening my couch crater and watching a chick-flick in yoga pants like a typical girl, which made him laugh. He typed "lol" at least. Then I asked him what he was doing, and he'd just got back from church and planned to veg around his apartment since his roommate was gone for the weekend. A few more texts were exchanged back and forth. Maybe I was somewhat flirtatious."

I shrugged my shoulders mischievously.

"He mentioned he wouldn't mind helping even out the dent in my couch by joining me for a couch date soon, but we didn't actually plan anything."

Vicki and I ended up talking the full hour when one of us wasn't chewing and had to rush back to work. We laughed the entire way back to the office, sharing stories of all the bad dates we'd been on that made my flawless night seem even more perfect. I didn't want to switch back to work mode, but the day wasn't over, so I pulled up my big girl pants—as my mom used to say—and adult-ed through the next four hours.

* * * *

Aaron text me every night that week, asking how my day went, along with questions to help him get to know me better. I, in turn, asked him every question he asked me, as well as a few to satisfy my curiosity. It became a new routine I very much looked forward to. Every night around nine, my phone chime would go off. We text back and forth, some nights for hours until I grew too tired to stay up. We knew pretty much everything that happened in each other's week, as well as more facts and random details than I probably knew about anyone else currently in my life.

As planned, Vicki and I met in the late morning for pedicures on Saturday, ready for a much-needed girl's day. She already knew about our nightly text convos, so there wasn't much to catch her up on. I made it a point to learn more about her today.

The small, quiet lady waved us back to the pedicure stations and waited to make sure we liked the temperature of the water as we took off our shoes and eased our feet in. We handed her the polishes we picked for our toes and turned on the fabulous massage features on our chairs, enjoying every roll of the massagers as they circled their way up and down our backs. It was quiet for a few minutes before we broke the silence with laughter as the full-body mode on the chairs began shaking our stomachs in a most unattractive way—mine more than hers. We both covered our stomachs in an attempt to still seem ladylike.

"So sexy, right?" I insecurely pointed out my flaw.

"Everyone has some hidden jiggle revealed. These chairs don't play favorites."

"Okay, Miss Vicki, your turn to dish the deets. I want to know how long it's been since your last date and what type of guy you're looking for, so I can keep my eyes open for potential mates for my bestie." I tallied the requests on my fingers.

"Oh man. An official or unofficial date?"

"Either. Whichever was the last one you remember?"

She leaned her head back against the large leather chair. "Well, I guess part of the problem was we stopped dating. I honestly don't remember our last date, but I'd have to say it's probably close to three years ago." A straight, tensed grin braced her face causing her dimples to fade ever so slightly. She took a deep breath, and I prepared for what she was about to unload. "I'm divorced, Maddy."

I tried to control my face from being anything other than loving and supportive, but I was pretty taken back. I knew Vicki for just over a year now, and it made me feel awful I didn't know such a significant part of her life.

"We got married when I was twenty-one, and it only lasted two years. I'm not sure if we weren't ready, maybe too young, or what else it could've been. We dated for three years, starting our junior year of high school. He was all I wanted." She paused, but in reflection, admiration, confusion, or frustration, I wasn't sure. "All my life plans were in accordance with what he wanted to do. His parents were willing to help with the rest of his tuition financial aid didn't cover if he attended full-time. I got a retail job so he could keep going to school.

"We started pulling apart before I knew it was happening. Looking back now, I guess there were some clues, I was just too blind to see them. He came home one day and told me he was sorry, but he shouldn't have gotten married so young before he knew what he wanted. He thought it was the next step we were supposed to take but didn't realize the weight of our commitment until some time had passed. *And* he met another girl at school. He swore nothing happened while we were married, but knowing he could start to fall for someone else when he had me at home, made him realize what we had wasn't enough to keep him happy for the rest of his life."

"Whoa" was all that came out, though many things were circling in my brain.

"I called him a coward and asked him why he was doing this to me. He apologized but didn't change his mind even though I was bawling in front of him. He walked out and didn't come back that night, called me the next day to see where I was, and came to get his stuff while I was at my mom's. It all happened so fast. He wasn't even willing to try and figure everything out—his mind was *made up*. I haven't had more than five conversations with Alex since."

"Vicki, I'm so sorry." Suddenly, I felt absolutely vile for gushing about Aaron to her. "I can't—"

"It's fine. I'm pretty sure I've mostly healed up. I stayed at our house, and he moved back in with his parents. While he reverted to more juvenile freedom back home, I continued to be responsible, like an adult. I worked my retail job while putting myself through design school, older than most of my classmates, and graduated on the dean's list. Perhaps I was trying to prove a point—maybe to him, maybe to myself—that I would make it. I was going to be the best person I could be, and giving up a few years of my life for him wasn't going to set me back."

I instantly felt like I understood Vicki more accurately. Many of the characteristics I witnessed at work made complete sense.

"Anyway, I've had some dates since then, but none of them turned into relationships. Maybe because I wasn't ready, or maybe because a piece of my heart will always long for him even though I keep trying to tell it otherwise. Those are some of the stories I've shared with you. I know how to pick winners." She laughed as if trying not to dwell on her heavy past and lighten the mood back up.

I wasn't sure if her comment meant she still loved him. I wasn't going to ask.

It was quiet for a minute as the tenseness of the conversation drifted away while we looked down at our feet, but also because I had no words to offer. I worked on putting together some type of encouraging statement in my head before we left.

"Well, my sweet friend, you are awesome. And I know you will find love again, and be happier than you could've ever imagined." My words weren't empty, either. I knew she would. My heart broke for her as I tried to picture all she'd been through. At such an early age, no less.

"Thanks. I haven't told my story to many people. Thank you for being a real friend." Her eyes filled with gratitude.

I was delighted we were becoming more than just work friends.

"You bet. I'm so glad we did this today. I didn't know how starved I was for girl time until I had a taste. And I'm just as thankful for you."

~ 7 ~

I remained a woman of my word, even though I was moderately nervous about going to church. Partly because I hadn't been in a long time, and mostly because I'd never been to *this* church, so I didn't know what to expect. But the thought of getting to hang out with Aaron for most of the day made me brave enough to face the awkward parts. Truthfully, I mostly stressed about my outfit and had changed a few times by eight forty-five. I wasn't sure if it was a traditional church with everyone dressed to the nine's, or a come-as-you-are modern church where I'd look dressed up if I wore nice shoes and a clean outfit. Finally, after changing for the fourth time, I shot a text to Aaron.

> ***Hey there, what are you wearing?***

As soon as I sent it, I realized it could be taken differently than I intended, so I quickly sent another.

> ***Because I'm not sure how dressy to get for church. ;)***

When in doubt, add a winky face. My go-to motto. *Please, Jesus, don't let him come back with an embarrassing flirtatious response.*

I look like I have almost every time you have seen me.

> ***Got it. See you soon.***

So you look like the hunkiest male model I've ever laid eyes on, and I'm going to have to try *very* hard not to be distracted while you're on stage. Great.

Can't wait.

We briefly talked about church Friday night over text. He was pleasantly surprised I planned on coming, and I hadn't said it in passing with no intention of actually following through. From our conversation, I knew the service started at ten and only about a fifteen-minute drive from my house.

Aaron was already there due to band practice held an hour and a half before service started. I hadn't had a handcrafted latte in a few days, so I decided to leave early and swing by the drive-thru.

I'm gonna get some coffee, want anything?

Oh and can we have drinks in church?

I already got one, but thank you for asking. So long as you don't walk in with your drink in a brown paper sack no one should say anything.

He was having too much fun with my nerves.

Very funny Mr! Ok, I'm headed out.

I took one last look in my full-length mirror to make sure I loved my final outfit: a loose fit, white three-quarters sleeve shirt that fell under my hips, skinny jeans cuffed at the bottom, and my favorite canvas gray camo flats with gold studs on the heel. My pedicured toes were fully covered—oh well. I topped the look with a long, brown leather knotted necklace with hanging feathers and metal beads. I spritzed myself with perfume and added my lip gloss before putting it back in my pocket—to be reapplied after coffee.

This was the earliest I'd been made up on a Sunday in probably a couple of years. Thankfully, I wasn't even as tired. Next stop, coffee. The idea of having something in my hand as I walked into the church made me less nervous for some reason.

Anxiously tapping my steering wheel, I waited longer than normal and began to second guess my plan to swing by before church. Making matters worse, the employee informed me they were out of my regular drink, and I had to order a cinnamon dolce latte. Much to my surprise, I actually enjoyed the alternate beverage when I finally took my first sip at a stoplight. Maybe it was time to change-up my coffee order for a while as well. *Bring on the change.*

A full-on what-in-the-world-am-I-about-to-do attack reared its head a few minutes before I arrived, so I played my music louder than usual in hopes singing along would help keep my anxiety at bay.

When I got to the church, the building was smaller than I anticipated. My childhood church probably sat around two hundred people and had two services to accommodate everyone. Granted, there weren't many churches to choose from in my small town, so they were all pretty much full every week. This location seemed like it might only hold half that amount, and they only had one service.

I pulled out my phone to let Aaron know I arrived.

> ***Just parked.***
> ***Any chance you want to meet me outside or are you busy with something?***

Only a couple of seconds passed before his response came through.

I'll be right out.

I went ahead and added a new coat of lip gloss, grabbed my purse and drink, and headed for the door. Still a few yards out, my handsome guy came out the double doors with a huge smile on his face. I kept my pace, even though I wanted to start running for him.

"Good morning. You look lovely. You'll fit in just fine," he said, still approaching. Aaron looked amazing as always in a blue and black plaid button-up shirt with the sleeves cuffed below his elbows. He looked great the black pants I'd never seen and sleek combat-style boots. He hugged me when we finally made it to each other. "I'm excited you're here. You have nothing to be nervous about, promise."

"I'm not too nervous, just psyched to be here." I spoke into his chest as we embraced, but I wasn't completely honest. *Forgive me, Jesus.* "Okay, I'm a little nervous."

He laughed and eased his arms free, grabbing my hand as if it was second nature now. And for everyone to see. Latte in my left hand, hunk in my right, today was going to be great.

I didn't know what to expect on the PDA level today. We weren't officially a couple yet unless he assumed we were without asking me—I hoped he would soon. We were on his turf with his people, so I'd already decided to keep my hands to myself.

I expected the inside to look churchy, but this place rivaled our coffee house. The decor was vintage yet modern, obviously well thought out and executed. Almost everyone appeared to be close to my age and looked like they just came from a coffee shop or were headed to some backwoods landscape, ready to fill Instagram to capacity. I did fit in. Well, maybe. I didn't feel as cool as all of these people. I blended in more here than I would have if I went back to the church I grew up, especially in jeans.

An ultra-fashionable, super gorgeous, young lady gleamed as she looked at us from across the room. Her ear to ear smile lit up the room. As Aaron led me over to her, I started to put together the reason for her illuminated expression.

"Maddison, this is Casey. Casey, this is Maddison, the one I was telling you about."

He was talking about me? To someone else? When I wasn't around? What was he saying?

"Oh no, I'm not sure what to make of that." I chuckled as I extended my hand. "Nice to meet you."

"Don't worry, all good things. It's a pleasure to finally meet you, Maddison." Casey seemed as sweet as she was beautiful.

"I've known Casey for a few years now. We're on the worship team together. She sings but also plays keys, even though she won't admit to it."

A new freak out started to brew, and I felt mighty insecure after learning they'd known each other for so long. He totally could have dated her if he wanted to. She was way prettier than me. *Oh no, did he date her?* I tortured myself again. *Shake it off, Maddison.* A quick glance down reminded me it was my hand he held.

"Oh, that's great!" I finally replied, hoping my silence didn't last too long. It wasn't shocking to me this woman who could easily fill a magazine cover had more things going on for her than just her looks.

"Maddison sings too. Or so she says. I've yet to hear it. I'm sure it's divine." Aaron turned playful, and it helped draw me the rest of the way back from What-If Land.

I laughed, no chuckle to it. "Man, I'm not getting out of that one, am I?"

"Never." He was for sure flirting now, and I ate it up. Aaron was much warmer in this environment than I'd seen, almost as if he came alive here. My attraction level ticked higher.

He excused us and led me to a few other important people in his life, always mentioning I was the one he told them about. I didn't remember any of their names after Casey and Devon.

We made our way into the auditorium, where he showed me his usual seat and left me there to go do his thing on stage, as the countdown on the screen approached zero. I was glad not much time remained before the service started, so I wouldn't have to face anyone alone. Everyone welcomed me with genuine hospitality, but I didn't consider myself a naturally confident person. I watched Aaron as he put his guitar on and got his gear situated. Every guy looked more attractive with a guitar on, but my guy, the one smiling back at me, just went from a ten to a fifteen.

He was in his element, at complete ease. Different from when he played alone at the coffee shop. This time he was illuminated, radiating. I loved seeing him like this, and if it was possible to be more into him than I already was, it happened that very moment.

The music was enjoyable. I didn't recognize the songs, but they were easy enough to follow when I forced my eyes to leave Aaron in order to read the words on the screen and remember why I was actually there.

Going back to church was probably the most significant change I needed in my life for years, and the fact that Aaron was here first, encouraging me and leading the way, was the icing on the cake. I shouldn't have allowed myself to get so disconnected from this major part of my life, but I was here now and fought not to let guilt take over. I was pretty sure God wouldn't want me to feel that way.

I looked around and took everything in. Friendly faces fully engaged in worship. Others with broken looks in their eyes had people embracing them in genuine adoration. Not that my church growing up wasn't great, and I was so grateful for how it helped mold me into the woman I'd become, but in my life now as a young adult, this place seemed like a better fit. I could picture myself drawn back to this feeling every week easily. Perhaps that was why Aaron looked so alive.

A business casual dressed man holding a cordless microphone in his hand made his way up the front steps of the stage as the music wound down. He swayed back and forth, letting the singers finish the last part of the song. When he started speaking, I realized he was actually praying.

"Thank you, God, that we can come into your presence, rejoicing or mourning, and you comfort us all to perfection. We're grateful you trade our brokenness and make us whole. Continue to work on every heart in this place as we seek you today, and in our lives. Amen."

A low roaring "amen" rolled through the room as everyone sat down as if on cue—I was only a couple seconds delayed. Aaron took off his guitar, set it on the stand, then made his way out of a back door I hadn't noticed before. I wasn't sure if he had something to do backstage but hoped he'd be at my side soon.

The same man was still on the stage speaking, so I deduced he must be the pastor. I scanned the room again and saw most of the faces were very engaged and obviously wanted to be here, give or take a few teenagers. I estimated slightly over a hundred people in attendance, not including kids who left for class, but it was hard to tell. The space was much larger on the inside than it appeared from the outside.

A smile grew on my face when I imagined the conversation I'd have later, and how thrilled my mom would be that I went to church today for the first time in ages. She finally stopped asking every week about two months after I moved away for college. Possibly because she got tired of her hopes being up, only to be let down.

"... hope. I'm telling you, get your hopes up! God can do big things."

I focused back in as the middle-aged pastor continued from the stage, a little freaked out he spoke a phrase that had just been in my mind. Maybe that's what grabbed my attention.

"I'm so glad you're here." Aaron whispered in my ear as he sat down next to me, causing me to jump. "I'm sorry, I didn't mean to startle you." He grabbed my hand and sandwiched it in between his.

"Me too. I'm a tidbit curious about what you've said about me though." I whispered back, trying not to be a distraction to the people around me. A memory flashed before me of my mom scolding me for talking during church.

"All good, I promise. Everyone here is always asking me when I'm going to get a girl, so I guess you could say they've been waiting for you for longer than we've even known each other." He winked with a grin.

Meaning not only did I think he was amazing but so did all these people who wanted him to have someone to share his life with. And so far, they all seemed to feel like I was good enough to hold that title.

I felt like I held the winning bingo ticket.

I wasn't catching everything the pastor said, but it wasn't intentional. I continued to soak everything in around me from the people, to the decor, to the sculpted hand holding my own. Pieces of my life were starting to make sense again. How many months had I felt like giving up? More than I cared to remember. I *would* get my hopes up. But not in anything, in particular, merely the fact that God had some awesome things in store for me. I was excited beyond words for the first time in a long time.

When the service was over, I met more people I wouldn't remember names for but looked forward to the day I'd not only know their names but details of their lives as well.

"How about some lunch?" Aaron asked after he finally finished introducing me to every person he knew longer than five minutes.

"I'd love that. I'm pretty hungry." I downplayed just how much my stomach alerted me of its needs. If we didn't leave soon, I'd be hangry, and I wasn't willing to risk messing our relationship up by letting him see a darker side of me just yet.

"Great. Want to ride together and come back for the other vehicle later?"

More time with Aaron was always the better choice.

"Sounds perfect. Mine or yours?"

"I'll drive." He led me to his car, a red Pontiac Grand Prix, and opened the passenger door like a proper gentleman. What a hot ride.

I leaned across the console and opened his door for him from the inside.

"Thank you, ma'am. Now, where are we headed?"

~ 8 ~

It was safe to say I saw Aaron almost every day, but if we didn't get together, we talked non-stop, unreal to think it'd only been three weeks since I met him. What was I even doing with my time before? Oh right, sitting at my apartment, existing alone. Thinking about those days didn't even feel like me now.

Church was precisely what I needed this past week. Like the sermon was somehow tailor-made for me. And lunch after was just as amazing. Aaron spent a good chunk of our time making more videos asking me to tell him something that would make him smile. I told him I had a crush on a cute boy. He pretended to be jealous. I also told him this was the best weekend I'd had in forever. He asked if it was even better than last Saturday, causing me to laugh and apologize, letting him know he was only second to Jesus, but he made up the good parts of the weekend too. He seemed to be pleased with my answer. I tried to make a video of him, but he told me it was his thing. He needed to see me anytime he wanted—or so he said.

He was going to arrive any minute now for our first couch date at my place. I cleaned more than I had in months and lit just about every candle I owned before realizing it might send the wrong impression. I blew them all out except for the one on the bar between my open kitchen and living room. Now my apartment was full of smoke. *I'm a mess.*

Aaron was bringing takeout from my favorite Chinese place. My contribution was picking the movie. Unsure if I was ready for him to see me in full veg-mode, I kept jeans on after work instead of my standard post-work attire.

I heard a rustle at the door and forcefully swung it open before he could knock, but found an older woman standing there instead. I recognized her from around the apartment complex.

"Oh! You startled me." She jumped back.

"Sorry. I'm expecting someone."

"It's all right. I got this mail of yours on accident and was trying to stick it into your doorjamb."

She handed me the thick, card-shaped envelope. I didn't get much mail other than junk or bills, and it wasn't close to my birthday, so I wasn't sure who it was from or what for.

"Thank you. I appreciate it." I closed the door and immediately opened the envelope because I had to know what it was right away. Obviously a wedding invitation from the looks of it, I read it over with a furrowed brow until I hit the names. The bride I didn't recognize, but the groom, that would be my ex. Garrett was getting married.

I tossed the invitation on the bar next to the candle, contemplating burning it. Okay, too dramatic. It wasn't so much I had any feelings left for him, *at all*, but more I wanted to be further along in our relationship than Garrett did back then, and here he was moving on past me with someone else. Apparently, it wasn't that he didn't want to be married, he just couldn't picture himself married to me. Which was fine, I guess, but it stung a little. Or a lot.

The knock at the door stole me away from my chaotic emotions. I needed to get out of this funk fast. I swung my arms around in the air like an enraged baboon trying to clear the rest of the lingering smoke. After evening my breath and putting the best smile I could manage on, I opened the door.

"Hey you!"

Aaron crossed over the threshold and squeezed me in a tight hug with his arms, a carryout bag in each hand. "Best thing I've heard all day. Where should I put these?" He lifted the takeout in the air.

"Uh, let's start in the kitchen. Welcome to my place." I led him through the short narrow hall that opened up to practically the entire apartment minus my bedroom. Because of the very open floor plan, there was no hiding my clinging sense of unease from him in the open.

"I rang the doorbell twice before knocking. Am I too early?"

"No, that thing only works when it wants to." My voice trembled ever so slightly.

Please don't notice.

He noticed. "Something wrong?" He appeared confused, probably because this was a side of me he hadn't experienced since I was always electrified around him. Evidently, I wasn't pulling off my fake smile successfully.

"Oh, uh, yeah. Just got some weird news a minute ago. I'm still processing, I guess."

"Everything okay?"

"Yeah, I um." Did I want him to know my ex getting married bothered me? How would he feel? In uncharted territory, I wasn't sure how to proceed, even with caution.

Forget it. "I received a wedding invitation. From my ex. He's part of Ethan and my group of friends. I'm not sad or anything, it's just kinda weird. I didn't know he was dating anyone, not that it bothers me, I just—" I grabbed the invitation, opened the cabinet door under my sink, and threw it away, turning my attention to the food without fully finishing the sentence I didn't even know how to complete.

I heard the cabinet door open again. "When is it?" He pulled out the invitation and was looking for details.

"I don't know if I read that far or already forgot. I literally opened it seconds before you got here." I was apprehensive with his response, but glad he didn't seem upset.

"Can I be your plus one? I mean, you were friends first and again after right? And Ethan will probably be there too." He put the invitation back down on the counter and stopped me from fumbling in the bags by grabbing my hands and turning me to face him. "Maddison, would you do me the honor of attending this wedding with me? I want to have the prettiest date there."

I didn't honestly know if I wanted to go, but a chance to spend time with Aaron was hard to pass up. "I'll *only* go if you go with me. There's no way I'd even considered going alone, but if you are with me?" I smiled the first real smile I had since he arrived. He leaned in and kissed my forehead.

"It's a date. We should have a few before then, though. I don't think I want to go that long without seeing you. It's still like two weeks away." He winked and turned to secure the invitation on my fridge with a magnet.

"What?!" I protested in shock. "Who sends a wedding invitation out so close to the wedding?" I grabbed the envelope and discovered a postmark from a month ago. I guess the nice little neighbor had this for a while before remembering to bring it to me. Not so nice after all.

It hit me then. If I received the invitation when it was supposed to make it to me, it would have most likely caused me to deepen my recluse lifestyle of work, home, repeat, with no social life whatsoever, spiraling even farther down. And possibly even resulting in not meeting Aaron at all. "Wow. I'm glad I didn't get this mail when it was originally sent out. Before I met you."

His dipping eyebrows conveyed he wasn't following.

"One of my neighbors got it by mistake and brought it to me moments before you got here. I scared her half to death dramatically swinging my door open, thinking it was you."

He laughed, and it cut the tension in the room with perfection. "Okay, enough of that. What movie did you pick?" he asked while helping me with the takeout.

"Beat-em-up, shoot-em-up, secret-spy, something or other. I can't remember the title."

We walked around the bar and set our food down on the coffee table and got situated. Sitting to the right of my normal dent, I hoped he wouldn't notice—or at least not say anything about my broken sofa. I grabbed the remote to start the movie, then my food, before pulling back into the couch, crossing my feet under my thighs.

"Thank you for being you." I looked at him with pure satisfaction in my gaze.

"That smile. It's the best when you don't know it's there. I hope I can always make you smile like that."

Pretty sure you don't have to worry there.

We watched the movie while eating our dinner, reminiscent of our first date. Only this time, we sat way closer, which I preferred. After Aaron finished his dinner, he snuggled down in his seat with his right arm on the back of the couch, seemingly as an invitation. I wasn't bold enough to assume his posture was intentional, but after I finished my food, I scooted closer to him, seeing how he would respond. To my delight, he pulled in toward me as well. I continued watching the movie with my knees curled up into my chest, leaning on the man of my dreams.

"This is perfect. I like the way you fit there." He kissed the top of my head.

I lost track of the movie and jolted awake when a loud explosion rattled the speakers. I didn't know I dozed off, and I wondered if he noticed.

"Sorry. That startled me."

"It's okay. You probably needed the nap." So he did notice.

"I just got so comfortable, I'm sorry. I promise you aren't boring."

He laughed. "Glad to hear. I'll enjoy my time with you any way I can get it, awake or asleep. Preferably awake."

The movie was practically over. I was sad our night would end soon, but we both had work in the morning.

"Would you like some ice cream?"

"Um, yeah. You've been holding out on me."

I laughed as I uncurled myself from the perfect curve in his side and rounded the bar into the kitchen. I dished us both two scoops into tall, thin coffee mugs and stuck a spoon in each one before rushing back to my favorite new seat on my couch.

"Thank you," he said, looking at the mug with one eyebrow raised.

"It's the only other thing I like in my coffee cups. Not sure which I like more."

As I tried to find the exact spot I'd been in, the hero saved the beautiful girl in the nick of time. They passionately kissed with danger still all around them, clothes tattered, the whole bit. If you've seen one action movie, you've seen them all. Both of us became interested in our ice cream as the on-screen kiss deepened.

"I'm glad we watched the movie this way. The theater was nice, but I do believe I like you closer."

I was definitely blushing and pleased the sun no longer came through the windows, keeping my altered composure a secret.

"I have to agree. Thank you for coming over."

When the credits started rolling, I got up to flip the lights on and went for our trash and empty mugs. Aaron quickly jumped up to help me.

"Thank you, but you don't have to help."

"Sure I do. I helped make the mess, so I can help clean it up too."

The more I got to know him, I realized I wasn't making excuses for the things I didn't like. Which was what I'd done in practically all of my previous relationships, desperate to force something that wasn't there. Or even worse, ignore the screaming red flags thinking, "I could change him." I knew something would inevitably come up eventually, but Aaron was easily the best guy I ever dated.

"Oh yeah, I almost forgot. Ethan suggested we do a double date if that's something you would be up for?"

"That'd be great. I still haven't had more than a two-minute conversation with Stacy. Did he say when?"

"Anytime this weekend. I prefer Friday if that's all right with you?"

"Done. I'll add it to my calendar."

"I'm glad you can pencil me in." He arched an eyebrow and slid his tongue across his teeth.

My heart skipped a beat. Or three. "Anytime."

As we finished clearing our little mess, I suspected he wasn't ready for our date to be over either.

After a moment of silence, he sighed. "Well, I better get." He grabbed my hand and pulled me with him down the hallway to the front door. "I guess I will see you on Friday then."

I opened the door for him after his failed attempt to figure out the correct combination of the three locks my dad insisted on.

"I look forward to it."

He stepped out, but turned around and leaned back into me, lifting his hand and gently placing it around the back of my neck. His thumb cradled my ear against my jaw. Ever so softly, he placed a tender kiss on my lips.

My mind stopped for a second then sped up to process what was happening in regular sequence.

Please do that again.

Moving to my other ear with his cheek pressed to mine, he whispered, "You'll hear from me before that, though. I can't be without you that long."

I felt the smile pull my face from under his hand.

He kissed me one more time on my cheek before saying, "Goodnight, Maddison."

"Goodnight, Aaron," I said, the smile still on my face.

That was the best first kiss I ever had. I'd be totally fine to have only those kisses for the rest of my life. He walked down the stairs, then looked back up and winked at me. Consider me completely smitten by him. There was no doubt.

I closed the door and leaned my back against it, having a hard time believing life could get any better as I faintly brushed my lips. I walked back toward the kitchen and saw the wedding invitation on the fridge. It no longer swayed my emotions. I'd attend with Aaron and be one hundred percent content with the man in my life.

I wanted Aaron. He made me feel completely different from how I felt with Garrett. The only thing going through my mind was how I wished I hadn't wasted so much grief on Garrett. I could be happy he found someone to marry, and I would find myself in a similar situation before another couple of years passed. I just couldn't rush things.

But first, I had to update Vicki.

First kiss. That just happened.

Yeeessss! Can't wait to hear about it!!

* * *

We met Ethan and Stacy at a local Italian place. If there was something I enjoyed almost as much as hamburgers, it was alfredo pasta. I was excited to dress up more than Aaron was used to seeing me for the semi-fancy restaurant. He turned to me all night telling me how nice—great, lovely, beautiful—I looked.

Ethan talked for ten minutes about some big opportunity his dad was offered but didn't want to take, and how it could launch the company into a whole new market. He lost me a long time ago. *Sorry, Ethan, I can't really force my brain to focus on anything other than Aaron.* Maybe I could, but I didn't want to. I was glad when the waitress showed up with our food, forcing him to stop. Before he could pick back up, I changed the topic.

"So, Stacy, are you planning on doing any more open mic nights?"

"Maybe. I get pretty nervous. I know the more I do, the more comfortable I'll become. And I've only done it twice," she admitted with a laugh, "but I've been battling allergies the last few weeks and couldn't sing if I wanted to. I probably need to check back in at Kristoph's and see when the next opening is."

"Tell them about the other thing." Even Ethan's eyes were smiling as he spoke.

She hesitated. "I also got an offer to play with another band, but I think they want a higher level of a commitment than I'm ready for."

"Stacy, that's great! What type of band?" I reminded myself in my excitement to eat carefully so I wouldn't mess up my outfit or my budding relationship with Aaron. This place was well-lit, and I already knew cheese hanging off my face wasn't my best look. Thank you, Patrick Lewis.

"Folk. The group is currently only a violin player and a guy on the upright bass. They tried to get a band going last year, but their lead singer and guitar player married each other and moved. The drummer didn't wait around, so now they're practically starting all over. The violinist saw me at the coffee house, actually. I'm pretty flattered, it's just that," she paused and looked over at Ethan, "I'm not sure I'm ready for that lifestyle. Or if I even want it as a career. I know I love music, but I've heard some bad stories."

Ethan cleared his throat quite obviously and looked at Aaron with *I'm sorry* oozing from his eyes.

"Oh, sorry. Never mind. Anything interesting coming up for you, Maddy?" Stacy grabbed her cup and took a quick practically-not-a-sip sip.

"Yup, I'm attending a wedding I only found out about this week."

Ethan almost choked on his food. "Garrett's wedding?" He didn't seem to try hiding his shock in the slightest.

"That's the one." I was heavy on the irony.

"He invited you?"

"He did. I wasn't sure what to make of it at first, but we were friends first and kind of after. I didn't plan on going, but Aaron talked me into it. He's coming with me."

He turned to Aaron like a bomb primed to explode. "You are taking her to her ex's wedding?" His eyes were practically popping out.

Everything finally registered in Stacy's eyes, who'd been looking back and forth between us, visibly trying to put it all together.

"Why not?" Aaron was as cool as the other side of the pillow. "I knew if she was invited, you were probably too. Besides, if he was dumb enough to let her go, I might just need to shake his hand and thank him."

Did he really just say that? Could this man get any better? I didn't think it was possible, but he kept surprising me.

"Well, you're a bigger man than I am," Ethan chuckled, obviously uncomfortable.

"Was it even a question?" Aaron teased.

"Ha, ha." Ethan hissed, unamused.

I, on the other hand, almost spit water out of my mouth.

"If you don't want to sit with us at the wedding or anything, that's fine. I'm going to enjoy a wonderful night with this lovely lady."

His confidence was so attractive.

"Oh, no, no. We can be together. Stacy will probably appreciate knowing someone other than me there now." He took a big gulp of his water and pretended to have it all together. "I was taken by surprise is all. It'll be fun."

Stacy smiled, but still had a minor look of confusion on her face. No doubt, she'd ask for more details and request an in-depth explanation from Ethan later.

I didn't have anything to hide, though, all in the past. Several months ago, I might not have felt the same, but Aaron changed things. I'd be on the arm of a total stud that night, and I was thrilled about it—sorry 'bout cha Garrett, *your* loss.

After developing a food baby, Ethan came back around to his normal self. Our night took on a more relaxing and enjoyable pace. Our first double date wasn't a disaster, and it looked like our second one was already planned—the wedding. I liked Stacy, but I was mostly delighted, however, that Ethan was with a girl who adored him. He deserved it.

My middle brother, Christopher, always told me I needed to get rid of Garrett and be with Ethan, but I never saw him as anything other than a friend. My brother was right about Garrett, though. He knew before I did. Guy intuition, I guess.

We said our goodbyes as we walked out of the restaurant. I was pleased to have some time alone with Aaron—even if it was just on the ride home. I reached my hand across the console and wrapped it around his bicep. *Hello!* Muscular bicep.

Vulnerability scratched the back of my throat. I didn't want to have the conversation, but not having it could prove worse in the long run. *Nothing to hide, right?* I took a deep breath to steel myself.

"I think I need to tell you something about Garrett. Because it might change your opinion about going to the wedding."

"If you feel like you need to, then that's fine, but I don't have to know anything. And I truly mean that." He glanced over at me, and I saw the honesty in his eyes.

Aaron was everything I wanted. And more.

"So," I sighed, "I found out after we finally broke up that part of the reason we were on-again-off-again was because I wouldn't sleep with him." I looked down into my lap and froze. It was quiet for every second of a long minute. "And apparently, he found another girl who would. After he got his fix, they would be off again, and he came back to me. I didn't know. I'd never go back to him if I did. The thought of it makes me sick.

"Ethan actually told me the truth. He'd known for a while and felt terrible for keeping it from me, he just didn't know how to handle the situation. I guess that's why he acted the way he did tonight. Maybe he figured I'd already informed you."

The drive was silent again. Desperate to know what was going on in his mind, I grew more and more uncomfortable. Eventually, I pulled my hand away and placed it back on my lap. I stared out my window, wondering if I should've brought my past up. At least this soon.

"Well, good."

Thankful he finally broke the silence, his choice of words confused me. I shifted my body back toward him. "Good?"

"Yes. Good for you. I'm glad you made a stand for yourself, and I'm glad he never pressured you. That's good."

I'd never thought of it that way. I told Garrett early on I wasn't going to have sex with him, so if that was what he was looking for, he should walk away in the beginning. It *was* good he never tried.

"That's very honorable, Maddison." He reached over and grabbed my hand. "Almost unheard of these days," he said, lifting my hand to his face and kissing the back of it. "And it doesn't change my feelings about attending the wedding. If you're still okay with going, I want to be there with you."

"Yeah?" My tone was shocked and full of desire.

"Of course. I want to be with you every chance I can get. Besides, if he invited everyone from your old crew, it'd be awkwardly obvious if he didn't invite you, don't you think?"

"Probably so."

"And you'd most likely be mad if he invited all the others and didn't invite you, even though you feel a little odd about it now, right?"

"Probably so." I was delighted he helped me take an outside perspective. I always got lost in my mind when I thought about all things Garrett, spiraling down into a depressing hole. "You are good for me."

He leaned in and kissed me while we were at a red light.

"Probably so," he said as he cracked a smile.

~ 9 ~

It took almost the entire lunch hour on Monday to catch Vicki up with everything from the last few days. She mostly sat there with wide eyes and raised eyebrows as if watching a soap opera while she ate her lunch and listened to me. I barely touched my food because I talked so much and had to go into scarf-mode, giving her a chance to finally talk.

"Wow. Very interesting. So when is the wedding?"

"This Saturday." I answered with food in my mouth—my mother would be disappointed. The time came to let Vicki know about my not-so-shiny phase. "After I found out about Garrett, I closed up and became a person I never thought I'd be. I didn't trust anyone, for far too long, but in the last couple of months, I decide to make changes. I think I'm starting to feel like me again. If I can forgive Garrett and mentally release all the darkness I felt after finding out about his side chick—*or chicks, yuck*—there will be nothing keeping me from embracing this new, well old, me."

"That's great. You're teaching me all kinds of things, Maddy. Thank you."

I smiled, mouth completely full, and continued chewing. I wasn't trying to be anybody's role model and actually felt like pushing myself to be close to Vicki was a major start to my change. "Thank you. I never realized how much I needed a girl best friend until you." Estrogen was practically floating above our table as we embraced the moment. "We need to get back!" I stood up after noticing the time, popping our bubble.

Now that I enjoyed life more, I found more fulfillment at work, which led to getting better at my skill, accomplishing more in a workday, and not dreading heading back to work after my lunch hour ended. We arrived a few minutes late. I didn't feel too bad about myself, more for Vicki, who I caused to be late as well.

I hurried to my desk and discovered a handsome man waiting for me, holding two cups of coffee in his hands. One with a straw and dome lid, the other with a heat sleeve. "Hey you!" I smiled and rounded my desk, hurrying to clock back in before going back to hug him.

"Hot or cold?"

"Hmmm, tough choice. I think I'll go with cold." I raised on my toes to kiss his cheek. "To what do I owe this awesome surprise?"

He took a sip of the hot drink. "I was just thinking about you and wanted to see you before heading back to work."

"Sorry I was late. Have you been here long?"

"Just a couple of minutes, but you're worth the wait."

Vicki sat at her desk and practically had fireworks coming out of her head. Her smile was so large it looked like it could break her face.

"Thank you," I gushed. "You remember Vicki, right?" I motioned to her desk a few feet away perpendicular to mine.

"Yes, from the coffee place. Nice to see you again, Vicki."

"Likewise." She looked paralyzed from shock, running her hands over her keyboard without actually typing.

"I don't want to get you in trouble, and I need to get back to work, but I hope you have a fabulous rest of your day." He kissed me on my forehead as I hugged him goodbye. We still hadn't kissed in front of anyone, and I was thankful he didn't attempt to at my work.

He left, even though I wanted him to stay. Being an adult was no fun sometimes. I still smiled as I sat down at my desk, taking a sip of my blended coffee dessert.

"Does he have a brother?" Vicki asked from across the room.

"You know what, it hasn't come up, but I'll find out for you." I made a mental note. "Would you be interested in going shopping to help me pick a dress for the wedding?"

"Absolutely. How about tonight?"

"That should work." I pulled my phone out of my purse to text Aaron, mere seconds after he left.

Thank you for my drink. Best part of my day. I'm gonna go dress shopping

> *with Vicki tonight unless you had any plans for us?*

**I guess I can share you, have fun.
Pick a good one.**

> *Will do. ;)*

"Let's go right after work!" I confirmed.

"Awesome."

* * * *

"I don't like that dress as much as the red one. It's still my favorite," Vicki commented, not yet annoyed with me because she was in her element. I'd tried on seven dresses by that point. If the tables were turned, I'd be bored.

"Okay. I have one left in there, so it's either gonna be the last one or the red one." I went back into the changing room and eased out of the seventh dress. I saved my favorite for last. As I slipped it on and got the zipper as high as I could, about an inch was still lacking. I turned to look in the mirror and instantly knew this was the one, hoping that Vicki would love the dress too.

The three-quarter sleeve dress, mostly dark, rich navy lace, gave a perfect blend of exquisite and modest. A solid navy bodice with a sweetheart neckline continued down to just above the knees giving the cover I desired. The top layer of lace created a mermaid fit with a small train trailing behind me.

"I think this is the one!" I shouted from inside the room. Before opening the door, I took a deep breath then stepped out.

Vicki's jaw dropped as she caught a glimpse of me turning the corner. "It sure is. You look amazing, Maddison. I can't even remember the red one anymore."

"Can you get the last of the zipper. I think I missed a bit." I turned around to show her my back.

"Oh, yep. Got it."

"This is the one?"

"No doubt. You can walk up to *anyone* there with total confidence. You better not hang your head in that dress, I forbid it."

"I think I can manage that." Because I truly felt beautiful for maybe the first time ever.

"Aaron is going to love it."

"I hope so. My cynical brain is still waiting for some bomb to drop with how great everything is going, but I really do feel like the luckiest girl ever."

"Get out of your head. You two seem perfect for each other."

"Fine, stop it before I start crying." I walked back into the changing room and pulled out my phone to take a picture of myself. If there was anyone who'd tell me if this dress was too much, it was my mom. I made sure the image did justice to reality and planned to send it to her later, but before I put my phone down to change back into my clothes, I sent a text to Aaron.

I found my dress!

I bet you look breathtaking.
You always do.

I managed to get the zipper down on my own and hoped it wouldn't give me any trouble this weekend. Fully dressed in my own attire with the winning dress hanging over my arm, I came out to Vicki, scrolling through her phone. "You ready?"

"Yep."

"Thanks for coming with me. We both know I wouldn't have found a gown this nice if I came alone."

"And that's why I didn't allow it."

I laughed at her honesty. "I don't know about you, but I'm getting hungry. I hope I didn't keep you too long. You can go ahead and go, no need for you to wait with me to pay."

"Okay, sounds good. You've *got* to take tons of pictures at the wedding. I can't wait to see them and hear all about it." She hugged me and walked away, looking back at her phone.

Seconds after she was out of view, my phone chimed in my purse.

So does that mean you're free
and ready to eat dinner?

It sure does. Just checking out.

Can I pick something up and
meet you back at your place?

That would be amazing.
How about burgers?

You read my mind. See you soon.

I now had the perfect dress and the perfect man bringing me dinner. Great day. Fabulous day. I spent my drive home silently contemplating all the changes from the last few months, so happy to finally be where I was. Not to mention truly grateful God hadn't given up on me while I selfishly put him on the back burner for far too long. I couldn't fathom returning to the way I lived before—empty, a mere shell, watching others thrive while I floated in and out when needed.

It broke me when I found out how Garrett deceived me. Completely shattered me, actually. We weren't even together at the time, but I felt so worthless. Thus, dating seemed worthless. I even questioned my friendships because it cut deep Ethan knew the truth but didn't tell me sooner—we knew each other for half of our lives. It caused me not to be able to trust people for a good while. Everyone was hiding something.

But look at me now. Headed to that man's wedding in a few days along with the friend who broke my trust, on the arm of a new man who's far better than I ever thought I'd have. I wasn't sure if Garrett knew I found out the accuracy of his actions because I was never able to confront him. Seemed pointless after the fact. *How quickly everything can change.*

I raced up the stairs, trying not to trip over the dress in my hands, to make sure my apartment looked decent enough for company. Thankfully, my place was still clean since I returned to a better headspace and cleaned up after myself again. Add in the fact I hadn't spent as much time here either: tidy apartment. I lit the candle on the bar to make it feel homier, then ran into my bathroom to check my makeup. I knew Aaron wouldn't notice the difference in a fresh look and the end-of-the-day-look, but I did. The knock on the door sent the butterflies in my stomach into a frenzy.

"There she is." He flashed his perfect teeth at me when I opened the door.

"There *he* is. Thank you for dinner. Need help?"

"Nope." He kissed me on the forehead before walking in. I was the perfect height for his forehead kisses. "So, am I gonna like your dress?" he asked.

"Vicki says you're going to love it."

"Mercy," he let out slowly.

I laughed at his response. "How was your day, after you made mine by surprising me at the office?"

"Good, but it's even better now that I'm here. Can we sit on the couch to eat? And talk."

"Sure." Him asking to talk made me nervous. *Here comes the bomb.* I rushed to the couch with my food. "Is everything okay?"

"Yeah, it's great."

Oh good. I overreacted yet again. Hopefully, this wasn't going to be a big deal.

He followed me to the couch, set his food down, and sat next to me. I looked at him with a curious blank stare, and I think he caught on to my insecurity.

"I just wanted to tell you some of my story. You told me more details of your past, and I thought it might be fair if I reciprocated if you wanted to know. No matter what's happened in your past, I don't have to know anything unless you want me to. I will leave that decision up to you. And it doesn't matter what you tell me; you aren't going to scare me away. I genuinely mean that.

"I'm an open book. You can ask me anything you want to know, and I'll answer, but I'm not the same man I used to be. I'd understand if it changes your feelings toward me, but I hope it won't."

His little speech was so genuine. I couldn't imagine feeling any different about him, but curiosity grew as to what he thought would possibly cause that. "Okay. Do you want me to ask questions, or was there something you already had in mind? And is it still safe to eat during this conversation?"

He chuckled at my awkwardness and took a bite of his burger. "Yup," came out muffled.

"Good, cuz I'm starving." I unwrapped my burger like a present and started attacking it.

"There was something I had in mind." He took a sip of his drink and used a napkin to wipe his mouth. "You already asked me, but I gave you the simple answer."

I looked up at him with a curious face still chewing, unable to remember asking him anything.

"At Kristoph's, you asked me what my tattoo was. I gave you the short answer, the one I'd give a stranger. There's a lot more to it than that."

"Well then, do tell." I marveled between bites, beyond excited he wanted to share something about his life with me.

"I haven't always been this guy. I grew up seeing my dad as an extremely talented musician, going on tour, and living a life driven by the desire to have his name in lights. I knew he left a bunch when I was a kid, but I didn't really understand its weight. All I knew was I wanted to be like him. He's why I picked up the guitar. Merely a way to connect with him at first, but slowly, his dream became my dream too.

"It was hard on my mom when he traveled, but she never let us see how deeply it affected her when we were young. When I turned nineteen, I found out my dad had more affairs than he could remember during his career. I was angry, so angry he did that to my mom. To us. I didn't want anything to do with him for a while and was desperate to live out the real dream I thought he lived. Only do it the right way, you know? To prove I was a better man than him.

"I failed. I got into a band with ladies and drugs around after every show. It wasn't long before I was in it too. For a couple of years. I hated my dad, and I hated myself for being like him. But even worse, I became an addict on top of everything else. I realized I let pride tell me I could make it when he didn't because I thought I was somehow stronger than him."

I drew a blank on what to say—if anything—and my face most definitely showed it. Not that I was unaccepting of his past, I couldn't even picture Aaron being that guy. *He* wasn't the man sitting in front of me.

"Are you okay?" Aaron touched my arm, worry his honesty crushed me quivering his bottom lip.

"Yeah, I—I'm fine. I just can't picture you like that is all."

"I was a totally different person, driven by pride and greed and hate and lust. While I was in the depths of it, my dad went through a recovery program that changed his life. When God restored my parents' marriage, my dad begged me to go through the same treatment, but I wasn't having it. I remained bitter for a long time.

"My lowest point was when a girl reached out to tell me she was pregnant, but she wasn't sure which of my bandmates was the father. We actually had to have DNA tests done." His gaze wandered off. Perhaps he was reliving the vastness of the day. "That was one of the strangest feelings. Not so much to think I might be a father, but to know it could only be one of the handful of guys who sat in the waiting room. We waited in silence, no one admitting what we all knew—none of us treated that poor girl right."

So he has a kid. Not a deal-breaker, right?

"How old is your child?"

"Oh no, the baby wasn't mine. But I thought of my mom as I sat there, stressing, and I broke. I called her the next morning and asked her to help me get into rehab. The program lasted a year. I lived with other men overcoming similar and other addictions. Throughout the process, I surrendered my life to God and never looked back."

"Wow" was all I had, and it didn't even come out at full volume.

"I know. It's kind of heavy. I hoped the burgers would help." He chuckled again.

"It is heavy, but that's okay. I'm really glad you told me. I want to know all about you, not just the perfect things."

"And my favorite color is blue."

I laughed at his attempt to lighten the mood, unsure of what to say.

"What is the tattoo of, then?" Since he wore a short-sleeve shirt, the full tattoo was visible. I grabbed his arm and ran my fingers over it, more confident in my touch with him this time around.

"Oh, right." He looked down and extended his arm. "It's a scripture reference from Romans. 'With grace, I warn you: Don't think of yourself more highly than you really are but instead use sober judgment, measuring yourselves by the faith God gave you.' Or that's my paraphrase, at least. Each translation says it a little different from the others."

The quote was a perfect fit. I couldn't remember hearing the scripture before or hadn't processed it that way—the words registered with his situation perfectly. "I love that. What a great reminder." I continued to run my fingers across his arm. He didn't seem to mind, either.

"Music will always be a part of my life, but now I get to direct it. It won't lead me anymore. That's why I love working with Simon and playing at church."

"Nice. You are so good at it too. Maybe you can teach me. And I say *maybe* loosely because I already tried before. It was a flop. My fingers are pretty short." I held out my hand for reference.

"You probably just didn't have a good teacher."

"I was teaching myself." I couldn't help but laugh. Hard.

"Oh, well." He laughed too. Not at me, but with me. He grabbed my small hand, pulling it in for a kiss.

"It *would* make more sense to learn from someone who knew what they were doing, though. Okay, now I want to know more. Do you have siblings?" I was curious in general but also had Vicki in mind.

"Yes, two sisters and a brother."

"Are you close to them? Do you see them often?" I asked, attempting my investigation skills without giving away what I actually wanted to figure out.

"I'm closer to the sister just above me, and my younger brother because my oldest sister had already moved out before I was a teenager. I still see them pretty often. Only the oldest doesn't live here." So he did have a brother, but Vicki might have to cougar it. I added a to-be-continued to the mental note on file.

"When is your birthday?"

"April sixteenth. Yours?"

"August third. And you are?"

"Twenty-six. Well, about to be twenty-seven. You?"

"Twenty-three." A smirk curled my lips. I figured he was older, but hearing it made me happy. I stored his soon approaching birthday on a purple sticky note in my mind. "Wait! Isn't that the day of the wedding?"

"It is."

"You want to go with me. To my ex's wedding. On your birthday? And why didn't you tell me when we made our plans?"

"Why not? I get to spend the night with you all dressed up, food and entertainment provided. Sounds like a great date to me. Plus, I didn't want it to sway your decision on attending."

"Are you sure? We can do something else, *anything* else."

"I'm sure," he said with honest charm on his face.

"Favorite season?" I continued with a huff, still unsure about the wedding situation even though I already bought a dress.

"Fall. You?"

"Same." I lit up at the thought of spending fall with him. There was something so romantic about the temperatures dropping and everything turning pumpkin. "Did you grow up here?"

"Yes. Did you?"

"No. I came out here for college. I grew up in Wimberlake, a small town in Texas. My parents are still there." I knew he wouldn't have heard of it. No one ever had.

"Right. Wimberlake. With Ethan, right? That's where the guitar shop started."

"Exactly. I forgot you'd know that."

"Are y'all close?"

"Not as close as we used to be." *The whole secret thing and all.*

"Not Ethan. You and your parents."

"Oh, same. I crawled into a cave a while back. I probably need to do some mending there."

Mental Note: *Catch Mom up and tell her about Aaron.*

My confession seemed to cause the mood to drop. The room grew quiet. *Dang it.*

"Do you have a secret talent?" he asked.

"A what?" I laughed, full of timidity.

"Come on. Everyone has something cool they can do. You know, like a party trick. A show stopper? I'm double-jointed in my arms. I can pull my hands from behind my back over the top of my head and back down in front without letting go."

"No, you can't." I gasped, not sure I wanted to see it.

"Oh, yes, I can." He stood up, clasped his hands with his arms fully extended behind him, and raised them toward the ceiling. Just when an average person would have hit the limit of mobility, his shoulder blades popped out—the right and then the left—with his hands still clasped as he said, now above his head. I jumped back and squealed with a huge grimace on my face. As he brought his arms easily back down toward the floor, his shoulder blades rolled back into the normal place in a mind-boggling contortion maneuver.

I was pretty sure I heard a pop.

"That's insane. No, I can not do anything like *that*."

"Maybe not as drastic, but I bet there's something."

I thought for a minute, then started to chuckle.

"See. What is it?"

"You'll make fun of me."

"I swear, I won't."

"Fine." I left a good pause before admitting, "I can sing with my mouth closed."

"How does that work?"

"I don't know. I did it all the time as a kid and didn't even think anything of it until my mom caught me once and told me not everyone could do that."

"Let's hear it. I need proof."

"Okay. But it doesn't work if I laugh, so you can't make me lose it."

He postured with eager anticipation tickling his face.

I took a deep breath, filled my cheeks with air, leaving the tiniest crack in my lips for air to escape, and started singing "You Are My Sunshine."

As soon as I hit the higher note on "hap-PY," he started full-on belly-laughing.

"What in the world? That's awesome!"

"I'm weird, I know."

"Finally heard you sing." His laughter subsided, leaving a goofy grin on his face. "Well, kinda."

We went on for a good hour, asking each other important and not so important questions, learning as much as we could about each other. I was ecstatic to be wearing some new grooves in my lumpy couch, and staring at this strikingly handsome man who wanted to get to know me, wildly blew my mind. I could picture myself doing this for years and never growing tired of it. I wanted to know Aaron more than I'd known anyone before.

Our food was long gone as we talked and laughed. Aaron gently rubbed my palms and the back of my hands, running his fingers up and down mine. The motion relaxed me so thoroughly, he rivaled the manicurist at the salon. Minus the polish talent, of course. But who's to say he couldn't be good at that too?

"I didn't realize it's almost ten. I should probably go."

I knew two things: I didn't want him to go, but he had to. I hoped there'd be a day I didn't have to say goodbye, only goodnight, but that was surely far away.

"Yeah, work tomorrow." I agreed. "But I'm super excited for this weekend."

"I can't wait to see you in this dress I'm going to *love*." He helped with our trash again. After the cabinet door for the trash can closed and I stood back up fully, he cupped my face with his hands. He peered so deep into my eyes as if trying to find the answer to some question he was too nervous to ask. "Thank you for letting me get to know you, even after you found out about my past."

"I'm not going anywhere." There was nothing to go back to. And as far as a future, I didn't want one with anyone else.

He covered my mouth with his, and for the first time, we shared more than a simple brush of our lips.

I fell. Farther. Harder.

He stopped before I wanted him to. But it was late, and we were alone. I knew the trouble that could lead to.

"I need to go," he said, still inches from my face.

"Probably so," left my lips in a breath.

He hugged me tight and kissed me on the forehead. We walked to the door at a snail's pace, not ready to be away from each other. He opened the door with his free hand I didn't have enclosed between my own.

"Goodnight, Maddison."

"Goodnight, Aaron."

He ended the night with one more, too short, kiss, and finally let go.

~ 10 ~

My amount of excitement for the day was odd—my ex's wedding day—but Garrett barely crossed my mind. I thought about spending the entire night with Aaron on his birthday and almost felt bad for using the wedding as a reason to have a super fancy date with my favorite guy. Not bad enough to care, however. Garrett did worse to me. Way worse.

Over the moon, I'd probably spend the same amount of time as the bride did today, pampering, prepping, and soaking everything in. I laughed at myself as I got my day started with a pedicure, knowing I'd gone overboard, but when you were happy in life, you did things on a grander scale, right?

"I tickle you?" the same petite woman who did my pedicure a few weeks ago asked. She probably noticed I didn't need another treatment, but glad I kept them in business.

"Oh, no. Sorry. Just laughing."

She finished rather quickly, considering she only needed to switch my polish to a deep red color. I could've done it myself at home, but I didn't have a massage chair. Since she worked so fast, I actually said yes for the first time ever when she suggested a manicure.

She uttered words in a different language, and another employee came up beside me and started working on my hands. This had to be better than getting your nails done in those tiny swivel office chairs at the manicure stations. I used my free hand to start the massage chair feature a second time and closed my eyes.

The two ladies talked back and forth in their native tongue so low I barely heard them over the sound of the chair. I, of course, wondered if they were talking about me. One of them laughed as the other asked, "Special day?"

I lifted my head and opened my eyes with a big smile. "I have a wedding."

"Oh, congratulations! You are beautiful bride."

"No, no, I'm not the bride. I'm going to a wedding, a friend's wedding."

"Your smile. You in love."

That obvious, huh? Did my face even give me away to a complete stranger? Granted, people who worked in salons could hypothetically open a side business for counseling with all the stories they heard over the years, along with the advice they'd given—trial and error if nothing else.

"Yes, I think I *am*." I hadn't admitted it out loud before. I was thankful when I did, it was to a person who had no way of getting it back to Aaron. Scaring him off wasn't an option. Guys could be weird about the L-word. One perk of growing up with only brothers was learning what *not* to do in a relationship if you didn't want to screw it up.

Both ladies giggled.

If I thought about who I wanted to laugh with, it was Aaron. If I thought about who I wanted to hold me while I cried, it was Aaron. If I thought about who I wanted to sit around and do nothing with, travel the world with, grow old with, it was Aaron. No denying it really, if I was honest with myself, I was in love. I wanted everything in my life from here on out to involve Aaron.

Lost in my thoughts longer than I realized, the second lady had not only moved to my other hand, but she'd practically finished. The massage rollers made their final descent, and they coached me to sit under the special lights—whatever it was that they did to finalize the job. I waited for the timer she set to ding as I daydreamed about Aaron some more, then made my way to pay.

"Thank you, ladies!" I headed out to my car in the oversized thin foam sandals, not wanting to mess up my perfect toes, thus waddling like a woman nine months pregnant, and feeling every piece of the pointy asphalt on my feet. I carefully grabbed my keys and phone from my purse as not to mess up my fingernails and discovered the missed text from my favorite person.

Can't wait to see you tonight!

I was glad I wasn't the only one already thinking about this evening.

You read my mind! ;)
Happy Birthday! I would have text you
sooner but I didn't want to wake you.

It would have been an okay thing to wake up to.

I went through the drive-thru of the very place I met my new infatuation and ordered the largest cinnamon dolce they made. The first sip filled me with warmth, traveling down my throat, and reaching my soul. I wasn't dramatic in the slightest as I let out a long "mmm" alone in my car. The idea of filling my day with overly-girly primping was so I didn't sit there watching the clock slowly tick by, seemingly taking five minutes for the second hand to make one full rotation.

I swung by the front office to pick up Aaron's birthday gift I ordered, thankful the delivery guy took it to the receptionist when I wasn't there to sign for the package because I didn't have a backup plan.

Now home, I started the avocado mask I found on PinBoard. I made a turkey and avocado sandwich for lunch, saving a quarter for the facial mask recipe. I mashed my sliced chunk of avocado with a teaspoon of olive oil, one tablespoon of honey, and a squeeze of a lemon until it was a goopy green concoction. I quickly finished my sandwich so I wouldn't accidentally eat any of the mask by mistake, although it was technically edible.

I took the mixture in the bowl to my bathroom and started reading aloud to myself since no one was here to make fun of me. "Before applying, hold a warm wet towel over your clean face for two to three minutes to open your pores."

I turned on the hot water, knowing it'd take a minute to heat up, and grabbed a washcloth from the cabinet above the toilet. I gave my face a good scrub with the face wash I didn't use nearly enough and prayed I wouldn't get any in my eyes like I usually did. Last time the whites of my eyes stayed red for hours. That look wouldn't complement my beautiful dress and perfectly mani-pedied nails tonight. I splashed my face with water to clear the soap like I was in one of those face wash commercials that never seemed to get water everywhere, being careful not to drench my bathroom. The sound of water colliding with the tile floor taunted me, declaring my life a failed fantasy.

I inspected my face in the mirror to make sure I cleared away all of the soap, then soaked and squeezed out the washcloth, placing it on my face. I walked—face covered, head tilted back—to my bed, hoping I wouldn't trip over anything, liken to a zombie. "Set timer for three minutes." I ordered my phone with a muffled voice.

"Okay, three minutes and counting," my virtual assistant answered back.

Once again, the catchy Black Eyed Peas song popped into my head. I started singing to myself, but practically suffocated trying to sing with a wet rag over my face and went with humming instead. When the timer ran out, I pulled the now cold rag off my face and grabbed my phone to end the alarm melody, then flipped back over to the app with my mask directions.

"'Using your fingers, apply the mask evenly to your face, avoiding the eyes.' Noted. 'The mask may drip, so make sure you're wearing a shirt that's easy to wash.' Hmph, I'm not worried about it." I rubbed the green slime all over my face, wondering if it would make any noticeable difference. Oddly enough, I enjoyed myself. "'Leave mask on for ten to fifteen minutes then wash well with warm water.' Done." I made sure none dripped before grabbing my phone and heading back to my bed, laying on my stomach with my ankles crossed up in the air. I knew a great way to spend ten to fifteen minutes.

The phone rang as I put it on speaker and placed it on my bed—no need to ruin my phone with an avocado mask.

"Hello?" How did her voice have the ability to be so soothing with one simple word?

"Hey, Mom."

"Maddison! How ya doin'?" Of course, she knew it was me. I was her favorite and only daughter.

"Good. Really good, actually. How are you?"

"Better now tha-cha called. It's been a while."

"I know, sorry. That's why I called. I have to catch you up on some things." And some-ones.

"Oh?" I knew by her tone she assumed what was coming, but chose to start with the news she'd be the happiest about.

"First of all, I've gone to church for several weeks now. It's pretty different from our church back home, but I really like it."

"That's great, honey. Yew have no idea how happy that makes me." I could hear the smile on her face.

"And work is going great. I think I finally found a good rhythm that doesn't leave me feeling completely lost or employed at the wrong place."

"That's fantastic. And?"

"And ... I met a boy."

"I figured there was somethin' yew were saving. Did ya meet him at church, I hope?" Mom hadn't been a fan of some of the boys I dated in the past. She always asked if I met him at church.

"No, I didn't. But he's the one who invited me to the church I've been attending. He plays guitar there."

"That's splendid!" I pictured her raising her hand in praise to Jesus, mouthing *thank you* because she knew I couldn't see her. Her sweet southern charm and all. "Well, go on then. Tell me 'bout him."

I let out a sigh full of admiration. "His name is Aaron, and I met him at a coffee place. He actually knows Ethan."

"Oh, does he now?" Which meant she was waiting to hear more before giving her approval. My mom knew Ethan also knew Garrett—both sides of him—who she wasn't the biggest fan of.

"Yes, he works for Ethan's dad. You remember him, right?" Of course, she did. Wimberlake only had about four thousand people. Simon followed Ethan to the metroplex for greater potential with a music business and more exposure to clientele. Boy, was he right.

"That explains him playin' guitar at church. What else 'bout him?"

The verdict was still out.

Good thing I could talk about Aaron until I was out of breath.

"He is tall, probably about six one, and in great shape." I didn't know how to explain his body, especially to my mom. Saying that much made me blush. "His hair is more cider than blonde, longer on top and kind of wavy, bright blue eyes, and perfect teeth you'd love."

My mom was a retired dental hygienist.

"I see. He sure sounds mighty handsome. Are y'all pretty serious?"

"I think so, and I hope he does too, but we aren't official yet. We've been on a few dates and—" I stopped there.

"He already kissed yew."

"How'd you know I was about to say that?"

"Yer my daughter, sweetie. I know yew."

"Yes we've kissed. But only a couple of times. Innocently too." I tried to reassure my mother, the woman who only kissed one man her whole life — my dad.

"Good. He sounds like a gentleman then. Anythin' else I need-ta know?" No doubt she pried to find out if he was anything like Garrett.

My mom wasn't judgmental. In fact, she was very loving, accepting, and forgiving, but I wanted her to meet him before she knew about his past. The past that didn't bother me at all and had no reflection on his life now. Not the type of thing you lead out with for a first impression.

"I'm sitting here with a fancy, all-natural, avocado mask on my face because tonight we're attending a wedding together."

"Sounds fun. Anyone I know of?"

I couldn't help the chuckle that escaped. "Uh, yeah. It's Garrett's wedding."

"Idn't that interesting. I wasn't sure he'd ever have a wedding, doubted you'd ever go if he did, let alone uh-nuther boy would be willin' to escort you there. Sure sounds like he has his head on straight tuh-me. Hopefully, I c'n meet him before too long." I was pleased she seemed impressed with him thus far.

"You know what Mom, I forgot to set the timer on my phone, but my face is feeling awfully tight. I should probably get off the phone and finish getting ready. Promise I'll call back soon." *And ask you how your life is going.*

"All right, hon. Be good t'night, to that Garrett boy."

I laughed because she knew I could go from sweet to nasty in two-point four seconds flat better than anyone. "Will do, Mom. Love yew." Her accent brought mine back to life.

"Love yew, too, sweetie."

Mental note removed.

I rushed into the bathroom, not knowing how long this mask had been on and prayed it wasn't going to leave me with some awful irritation all over my face. Thankfully, when I rinsed it off, everything looked normal, only a hint fresher—one point for the avocado mask.

I created an entire PinBoard event for today with all the techniques I wanted to do. I left plenty of time to *try* the various methods in case I needed to wash my face and start all over. The elegant hairdo I picked would show off the lower back line of my dress my hair would typically cover if I left it down. I wasn't great at doing my hair, so I picked one with a step by step video. All the hours I spent searching for how to perfect my look also led me to where I found the gift I ordered for Aaron.

With a clean face, I changed into a button-up shirt that wouldn't mess up my hair or makeup after I was done, feeling like I should've asked Vicki to come help me execute my semblance. She was more of a natural at these things.

I applied my makeup the way I usually did, focusing mostly on the smokey-eye technique I wanted to achieve. I felt like I did a pretty good job, although it didn't look exactly like the picture on the screen. My eye shape was different, I guess—I had big eyes, or so I'd been told all my life. The eyeshadow still looked good to me, probably the best and most eye makeup I'd ever worn, so I considered it a success. I highlighted my cheeks with blush and added lip gloss even though I'd reapply closer to leaving.

Taking a deep breath and feeling victorious thus far, I plugged in the large barrel curling iron. The look I went for was a low side ponytail I thought would do my dress justice. I followed the steps while watching the video as best as possible, but it looked much easier when you weren't working on yourself. The majority of my hair was pinned just above my neck over my right shoulder and then secured it into a low ponytail. I loosely pulled strands from the left and then the right and wrapped them around the black hair tie. It gave the illusion my hair was tied up by itself and kept my bangs swept across my forehead as they always were, agreeing with my natural part.

I used a hand mirror to make sure it looked good from every angle and felt pretty good about my work. The last steps were to curl the ponytail, then tug and tease until just the right fullness occurred. And enough hairspray to fuel a fire to hold everything in place. I accidentally burned my pinky finger on the last curl and winced as I shouted out in pain. The mark wasn't too bad, and it wasn't surprising I didn't make it through all this process without at least one mishap.

Finally ready to slip into the dress, I retrieved it from my closet and removed the thin plastic wrap. I carefully removed the tag so I wouldn't put a hole in this gorgeous gown. Treating it like it could tear any second, I gently pulled the dress up around my thighs, waist, then eased my arms in one at a time, securing the dress above each shoulder. I zipped as high as I could reach and turned to look in the mirror.

The zipper lacked the same inch as the day I tried it on. I shifted my weight, hoping it would allow me to lift my arm higher, but it didn't work. What was I going to do now? I almost cried but thought about how long it took for me to do my makeup. If my eyes messed up, I'd cry even more and potentially back out.

There wasn't enough time for Vicki to come over, so I'd have to ask Aaron to do it when he got here, or wait until we got to the wedding and ask Stacy. Either way would be awkward, but I settled on Aaron.

When I sat down on the edge of my bed to slip into my nude heels, the only thing I lacked was my silver cuff bracelet. I wrapped it around my wrist and stared down for a few minutes, not ready to look up at the finished results of my day's work. Hard work. I braced myself, walking over toward the mirror, and slowly lifted my head. I barely recognized the woman looking back at me.

Two months ago she didn't live here. I was glad I evicted that borderline recluse who weaseled her way into my thoughts.

Next time I'd do all this prepping and look this beautiful, the woman looking back at me would most likely be wearing white. The day would be filled with friends and laughter following these PinBoard activities together. My name would change that day.

But there I was, getting ahead of myself again.

The only thing missing was a fresh coat of lip gloss for extra shine. I carefully walked back to my bathroom to retrieve the tube and returned to the mirror to apply, even though I didn't need to look—I could gloss with my eyes closed.

Just then there was a knock at my door. My heart started racing, and I had to place my hands on my stomach to calm the jitters. I grabbed my clutch from the bed, stuck my keys, phone, and gloss in there, and headed to the door.

~ 11 ~

I took my time walking to the door; my pace drastically slower than my heart rate. The small lace train on this dress could easily get tangled up in my heel and cause me to face plant right into the floor. Another knock resounded, considerably louder this time, most likely if the first hadn't been heard or possibly after the doorbell failed. Just as the beat ended, I opened the door with raised eyebrows and a miniature sanguine smile.

"Wow" was slow and breathy, leaving his lips. "You look astonishing. I do believe you're the most beautiful thing I've ever seen."

"You." I took my time taking in every detail of him. He wore a black suit that fit like a glove and looked like he came from a professional menswear photo shoot. A thin black tie rested over his white button-up shirt, and his jacket was buttoned, but only one. His flat leather shoes came to a rounded point, making even his feet look attractive. I hoped I looked as good to him as he did to me.

"Happy birthday! Come in for a second." I took a few steps back to make way for him. "I have to ask you a favor, but I'm kinda embarrassed about it." I hesitated to ask.

"You don't have to be embarrassed to ask me anything. What is it?"

"I couldn't get my zipper all the way up. It isn't revealing anything. If only I were double-jointed like you are, this wouldn't be an issue." I spoke way too fast and rambled through the sentence.

He chuckled at my nervousness and motioned for me to turn around. "Helping you zip your dress up, I can do. However, I won't be the one unzipping it for you, so you'll have to figure that one out later." He gently closed my dress the few notches, with one hand on the zipper and the other on my waist.

I was sure my face was a lovely shade of pink as I turned back around, musing he'd be the one to do this for me for years to come, causing butterflies to erupt in my stomach. "Thank you, I tried. I wasn't just—"

"It's fine. Don't mention it again." He cut me off from my groveling and leaned in to kiss my rosy cheek. "Are you ready?"

"Almost. I have something for you. At least one part of tonight needs to be completely about you." I grabbed the small red box from the bar and handed it to him.

"You got me a present?"

"I did. Open it," I exclaimed, eager to know if he'd like it.

He purposefully opened the box slowly while looking straight at me, making me more anxious. As Aaron pulled out the wooden guitar pick key chain, a smile grew on his face. "How cool. What is this part?" he asked, inspecting the engraved portion.

"It's a sound wave. Of me."

"For real?" He ran his thumb over it. "What're you saying?"

"Well, I put a lot of thought into it, but it isn't deep or anything—"

"Just tell me."

"It's 'hey you' because we say that to each other often." The part I was nervous about. "There's an app that scans it and playbacks my voice for you. Now you can hear me anytime you want."

"Really? It's perfect, thank you. This is the coolest present I've ever received." He pulled his keys out of his pocket and added my gift to the bunch.

"The website said you could use it as an actual pick too, but I'm not sure about that. It seems pretty thick."

"It can be my emergency back up. I'll never be without one."

"Okay. Now I'm ready."

"I do believe you will be turning heads all night, Miss Miller." He beamed, looking me over before pulling me in close with one arm around my waist.

"No doubt with you on my arm."

He helped me down the stairs, which was nice since I feared to break an ankle. I think a sloth could've made it down faster, but he didn't seem to rush me. Aaron opened the passenger door for me and carefully helped me into the car, making sure no parts of my dress would get caught. After he sat and buckled, he looked up at me.

"You really are breathtaking."

I smiled his favorite smile and looked down at the clutch in my lap, slightly embarrassed and unsure how to respond. I felt like a young girl with her first crush.

"What did you do today?" he asked, firing up the car and hitting the road.

"Lots of girly things," I admitted, not wanting him to know just how much prep work went into this look. "I got a manicure." I dangled my fingers out in front of me so he could see them.

"Nice." He grabbed my hand, kissed it, then laced his fingers into mine, and lowered our hands to my lap, stretching his arm over the console.

"What did you do today, Birthday Boy?"

"I saw my brother, which was great because it's been a while."

"That's fantastic. What did you guys do?"

"He took me to get some hot wings for a birthday lunch. We spent a long time talking too. He needed some advice. Not that I have an overabundance of experience with relationships or anything. He's always looked up to me as his older brother and wanted to know what I'd do in his situation."

"I see. So he's in a relationship?"

"Yeah."

Sorry, Vicki.

"Michael's been with his girlfriend for almost a year, and she told him they either needed to get engaged or break up. He just isn't there yet but also doesn't want to lose her."

"Oh man, that's a difficult situation. What did you tell him?" I was more interested in Aaron's advice, and what I could learn about him from it than I honestly was his brother's situation.

"Well, I told him it wasn't that cut and dry. If she loves him and truly wants to be with him forever, then she wouldn't give him up based on a time frame. I also told him if he knew she was the one and wanted to marry

Mental Notes

her eventually, they should compromise on a date they both liked. But he had to know for sure if she was his one."

His one.

I liked how he conveyed that and tried to close my mouth because it felt like it gaped open. Graciously, it was only open in my mind. I was beyond thrilled with his sound advice and ability to reason so well. "Good advice. Did he come to a conclusion yet?"

"Not sure exactly, but I think he might be single soon if I had to pick which way he'll end up."

Maybe Vicki had a chance after all.

"I just think it's awful he's in that predicament, but better now than in five years of continued ultimatums."

"Very true. I hope he makes the right choice for himself."

The drive to the venue where the ceremony and reception were being held wasn't long at all, and our conversation made the ride seem even faster—we were already pulling into the parking lot that was mostly filled. Aaron found a spot as close as possible, probably not wanting me to have to walk too far on the gravel parking lot. He shut down the engine and turned to me.

"I want you to know that if at any point you feel uncomfortable and want to leave, all you have to do is let me know. I'm here for *you*. I have no attachment to this situation. You can say something, like a code word, and I'll get us out of here. We can go eat somewhere else or whatever you want to do."

"A code word, huh?"

"Yup." He smirked with pride of his idea.

"How about bananas?"

"Bananas. Got it. Now let's enjoy ourselves. I do plan on giving you an unforgettable night."

"Deal." The smile on my face couldn't get any bigger.

When he got out to come around to help me, I inhaled and exhaled deeply while alone. *I can do this.*

"I'm sorry, I should've dropped you off at the door. This parking lot is probably tough in those heels."

"I wouldn't have wanted to stand there without you anyway. We're good if we keep this pace." Which wasn't fast. I used it as an excuse to pull myself closer to him, my arm linked in his—the train of my dress in the other.

"Sounds good. We don't have to hurry. Ethan and Stacy saved us seats, and we have," he looked at his watch, "ten minutes until the ceremony is supposed to start."

"Perfect."

We made our way across the parking lot and passed the mighty, ornate wooden door. The place was beautifully covered in various sizes of fresh, white flower bouquets and tulle. Everything looked clean and crisp against the dark wood floors. The ceiling was high, and the main lobby's acoustics echoed the sounds of chatter and heels colliding with the floor. We walked passed the sign-in book because I wasn't planning on signing it when Aaron pulled me back and wrote:

Aaron & Maddison

No last names. Our names looked so good together, especially in his handwriting. I laughed and rolled my eyes, picturing Garrett reading it later, and glad it didn't say Maddison. The double doors leading into the hall were still open as ushers herded people in like cattle. Fancy dressed up cattle. We got caught up in the crowd, but Ethan saw us and flagged us over to our saved seats.

"This place is beautiful," I said as I sat next to Stacy, Ethan on her left. I was glad I got to sit next to her, almost positive Ethan would be cracking jokes the whole time with whoever was next to him. Which would've driven me mad.

"I know. And it smells amazing. I bet there's a million flowers in here."

"You look beautiful." Stacy's tight fitted black halter dress had an asymmetrical bottom—or at least it appeared to while she sat down. It wrapped around her waist, leaving an open slit above her knees.

"Me? Oh my gosh, you! That dress was made for you." She replied way too loud for my liking.

"That's what I'm saying," Aaron butted in. I hadn't noticed he was paying attention to our conversation.

The music started playing, signaling the beginning of the ceremony, and cueing the ushers in the back to close the double doors. Out of a side door, the officiant led the way, followed by Garrett and his groomsmen.

The first time I laid eyes on him in over two years. He looked a bit different to me. Maybe it was love in his eyes, and I'd never seen it before.

One by one, we watched the bridesmaids, of whom I knew none, walk down the aisle followed by an adorable little flower girl. If she was Garrett's niece, she aged quicker than I thought possible.

The music changed, alerting everyone to rise to their feet and face the back, awaiting the bride. The doors opened to a father and radiant bride in a pearl dress. Her skin was olive, and her hair black as night. The smile on her face appeared excited yet nervous, and tears trembled not to break the lid barrier—all of which I could see from our seats close to the back.

I couldn't stop my brain as I compared myself to her. What did she have that I didn't? What was it about her Garrett loved and couldn't find in me? I wouldn't say she was vastly prettier than me; we were both quite equal, really.

Aaron reached over and grabbed my hand, pulling me out of my destructive thoughts, and once again, I was glad he was in my life. I smiled and wondered if he saw something on my face that gave away my inner turmoil.

"Who gives this woman to be married to this man?" The officiant's voice boomed in the vaulted ceilings.

"Her mother and I." We could barely hear her father since he was so far away from the microphone on the small stage.

The father handed the bride off to Garrett, who looked better than I'd ever seen him. His face was full of life—a stab to my gut in all honesty. The officiant started talking about the importance of marriage and the meaning of two becoming one, but I only caught about half of it. I watched the bride and groom as they looked at each other in deepest admiration like they were the only two in the room.

Really starting to question why I came but doubting a "bananas" and an exit this early was a good idea, I knew I needed to muster through my conflicting emotions. I focused my attention elsewhere and looked down the row of bridesmaids, all beaming for their friend—or family member for all I knew. Their long mint gowns flowed smoothly and elegantly. All of the dresses were floor-length and cinched at the waist, but each girl had a slightly different cut to the top. A simple sleeveless v-neck stood next to a strapless sweetheart cut. In front of her was a high neckline covering only one shoulder, and the maid of honor had on a beautiful sweetheart neckline covered with a top layer of chiffon, creating cap sleeves. They all looked stunning with low buns over their left shoulders.

The groomsmen were in gray tuxes with open jackets, exposing a vest over pale lavender shirts and deep eggplant ties. Everyone looked sharp except for the one guy on the end who'd probably never worn a suit—and never would again. He constantly fidgeted, picking at the various parts that appeared too tight for comfort. I was uncomfortable with him.

"Garrett, do you promise to be faithful, putting Lacy before yourself always?" The thunderous voice drew me back into the here and now. The verbiage of Garrett and faithful weren't words I would've put into a sentence of my own forming. I looked down and started tracing the flowered lace pattern on my dress. When he said, "I do," I tensed up.

"Hey, you okay?" Aaron whispered into my ear.

"Think so. I got so caught up in my date with you today I forgot some of this might get awkward, but I'm fine."

He leaned so far in there wasn't a gap left between us and wrapped his left arm around extra tight. Pulling me away from Stacy grabbed her attention, but only for a second.

"It wasn't about you. His issues were his own. You're far greater than all that." His cheek was pressed against mine as he continued to whisper in my ear, his words filling all the negative voids with soothing golden oil. He definitely knew I was trapped in my thoughts now and was fighting to dig me out of the treacherous pit that sucked me in.

"Thank you. You're right."

The room exploded into applause, and I looked up to see Garrett kissing his now wife. I gave a clap I wished I meant more genuinely. The worst was over. The rest of the night would be like a crowded restaurant club combo. Or so I tried to believe.

"It is my honor to present to you for the first time, Mr. & Mrs. Garrett Hall." The maid of honor handed the lavish bouquet back to the bride, and the newlywed couple sped through the double doors. The pairs of the wedding court followed them out one at a time, much faster than they came in. "The bride and groom have asked me to announce dinner will start in one hour. In the meantime, they'd love for you to enjoy the cocktails and refreshments in the lobby. If you wouldn't mind, please head out there now to allow the staff time to set up for the meal."

"Sounds good to me." Ethan exploded from his seat, obviously still not the sit-still-and-be-quiet type. He was up before anyone else, dragging poor Stacy out the opposite end of our row.

Aaron chuckled under his breath, standing and offering me his hand. "Shall we?"

The lobby looked totally different from our arrival. During the ceremony, about twenty bar height tables and a mobile bar stand on wheels were set up. Two buffet tables stood in the middle with fruit and vegetable trays, crackers and cheese, and meatballs.

I was confident the meatballs were Garrett's idea—the memory they were one of his favorite foods tormented me. I never cared much for them anyway, but wouldn't dare eat one of those barbecue drenched hazards in this dress.

"Do you want anything?" Aaron asked as we walked around the quickly crowding lobby.

"I think I might grab some fruit and cheese. Are you gonna get something?"

"No, I'm saving my appetite for dinner. Ethan said Garrett went on and on about the caterer they hired."

"Fancy," came out, seeping with sarcasm.

Aaron laughed.

"Do you want a drink then?" I asked. We hadn't disgusted the topic before, so I wasn't sure if he drank, socially or otherwise.

"Nah, I'm good. I can get you something, though, if you'd like."

"It's ok. I don't drink much." *Especially if you aren't.*

"Not even a coke?" He joked but looked relieved at my answer.

"Nah, I'm good." I tried to match his voice from seconds before. "So you don't drink?"

"I used to. A lot, actually. During recovery, I decided to step away from all of it. Haven't touched alcohol in three years. You?"

"I have, but can't say it's for me. The only alcohol drank in my house growing up was found in cough medicine."

He laughed again.

It was a good sign I was able to be playful for the first time tonight. I was thankful the chaos of emotions tumbling around inside of me appeared settled. I was also relieved I hadn't tried to alter my current anxieties by nursing on five ounces of liquor since it was something from Aaron's past he had to break free from. Simply being around him was enough to alter my anxieties.

~ 12 ~

The hour didn't go by as painfully slow as I thought it would, but we lost Ethan practically the entire time. He was trying to find and catch up with our old group in attendance while I was hiding in the corner from the exact same people. Most of the guests here, probably two hundred or so, were strangers to me. I hoped I was another face to them and not "the ex" every time I caught someone staring at me.

When my eyes almost bulged out of my skull, and I looked down for the twentieth time, Aaron leaned in and whispered, "It's the dress they're looking at. I told you I wanted to have the prettiest date here, and now everyone knows it's true."

I never drifted too far off into my realm of ridiculous over analyzing before Aaron reeled me back to reality. He acted as my anchor, and he was succeeding.

Moments later, we were back in the main room, seated at a table for eight. I sat between Aaron and Stacy again, Ethan on her left. Billy, Ethan's best friend and member of our old crew, sat next to Ethan. His date, who I didn't know, was next to him, and two seats were left unoccupied.

The staff transformed the venue from a church like rowed seating and small stage, into an open banquet room with large round tables covered in black tablecloths and a dance floor in the middle. The centerpieces on the tables looked like the large white bouquets that adorned the end of each row down the center aisle an hour ago, now in sparkling crystal vases. Each seat had a formal place setting comprising a white salad plate rimmed with gold polka dots, a mint dinner plate, a large white petal-shaped charger, and shiny gold utensils. I liked how she—I couldn't remember the bride's name—tied the mint theme into the dinnerware. Surely Garrett had nothing to do with that.

The waiter came around dressed in black slacks, a white button-up shirt covered with a fastened black vest, and a half apron tied around his waist. Very formal. "Chicken, beef, or fish?" He started with Stacy.

"I'll go with Chicken," she politely responded.

He looked at me, "Ma'am?"

"What cut of beef?" I had to ask. Sometimes beef grossed me out.

"It's a round steak."

"Oh yes, beef, please. Medium-well." I prayed the other girl wouldn't get chicken as well and leave me looking like one of the guys.

He turned to Billy's date and received a hand in the air. Rude. Maybe she hadn't decided.

"Beef. Medium, please." Aaron offered up to the waiter and then looked back at me and winked. This was much fancier than our last beef—hamburger cut—couch date. The waiter continued around the table, taking down two more beef and finally a fish for Billy's date. Even worse. Once again, I was just one of the guys.

I could see Garrett and L-something making their rounds to the tables to thank everyone for coming. I picked at my salad and prepared for my inevitable interaction with him. Aaron already finished his—he practically inhaled it—probably since he skipped the hors d'oeuvres. He wiped his mouth with the cloth napkin and started a conversation with the guys from across the table.

"So, Billy, was Ethan just as annoying in college too?"

Billy laughed but paused to finish his bite before responding. "Worse." Everyone joined in his laughter, but only Billy and I knew it was accurate. Ethan was great, but he could also be overbearing at times.

"Ha, ha, ha." Ethan shared his amusement or lack thereof.

"What's so funny?" Garrett came up as our snickering faded, standing in front of the vacant seats.

I was done laughing. I could barely breathe.

He looked around the table at all who sat there. "Maddison. I'm so glad you came."

Aaron reached over and grabbed my hand. Garrett's eyes dropped in recognition before his gaze returned to my face.

"They're laughing at how awesome I was in college." Ethan objected, trading out a word for one he preferred.

"Super awesome," Garrett said with a chuckle. "Hi, I'm Garrett." He leaned his hand across the table toward Aaron.

"Aaron. Pleasure to meet you. Congratulations." Aaron stood halfway and gave a visibly firm handshake, drenched in testosterone.

"Thank you. Are y'all togeth—"

"Yes, sir." I was pretty sure Garrett asked me, but Aaron offered the answer.

"That's great. Maddison deserves the best." A weird thing to say considering our past.

Now I do, but not when you were with me? Do you know that I know? I had yet to say anything.

"You look great, Maddison."

I had to say something now. Everyone looked at me, waiting for my response. I went for genuine honesty, even though I'd rather poke myself in the eye with my polished fork. "Thank you, Garrett. So do you. I don't think I've ever seen you happier." Which was true, but extremely sour in my mouth to admit.

"I'm extremely happy." He smiled as if somehow we'd resolved all of our issues in this brief conversation. Perhaps it was that easy for him. It wasn't for me.

"Beef, medium-well?" One of the servers asked, attempting to pass out the food. I raised my hand, along with Ethan and Billy. "Ladies first." The waiter lowered the plate in front of me.

"I'll let you all eat. Thanks for being here. Nice to meet you, Aaron." Either he already knew Stacy and Billy's date, or he was seriously honed in on Aaron. For obvious reasons.

"Likewise," Aaron responded.

I looked over at my date with relief in my eyes and a one-sided smile. He winked.

That could have gone worse. I was glad it was over with. I banked on most likely not having to interact with Garrett again and planned to enjoy my food and dance with this super gorgeous man who just boldly claimed me to my ex—*whew, that was attractive.* Replaying Aaron's actions from the last several minutes caused a smile to transform my face.

The food was worth raving about—I tried not to be annoyed—and everyone did so except for Miss Fish, who barely said anything all night. If I had to guess, I'd say she and Billy weren't a serious item, or she wasn't thrilled about feeling the odd one out all night.

"You know what we need to do?" Ethan blurted out of nowhere. "We need to do another road trip!"

"That could be fun." I used *could* because it'd all depend on who came.

"Totally." Billy spouted off, looking at his unimpressed date, who said nothing. No surprise there.

"You in, Aaron? Babe?" Ethan asked around the table.

"If Maddison goes, I'll be there," Aaron replied.

"I'm in." Stacy agreed.

"Awesome. I'll see if I can locate the information for those cabins we stayed in on the lake close to Austin. It's almost warm enough for a nice day of floating down the river." Ethan pulled out his phone and created a reminder.

The first dance started, followed by the father of the bride and the mother of the groom dance. Quickly after, the deejay played lively music and invited everyone to the dance floor. I didn't move at first, unsure what everyone else was going to do, or if Aaron considered himself the dancing type. Ethan was the first person up again, always the one you could count on to get a party started.

"Would you like to dance?" Aaron asked. "I'm not the best, but I'm in if you are."

"Oh, I'm in." I'd looked forward to this portion of the night the most. Simply letting go and having fun with some of my favorite people.

The majority of the guests looked close to my age, and practically all of them moved to the dance floor. Everyone was living it up, laughing, and no one seemed out-of-place.

Even me.

All of these people were here to celebrate love. Some had it for themselves, others probably hoping to find it tonight or in the near future, but I'd found mine. With every new song that played, I shook off another damaged part of me caused by the betrayal of the man I used to love who everyone was celebrating tonight.

The crowd was electric. I even saw a guy wearing his tie sideways around his forehead. Aaron told the truth about not being the best dancer. He had a few solid moves but resembled a junior high boy next to Ethan, who was often in the middle of the dance floor commanding everyone's attention.

I noticed some beads of sweat forming around Aaron's hairline and suggested, "Let's take a break. I need some water, and I'm probably gonna ditch these shoes at the table," over the music.

"Good idea, my feet are killing me," Stacy agreed. Her heels were even taller than mine. We lost Billy several songs ago, and when we made it back to the table, all of their things were gone. Poor Billy.

"Have a seat, I'll grab you some water," Aaron said, leaning in close enough so I could hear him while placing his hand on the small of my back. His touch made my heart skip, and I instinctively turned around, almost colliding faces with him. "Sorry. I didn't mean to startle you, but since I have your attention." He took full advantage of my face being so close to his, kissed me, then smirked.

A smile grew on my face to match his. He took it as a welcoming gesture and leaned in for one more. He was right.

My feet seemed to have perfect timing, as the deejay announced the bride and groom were heading over to cut the cake. I enjoyed the part at weddings, watching to see if the couple would be sweet and gentle or take full advantage of the opportunity to shove cake in their spouse's face. I had a theory you could tell a lot about how a marriage would turn out based on this very act.

Garrett would most likely make a mess of it, or at least taunt her with it. Lacy, I finally remembered her name, was all giggles as they cut their tiny bites of cake. Garrett carefully placed one hand under her chin and fed Lacy the cake sweetly, then kissed her to prevent any crumbs. Well? Another reminder he wasn't the man I knew—and dated. Projecting things on him kept coming up void.

Lacy grabbed her much larger piece, started slow, and then shoved it in Garrett's mouth, breaking the cake and smearing icing all over his chin and cheeks. I didn't know anything about her before, but I knew more than I did five minutes ago. Garrett picked a feisty one.

People laughed and clapped as Garrett pulled some more icing off the bottom tier and rubbed it on her cheek. I knew there had to be some degree left in him and finally laughed with everyone else. He wasn't my mess anymore.

"I hate when couples do that," Aaron whispered in my ear before setting down our waters and taking his seat.

And now I know more about you too.

How did he keep doing that? I seriously wondered if he had a way to read my mind. "Yeah?" I leaned my head in and rested against his shoulder. He told me more in one statement than he could've ever imagined. I closed my eyes and leaned into him for a minute longer, taking in his wonderful scent paired slightly with sweat. Perfection. The music started again, but I wasn't ready to give up our position. It felt like he wasn't either.

"Cake?" The waiter barked, forcing me out of my own little paradise.

"Please." I never passed up cake.

"Yes, sir." Aaron answered the waiter's motion with a small, clear plastic plate. Ethan and Stacy also stayed for cake.

"Y'all are getting pretty serious, huh?" Ethan's bold question wasn't one I felt comfortable answering on the spot. I guess after watching us all evening, including our first kiss in public, I couldn't blame him for wondering. Asking maybe, but not wondering.

I turned to Aaron, who looked at me for a reaction. I must've looked like a deer in headlights because he rescued me for about the fifth time tonight.

"I hope so," he replied, still looking at me with a grin before turning to Ethan.

Stacy caught my glance first and smiled before looking down at her cake.

"Me too." I responded to Ethan, who I felt burning holes into my skin without even looking at him.

"All right, folks. We're going to take it down for just a few more songs before we send off the newlyweds in their getaway car." The deejay roared over the microphone.

"That's my cue. Time to trash Garrett's car with some of the groomsmen. I'll be back, babe." Ethan kissed Stacy and shoved his last bite of cake into his mouth as he stood to leave.

A slow song played in the background. I hoped to dance at least one more time with my favorite person as I finished my cake, but tried not to look like I was rushing.

"Do you have a few more in you?" Aaron asked, after wiping his mouth and tossing the napkin onto the table.

"I do if you do." I gushed, sending him a flirtatious glance.

"Please excuse us, Stacy." He confirmed even further he was a true gentleman—my mother would be elated to hear.

I, on the other hand, was so caught up in Aaron, I hadn't even thought about leaving her there alone. "Oh, we can stay," I offered.

"No. Please, go. I'm gonna ask Ethan if we can leave when he's done. My feet are so mad at me. I was overzealous with those shoes."

"Okay, we'll see you soon." I leaned over in my chair to hug her before standing.

Aaron stood as I did. I grabbed his hand, pulling him to the dance floor a few inches shorter without my shoes. I placed my hands around his neck, and his forearms rested courteously around my hips, his hands clasped behind my back—I wouldn't have minded if they held me though. My eyes took him in with pure amazement, my view farther away than before.

"Do you see yourself doing all of this? Getting married?" he inquired.

"I do. I see the love my parents have had all these years and know it's still possible if you're willing to fight for it. You?"

"I do. Not sure I care to go this fancy, though." He motioned around with his head, lifting his eyebrows. "Not that this is bad. I just don't think you need it all. Did you have a good time tonight?" He fixed my bangs by brushing them into the correct position.

"I did. Thank you for forcing me into this. You did more for me than you know."

"Force is a strong word."

"Nudged." I winked.

I truly felt my healing process from all things Garrett had finally completed. I committed to working hard to get back to a better version of my old self. It was pretty remarkable how Aaron was the one to help me once I stopped trying to control being hurt by isolating myself. Especially considering a guy was usually the cause of my issues. And just when I wasn't sure I'd ever trust men again. Sometimes I thought God had an ironic sense of humor.

"Honored to do so. You're pretty amazing, you know?" Aaron looked into my eyes with genuine affection.

"You think so, huh?" My heart picked up its pace, considerably swifter than the music.

"I do. You know, I've spent a long time single—a *long time*. My friends kept trying to set me up and never stopped asking when I was going to settle down with someone, but ... I just prayed. A lot." He chuckled. "I didn't want to be with someone just so I wasn't alone or people would stop asking. I wanted to get my life in focus so I could be the kind of husband my dad is now, and make sure I'd never be the husband he used to be."

His words were one hundred percent candid and vulnerable. In that instant, I was hands down the most attracted to him I'd ever been—and falling even deeper. "That's amazing."

"I'd like to make my intentions known if that's okay?"

"Yes, please do." I had to take a breath before my brain forgot how to breathe.

"I don't just want to date you casually. I want to pursue you." He stopped for a brief second, pondering his next words. "Because I think you are my one. The one I've prepared for. Is that okay with you?"

His favorite kind of smile grew on my face as my eyes most likely began twinkling. "Absolutely." We continued swaying to the music, and I laid my head against his chest, hearing the faster rhythm of his heartbeat. He kissed me on the top of my head.

"Thank you," he said tenderly.

"Thank *you*." I couldn't help but feel like my life would never be the same. Finally.

"I knew you were a keeper when you opened my car door for me after church," he admitted.

"Oh, really?" I couldn't help but snicker. That happened a long time ago, making me wonder why he waited so long to finally ask.

"Ladies and gents, as requested by the Halls, this is the last song of the night. The bride and groom are going to say their goodbyes for the evening before heading out." The voice over the speakers informed everyone, interrupting our special moment.

A familiar song from a movie I saw dozens of times on tv as a teenager —*Dirty Dancing*—filled the room. Aaron started singing to me as we danced.

I looked up at him in pure joy and sang back to him along with the female vocalist portion of the duet, gazing into his warm cobalt eyes. Our pace picked up to match the new tempo as we sang back and forth the lyrics we knew, laughing and mumbling through the others we didn't or that were mildly inappropriate.

People around the room began putting on their best acting impersonations, a few even trying the iconic lift and laughing all the way through.

"Take a sparkler and head outside, please." The bridesmaid in the single shoulder dress passed the sticks out for the send-off before the last song ended.

Aaron took them from her as she hurried along, repeating her phrase. "You want to do this?" he asked.

"Uhhh." *Not really*, but I didn't admit it.

"Me either. Let's go."

We put the sparklers down on our table, grabbed our things, and hurried out the side door, to prevent anyone noticing us ditching as the final song came to an end. He pulled me behind him, checking to make sure he wasn't going too fast so I wouldn't stumble in my heels. We laughed all the while, like a couple of school-aged kids skipping last period as we made our way into the darkness toward his car.

"This has not only been an amazing birthday, but it has also been one of the best nights of my life. I truly mean it," he confessed as we leaned against the passenger side.

"Mine too." A light shiver took over my body. With the sun long gone, my lace dress didn't offer much warmth. Aaron rubbed his hands up and down my arms to warm me up. "We are official now, right?"

"Officially official," he said. I could see his perfect teeth gleaming in the moonlight.

"Yesssss!" I tipped my head backward and raised my hands in victory. Letting out more of my quirkiness than he'd seen thus far felt safe now in our solidified relationship.

He laughed and grabbed both sides of my face to kiss me.

I let my arms fall back down around him.

It was pure magic as the sparklers began lighting up behind us, the perfect ending to a perfect night. Another chill ran through my body, ending our kiss, but I wasn't sure if it was from the cold or his touch.

"Happy birthday, Aaron."

"Thank you. You have a beautiful voice, by the way." He pulled me into a tight hug, transferring his warmth to me. "Okay, let's get you home before you freeze."

~ 13 ~

Vicki and I were long overdue for some girl-time. We hadn't spent any time together outside of work since she helped me dress shop a couple of weeks ago. Our hands were full at work, with customers wanting to get their ads in time to run all summer long. We even had a joint project—my first ever two-page spread—Jerry wanted her to coach me through. I was glad he didn't throw me to the wolves on my first attempt, and there was no better teacher than Vicki. Which he knew, of course.

Vicki's mom, Patricia, recently became a beauty consultant/saleswoman and needed to practice her facial parties. She asked Vicki to get a few girls together for a dry run in order to feel more prepared. I obliged but warned Vicki I wasn't the super girly type when it came to beauty regimens. It'd probably be good to learn more makeup tricks than the few I used, which was like two. A win-win as far as I was concerned: time to hang out with Vicki, helping out Patricia, and a free facial. Win-win-win, actually.

Patricia wanted to practice everything, including what to pack and commuting with the supplies, so they were coming over to my apartment after work. I grabbed the refreshment trays from the fridge and placed them out on the bar with a few plates and napkins. I knew I'd be hungry not eating dinner at my normal time, and I figured the snacks were a nice touch to the evening as well. I heard a knock at the door, and yelled, "Come in," since I was expecting them.

"Knock knock. We're here." Patricia walked in, toting a cute pink luggage box on wheels. Vicki favored her mother in looks.

"Welcome. Please let me know if you need help setting anything up. Sorry, my table is so small." Living alone, I had no need for larger furniture. My small breakfast nook table for two wouldn't have worked for a larger party.

"No, ma'am. I got this." I couldn't tell if she was responding to me or giving herself a pep talk. "Just point me in the right direction, and I'll be ready to go in about ten minutes." As Patricia parked and began to unload, Vicki walked in with even more pink containers.

"Oh my goodness, let me help you." I rushed over to the door to my out of breath friend.

"Mom, how're you going to do this alone next time?" Vicki stumbled through my hallway like she was hauling enough luggage for a month-long vacation.

"Well, honey, I probably don't *actually* need all of it. I brought *all* of my things, just in case. I won't do this every time, you know." She chuckled as she set up the few items from her one small bag on wheels.

Vicki somehow managed to drop every bag to the ground with one quick body shake, creating quite the commotion. "Hey," she sighed as she lost twenty pounds, "thanks for helping."

"I'm happy to offer up my 'unskilled with makeup services.' Need something to drink after that workout?" We joked about the situation because it was better than getting mad or crying about it.

"I'd love some water," she said, pretending to wipe her brow as if she'd finished a grueling exercise session. "And I'm totally going to devour some of these veggies." Vicki dipped a carrot in the ranch and bit it in half with her back teeth, causing a loud snap to fill the room.

"Victoria Lynne! Where are your manners?" Patricia spouted off. We never outgrew the use of our middle name from time to time, did we? At least in our mothers' opinion.

Vicki clenched her teeth and forced an awkward smile.

"Patricia, do you need something to drink?"

"Please, call me Patti. I'd love some, thank you."

I set a glass on the counter for her and joined Vicki, who was sprawled out on my couch, right in my crater.

"Your place is so cute," she huffed, still trying to catch her breath and causing me to laugh. "What? Those things were heavy! Anyway, continue.

You'd just told me about when your ex came over, and Aaron grabbed your hand."

Between all of our time spent on the project at work, Vicki still needed the remainder of the recap she'd only got in pieces.

"Right, he was just *there*. All night. Every time I was about to crumble. I don't know if he saw it on my face or felt it coming or what. He was just —"

"Perfect," she interrupted.

"I guess you could say that, but it's unfair to set him up for failure that way, don't you think?"

"Oh, come on. You know what I mean."

I went on to tell her the highlights of the evening, beaming at my favorite parts, which was practically all of it. Vicki liked more in-depth retelling, but I knew her mom would be calling us over any minute.

"Oh! And he does have a brother that's newly single. But," I paused, "he's younger. Not sure if you want to hold a cougar card or not."

She laughed but didn't answer. Was that a yes or a no?

"All right, ladies. I'm ready." Patti called from my kitchen, excitement lighting her face and nerves wringing her hands.

We took our places around my tiny table and let Patti begin with her entire spiel. Vicki and I tried to be good participants, but the idea of it being a practice session seemed to bring out our goofy pre-teen sides. After Patti gave Vicki the famous mother's eye for the third time, we tried to keep our silliness at a minimum.

Patti guided us through all the different cleansing creams on our small trays, then handed us an incredibly soft makeup removal cloth. She specifically noted we could buy the wipes for six ninety-nine for a month's supply. Must've been part of her presentation. It didn't take me very long to clear my face because most days, I only had on the basics anyway.

"Now, starting with cream one, gently rub a dab at a time onto your face in small circles, avoiding your eyes." She checked back down to look at her note cards, making sure she got it right.

"Oh, I feel all the little scrubbers. That's almost painful." Vicki looked up at her mom.

Patti peered at her note card with worry in her eyes, looking for an answer. "Just ... try not to rub as hard, probably."

The exfoliating cream didn't seem to bother me.

"Now I'm going to give you a warm washcloth, and you will gently wipe your face until it's clear." She asked to warm the towels in my microwave, and I was glad I recently cleaned out the inside. My mother would be proud.

"This is heavenly. My face feels so soft." Maybe my face was always supposed to feel this nice, causing me to recognize the need for implementing a better skincare routine.

"Yes! You just removed all of your dead skin that also aged your appearance." Delighted mark Patti's grin as she used one of the facts she didn't need the card to remember. "Now take cream two and apply it all over your face. This is a moisturizer." She looked down, flipping the card to the next. "It's important to re-hydrate your face. Now, while your faces dry, we'll pick out the colors that best complement your complexions."

This should be good. I probably used the wrong color because I just did what I always saw my mom do—try a small dot from the bottle in the beauty section on the back of my hand and rub it in.

We discovered I was ivory cream, and gold, gray, and plum were good shades for my eyes. I followed Patti's instructions step by step, questioning how I didn't know some of the things I'd done for years were considered "wrong." I wondered if people thought I looked as clueless as I felt. I used up the small samples to the fullest of their potential and felt quite pleased with my look. The only thing I'd probably change was the lip color—I didn't love lipstick on myself.

"All done. I'd love to take a picture of each of you for my client files." Patti bragged, pleasure with her educating and coaching tonight marking her face instead of the anxiety from earlier. She took Vicki's picture—as if she needed the reference—then one of me with her slightly outdated smartphone.

At least it wasn't a flip phone like my dad still had.

"My turn, Vicki. Let's take a selfie." I grabbed my phone off the bar and stood next to Vicki, who attacked the veggie tray again.

She chuckled, making sure there wasn't ranch dripping from her lip. We made our best teenager pose, showing off our made-over look. Aaron joked about being jealous of giving up his time with me tonight for Vicki but said it was important for me to have girl time. I figured he'd appreciate the fact I still thought about him and sent him the silly pictures.

Do we look like models or what?!

You look beautiful! Tell Vicki she looks great as well.

Miss you.

"Aaron says, you look great. Should I tell him to show the picture to his brother?"

When she snickered without answering, I decided not to bring it up anymore.

Call me when they leave?

I'd love to! ;)

We helped Patti clean up and put away all the things she used. Vicki was *not* thrilled the multiple bags she brought up weren't touched, but it was further proof Patti was ready for her first real presentation. I didn't want to listen to Vicki complaining of sore muscles at work, so I helped her carry the extra bags back down to her mother's car. We said our goodbyes, and I ran back upstairs to call my favorite person in the world.

I tossed a hot pocket in the microwave and grabbed the veggie tray's remnants for dinner before touching his name in my recent calls list.

"Hello, you!" His voice was always a touch deeper on the phone, causing comfort to cover me like a blanket.

"Hey! Did you have a good day?" I asked as the microwave timer went off.

"I did, although it's better now." He always seemed genuine when he said the lines I used to think were cheesy when they left anyone else's mouth. "Ethan brought up the trip at work today and wanted me to make sure you were still up for it?"

"Absolutely! I just need to request the days off if it's longer than Saturday and Sunday."

"He was thinking of the fourth of July weekend. We'd only have to take off Thursday, and it would be a four-day trip."

"Sounds good to me. Far out enough to ask for it off and not too far away to get excited! I think you deserve a fair warning. Ethan can be kinda crazy on these trips."

He chuckled. "Oh, he talked my ear off today. All about some of y'all's previous trips and some of his ideas for this one. There's already a list, but we can always ditch the activities we don't care for."

"Deal."

"He said Billy already backed out though, not wanting to be the only single guy there. Just Ethan and Stacy and us now. A guy's cabin and a girl's cabin."

No surprise, Billy's date from the wedding was already out of the picture. I didn't know Ethan and Stacy's stance on sharing a cabin, but Aaron and I had pretty clear boundaries for our relationship. Sharing a bed was a no-go.

"Sounds perfect."

"Great. The river will be pretty packed on a holiday, but it'll be fun. Ethan asked if we could take my car, bigger trunk. You up to be my co-pilot?"

"You know I am. But do you really think he's going to sit in the back seat the whole time?" I had a hard time believing he would.

"My car, my rules. If he doesn't drive, he loses the say."

"Well, all right then." I laughed. "This trip is going to be interesting with the two of you." Ethan was pretty crazy, and Aaron was definitely the calmer, laid back type, but he was strong on his opinions. There was a high possibility of at least one argument or tense situation.

"Eh, Ethan knows me pretty well. I don't think he'll push it." Aaron countered my statement. "I'm just excited to have my first road trip with you."

"Me too. All my favorite people together, except for Vicki."

"Invite her then."

"Yeah? But we'd be an odd amount again. I guess we could tell Billy." I knew Vicki wouldn't be interested in Billy, although I couldn't say why exactly.

"No. I think I want it to be our group, doing our things. Honestly, I don't want it to be some glory-days trip with people I barely know. Is that mean?"

"No. I'm with you there."

"I can ask my brother. He needs some social interaction."

Maybe it was a good idea, but with how Vicki blew off the subject already, I wasn't sure.

"Um, let me check with her before you invite your brother. If she doesn't want to go, and you've already asked him, he might feel like a fifth wheel. Having his singleness thrown in his face would be no fun."

"Good point. You're always thinking."

Knock, knock, knock.

Patti or Vicki must've left something. I scanned my eyes around my kitchen but found nothing. "Just a second. I think Vicki's back." I headed to the door, still not seeing anything left behind.

"Hi." I heard the velvet voice in surround sound, Aaron still holding his phone to his ear.

"Hey you! What a good surprise," I said before ending the call.

"If you're too spent, let me know, but I wanted to see you. I can kiss you and leave."

"You drove all the way over here just to kiss me?"

"Well, yeah. It's more than worth it."

"You're something else." I wrapped my hands around his face and rose on my tiptoes to kiss him.

He smiled at his successful mission.

"I was about to veg out and watch some tv. Care to join me?"

"I mean, since I'm already here." His playful tone sent shivers down my spine. Surely, he knew I'd invite him in. I had a hard time believing he'd drive over here just to kiss me and leave, no matter how romantic it sounded.

~ 14 ~

Vicki and I finished the joint project after one more full day of work and submitted it to Jerry, pretty sure it'd bounce back at least once. No doubt she would've finished much quicker if she worked alone. The full double-page spread for an up and coming travel agency was a beautiful ocean landscape with clear light green tropical waters. A single palm tree on the beach started on the bottom of the right page and grew at a curved angle into the left page. A clean, bold white lettering said, "Being here in six weeks is more affordable than you think" on the top of the right page. The travel agency's name and information scrolled across the entire bottom of both pages in a thin black font above the sandy beach. I mentally gave myself a pat on the back.

Negativity crept in seconds later. *How did something so simple take me so long?* My inner mean girl was hard to get rid of.

"Did I tell you about Ethan suggesting a road trip at the wedding?" I wasn't sure how to bring up Aaron's younger brother again, so I started broad, especially since I previously decided not to mention him after my "O and two" record.

"Cool. I don't think you did. Where are you guys going?"

"A place a couple of hours away. It has small cabins within walking distance of the water. We're going to spend at least one day floating the river. Our college group did it several years back and had a blast. We're going on the fourth of July weekend. I'll only miss one day of work."

"That's great. Is everyone in one big cabin?"

"No, we'll have two cabins, guys and girls. I mentioned to Aaron that my only favorite person who wouldn't be there was you, and he suggested

I invite you." I hoped to butter her up so she'd be less likely to turn me down, even though my statement was true.

"Really?"

I think it's working.

"I'd love to go! I need some get-away time." Vicki's dimples appeared. "Plus, constructing this ad gave me a major travel bug."

"Awesome. There's just one other thing. Aaron wants to invite his brother, Michael." Before she could protest, I added, "I swear this isn't a setup."

"Mmhmm." She laughed. Again.

"What's so funny about it?"

"Do you honestly think a younger guy's gonna want a *divorced* older woman? I'm practically the fifth Golden Girl."

She disqualified herself prematurely—not to mention, dramatically.

"You're ridiculous. I say anything can happen. Why not let him decide?" I hoped my optimism would encourage her to be more open on the topic.

An enormous huff left her lungs. "Fine. But if the weekend turns into a disaster, you owe me. BIG."

"Deal!" I said too loud for the office and slumped in my seat. "It's going to be so much fun, I promise." I continued with a lower voice. "And I haven't even met Michael yet either. I'm nervous but really excited about meeting some of Aaron's family."

"I sure hope he's a hottie like his brother. No offense. After hearing all of your stories, my hopes are set pretty high."

For a minute, I pictured Michael as an ultra nerd who talked cosplay and tech all day. I cringed at the thought of Vicki being stuck with him all weekend as the third pair if that were the case, but I was pretty confident if he had a girl wanting to marry him, he was suitable husband material.

"I bet he's just as awesome. Their momma seemed to raise them right." I gushed, somewhat unsure, but mostly confident. "We need to get another pedicure before we go. Our feet will be in close proximity to faces as we float down the river." I knew from experience and previous embarrassment. I pulled out my phone from my desk drawer to shoot Aaron a quick text.

Invite Michael. Vicki is in!

When I looked back up at her, unease gripped her face. I came up with an idea to possibly calm Vicki's nerves. If it didn't work how I planned, I wouldn't tell her in fear she'd back out.

> *Any chance you have apicture of Michael on your phone? She's a bit nervous.*
> *And maybe five fun facts about him too.*

A few minutes later, I got a reply. A picture with facts included. I was blown away by how similar they looked. I knew it would make Vicki happy since she agreed Aaron was handsome the first time she saw him.

"Okay, Vicki, don't be mad. I told Aaron to send me five facts about Michael since we both know nothing about him. You ready for this?" I asked, unsure if she would be excited, mad, or unimpressed.

"Let's hear it." Her tone was pretty level, giving me no pulse on the situation.

"One. 'They're only eleven months apart.' Which makes Micahel twenty-six because Aaron just turned twenty-seven."

"Really? That's a good start. I'm only a year older." Interesting. Vicki was younger than I thought. She must've graduated high school early. "Next?"

Score. She's into this.

"'He is taller than Aaron. Six foot three.' Ooh, tall is always a plus."

A smirk grew on Vicki's face, but not enough to reveal her dimples. She waved her hand in the air for the next fact.

"Three. 'He's left-handed.' That isn't a deal-breaker or anything, right? Four. 'He can't beat Aaron in arm wrestling.' Sorry, girl. Looks like I got the buffer brother. I bet Michael wouldn't have offered that fact."

We laughed.

"And finally, 'He was the valedictorian of his high school class.' Wow, pretty impressive. Want to see the picture now?"

She jumped up from her desk and darted over to mine. My idea was working.

"Sure." She downplayed her response even though her body langue was loud and clear. "Oh my gosh. They're like twins. Okay, maybe I'm interested."

A smirk grew on my face. I couldn't blame her for being attracted to Aaron's stunt double.

"Do you want to send him a picture of you?" I asked with raised eyebrows and squinted eyes. "You're drop-dead gorgeous, you know. It's not like you have anything to worry about."

"I don't know. Does he even know I'm coming? You said he's newly single, right? Will he think it's a lame set up?" She messed with her hair.

My phone vibrated on my desk.

Michael said he's excited to meet and she's gorgeous!

"He's excited to meet you, and thinks you are gorgeous." I wore a strained smile and bottled my excitement.

"Did you just take my picture and send it? MADDISON! I have to approve these things."

"I didn't. I have no clue how Michael saw you. Maybe they looked you up online or something. I'll ask." Hoping to escape the wrath of Vicki, I hoped Aaron could clarify and spare my plan.

Gorgeous? Y'all creepin online?

His response seemed to take an eternity, especially with Vicki's eyes shooting lasers through me.

No. I don't do social media. Remember? You sent a picture after your makeover.

That's right. "So I know what picture he saw. Remember the post-makeover selfie the other day at my apartment?" I pulled up my shoulders and leaned back, preparing for a punch I knew she wouldn't actually throw, but it conveyed my worry about her retaliation.

"Let me see it." She barked.

I scrolled back up in the conversation to find the picture and turned my phone for her to see.

"I guess it could be worse. I hope it's obvious we were being silly, and he doesn't think I'm a dumb blonde."

"Aaron knows you. He wouldn't let Michael think that." She glared at me with an unamused face. "I'm serious."

He wants five facts now, says it's only fair.

The text conversation pulled from the picture to his new response. We turned into a couple of teenagers reading a *Seventeen* magazine quiz in a heartbeat. Frustration melted off Vicki's face. "Should I? Or do you want to give your own facts. I mean, I'm pretty sure Aaron did it for Michael, so —"

"Give me that." She snatched the phone out of my hands and started texting at a fiery pace, releasing a thunderstorm of clicks before passing my phone back to me.

"Ladies, you're still on my clock for ten more minutes. Phones away." Jerry scolded us as he passed by us on his way back to his personal office, north of Cubical-Land. "Great job on the ad. No revisions requested by the client."

I didn't have anything else to work on for the day, but I pretended to look busy on my computer by checking my email. My inbox typically contained spam mail for the most part, but a message with "Request for Interview" in the subject line grabbed my attention. Before assuming it was junk and deleting it, I clicked the heading.

> *Ms. Miller,*
>
> *This response may come as a surprise to you so many months later. However, thank you for sending your résumé to us. We are now under new management and currently replacing a large amount of our staff. If you are still interested in working for Hands of Hope in our counseling department, please give me a call to set up an interview as soon as possible. I look forward to hearing from you.*

What was this? I applied at so many places the name didn't ring a bell. I searched Hands of Hope online, finding it to be a non-profit counseling agency that worked with recently adoptive families and children. *What do I do with this information?* There was no way I could mention it to Vicki with all this vacation and Michael talk going on, but I knew who'd give some pretty excellent advice. Two people actually.

"Let me know if he replies anything. I'm undecided if it's a good idea to meet him before the trip or not," Vicki said as she stood in front of my desk with her bags, indicating our workday had ended. I quickly clicked off my email screen, hoping not to look suspicious.

"You got it. I know a great couple you can double date with if you make up your mind." I collected my things, including my phone from the drawer, and read her five facts. Maddison's fashion advisor, super hard-working, easygoing, up for an adventure, loves to read. "Really? My fashion advisor?"

"It's happened more than once. Am I wrong?"

"You're a mess."

"Psh."

"A hot mess." I clarified. "See you tomorrow. And yes, I'll tell you if anything else is said."

My plan succeeded. Vicki was obviously interested.

* * * *

It was my night to decide our dinner plans, so I made my favorite crockpot recipe and told Aaron to head over after work. The timer beeped as I walked into my apartment. The rich scent of garlic parmesan chicken and potatoes filled the air as if I'd lit a southern-home-cooked-meal flavored candle. After kicking off my shoes, I set the table for dinner even though I didn't have to do anything fancy these days. I still liked making Aaron feel welcome and special in my little home.

I didn't know how to bring up the interview topic and weighed the options of blurting it out first thing, waiting until he asked about my day, or seeing if it came up somewhat organically. This was a big deal for me. Switching jobs after I finally got the hang of—and becoming more successful at—the one I didn't necessarily want several months ago. The timing didn't seem great. What if I switched and failed at my new job and couldn't return to my current position? What if I wasn't even good at being a counselor? I knew all the book smarts of counseling and psychology, but I hadn't actually *done it* yet. What if....

My brain never stopped.

The knock at the door pulled me from the potentially hazardous train of thought I was on, so I jumped off and stumbled to the door.

"Aren't you the best part of my day?" I crossed the threshold and leaped into a hug before he even walked in.

"That's quite the welcome. Any particular reason?"

I'll take that as my cue. "That obvious, huh? I need some advice. Well, input. I don't know what I need." The weight of my thoughts tumbled out of my mouth.

"You know, I do have a good record with advice-giving." He kissed my forehead and was drawn down the entryway by his nose like something from a cartoon. "Smells amazing! Did you cook this?" he asked, opening the crockpot lid.

"I did." I acted up to his question. "I'm becoming quite the homemaker." I winked, hoping he caught my unsubtle, subtle comment.

"Fantastic." He grabbed a plate, not even waiting for me to serve him.

"Someone's hungry. I got this, go sit down."

My quaint table was the perfect size for us, and he looked *perfect* sitting there.

"So, what's this crisis you're facing?"

"I got an email today."

"Oh, no! An email?" He shrieked, picking on me. He probably considered it flirting. I shot him a snide look. "Sorry, go ahead. What email?"

"It was from a company I applied at last year. I didn't even remember it in particular, really. I sent out a thousand."

"That's great."

"Is it? Do you think I should be switching professions right now? It's for a counselor position working with families that have adopted. It couldn't be more different from what I'm currently doing. I feel like I can only handle so much change at once. And trust me, I've already had a ton." I set the food down in front of him harder than I intended and joined him.

"But that's what you went to school for, right? It's obviously something you wanted to do at one point in your life. You can always go to the interview and feel it out."

"I don't know. What if—what if I'm not good at it. I'm just *now* getting good at my current job after months of *hard* work."

"Don't disqualify yourself, cutie," he said before taking a bite of his food. His eyes closed as his head tipped back. "Oh my goodness. Thank you, Jesus, for this food." He spoke out of the side of his full mouth. "And Maddison."

I laughed and started eating myself.

"What's the real reason you are hesitant?"

I pondered as we ate, Aaron quicker than me. After really thinking, I only came up with two things. "I guess I'm just afraid I'll be bad at it, and I feel guilty about leaving Vicki. She's helped me so much and become my best friend."

"Okay, Vicki first. If she's your best friend, do you really think not working together will change that? It isn't like you can't keep your relationship going without the same job. You just won't see her every day. And if she cares for you as you do her, then she'll be happy and supportive of you pursuing this, right?"

"Probably so." But the thought of not seeing Vicki everyday wrenched.

"And I already told you, don't sell yourself short. You have no idea how spectacular you can be at this. You had enough passion to suffer through five years of college. I'm certain you'll be amazing. Plus, you won't even know until you try it, so don't go there yet. Be optimistic." *For once* was what my mind added though the words didn't leave his lips.

Optimistic wasn't a common word in my vocabulary.

But he was right. I'd done horrible damage after the whole Garrett thing came to light and had to work hard for months to get myself out of that awful mindset. A similar thought pattern was trying to rear its ugly head again.

"You're right, sir. Are you sure *you* didn't go to school for psychology?" I smirked and took a bite from my full plate.

It was often easier to see a situation more clearly from an outside perspective—something I learned in college. I was thankful my boyfriend helped me see mine through different eyes.

Aaron got up for seconds.

"I'll return her email tomorrow," I said with equal excitement and hesitation. "Michael and Vicki, huh?" I changed the topic in an attempt to enjoy our time together. "Anything y'all talk about that I should know?"

"I'd probably be breaking some kind of 'bro-code' by telling you too much, but he's very excited to meet her and thinks she's a knockout!" His words led me to believe they talked more than a simple sentence could sum up.

"Do you think he's past the post-breakup re-bound stage?" I didn't want my friend to only be a fling for him. She deserved way better than that. Vicki had been through enough drama and needed promising potential for something long-term.

"Oh yeah. After she gave him the life ultimatum, he was grateful to see her true colors and the miserable future he was saving himself from. I just hope Vicki doesn't want to get married this year or anything."

I laughed. "I don't think she's in a rush." I didn't want to give away too much about her. It was her information to share when, and with whomever, she wanted to. "You know she's older than him, though, right?" I stroked my hand forward in a claw motion like a cougar.

"You are adorable, Maddison!"

I loved how Aaron always called me by my full name. I never really told people they could call me Maddy—which I wasn't particularly fond of, actually. Shortening any name longer than two syllables seemed to be a societal norm. Him saying my full name, every time, made me feel extra special.

"Who me?" I tilted my head and batted my eyes as fast as I could.

He pulled out his phone and started a video like he often did.

"Yes, you. Quite adorable."

"I'm pretty smitten by you as well, Mr. Walker." I winked at the camera.

"Are you now? Tell me something that will make me smile."

I knew that was coming. "You're my favorite person."

"Mmmm." He tilted his head. "What else?"

"What else? Let's see. I want you to be in my life for a long, long time."

A smile spread across his face. "Me too."

* * * *

The next day at work, after emailing Hands of Hope, I asked Vicki to go to lunch with me so I could fill her in on Michael and the job offer. We went downtown to Food Truck Row, a fun and delicious place to eat if the lines weren't already around the block. We picked the taco truck because, when's it not a good idea to eat tacos? I enjoyed them up there with hamburgers and pasta.

"I have good news and bad news, which do you want first?" I broke the ice while we waited in line.

"Michael backed out?" She looked defeated but not surprised.

"No, he didn't." I smiled.

"Okay. Good news first."

"Michael thinks you're a knockout and can't wait to meet you." I tried not to add anything to the brother's conversation, although I was sure there was more to it, grinning at her and raising my eyebrows a few times.

"Yeah? So like, soon?" She leaned in and grabbed my arm.

"I guess it's up to you. We didn't talk about it or plan anything if that's what you are thinking. But we can."

The thought of a double date with Vicki and Michael seemed more intriguing to me than the ones we had been on with Ethan and Stacy, but I felt bad admitting that to myself. Not that I didn't love being around Ethan and Stacy, I'd just grown so close to Vicki over the last year, and Ethan didn't provide the same support in my life anymore.

"Fine, to be continued. What's the bad news?"

I still wasn't exactly sure how to present the other part. I hesitated, then took a big breath and let it flow. "I was asked to come in for an interview for a counseling job."

"What? Maddy, that isn't bad news; it's awesome." She cheered.

"You think so?" I mostly worried about leaving Vicki, but she didn't seem to think anything of it. Or at least she wasn't letting it show.

"Of course. Why wouldn't it be?"

"I've just worked so hard to get good at this job, and you've helped me so much. Now I'll possibly switch to a career in a totally different field. It's kinda scary to start all over."

"Oh no, don't think like that. I was glad to help you learn and look at how it turned out," she motioned to me, acknowledging our friendship. "You don't worry about me at all when it comes to this decision."

135

That's when I knew. Vicki was the best girlfriend I ever had. I swept through the Rolodex of past friends in my mind, trying to find someone who wasn't motivated by what I could bring to the table in advancing them rather than caring for my best interests. Never found one.

"Thank you. I still don't know if they'll even hire me since I have no experience outside of my internship, but I emailed back this morning."

"That's fantastic. Keep me posted."

We made it to the front of the line and dropped our conversation as the smells from the taco truck filled our noses.

~ 15 ~

The day of our double date arrived. We asked the guys to pick where we went because Vicki wanted to get a feel for Michael's sense of planing a good date. I even told Aaron not to offer up much and leave most of it to Michael. He figured it was some kind of weird girl thing and left it alone. The date would also be my first time meeting anyone from Aaron's family, so I was the tiniest bit nervous. Nothing like Vicki though, currently found biting her nails at her desk.

Vicki hadn't been excited for a date in a few years, so it was her turn to be anxious about her outfit and have a hard time focusing. I giggled as she mindlessly tried to complete tasks that typically presented her with no issues whatsoever.

"Hey, stop that. Chewed nails aren't cute," I said from my desk, trying to ease her jitters.

"This is ridiculous. You'd think I was about to meet a long-lost twin I never knew I had."

I laughed. "It's going to be fine. There's nothing to be nervous about. I sure hope I wasn't this ridiculous." My comment triggered a colossal roll of her eyes.

"Tell me one more time what he already knows about me." She kept asking like I was going to finally tell her a new truth I'd been hiding.

"That you're a gorgeous blonde, most likely several months older than him. I honestly don't know what else he knows. Aaron might've said something to him, but it isn't like Aaron knows much about you either. Only what I've said, which isn't anything."

"So he doesn't know abou—"

"No." Her divorce. "And don't worry about any of that. It isn't like you have to introduce yourself and set out all your issues on the table like trophies."

"You're right. One day at a time. He'd freak me out if he spilled his life story tonight, so there's no need for me to do it."

"Exactly."

Almost time to clock out, I was thrilled for Vicki. Not to mention my day was always better when I got to be within touching distance of Aaron.

"Vicki, Jerry wants to see you in his office real quick." One of our co-workers barked as he passed from Jerry's office in between our desks. She looked at me as if she'd done something wrong, expecting some type of scolding, and hurried from her desk into the boss's office.

I took the last few minutes to check and see if Suzanne from Hands of Hope had emailed me back. Still nothing. Maybe she sent out requests for interviews to several people. Maybe they already hired someone. I was glad I hadn't mentioned a word of it to anyone here except for Vicki because all I needed was to be let go for a new job I didn't actually have.

Mental Note: *Check with Suzanne if you haven't heard anything by Monday.*

It was practically the weekend, so it made sense she hadn't responded yet—I tried to convince myself.

Vicki quickly sat back at her desk with a look of defeat in her eyes.

"What is it?"

"Jerry just gave me a last-minute ad that has to be finished today. He said I was the best one to nail it out fast." She started opening all the programs on her computer without even looking over at me as she talked.

"What? No. You can't stay late today. Let me do it?" I got up from my desk and started walking to Jerry's office before she could say anything.

"How can I help you, Maddy?" Jerry asked, seeming unamused I was in his office.

"Can I do the ad you just gave to Vicki, please? I think she has somewhere she needs to be, and I'd like the challenge." I knew exactly where she needed to be, but I wasn't giving him any of her personal details. Besides, if the job interview didn't pan out, it couldn't hurt to have some brownie points up my sleeve.

"I guess that would be fine. But they want it in less than an hour. You think you can manage?" He didn't sound like he had much confidence in me.

"Yes, sir. Thank you." I practically ran back to Vicki's desk after exiting his office. "Listen. I asked Jerry to let me do the ad. You're not going to be late for this date. I want you to tell me what you were already planning on doing, and I'll finish it. You go home and get ready, and we'll meet up soon. I'll be fine to go straight from here." My outfit wasn't first date material, but it didn't matter. Aaron didn't care whether I put in five or fifty minutes into getting ready.

"Are you sure?" I nodded. "You're the best." She already started and had a vision like I knew she would. She handed me the info form Jerry gave her mere minutes ago. I was shocked at how much she'd already accomplished.

"Got it, now move. I'm going to work on your laptop. I'll bring it to you in a bit. Go get ready for your hot date." She collected her belongings I wasn't using and hurried out. "And don't bite your nails," I said one more time before she couldn't hear me.

"Thank you!" she yelled without turning before the door closed behind her.

I called Aaron to let him know I'd be a few minutes late, having something to finish at work, but I couldn't wait to see him. Sweet as always, he assured me I was worth the holdup. There was no way I'd finish this ad as quickly as Vicki, but I hoped I'd do justice to her idea.

After working on the layout for about fifteen minutes, I took a picture of the screen and text it to her to make sure I executed the plan well. She called, talking me through a few tweaks and had me submit it to Jerry, who was also staying late for this ad in order to lock up. Another reason he probably asked Vicki. No one wanted to stay late on a Friday.

"Great job, Maddy." Jerry walked up to me, still at Vicki's desk. "Client loved it. I'm impressed."

"I can't take all of the credit, sir. Vicki's creation, I just finished it. She's helped me tremendously." I threw out a compliment, hoping he'd see more value in her than he might've previously.

"Thank you for your help. Now let's get out of here." Jerry wasn't a bad boss, but he wasn't what one might call a friendly boss either. The word intimidating was probably a better fit, so I was glad to earn some credibility.

I collected Vicki's laptop and charger before going to my desk and gathering all of my things. The extra half hour I spent here was nothing compared to the pleasure I took in knowing Vicki didn't have to. I called my man to find out where we were supposed to meet them before heading to pick Vicki up from her place. We planned to go together because she didn't want to be there completely alone or with Michael. She wanted a buffer—me.

"You ready, Miss America?" I joked over the phone.

"Just about. You almost here?" I could tell by the echo she had me on speaker, probably finishing her last bit of primping.

"Map says four minutes till arrival." I hadn't been to her house before, but it wasn't far from my apartment. "Should I honk when I get there?"

"That works. See you in a sec." She hung up before I could respond. So she *was* still a bit nervous. I chuckled and said bye to myself knowing she wouldn't hear.

I arrived at her house exactly four minutes later, thanks to my trusty GPS. Her house was charming, every bit a young couple's starter home. Petite, single car garage. Burnt red siding with white trim and a gray roof. Several steps led up to the small porch framed in with white pillars. A large double window had light shining out through the sheer curtains.

I gave a *beep, beep* of my horn to let her know I arrived. Seconds later, she emerged, locked the door behind her, and bounced down the steps to my car.

"Don't you look cute?" I hadn't seen her dressed up in anything other than her work or casual attire. A classic black blazer hit right under the elbow over a loose-fit white T-shirt paired with dark blue jeans cuffed just above super cute nude peep-toe heels. Her large bangle bracelets and oversized rose gold watch were the cherries on top.

"Thanks. I hope I'm not overdressed." She looked at me, still in my work clothes. A guilty look overtook her face.

"No way. You look great no matter what anyone else is wearing. Want to know where we're going?"

"Yes!" She looked ready to explode.

"Michael picked the hibachi grill in the shopping district." The same area where Aaron and I had our first date. I looked over at her quickly and smiled before turning back to the road.

I dialed Aaron at the stoplight, connecting to the bluetooth. He answered after only two rings.

"Hey cutie." His voice filled my entire car with a divine presence.

I perked up. "Hey you. We're close. Have you been waiting long?"

"Nope, just got here. We're sitting on the benches by the fountain."

The outdoor mall was so huge, I often got lost remembering which section I needed to head to. I was thankful he mentioned the fountain because I knew exactly where that was.

"Great, see you in a few."

"Can't wait."

After I ended the call, Vicki looked at me with puppy dog eyes.

"I sure hope Michael is as sweet. I can't believe I'm doing this. Good thing you're driving, or I might've turned around and claimed a horrendous case of the tummy bug or something."

Her antics made me chuckle. "You got this. Just be you. You are beyond great, and if Michael doesn't see that, my boyfriend's brother or not, he's crazy. And if nothing more comes of it, you got to dress cute and get treated to dinner, right?" I gave my best pre-game speech.

"Right. What is there to lose?" She whispered more to herself than to me. I wasn't sure if it was a rhetorical question or if she needed more encouragement from me, but before I could say anything, she continued with a shrug of her shoulders. "Nothing, really."

And with those words, the last bit of a protective shell she built around herself over the last few years seemed to crack and fall to my car's floorboard. She sat up straighter and checked herself in the mirror, illuminating my car with light—from the visor mirror and her smile.

I prayed her sudden confidence boost wouldn't waver in the next few minutes.

"You look good, for real. I'm glad Aaron is already mine, and this isn't a double-blind date." I chuckled, mostly joking, but also a bit insecure. Her ex was crazy for leaving her, not to mention selfish.

Thankfully the parking lot wasn't too crowded yet, and I saw an open spot close to where the guys sat. Aaron waved at us as we pulled in.

Michael had a huge smile on his face, turning his head to say something to Aaron but not taking his eyes off of Vicki.

"Ready?" I asked, grabbing her hand before we got out of the car, not expecting an answer. We walked toward the guys, a few parking spots length away. They stood up as we approached. Michael was taller than Aaron, but not in a towering way, barely noticeable.

"Mmm." Aaron wrapped his arms around me in a firm embrace. He took a deep whiff of my hair before kissing my head, then leaned back to kiss me. During our moment, I forgot Vicki and Michael, although knowing *of* each other, hadn't been introduced. When I turned, they were just standing there.

"Oh, sorry. Vicki, Michael. Michael, Vicki." I technically didn't know Michael either. After they gave a quick awkward hug and greeting, I also introduced myself to him. "It's nice to finally meet some of Aaron's family."

"We're pretty awesome," Michael said with a blend of confidence and humor. Vicki laughed, holding her small strapless purse in front of her with both hands while looking down.

"Let's go eat. Shall we?" Aaron started walking forward, and we all followed. "You look cute," he said to me quieter, no longer talking to the group.

"My fancy work attire. Only the best for you." I responded with wit but was glad he still complimented me. I turned around and saw Michael and Vicki making small talk as we made our way inside.

The restaurant was pretty empty before the dinner rush, so we were seated right away. Having to sit in a straight line in front of the hibachi grill probably wasn't how we would've sat any other place. After a minute of discussion, we decided on ladies on the inside and the guys on the outside.

"Have you been here before?" Michael kept the conversation fluid with Vicki.

"Not this particular one, but I've been to one of these places before."

I saw a nervous tick in her eye and wondered if she remembered who she went with—possibly her ex-husband. I willed Michael not to ask that information.

"What're you going to get?" I asked Aaron to derail another question that might involve Vicki's past. We looked at our simple menus, deciding which meat, rice, and veggie combo we wanted.

"Beef, white rice, and broccoli." Aaron responded with certainty.

"Me too. Great minds think alike." I leaned in and rested my head on his shoulder, trying not to be too affectionate and possibly make it more awkward for the other pair.

The chef made his way into our little section of the restaurant. We were the only people at the grill. He turned on the grill and did some fancy spinning and clanking tricks with his utensils, pausing with a cheesy grin on his face when he wanted an applause. I was sure he'd done this routine thousands of times. Starting with Aaron, who was to the chef's right, he tapped his long flat thin spatula down on the grill, raising his eyebrows as to take the order.

"Beef."

He then tapped in front of me.

"Beef."

Moving to Vicki.

"Chicken." She smiled, being the first different order.

He tapped the last time in front of Michael.

"Beef," he said, looking like he felt bad that Vicki was the odd one.

Maddison, ladies and gentlemen. Just one of the guys. I snickered to myself.

After several more clanks, the chef placed a large pile of beef and a smaller pile of chicken on the grill. We finished giving him our order and tried to talk over the explosions of steam, flames, and the clinking metal tools. The chef was almost done when he made a small volcano out of stacked onion rings, filling it with oil and lighting it on fire.

"Choo, choo. Choo, choo."

His goofy grin came again, awaiting our applause. I was thankful the chef didn't try tossing a chunk of rice into our mouths like the other place I went to as a teenager. For myself, who could never catch it, but mostly for Vicki being on a first date and all.

The chef separated everything onto our plates before turning off the grill and scraping it down clean. We thanked him as he finished.

"So, Michael, what is it that you do?" I asked for myself and Vicki, hoping to get a good conversation going.

"I work in I.T. for a bank chain here in the metroplex. I go to whichever site needs fixing or upgrading."

It made sense to me if Aaron was the more musical one, then Michael would be more of the brain of the family. It wasn't super common to see siblings doing the same thing unless they were involved in a family business or something.

"I bet that's fun. Having a similar but different job each day. Kind of keeps it new, right?" Vicki chimed in.

"Exactly." Michael smiled at her agreeable response.

We ate and talked, getting to know each other better. Aaron and I sometimes engaged in our conversation, leaving Michael and Vicki to do the same. They seemed to be hitting it off great. I was elated for her. I discovered a whole new side to my friend, including a super cute side smile I'd never seen before.

"What do you think?" I asked Aaron quietly, nodding my head in their direction.

"From what I can tell, he's totally into her. When you guys pulled up, he turned to me and said she was even hotter in person." He spoke barely above a whisper. My face lit up in excitement, earning a kiss on the forehead.

As dinner wound down, I hoped someone, mainly Michael, would suggest coffee or ice cream. There were several places within walking distance, after all.

"All done?" I asked Vicki.

"Yes. I'm so full. I can't eat anymore." Whether that was the complete truth or if she was more concerned with looking bad cleaning her entire plate on a first date, I wasn't sure. Been there, done that.

"Too full? I was going to suggest we go for coffee or something?"

Good job, Michael. I guess he didn't want the night to end yet either.

"Sure" rolled out as a smile graced her face.

"I could go for coffee." I agreed, knowing Aaron would go wherever I wanted to.

"Then let's go. Be right back." Aaron stood up, and Michael followed him to pay for our meals.

"Sooo?" I questioned in a higher pitch, dripping with curious tone.

"I'm very interested." She replied, bright as a lightbulb.

"I thought so. He seems pretty great." Which I meant, although I was glad to have the artsy brother who better complemented me.

"Yes, he does. I really hope he wants to go out again."

"I bet he will. Aaron seems to think so."

The guys made their way back to us, finished with the bill. "Ready?" Aaron asked.

"Yup." I stood up just before Vicki as we pushed away from the grill.

Aaron offered me his hand, which I took, and Michael guided Vicki by placing his hand on the small of her back a few steps ahead of us. I couldn't see her face, but I knew she was smiling.

~ 16 ~

I found myself looking forward to Sundays now, and it wasn't just because I spent most of the day with Aaron. I missed being active at church. No one was meant to do life alone in their own little world, confined into small physical and mental spaces. It took me getting more involved to remember I already knew that truth all along.

Aaron was on his way to pick me up today since he had the week off from the band. I checked myself in the mirror one more time, thankful I was able to dress more casual, stylish, and like myself at my new church.

My phone rang, letting me know he was downstairs. No one else called me this early on a Sunday morning.

"Hello?" I answered with a flirty voice.

"Good morning, beautiful. I'm here." I heard the smile on his face.

"I'll be right down." Grabbing my purse, lip gloss, and keys, I made my way out and took the stairs as fast as possible to the hunk in the fast red car sitting curbside. I let myself in on the passenger side to find my handsome boyfriend holding a latte for me.

"Here you go." He offered me the cup with a pucker.

"Thank you." I took the latte and the kiss. "Good morning. You look nice." He always did. Today he wore a cream henley and dark jeans.

"As do you."

I didn't waste any time on our short drive to the church. "Give me the scoop. Did you and Michael stay up all night talking about us girls?"

He laughed at my assumption that guys acted like girls when no one was looking. "Not quite, but we did talk about it on the car ride home."

Mental Notes

"Aaand? I need something here, babe." I had to know how Michael felt about Vicki. Would there be another date? Did they swap numbers? I knew I'd get an overload of info from Vicki, but the stuff that came from Michael was more insightful.

"He's excited to see where it goes and wants to go out again." He stated the information like it wasn't a huge deal, but to me, it was.

"That's all. On a twenty-minute ride home, that's all he said?"

"Pretty much."

Oh man, guys are so different from girls. I pictured the brothers talking about moments of their evening in greater detail like Vicki and I would, trying to imagine what they'd say as they giggled and talked with their hands, and then a scene of them saying almost nothing the entire drive. I knew he was probably honest; I simply didn't understand the male brain. But then again, I barely understood my own brain.

"Fine, I'll get more details from Vicki at work tomorrow." We both chuckled. "I'm excited for her. She's been single for a long time. I'm sure she'll share her story with Michael soon, and then he'll share it with you. In way fewer words, I'm sure." We laughed again. I enjoyed a few sips of my latte and wrapped my hand around Aaron's bicep—my favorite place to rest my hand. He gave a quick flex as he often did under my touch.

"Any word on the interview?" He was only making conversation, but it wasn't something I wanted to talk about.

"Ugh, no. I keep trying to think of all the different reasons why I haven't heard back. Especially since she was the one that reached out to me. I've come up with dozens of possibilities, and now of them make me feel any better. It's on my 'Do Not Think About' list for the day." My sour mood altered the atmosphere.

"Got it. Did Vicki tell you anything about Michael I should know?" He switched back to the topic I was excited about. He knew how to make me happy.

"She's very excited but nervous that he'll back off once they get to know each other more. I have to keep reminding her how awesome she is and to stop being so negative. Easier said than done, right? It seems like the very conversation we had not too long ago about me and you." I looked over at him, not sure I was ready to talk about that first meeting again.

"Whaaat? Y'all talked about me. Tell me. I want to know." He gave my thigh a squeeze and shook his grip.

"Kinda. More about me, I guess, and how I totally made a fool of myself the first time I met you."

He glanced over at me for a second, then back to the road. "What do you mean?"

How could he not remember?

"Really? It was awful. I curtsied for crying out loud." My hands flew around in grand gesture.

"That's right!" He laughed, hard, lifting his hand from my thigh and holding his stomach. "I honestly forgot. It wasn't the defining moment I remember from that night."

"What do you remember then?" It blew my mind how he could possibly have a different perspective of the night we met.

"I remember Ethan seeing you and excusing himself for a minute while I sat there and listened to your conversation, trying to imagine what you looked like. I listened to your voice, at how easily you talked to Ethan, warm and genuine. When I couldn't handle not knowing any longer, I turned around to discover you were even more beautiful than I pictured. I had to know more about you. I asked Ethan question after question, trying not to make it super obvious, but once he started getting annoyed I was interrupting Stacy's singing, I stopped. That was when I started looking across the room at you, over and over. I planned on talking to you afterward, but as soon as the music ended, you disappeared. That's why I asked Ethan if he had a way to get back in contact with you."

Somewhere during his speech, he stopped at a light and took my breath away with the honesty in his eyes. I beat myself up for days, and there he was in his own little world needing me like air. "Wow" came out barely audible.

"It turned out pretty good, right?" He touched my knee again.

"Yes, it did. I like your memory of that night way better than mine." How often did I do that to myself? Make things worse in my mind than they actually were. No doubt, it happened more than it needed to.

He replaced his hand on the wheel when the light changed and drove us the last few blocks to the church. I unintentionally started singing until he acknowledged it.

Mental Notes

"I love your voice. You should audition for the worship team." His compliment made me smile.

"Maybe, but don't out me. I'll do it when I'm ready." Another change could break me now.

We made our way inside hand-in-hand. I soaked it up because most weeks I walked in alone. However, it was getting less awkward since I'd gotten to know more of the crowd.

We found our regular seats and talked to some people nearby while the countdown rolled. All the lights faded out, cueing us to end our conversations as the band started the first song. It was equally distracting having Aaron next to me within touching distance as up on the stage to look at, but by the middle of the first song, I was always able to get my focus in the right place.

The pastor shared a great message on how to handle disappointment. If only I would've heard this message a few years ago, I had a better grip on things now. I took notes in my phone to remind me later if things didn't go the way I wanted—because they would—I'd be able to make it through if I trusted God. Applying this to the fact that I hadn't heard back on the interview, I decided not to be so worried and be thankful I already had a job. If this new job panned out: fine. If it didn't: that was all right too.

"And can someone please tell me when we started blaming God for everything? The last time I checked, the Bible said the *devil* came to kill, steal, and destroy, but Jesus came so that we would have *life and life more abundantly!* When are we going to stop pulling the God card when something goes wrong, saying He did something against His nature, *hello?* Don't be flashing God's i.d. when you get pulled over if you were the one speeding. Don't flash God's i.d. when the doctor says it's cancer, claiming God gave you sickness to teach you something. That's identity theft! You give credit where credit is due. Steal, kill, destroy- devil ministry. Life, and life abundantly- Jesus ministry."

The room erupted with "amen" and "preach it" and many other shouts of agreement—what a great reminder. Our pastor was young and vibrant and spoke things in a way that made it real. Challenging us to seek God for all He had to offer, not only the preconceived ideas passed down over the years resulting in poor theology. I loved feeling encouraged to encounter Jesus on His terms, not my own.

"This is so good." I turned and whispered to Aaron.

"Agreed."

Once again, I was grateful getting to know Aaron better also led me to be here today, hearing this message. It was embarrassing to admit I'd questioned God's goodness while attempting to recover from heartbreak and trust issues. Probably the wedge that started the separation, and later the reason I never went back to church in if I was honest. I continued taking notes on my phone like a madwoman, knowing this was something I'd want to look back on if I found myself questioning again.

A whole day with Aaron was my favorite kind of day. Church was fantastic, proven by the novella of notes on my phone. The hardest part of Sundays was the weighty decision of where to eat that no one wanted to make, but every decision seemed easier when I got lost in his ocean-blue eyes. I typically threw out a few suggestions, and he ended up deciding anyway.

This particular week, some worship team friends joined us for lunch, and then the two of us went back to my place to relax. We decided to start binge-watching the most random show we could find on Netflix. A modern sci-fi, something about people who were suddenly linked in their thoughts, was the winner. I wasn't huge on sci-fi. It usually turned more into a comedy to me personally, but Aaron seemed like more of a sci-fi fan than he wanted to admit.

By the third episode, I zoned out and decided to check my email on my phone. I didn't expect to find anything but saw no harm in checking anyway, considering I hadn't since yesterday evening. The contents of my inbox made me jump up to grab my computer, wanting to read the email full-screen.

"What's wrong?" Aaron asked, startled from my movement that caused an abrupt ending to our cuddling position.

"She emailed me!" I yelled like a professional cheerleader as I ran into my room, grabbed my laptop, then rushed back to the couch to read the reply with Aaron. "'Thank you so much for your response. We are very excited about the opportunity to interview you for our counselor position. Please check your schedule and let me know if Wednesday at one thirty works for you. I look forward to hearing from you. Suzanne.'" I smacked his thigh thirteen times. "Can you believe she emailed me over the weekend? I figured I wouldn't hear from her until tomorrow at the earliest. Aaaahhh! Oh my gosh, I'm nervous." The excited energy left me like a draining tub.

"Nervous, already? Don't be. You'll do great." He closed my laptop, placed it on the coffee table, then wrapped his arm around me again, forcing me to be with him, and handle it later. Although I wanted to email her back immediately, I sure didn't want to make Aaron feel like I didn't put him first. I snuggled back into the perfect Maddison sized curve in Aaron's side and tried not to laugh too hard at all of the serious parts I wasn't supposed to find humorous.

* * *

Nerves pricked my spine when I asked Jerry for some personal time off from work and prayed he wouldn't ask any questions. When he approved my request for half-day without a second thought, I wasn't all that relieved. Vicki gave me a great, much-needed pep talk at lunch on Wednesday, and I was on my way, anxiety in tow.

The upside to this interview was I already had a job. I wasn't desperate for anything to pay my bills and didn't have to take something I didn't really want—my situation a year ago. Having the ball in my court helped me not to feel like the pee-wee league challenging the pros. But I couldn't really dribble.

When I pulled up to where my map directed me for Hands of Hope, the large building had at least a dozen floors. Either this company was way bigger than I thought, or this monolith had multiple businesses inside, Hands of Hope, only one unit. I shot up a prayer for the latter because working for a significant company wasn't something I felt qualified for. Having to find which floor and suite I needed made me further uneasy— large buildings always did that to me.

I grabbed my things and approached the building with as much confidence as I could muster. The inside of the main lobby was modern and sleek with an enormous information board front and center listing all the units inside by name. *Thank God.* I found Hands of Hope located on the third floor, Suite C. When the elevator opened, I pushed the correct button, happy to be alone for one last moment to collect myself. Everything started functioning in slow motion. Or perhaps my brain flipped to autopilot.

You've got this. This is what you want to do. If it doesn't work out, that's okay. Jesus, give me favor, sounded in my head as I closed my eyes.

As the doors retracted opened, suite C was within sight of the elevator. Glass walls and doors were all around me. Hands of Hope labeled the door in a bold font, all caps. The few steps I took felt like hundreds.

The pretty young lady at the front desk greeted me. "Hello, can I help you?"

"Yeah. I'm here for an interview with Suzanne," came out, but it wasn't my most confident voice. Clearing my throat, I had to do better.

"Oh, yes. She's expecting you. Maddison, correct?" I nodded. "Let me check real quick and make sure she's ready for you."

I took a minute to scan the place as I stood mere inches from the entry. Behind the receptionist, I saw the logo for Hands of Hope. At first, it looked like a fall tree that already shed its leaves, but after gazing for a moment, I noticed the trunk was two people, and their raised arms were the branches. The polished counter had a white top on light color wood with gray panels bolted across the bottom. Two modern pendant lights illuminated the check-in desk. The colors of the room were neutral, creating a relaxing atmosphere—most likely intentional, seeing as this was a counseling center and all.

"Okay, she's ready." The lady at the front desk informed me as she hung up the phone. "It's down this hall, first door on the right." She motioned to my left.

"Thank you." I walked down the hall slowly, making sure not to rush and trip. I knocked on the closed door and heard her call me in. "Hello, Suzanne?" I confirmed I didn't head into the wrong office in my anxiousness.

"Yes, come in. Please have a seat. Thank you for coming." She cleared some things from her desk, grabbing what I assumed was my dated résumé. It looked vaguely familiar, even though I hadn't seen it in over a year.

I sat in one of the chairs opposite her desk, sliding to the edge of the seat, and sitting up as straight as possible.

"Let me start by saying we recently had some changes in-house due to opening another location."

Knowing the positive cause of the changes mentioned in our correspondence lifted my spirits. "That's fantastic."

"Yes, we're very proud. The manager took a handful of the staff and chose me to run this location. I started looking through the résumés we had on file, needing to build my team, and was very impressed with yours. Please tell me a little more about yourself that I can't find on this paper."

Here we go.

The part I wasn't great at: talking about myself. "I decided to pursue counseling after realizing I liked helping people through emotions—which happened pretty often in my small town." I chucked. "But after graduating college, I somehow seemed to fall into the pool of people unable to find a job in my field and ended up working at an advertising agency. I've been there for most of the last year." I mentioned my current job since it wasn't listed in my out-of-date job history.

"Great. I see here you did some volunteering and internships through college. Tell me more about those."

"I did. We focused on a lower-income area of town. Most of the kids were left to fend for themselves all summer with parents at work or on the streets. We held a camp-like program, hosting fun activities, sports, crafts, and equipped them with hygiene supplies and the importance of self-care. I really enjoyed it. I can easily see how that experience could help me work with the children who come here." I added in an attempt to make my résumé seem more applicable.

"What a great idea." She scribbled something down on a notepad beside her, asking me a few more questions about myself, and clarifying information she'd read. I felt like it was going pretty well based on her facial expressions and our interaction.

"I have to be honest. You were the one I hoped would respond based on your experience. It doesn't bother me that this will be your first job in our field because it will allow us to show you how we do things. We run a bit different here, being Christian based first of all. I wanted to be able to have someone fresh come on board, ready to learn how we function at Hands of Hope.

"We work with amazing families here. Bringing a child into your home is a big step, but we feel like it's a perfect example of what God did for us. Often times there's a period of adjustment and the need for counsel, so that's why we exist, to support the families. Those bringing a child in, and the child who just had their whole world flipped upside down."

"I love that. It isn't something I ever thought of before, but now that you say it, I see the huge need for adoptive families."

"Does that mean you'd be interested in joining the team?"

I was taken aback for a second, not expecting to be offered the job on the spot. *Answer her!* "Absolutely."

"Great. When can you start?" Suzanne sounded eager to add me to her staff.

"I'd like to give my two weeks' notice at my current job if you're all right with that. My boss doesn't know I came to an interview today."

"That's fine. If they let you off sooner, just let me know." I could tell she wanted me to end well with Jerry, but would also be thrilled if I started sooner than later.

"Yes, ma'am. I'll let you know. Thank you. I look forward to starting here." I stood up and shook her hand before exiting with a giant smile on my face.

"See you soon," I said to the unnamed receptionist as I passed by, knowing I'd learn her name soon enough.

I called Aaron first thing when I made it down the elevator and back to my car.

"Hey you." His voice was a spark that lit the firework already in my system.

"I got it! She offered me the job on the spot. Can you believe it?" I spouted out so fast I wasn't sure if he caught it all.

"Of course she did. Celebratory dinner on me!"

I could hear the pride in his tone.

~ 17 ~

Jerry took my notice like no big deal. I tried not to take it personally. I sort of expected him to ask me to stay or to maybe seem sad to lose me. He thanked me for the two weeks' notice but said one week would be fine to wrap up all orders left on my desk. I was thankful for that part, at least, because I was excited to get my new job started. The only thing I'd miss from this place was Vicki, but I was confident I'd see her more often since our relationship had reached bestie status on my life team. Plus, dating Aaron's younger brother didn't hurt.

On my last day, Vicki managed to get the approval from Jerry to share a small cake with everyone in the break room during lunch. The bakery forgot the apostrophe on the cake, so instead of "We'll miss you," it read, "Well miss you." Which seemed fitting, seeing as how I barely made any connections.

I didn't have much left to do after the lunch hour, so I took my time cleaning my desk and thanking everyone for their kind words. Vicki got a bit misty at the end of the day, stating I wouldn't be within talking distance from her desk eight hours a day, five times a week, anymore.

I took my super girly pink feather, practically a prop from the set of *Legally Blonde,* that Vicki always laughed at, and stuck in the organizer on her desk. "For a rainy day." I winked. An actual tear bubbled on her lid.

"Stop it. We'll still see each other all the time. We're practically on course to becoming sisters-in-law." Vicki chuckled through the lump in her throat and wiped her cheekbone with the back of her hand.

"Whoa. That serious already, is it?" I laughed. "Now we have even more to look forward to on our little vacation." Which was just around the corner.

"Yes, I can't wait. Thank you, thank you. For being a true friend, a great co-worker, introducing me to Michael, for—" She full-on cried now.

"Don't start. You'll get me going too!" I tried to laugh through swimming eyeballs.

"Wa waa. You girls are so funny." Jerry came to break up our XX powwow with his Y chromosome. I was actually glad for once. "It's been a pleasure, Maddison. If you decide you aren't a fit over there, you'll always have a desk waiting for you here."

So he did see me as a valuable asset. His words brought a smile to my face. "Thanks, Jerry. I'll keep that in mind." I could tell by Vicki's face that her emotions were conflicted, probably not wanting me to fail at my new endeavor, but glad for Jerry's offer.

I was thankful for this job I never thought I'd have because it brought me Vicki, an eye that paid greater attention to detail, and helped me start crawling out of a dark season of my life. It was a good chapter, but my story was about to get a whole lot better.

I walked back to my desk and finished cleaning everything out, trying to remember what was mine and what was there when I came to this only partially empty cubicle. Anytime I looked up, I caught a glimpse of Vicki switching back and forth from smiling to the verge of tears, trying to focus on her work unsuccessfully. Seeing as it was almost time to leave on a Friday, I was sure she was already done with her tasks for the week like always.

With time to kill, even though I was pretty sure Jerry wouldn't dock my paycheck if I left early, I wanted to finish strong. I decided to go clean out the break room after my farewell dessert social. Then moved the refrigerator, which I quickly regretted. I tried not to gag at the unrecognizable couple of containers with an elementary schooler's science project growth and figured if it got that bad, the owners didn't miss the boxes. Straight into the trash. I laughed at the note my passive-aggressive co-worker put on his lunch.

"Steve's lunch. Don't eat unless your name is Steve."

Mental Notes

I quickly wiped the shelf under his tupperware and placed it back down, hoping he wouldn't notice the millimeter of movement. Despite a couple of gag moments, I was glad I tidied up the break room because I saw my coffee mug for days I took advantage of the office Keurig. No doubt, I would've forgotten it.

My arms were suddenly pinned down to my sides while someone hugged me from behind. If it was anyone other than Vicki, we had a problem.

"I'm really going to miss seeing you every day." She must've seen me head into the break room and took advantage of the privacy.

"We'll still see each other often. I'll make sure of it." I hugged her and ended our embrace with a good squeeze before needing a clean up on aisle one from the puddle of our tears. "Okay, I'm officially done here—time for me to clock out. Aaron is making dinner for me at his place. I'm excited to finally see it." I patted away the tears that threatened to escape.

Vicki did the same. "Have fun. Let me know how it goes."

"Will do." I walked back to my desk and clocked out for the last time before closing the software program I'd no longer need. I grabbed my overstuffed bag and the small box I brought, which was also filled to the top with my belongings. I didn't stop to say anything to Vicki—or anyone else. Goodbyes were already excessive by that point.

Looking back at the building one last time for a mental memory snapshot, I put everything in my back seat and called Aaron.

"Hey you."

"Hey. I'm leaving work now. Should I run my stuff home first, so you aren't rushed?"

"No, you can head on over. I'm already home. I left early today because there wasn't anything left to do. Oh. Well, actually, can you go get some ice?" The confidence in his voice wavered.

"Sure, I'll do that and be right over." I pictured him getting everything for our dinner at his place, only to realize he forgot to get something as simple as ice. He was too cute.

"Can't wait to hear about your last day."

"Ugh, it was an emotional mess." I chuckled.

"Vicki," we said at the same time, causing him to laugh.

"Okay, see you in a few, cutie," he said, illuminating my face with a smile, and sealed our conversation with a "bye" before hanging up.

I ran by the convenience store with a large freezer out front, grabbed a bag of ice, and hurried in to pay. How many bags of ice had been easily stolen entered my mind and made me sad for the owner.

I was on a rollercoaster of emotions today for various—and ridiculous—reasons. Last day at work. First time to see Aaron's place. The back and forth that was Vicki. Stolen ice. The underlying excitement of my new job I'd be starting on Monday. And an overall gratitude for all the good occurring in my life.

The cashier said, "Ready," with a questioning tone like it wasn't his first time saying so.

"Oh, sorry." I lifted the still perfectly frozen bag of ice up onto the counter—so I hadn't drifted off for too long.

I left in a hurry to see my favorite human and felt butterflies start to flutter around in my stomach as my GPS escorted me closer to my destination. I wasn't sure what to expect of his apartment. All I knew was he had a two-bedroom and a roommate he wasn't particularly fond of.

Going to an apartment complex for the first time, and figuring out how the apartment buildings were laid out was so stressful for me. Each one was different. After my map said "redirecting" a few times, I almost screamed and called Aaron for help when I saw the right unit.

I sat there for a minute and tried to shake off the frazzled nerves that multiplied while I circled the complex repeatedly. Like the habit it was, I looked in the visor mirror and added more lip gloss. A few deeps breaths later, I walked up to his building. After reading the sign for grouped units and figuring out where to go, I finally found 808B and knocked on the door. It seemed like minutes passed as I waited, even though it was only seconds before the door actually opened.

"Hello, beautiful!" His phone in hand, he was recording.

"Hi," I said before releasing a huge sigh and allowing a smile to breakthrough.

"There's my girl. Come in here." He grabbed me into a tight hug and kissed my lips. Once. Twice. Probably recording the floor. "Welcome to my place."

Mental Notes

I scanned the room to soak it all in. Unlike my apartment, the front door opened right into the living area. The first thing I noticed was his mismatched couch, love seat, and chair that still looked great paired together. Behind him, to the left of the front door, was a small entertainment station centered on the wall with a flat-screen tv sitting on it. The television was bigger than mine—man toys. Straight ahead was a half wall dividing the living area and the kitchen. Just to the right of the kitchen was a small round kitchen table with four chairs prepared for dinner.

As my eyes panned a degree farther, I saw an opening to the hallway and figured it led to the bedrooms. Aaron's apartment seemed older than my place with small indicators of dated architecture.

"I love it! Super cozy." I looked back at Aaron, who still recorded me. "You're lucky that doesn't freak me out," I added with a smile.

"SURPRISE!" Vicki and Michael popped up from behind the half wall in the kitchen.

"What? Surprise for what?"

"We wanted to celebrate with you on this last day of your old job and the beginning of something new." Aaron cheered, beaming from ear to ear.

Vicki ran around the bar and practically tackled me in a hug.

"You knew this was coming, and you still hugged me a hundred times at work today?" Okay, I exaggerated the amount by a few. "How did you even beat me here?"

"We sent you for ice," she said, looking at my empty hands.

"Oh my gosh. I left it in my car. I hope it isn't melting."

"I'll go get it. Give me your keys." Aaron offered and ended his video, darting out the door to get the stall-tactic ice we probably didn't even need.

"Congratulations," Michael spoke as he leaned in for a hug.

I was still slightly awkward with Michael. He looked so much like Aaron, but nothing came alive inside me when I was around him, reminding me of the main difference between them.

"Thank you. I can't believe y'all did this." I saw the prepared food as I entered the kitchen.

"It was Aaron's idea," Michael responded, giving credit where credit was due.

Of course, it was. Aaron was amazing, and knew exactly how to make me feel special. A full spread of a large salad and a pasta casserole was assembled on the stove next to a stack of plates.

"Mmm. Smells good," I said.

"Thank you, cutie," Aaron replied, ice in hand, as he re-entered his apartment. "It's my mom's chicken spaghetti recipe. One of the few things I'm good at making." He walked over to the freezer to put the bag away. That's when I saw the bowl of ice already out on the counter, confirming my unneeded purchase. "Let's eat. I'm hungry!" He kept two plates and passed the other two to Michael. They could serve us ladies.

"You did an excellent job not tipping me off at work today." I nudged Vicki with my elbow.

"It wasn't easy, but I think the continual sway between not blowing the surprise and sadness masked everything."

"You're probably right." I laughed.

"But tonight is about celebrating. No more tears, I promise."

"Deal."

The brothers handed us our food, and we all sat down at the table, a perfect fit for the four of us. I grabbed Aaron's hand and looked at him in pure adoration. "Thank you for this."

"It's my pleasure. I love making you smile. And the weekend is just beginning." He grinned.

"Is it now?"

"Yes. You, my dear, are going to have an excellent weekend and possibly be tired of me by the end."

"Impossible." I leaned over and kissed him.

"Bless the food so we can eat already." Michael interrupted our moment.

"Thank you, Lord, for Maddison and the new journey she has before her. Thank you for this food, and bless the hands that made it. Amen." Aaron made us all chuckle with his self-mentioning prayer.

No one hesitated to dig in.

"*Almost* like mom used to make." Michael broke the chewing sounds with his half compliment.

"It's delicious." I offered up.

"Yes, it is," Vicki agreed, looking over at Michael, who seemed to feel pressured.

"I'm just as good, if not a better cook than him." Michael spouted as he puffed his chest.

"Not even on your best day, bro."

"Whatever." Michael huffed, unable to find a come back for his older brother. Somehow I knew there'd always be some brotherly competition between these two.

I tried to hide a laugh behind my napkin and noticed Vicki attempting to conceal her smile behind a fist as well.

When we finished our dinner, I helped clear the table like Aaron always did when he was at my place.

"To the couch, everyone. I have a game I want to play." Aaron ordered us.

Michael sighed, but I was excited. "What game?"

"Charades, but it's on my phone. It records the player as they act it out," Aaron answered me.

"Seriously?" I asked.

"Uh, if you're up to it, I am." He hesitated for a minute, probably thinking I was over the recordings already.

"I'm about to show you all how the Queen of Charades plays the game!" I bragged, confident in my skills, and super stoked.

"I don't know if I'm ready for this." Michael plopped onto the couch.

"Come on, it will be fun." Vicki tried to encourage him with heavy persuasion—also known as coercion.

"Fine. Us against you two." Michael agreed, only after turning it into a brother competition again.

"Oh, you guys are going down!" I said, slightly cocky.

~ 18 ~

The celebratory weekend continued Saturday afternoon, and I was eager to see what surprise Aaron planned. All he was willing to tell me was to eat a snack before, dress comfortably, and bring my smile that he adored.

My apartment wasn't in its cleanest state since I'd barely been home to tend to it, but I was no longer insecure about him seeing my apartment in any state it might be after seeing his place. Aaron was neat and organized, but he couldn't always ensure if his roommate would be there, clean, or appropriate. Not all musicians were as charming as my guy. Which was why he preferred coming to my place.

Knowing he'd arrive any minute, I checked my appearance one last time after finishing a protein bar. The knock on the door came while I was in the bathroom. I rushed through my apartment with intoxicating excitement like a kid rounding the corner on Christmas morning, and opened the door with a huge welcoming smile on my face.

"There he is!" I still couldn't get enough of him and hoped the feeling rushing through me would never go away.

He leaned in and planted a tender kiss on my lips. It was electric, another feeling I never get used to.

"There *she* is. You all ready?"

"Yup, I just need to grab my purse. Now can you tell me what we are doing?"

"Nope." He pulled me toward him holding my hand and laughed.

I smacked him on the chest. "Fine. Let's hurry so I can find out on my own. I'm super excited." I retrieved my purse and locked the door.

As he drove, I stared at him, questioning how I landed such a man and feeling so blessed to call him my boyfriend. Being his co-pilot was my favorite, especially when I held his hand or wrapped my hand around his bicep.

Without the slightest clue about what we'd be doing today, the fact that he planned something special and kept it a surprise only made me even more pumped.

When he came to a stop in a large parking lot, he got out first and came around to open my door for me, offering his hand. As soon as my feet hit the ground, I started reading all the signs on the strip center.

"Did you guess correctly?" he asked with a nervous squint to his eyes and raised brows.

"Still in the dark." I continued reading landing on a colorful sign that said, "Paint With Me!" The exclamation point was an upside-down paintbrush. "Eeeek. Are we going to paint?"

"Yes, ma'am." Pleasure filled his face, and he kissed me on my forehead. "You're too cute."

I mentioned once in a late-night phone conversation that I wasn't an artist, but ever since these places started popping up, I wanted to try it out. Who better to experience it with than my most handsome boyfriend?

"Let's go." I practically ran, dragging him behind me. Not like he'd rather have his teeth pulled one at a time or anything, I was just as excited as a puppy chasing her favorite ball.

He opened the door for me like the perfect gentleman he was, unfazed by my giddiness. The place was illuminated and filled with paintings of various styles everywhere you turned. I saw sports team logos, nature scenes, and random things I couldn't quite make out. I decided they fell under the category of "artistic expression"—of which I had none.

The open room had long tables with mini easels containing blank canvases. Several different size and shape paintbrushes sat at each station.

"I'm so excited." I clapped my hands against my chest, entirely free to let Aaron see my quirky side under my chin. And I loved him for his acceptance.

"Welcome. What name is your reservation under?" The woman behind the counter *totally* worked here. She wore a white apron decorated in layers of paint projects gone by and had on artsy thick-rimmed black glasses that fit her face well. Her hair was in a loosening messy bun held in place by a paintbrush, which was most likely the reason it flopped over to the side and needed to be redone. A few strands of hair already fell, framing her face.

"Aaron Walker."

I hadn't noticed at first, but everyone seemed to be in pairs. Several couples already sat by empty canvases. "Is this a couples class?" I whispered into his ear.

"Yes, it is." He answered with a wink.

My eyes grew bigger as I rose on my tiptoes to kiss his cheek. "You're learning me well."

"That's my goal. I want to know all about you." His statement was honest and longing, causing my heart to beat faster. Way faster. The fact that our twitterpated-ness was mutual left me speechless.

"All right, I got you all checked in. Here's the sheet of what you guys need to get. The aprons are over there on the left, and you'll find a stack of paper plates next to them. Please get the following amounts of paint on your plate, then pick a seat." The sentences rolled out of her mouth like she'd said them a thousand times. I was confident she'd be the one leading the class momentarily. I wondered if she could even be the owner.

We rounded the check-in counter and found everything as she described. The paper in Aaron's hand read "Lovebirds" and listed the colors we needed. It was kind of hard to make out the small black and white photocopied image, but I was pretty sure our two pictures would make one larger image when placed side by side.

After pumping the indicated amount of each color onto our plates, we headed to seats closer to the front because I didn't want to have a hard time seeing. I also wanted to soak up every detail of the experience. A painting class was a yellow sticky note in my brain for months. I never would've gone back then though—no one to go with, and rarely a reason got me to leave my apartment whether a mental note was involved or not.

"Thank you so much for bringing me here. I'm glad I get to experience it with you. A perfect date with my perfect stud." I winked at him.

"I'm not perfect, Maddison."

"Closest thing I've found."

"I'm thrilled you're so pumped about this, but I'm setting you up for disappointment. Hopefully, my artist skills don't ruin the image you have of me." He teased.

"I couldn't care less how it turns out. It's something we're doing together, and that's priceless. These bad boys are going up in my living room."

"Guess I better take this seriously, then." He chuckled at my antics, but I was pretty sure he wouldn't want something utterly horrendous hanging in my apartment where he frequented.

"That would be great."

The artist made her way up to the platform and stood beside the full-length easel. "Everyone ready?"

"Yes" and "yeah" were heard from around the room.

"Great. My name is Alice, and I'll be your teacher today. I want to thank everyone for coming to our couples' class. In this session, we will be painting The Lovebirds." She lifted the cover from a second easel with the final artwork. "Please take a minute to decide who wants to do the left canvas and who wants to do the right canvas. They vary in detail to some extent."

A moon joined the pictures together, half of the circle on each canvas. Both paintings had a bird sitting on a branch, but the left one contained more details of the tree. I looked over at Aaron in question, assuming he wouldn't want to paint the more elaborate picture but wanted to make sure.

"I don't mind. You can pick," he said, considerate of me.

"I'll do the left one. I'm up for the challenge." I held up a brush with determination. If I was going to try something new, why not stretch myself —my new norm, apparently.

The room was filled with murmuring discussion, then shuffling to the appropriate seat if needed. I just so happened to be on the left already, so we waited for the instructor to start again. I looked Aaron over in all his splendor. *He* was a masterpiece, even though he looked drastically out of his comfort zone.

"First things first, you'll find four brushes in front of you," Alice started, drawing my attention away from Aaron. "To prevent confusion, I'll call them the large angled brush, the large flat brush, the small thin brush, and the small round brush." She held each one up as she described it.

"This painting is mostly black and white, so you should have eight pumps of each color and two red pumps on your plate. Everyone grab your large flat brush and start with black. Paint all the way around the side edges of your canvas. When you're done, cover the top of your canvas in black about an inch down. Don't worry if it comes on the front to the canvas while you paint the sides. We'll blend everything in a later step."

Faint giggles could be heard while others talked loudly around the room as everyone followed the directions.

"Now take some of the black and white and mix them together on your plate. Begin with even amounts, and don't clean your brush. Start where you left off on your canvas, blending the gray in and bring it down," she pondered as she painted, "about another two inches. Next, add some more white to your gray on your plate to lighten it up and keep blending onto your canvas the rest of the way down. Simple strokes, back and forth, are all you need until the entire canvas is covered. When you get to the very bottom, blend in one more thin line of black."

I leaned over to look at Aaron's canvas. "I think I'm doing pretty good. How're you doing?"

He chuckled. "I mean, there's nothing artistic on there yet, but I think my painting looks like it's supposed to."

Even though both of us could be considered creative in other areas of our lives, neither one of us had any clue what we were doing.

"Yours looks better than mine. You blended better." I wasn't surprised he was better at this than me. What wasn't he better at?

"No, yours looks good. Just blend it right ... here." He leaned over and stretched his brush across my canvas to work on an area I hadn't noticed from my straight-on view. Like many things in my life, he always saw from a different angle and helped me fix my dilemmas. We made such a great team. I took advantage of his closeness and planted a quick kiss on his cheek.

"Thanks, I didn't see that."

Our next step was to add the half-moon in white, then pull our canvas off the easel and gently fan them dry before we could layer the bird on top, creating the natural sense of depth in the landscape. The class got trickier with this step. Alice made it all look so easy, painting both simultaneously with ease. I made a point to focus on her instructions carefully since I had several more steps than Aaron.

"You're adorable," Aaron said, interrupting my focus. He beamed with pleasure as he watched me grow in tune with my artwork. I smiled and looked back at my canvas. "You missed another spot here." He laughed.

Something wet collided with my arm. I looked down at a gray streak trailing my forearm.

"You punk."

I laughed, but quickly pulled up my brush to return the attack. He was too quick, causing me to mostly get paint all over my hands in my attempted retaliation.

We were in our own little world, full of joy and young love, although the L-word hadn't been spoken between us yet. I often said it in my head, or out loud after I ended—and double-checked—our call.

"Good one." I wiped my hands off on the already paint-stained apron, hoping we wouldn't be short on paint after our little battle.

Turning my attention back to the canvas, I listened to the last few instructions, afraid to make eye contact and earn myself a mothering scold from Alice.

Once we completed the steps, we sat back and looked at our handy work. I was extremely pleased with how they turned out. Aaron grinned as he pushed his right next to mine to form the single image.

A bright white moon filled the center. A skinny, curvy tree on the far left side had a branch extending all the way across the entire scene from my picture onto his. Lovebirds perched in the moonlight on the branch. His bird on the right barely larger than mine. The limb had smaller branches coming off of it with little cherry blossom like flowers in various shades of red and pink, white accents reflecting the full moon's light.

It was beautiful. It was us. And we made it together.

"I love it. Thank you for doing this with me." The smile on my face shined brighter than the moon we created.

With a smile matching mine, Aaron leaned in close to my face and whispered, "You're welcome. I love you." He gently brushed his lips against the top of my jaw under my ear.

Three simple words pulled all the air out of my lungs, causing me to gasp and fill them back up. I turned to look at him, my face giving me away as always—glistening eyes and flushed cheeks. "You do? I mean, I know that I love you, I have for some time, but you love me?" I eagerly rambled with shock in my voice, almost ruining the moment.

My response elated him. "I do. Like, a lot." His words melted me like wax under a flame.

"I love you too."

I leaned in for a kiss. Aaron's lips lingered before my brain remembered we were in public. I didn't want anyone watching us, so I ended the kiss before I wanted to, but not before going back for one more —because I couldn't get enough of him. "Best. Surprise. Ever."

As he grinned, I had to reach up and wipe off the lip gloss he now wore. It was becoming a post-kiss habit.

While awaiting further instruction, I looked around the room, checking out the other couples' art, convinced ours was the best. But maybe I was biased.

"Thank you all for coming tonight. I hope you had a great time and enjoy your paintings. Please leave all of your supplies on the table and feel free to take your canvas with you whenever you are ready." Alice gave the closure we needed to leave.

Aaron and I walked out of the studio, each of us with half of the painting in hand. It was awesome how each canvas was a picture of its own, yet it made an even better image together with the birds leaning into each other. Just like these pictures, I liked my life better with him in it.

Better together. Complete.

We set the paintings in the back seat of his car before he opened the door for me.

"So I did good?" he asked as he sat down.

"You did fantastic. You just keep amazing me, Mr. Walker. I'm so grateful to have you."

He leaned across the console and kissed me again.

"I love you," I said through a smile as our lips were still close enough to touch.

Now that he already broke the ice, I felt it was my turn to say it first. The utterance felt right, natural coming off my lips.

~ 19 ~

The weekend ended with another full day around town with Aaron. Which was the best way to spend a day before I started my new job because it didn't allow me to have much time to freak out. Probably his goal—how well he knew me.

But Monday morning arrived, and I was frea-king out.

After tossing and turning most of the night, I finally gave up the fight and decided to get my day going. Being up almost two hours early, I had plenty of time to pick out the right attire. I changed my outfit three times before deciding a cardigan and flats said, "I'm a comfortable person who's easy to talk to." I didn't know if we had a dress code, but I was sure I'd find out soon.

I took my time fixing my hair and makeup while playing my worship station on Pandora. I sang along, trying to prevent myself from running away with anxious thoughts in my mind. I loved singing, and now that I was involved in church again, I realized just how much I missed being on the worship team.

Mental Note: *Talk to Aaron about the worship team protocol soon.*

After completing my hair in a soft curl and my makeup somewhere between the natural look and the more glamorous look, I made my way into the kitchen to kill some more time by packing a lunch, toting my laptop along so I could still hear the music. I paused for a minute, listening with eyes closed, grounding into the peace of the moment.

The knock at my door sprung my eyes open.

It was either Vicki, a neighbor who accidentally got my mail again, or my most favorite person. A smile grew on my face, and my heart sped up as I headed to the door, knowing who I wanted it to be.

"I hoped it was you." I greeted the most handsome man I'd ever seen.

"Who else would it be?" He chuckled, holding a pastry bag in one hand and a latte in the other.

"Vicki. Or a neighbor. But of course, it's you." I stepped aside to let him in.

"My last surprise for your new job celebration. I hope you haven't already made yourself coffee this morning." He kissed my cheek as he handed me my favorite drink.

"You're simply the best. You know that?" The fact I was able to catch such an amazing guy had finally settled into my brain without much shock. But here he was, causing electricity to spark my thoughts again. I took a sip and felt my jitters melt away as the warm drink slid down my throat.

"I think you're pretty amazing yourself, Ms. Maddison." He set my breakfast down on the bar. "I wasn't sure how far along in your morning routine you'd be, but I wanted to swing by before you were ready to walk out the door."

"I've been up for a while because I couldn't sleep. So I've taken my time getting ready. I keep finding ways to kill time, but this is the best way to do so."

I set my coffee down and wrapped my arms around his waist, laying my head against his chest. The rhythm of his heartbeat was the final dose to cure my anxiety. His long arms wrapped around my shoulders and mid-back. We stayed there in silence for a good while. Aaron didn't seem in a rush to let go either.

"Thank you," I said, my head still pressed firmly against his chest.

"This is definitely the best way to start my day too." He kissed the top of my head then rested his chin there. "You're gonna be great, you know. This is exactly where you are supposed to be."

"I agree." In his arms. That was where I was supposed to be.

I knew he meant my new job, though.

I held onto him a few seconds longer before finally pulling away. "I was about to make my lunch. Do you want me to make you one too?"

"Yes, please. What're you making?"

"Nothing fancy. A chicken salad sandwich and some carrot sticks."

"Sounds good to me. Need help?"

"Sure. Can you get the can opener out of that second drawer?" I pointed him in the right direction and continued collecting the other ingredients. "I don't make it special. It's just canned chicken, mayo, mustard, a tiny bit of relish, grapes, and pecans."

"Sounds delicious to me." He side bumped my hip with his own and placed down the can opener. "What else?"

"Uh, you can grab the carrots and bag them up. The ziplock bags are in the pantry on the bottom left." When he started to hum along with the song coming from my computer, I pictured this being our morning routine. I tried not to swoon into the bowl as I mixed the ingredients.

"What?" he asked through a laugh after seeing my fairytale-like countenance.

Would there ever be a day my uncontrollable emotions wouldn't betray me as they surfaced to my face? I wasn't about to freak him out with my mind's playground, so "This is fun" was all I fessed up to.

"You are fun." He quickly kissed my cheek like a young boy stealing a cookie, not wanting to interrupt my master culinary precision—or lack thereof.

I finished assembling and bagging the sandwiches then placed them with the carrots in a brown paper sack. Before passing Aaron his lunch, I drew a purple heart on the bag.

"I'd much rather stay here with you," I said with a flirty grin, "but I better get going. Thank you for everything this weekend." I grabbed my lunch sack and set it down on the bar next to the breakfast he brought me. "I just need to grab my things real quick, and we can leave."

Silence momentarily filled the space when I closed my laptop, abruptly ending the music, but Aaron continued singing where the song left off. I didn't get to hear his rich tone often, but his singing voice was easily one of my favorites.

"I love it when you sing. You should do it more often." I commented as I walked up behind him.

My words stopped his melody. "I love it when *you* sing. *You* should do it more often. Say, on Sundays...."

"Yeah, yeah. I've been thinking about it."

We made our way out of the apartment, down the stairs, and to our cars at a sloth's pace. He hugged me goodbye, causing our lunch sacks to crinkle between us.

"Have a great day, dear." He mimicked an old married man.

"You too, hon." I played along, giving him a content smile. "I could get used to this."

The thought slipped out before I fully processed the repercussions of admitting my deeper longings. *Please don't freak out!*

An almost shy, knowing smile pulled at his lips. "Good to know."

This. Right here. This was what I always wanted and hoped for but started to doubt still existed. My entire body sprang to life in delight. He went out of his way to make sure I got out of my head this morning and joined him in reality.

He was my best reality.

With a sigh, I forced myself to end my perfect morning. "I better get, I want to be early. Thanks again." I jumped into my car before I couldn't pull myself away from him. Aaron leaned in to kiss me goodbye before closing the door. After starting my car, I gave two flirtatious honks on my horn and took way too big of a bite of the banana-nut muffin he brought me, not thinking he was still watching.

He laughed and shook his head.

I smiled as crumbs fell from my mouth. *Yup! This is the real me. Sorry.*

I kept my radio off and gave myself a pep talk on the way, reminding my negative side of all the reasons why I'd succeed at this new adventure.

"You are awesome. You're great at helping people. You are easy to talk to, and you're going to be great at this place. Don't get too worked up, and enjoy what has been put in your lap. You got this!"

I arrived at the massive office building, not quite as intimidated as the last time. I only brought my laptop bag for today but was excited to figure out what I wanted to bring to decorate my office. I definitely didn't want to look like the new kid, decked out on the first day of school with an over the top collection of matching tie-dye supplies.

Telling myself to remember to breathe as I walked into the elevator, up to the third floor, then into suite C. My brain functioned partly on memory but mostly adrenaline. Now that my nerves were at bay, I was fired up. I didn't know how long the training phase would take, but I was ready for this transition.

I entered with a smile that grew brighter as I saw the faces of my new co-workers. Everything was just as I remembered it, but this time I belonged here too. The crisp and clean environment of my pristine workplace was a breath of fresh air in my life.

"Maddison, good morning." Suzanne greeted me from the counter. "Did you meet Lisa last time?" She motioned her hand to the receptionist I recognized from the day of my interview.

"Not officially. Hi. Maddison, nice to meet you." I extended my hand over the counter and down toward her seat.

"Lisa. Welcome to the team." Her words were warm and encouraging.

"Thank you. I'm excited to be here."

"Great! That's what we want to hear. Now come this way, I'll show you around." Suzanne started down the hallway to the left, passing the first door on the right that I remembered was her office. "This is the waiting room here on the left. Sometimes we send one of the clients out here to talk to the other in private before bringing the families back together." It was across from her office but didn't have a door, more like an open lounge.

"The other counselor isn't here yet, but this is her office next to mine. Her name is Rachel. And you'll be in this office here. It has some furniture already, but you can add to it what you like."

When I walked in, it was as if the room was glowing with expectation. Underneath a large window, a small desk was pushed up against the wall, not the usual set up you'd see in most offices. But it was more personable if you weren't looking across the table at someone you were counseling. Only a notepad calendar and a stapler sat on the desk. I looked forward to shopping for decor to make it my own. *My desk*. In *my office*. I was no longer just another worker at a cookie-cutter cubicle.

Mental Note: *Take a picture with Aaron to put on my desk.*

The large, cozy-looking leather chair almost didn't seem like a desk chair, but it was indeed on wheels. I guess that made it easier to go back and forth from work mode to counsel mode. Perpendicular to the desk was a small gray couch I wasn't sure could even fit three people, but considering this counseling establishment was for newly adoptive families, I bet parents and a child could fit on it perfectly. The only other thing in the office was a small bookshelf with a few books and knickknacks, most likely from the previous occupant.

"It's perfect." I set my things down on the empty desk and turned to look at Suzanne, unable to contain my excitement.

"Glad you like it. Come this way to finish the tour, then I'll let you get situated." Suzanne walked out and continued further down the hallway. "We only have two single restrooms, so they aren't men's and women's. The majority of the time it's just us ladies in the office that end up using them, but either way, they lock. They are both decorated the same. Personally, I prefer this one," she whispered as she pointed to the door closest to her office. The bathrooms were side by side at the top of the hall, right outside my office. I was glad they were close. Well, technically, everything was pretty close.

"And this is the mini kitchen." She went on about some of the guidelines of kitchen usage I probably should've been listening to, but my mind began to wander and focus inward.

This is right. This is where I'm supposed to be.

The small and more intimate building space was perfectly metaphoric of the type of connections made in these rooms. Hearts being healed. Hands providing hope.

I couldn't help but notice the drastic comparison between this place and my former office. The busy, loud, open room filled with cubicles served its own characteristics paired for its purpose, but it was never me. This was me. I wouldn't have to learn to fit in here.

Finally, the key piece of the puzzle my life lacked. I'd been trying for years, grasping and forcing situations together, relationships and jobs. Somehow it created a picture before, just not the right one. But now I saw it—the intended design—and it felt incredible.

I was back in my office, like a dream that changed scenes without rhyme or reason. Hopefully, I hadn't come off as rude while I spaced out. I took the time to inhale the moment as I sat at the desk.

Looking around my office, I began to picture all that would come to pass in this small room. The warm faces of the lives I would hopefully help. The bright smiles of innocent children learning the acceptance of a family.

Mental Notes

I probably needed to do something to make this space a little more kid-friendly and turned that thought into a mental note with question marks to resolve later. For now, I had some real notes to take.

The day went by too fast. Suzzane said most days, I'd see three to four families, each with different faces and unique circumstances. I sat in on two of Rachel's sessions to observe and take notes, which was majorly reminiscent of my intern days. She was skilled at her job. The calmness in her voice was soothing, and the genuine gleam in her gaze covered the families with an instant blanket of comfort. I took two pages full of notes during my time in her office. A few mental notes too.

Pick Rachel's brain.
Get to know Rachel more than just a co-worker.
Ask her what's it like to work for Suzanne.

The couple of hours I spent observing were quite possibly more effective than my entire senior year of "how to counsel" classes. And the flower doodles on the edges of my page told me just how happy—and relaxed—I was.

Everything was right.

My job.

My goals.

My focus.

My relationships. Aaron, in particular.

Thinking of myself a year ago was like picturing another person. As if I merely retold a story I heard once about a different woman whose thoughts were no longer my own. She was not me. I was not her. And that felt good.

~ 20 ~

I blinked, and it was July. I floated on cloud nine, practically daily. I even had to remind myself this was actually happening: dream job, dream man. A better routine, with a finer fit to my life goals and upbringing, helped me find pleasure in areas of my life that used to seem so empty and dull. I *loved* my new job, more fulfilled in life with a career I felt was a better match for me than advertisement design. I could be found almost every Sunday at church—singing alone during worship but linked by the arm next to the hot guitar player during the sermon. No longer wasting away alone in my apartment and deepening the size-six crater in the middle of my couch. I'd also successfully tackled many of the colorful sticky notes in my mind that had been there for who knows how long, leaving a more organized and smaller to-do list, mental or otherwise. It seemed like everything in my life had finally fallen into place.

Life was good.

People I hadn't seen in a while at frequented food locations noticed a difference in me and began asking what had changed. My usual response was something along the lines of "what hasn't?" This was the life I should've been living, even before the addition of Aaron.

Although it was short notice, Suzanne let me have the days off for the trip we'd already planned. She was a much more relational boss than Jerry, for which I was extremely grateful. A part of me felt guilty for taking days off after just starting, but not bad enough to cancel my get-a-way with my favorite person in the world, and the female runner-up.

I double-checked my mental list as I packed everything for our river retreat, passing over swimsuit more than once without crossing it off. I contemplated going to buy another one that covered even more than my already modest tankini, a tinge apprehensive about being in my swimsuit in front of Aaron. My lack of confidence in my body was a real thing. Not to mention Vicki could potentially be walking around looking like a model in a tiny two-piece, leaving me to look like a grandma no matter what I wore.

There I went again....

I pushed that thought from my mind as I packed my suit and focused on positive topics like how excited I was to spend time with Aaron, but also delighted to have a few days with Vicki. We kept up, I made sure of it, but not seeing my bestie every day was the only downside to my new job.

The knock on my door caused me to jump, an equal amount of nerves and excitement. I ran to the door like a goofy seven-year-old girl chasing her crush on the playground, laughing at myself and glad no one could see me, then composed myself back to an acceptable norm.

Plans had changed just this week when Ethan had to have an emergency appendectomy. Our party of six became a weekend-long double date. Aaron and Michael were coming to pick me up, and then we would get Vicki and make the three-hour drive together. Ethan was a part of many fond memories, but those were connected to the old me, so I was more than okay this trip would now be entirely about the new me.

"Hey you." My favorite words rolled off his lips before I leaned in to kiss them.

"Hey! Come in. I'm almost done." I knew I had to hurry when Michael wasn't behind him and must've been waiting in the car.

"Did you pack that snack bag?" he asked as he lingered by the bar while I darted back into my room.

"Yeah, it's the big red bag on the counter." I yelled from the other room.

"Ethan was right. You don't mess around. You are the Road Trip Snack Queen," he said, causing me to chuckle as I emerged with my small rolling suitcase, hefty gray and white beach tote, and a book. "When do you think you're going to have time to read? I'm going to spend every waking minute of this trip learning more about you."

I threw the book onto the coffee table, then pulled the sunglasses from the top of my head over my eyes. "Let's do this," I spouted off in the most serious and dramatic tone I could muster.

"You are so cute. Let me get that bag." He took the rolling suitcase from me and grabbed the snack bag from the counter. "Anything else?"

I kissed him on the cheek, confirming my cuteness. "Nope. Bye, Seabass. Behave yourself!"

He chuckled. "I doubt your fish will even notice you are gone."

I made it down the stairs much faster than Aaron since he had most of my bags.

"Back seat, bro." Aaron called out to Michael before he was down all the steps. It might bother him to give up his seat for me on another occasion, but seeing as the last person to make the group complete was his girlfriend who had him wrapped around her finger, Michael hopped out with eager anticipation.

Aaron threw the snack bag in the backseat as I climbed in the front. Michael caught it in his lap, although I was not sure that was its intended destination. His eyes grew to the size of saucers as he opened the bag and inspected its contents.

"Don't go crazy. Those snacks are for the way back too." I bossed him around, feeling like a scolding mother harnessing her ecstatic child in a candy store.

I heard the thud of the trunk and knew our mini vacay was almost in full swing. Aaron sat down, buckled in, shifted the car into gear, then plopped his forearm on the console. His hand was facing up as he looked at me. "This is where your hand will be for the foreseeable future. Don't let go."

I interlaced my thin fingers between his strong ones with pleasure. "That shouldn't be a problem." I tipped my head back against the rest and closed my eyes even though I wore sunglasses. He took our hands toward his face and kissed the back of my hand, drawing my attention back to him.

"Love you."

It still made my stomach clench and heart race every time he said it. I rolled my head back to its previous position. "I love you, Aaron Walker."

"Is this what I have to look forward to all weekend? Putting up with you two lovebirds." Michael griped just before taking a bite of a candy bar from my snack bag.

"Like you and Vicki aren't going to be the same." Aaron argued, looking at his brother in the rearview mirror.

"From what I've heard, you're pretty smitten, Michael." I joined Aaron on defense.

"Oh, really? What have you heard exactly?" Michael perked up and leaned forward, poking his head into the front seat, inches from ours.

"Put your seatbelt on, man. I never thought I'd still have to tell you that as an adult."

"Yeah, yeah. So let's hear it, Maddy?" The click from the buckle rang in my ears.

"Like I'd out my best friend. You'll have to ask her if you want to know."

"Whatever." Michael slumped in his seat, then shoved the rest of the candy bar in his mouth before messing with his phone.

Vicki was already waiting outside with her bags at her feet. Michael jumped out of the car and ran to her, picking her up and spinning her around. Her legs popped up behind her in unison as they kissed before he spoke something and set her back down. If there was anyone I knew who warranted to be cherished the way I was observing, it was Vicki.

"I don't know if I'm happier for him or myself," Aaron said as he turned back toward me.

"I'm glad he took your advice."

"Can't take much credit. I pretty much gave him an outside perspective."

"Sure, Dr. Phillip. Just admit you are amazing."

"Whatever. Definitely happier for myself, but Michael's a close second." He leaned in slowly about to kiss me, causing my stomach to flip in anticipation when Michael rapped on the window to pop the trunk.

Thankfully Aaron's car had a big trunk because Vicki packed even more than me. I pulled my hand away from its station and jumped out with my own enthusiasm to hug Vicki, whose face I hadn't seen in a few weeks. We all piled back into the car, high on expectations for a fantastic weekend. I grabbed Aaron's hand, still frozen, where I left it.

"Are we there yet?" Michael asked in a whiny kid voice, obviously to annoy his older brother.

"I will punch you," Aaron responded, making us all laugh.

Their banter reminded me of the relationship my older brothers had that I witnessed growing up yet never really understood. It would've been nice to have a sister to know all the treasures of a life counterpart. Fingers crossed, I'd gain one through marriage—hopefully Vicki.

* * * *

Aaron traced a thousand circles into the back of my hand as we drove down the highway. I gazed out my window and saw the sun far off, breaking through the clouds onto the hills. All the other clouds seemed drastically low and gray.

"I hope it isn't going to rain. That would ruin this whole trip." I fretted, still looking out the window.

"It would change up our plans for sure, but it wouldn't ruin anything." Aaron reassured me, as he often did, always choosing to stay optimistic. I loved him more because of it. Time with each other was never bad, and even if we spent our day indoors instead of out exploring nature, it would still be a great trip. Of course, he was right. "We're almost there. The map only shows thirty more minutes."

"Thank God, 'cause I have to pee." Michael roared from the back seat, causing all of us to laugh.

Most of Michael and Vicki's conversations had been quieter when they weren't talking to us. I didn't make anything out over the music and my chats with Aaron but was excited to ask her what they talked about later tonight when we were in our cabin.

A drop of rain hit the windshield. Hundreds more followed in a matter of seconds.

"It's better if it rains today than tomorrow anyway," Aaron said. He turned on the windshield wipers, rescuing me just as my hopes began to slide away with the droplets.

"True. Very true. Perhaps tonight can be a movie night." I suggested some alternative plans for this evening, trying to stay positive as well.

"I wouldn't mind that," Vicki said, looking at Michael.

"Sounds good to me." Michael agreed.

"All right, why don't we stop to eat soon? Then we can go get checked in and stay at the cabins for the rest of the day." Aaron took the initiative to solidify our evening events.

"Perfect." I gushed. His ideas, his hand in mine. All of it. Even the rain.

He pulled into a hole in the wall place with a sign advertising "Burgers, Fries, & Shakes," knowing how to pull me right back into this trip if I was still down about the weather. We all got out, giggling—well, Vicki and I, men don't really giggle—and ran inside, trying not to get too wet. It felt good to move my legs after a few hours in the same couple of positions.

The place was fuller than I expected, which made me hopeful. If the locals ate here, I was about to have a good meal.

But before we could find out how good the eating was, Vicki and I meandered toward the ladies room and the guys toward the men's room, all slightly dripping. Well, Michael was kind of rushing.

"Y'all sure seemed to be talking about something important back there." I noted to Vicki as we washed our hands and checked out the aftermath of the rain on our hair and makeup.

"I told him about my past. A few days ago actually, but over the phone. I hadn't seen him in person since. I was nervous that it would change how he saw me or that he wouldn't want to stay with me. That was probably why he greeted me so extravagantly today."

He reassured her, just like his older brother did so naturally to me.

"I'm thrilled to discover nothing seems to have changed. Michael had a few more questions about my ex he wanted to ask in person, which led to the more serious conversation in the car. But mostly, he just made sure I knew he wasn't going anywhere."

Good job, Michael.

"Glad to hear. Look at us, a hot mess, but two hunky men are still waiting for us. It doesn't get much better than this."

"No, it doesn't." She agreed with a content smile.

* * * *

The burgers and fries were better than I hoped, and the cabins were equally breathtaking as we pulled into the property. Either my memories of this place were inadequate, or they'd done some renovating in the last few years. Or maybe I never went by the office building last time, because I definitely didn't remember the massive pond with a fountain.

The guys went inside to check us in and get the keys. They'd only been gone for a few minutes when Aaron jogged out in the light rain and opened my door.

"When I gave her our names, the receptionist started acting nervous. After some awkward silence, she told me they'd accidentally double-booked our cabins. I told them about Ethan and Stacy not coming if that helped any."

The rain started to pick up, and Aaron had to wipe away the drops falling into his eyes. My heart sunk, and my shoulders slumped. How much more would go wrong before this trip was over?

"She has a larger two-bedroom cabin that's vacant and is wondering if we'd be willing to take that one instead. It actually saves us money and gets her out of their double booking mistake, but I told her I needed to come ask you."

I turned around to look at Vicki, but she didn't offer much with her body language. *What do I do here?* Was this okay? If I said no, would I be the one responsible for complicating the trip even further? Did I have a choice? I remained quiet as my thoughts began to suffocate me.

"Michael and I will stay in one room and you two in the other. The doors have locks, I already asked. But if you aren't comfortable with it, I can tell her no. We can find another place to stay." He disarmed my biggest fear. He wasn't trying to room with me.

I processed his last statement, thankful he was considerate of my sentiments on the matter. "I guess that's fine. Vicki, you okay with it?"

"As long as those stinky boys give us our own room, I'm good." Her attempt to lighten the mood brought a relieved grin to my face. Vicki knew I wouldn't want to room with Aaron, even if she might've been okay with sharing a room with Michael, so I was extremely thankful she didn't try to change my mind in the slightest.

"Are you positive?" Aaron asked one more time, wiping the rain from his face again and making eye contact with me only. Not Vicki.

"Yes, I'm sure. Sounds like we're helping them out of a bind. I guess it's a good thing Ethan and Stacy weren't able to come."

He leaned in and kissed my forehead. "Okay, I'll be right back with the keys."

I let out a sigh and tried to keep my thoughts positive about this trip even though everything was *not* going how I hoped. Why did this always happen to me? Vicki's hand touched my shoulder from the backseat.

"I know this might be an awkward situation for you, but I promise I won't let anything weird happen. Not that I think either of the guys would try anything anyway, but I got you."

"You are my best friend, did you know that?"

She nodded with a grin. I looked at myself in the visor mirror, mostly because I was nervous, and it gave me something to do.

This isn't like the time Garrett tried to see exactly how far you were willing to go on one of your road trips. I told myself, staring straight into my eyes. *Aaron isn't like that; he respects you.* I focused on the mental note I put up months ago, reminding me not to compare Aaron to my handful of previous horrible boyfriends. *He would never push the boundaries you've set up.*

I flipped the visor up just as the boys were back in sight, walking toward the car. When they got in, Aaron handed me the map of the grounds. "We're cabin 4A. We got quite the upgrade in all of this. It has a dock that goes right up to the river."

I looked down at the photocopied map with pen lines showing us which roads to navigate from the "You Are Here" star to our cabin.

"Sweet. That's pretty cool. Okay?" I tried my best to navigate the map and guide Aaron, not sure why he handed it to me and not Michael. I was only good at the companion side of co-piloting. My head still slightly spun from the assault of bad news and negative memories when he reached over and flipped the paper upside down in my hands and half-smiled. No wonder. That would've been bad.

Laughter spilled out of my lips, pouring balm on old wounds and helping me snap out of the funk. I was thankful he didn't acknowledge my frazzled actions in front of the others even though he recognized them. I linked my arm in his on the console and reread the map.

The drive through the winding roads was beautiful, but when we stopped at our cabin, I was pretty sure I failed to navigate the map correctly. Upgrade was an understatement. This place looked three times as big as the cabins we passed along the way.

"The lady said one bedroom is upstairs and one is downstairs. We each have a bathroom too. Which do you guys want?" Aaron inquired after he turned the engine off.

"I don't know. Let us check them out first, and then we'll decide." I snickered, glancing over my shoulder at Vicki with an excited grin.

"Go pick then. We'll get the bags." Michael instructed as he gave Vicki a flirtatious nudge toward the door.

The cabin was terrific, like walking into someone's fully-furnished home, decorated to perfection. Large leather couches with signs of comfortable wear sat in front of a fake, but lovely, fireplace. A large tv hung above the mantle. I saw the modern kitchen with all the dishes stacked in the open-faced cabinets.

The downstairs bedroom door was open, right next to the cabin entry. It was simple, with two full-size beds and a dresser in the middle. Probably the kids' room if it was someone's house. I passed the downstairs bathroom as I headed up the stairs and saw the open loft with another couch and games stacked on a coffee table. The second bedroom concealed the master suite. A king-size bed centered on one wall and an enormous vanity mirror spanned most of the wall to the left of the bed, next to the bathroom door.

"This is better for us since it has the bathroom in here, don't you think?" Vicki asked over my shoulder.

I wasn't sure how long she had been shadowing me, so her unexpected voice made me a little jumpy. "Sure, as long as you don't mind sharing a bed. Otherwise, I'm sure they've done it before, being brothers and all."

"Sounds good to me. We can stay up all night giggling about our boys."

I heard the bags hit the floor downstairs. "We'll take upstairs." I yelled as I came back down the stairs with a smile on my face as big as our cabin.

~ 21 ~

Our first evening was filled with immense laughter and board games in the loft, followed by a movie with cuddling and the fake fire on as the rain continued outside. Despite my earlier reservations, it wasn't awkward at bedtime. Vicki and I said our farewells after the movie was over, and the brothers kissed us goodnight at the bottom of the stairs. She and I then gabbed and gushed over our guys until we couldn't keep our eyes open.

Come morning, neither one of us was ready for our beau to see us in full-on morning mode. We freshened up enough that we didn't look like zombies, and not so much it was obvious we made ourselves over. We looked pretty good in our messy buns and stretchy pants if I said so myself.

So far in the day, there hadn't been any rain clouds in the sky, but we all knew the weather could change quickly in Texas. I expected a slow morning of relaxation and followed by deciding on the rest of the day's events as a group.

A knock on the front door caught my attention, and I wasn't sure if the guys were up yet, so I hurried down the last several steps to get it, pretty sure it was housekeeping of some sort or one of the guys who accidentally got locked out. I was surprised to open the door to a young woman. She had a high ponytail, sported a polo T-shirt promoting the resort's logo, and held a basket enclosed with shiny cellophane wrapping.

"Good morning. I'm from the front office. We wanted to apologize again, and thank you all for helping us out in our overbooking bind." Based on her looks that were a union of nervousness and relief, I bet she was extremely thankful to have her job still and might've even bought this basket herself after last night's shift.

Just as I reached my hands out for the basket, I felt something brush the small of my back. I turned to see Aaron standing behind the open door, sleepy-eyed and rumpled hair. Judging by his tousled state, the knock at the door woke him up. I assumed he wasn't ready to interact with visitors this early because he didn't budge.

"Oh, wow. Thanks. I'm glad it worked out for everyone." I truly was. Putting myself in her shoes for a minute, I would've been an anxious mess. "This isn't necessary, though."

"Sure, it is. It's just a little something to show my—our appreciation. Y'all have a great day," she said as she turned before I could refuse to keep the gift.

"You too." I closed the entry to reveal a groggy Aaron standing where the open door had been. Even first thing in the morning, he was attractive.

"Good morning, you look adorable today." He leaned in and kissed the top of my head. Maybe he was self-conscience of morning breath, or perhaps he hadn't even considered that since he kissed me there plenty. "Any goodies in that basket? I'm hungry."

"I see fruit on the top, but it looks like there's more underneath. Let's open it. Is Michael up yet?"

He shrugged his shoulders through a yawn as we walked over to the kitchen table to untie the bow. The plastic wrap echoed as I struggled to get it open. If Michael wasn't awake, he would be after that noisy ordeal. Aaron grabbed one of the apples, tossed it up in the air, and took a bite after catching it.

"Good morning, everyone," Vicki said from the top of the stairs. Her beauty was commanding enough, but she still gave an extravagant greeting. Not in an annoying way, though. We wouldn't be best friends if it was.

Just as she was about to take the last step, Michael jumped out of the bathroom to startle her. It worked, and we all laughed, even Vicki after she smacked his arm. They shared a sweet morning greeting as they embraced and swayed. I tried not to watch, but the show was too good.

"Come grab some breakfast. The front office brought us a thank you basket. Several options in there." I ate a tasty breakfast bar with nuts. "So, what's the plan for today?"

"I'm ready for a lazy day of floating down the river, myself," Michael said, digging through the snacks for something to eat. "I say we load up on several things from this stash, float the river, then go get lunch somewhere with some A/C. Beat the heat of the day."

"For sure. I don't want to be out there when it hits triple-digit weather. The river will probably be less crowded earlier as well." Vicki agreed.

"Did they tell you at the front desk about a shuttle? If they still do it, I think that's how we got back last time."

"Oh, yeah. It's on that map. She said they have a few different locations where people can get out, and the shuttle runs every thirty minutes." Aaron got up to grab the map. "It looks like the first stop is pretty close to us, and the farthest will take a few hours to reach. They're labeled with colored flags. I guess we can decide as we go when we're ready to be done."

"Perfect." I grabbed a banana from the gift basket. "I'll go get ready then."

To say I was nervous about being in a bathing suit in front of Aaron and suddenly wishing the rainclouds would return, was a gross understatement. Vicki must've picked up on my nerves when she followed me back to our room.

"You're gonna look great, stop worrying about it."

Maybe it was the fact that she had more experience than me in the intimacy department, or that she was smoking hot, but Vicki didn't seem to mind being in a swimsuit in front of Michael—or Aaron—at all. If I stood next to her and looked in the mirror, I'd probably cry and not leave the room, so I told myself to push the nerves away and focus on having a fun day.

I went into the bathroom with my suit and took a deep breath before changing. No matter how hard I tried in the past, only negative memories were associated with swimsuits. Insecure about how much was visible, my splotchy untanned skin, and self-conscious, to name a few. I decided not to look in the mirror after putting it on since I already knew how I looked—the full black tank on the top covered my wiggly stomach, and the brightly colored Aztec pattern bottoms covered my entire backside. I tried it on a few times stressing at my apartment, so looking again now, focusing on the parts of myself I hated the most, would do no good. I emerged from the bathroom, b-lining it to my suitcase for my swimsuit-cover, mostly self-conscious about my legs. The loose-fitting black tunic fell below the part of my thighs I disliked the most and would help me feel more comfortable walking around before the river.

Vicki whistled. "Nice legs."

"Shut it. You're crazy." S*top it, Maddison.* I closed my eyes and paused from frantically searching through my bag for the cover. The memory of Garrett pulling on my swimsuit bottoms at the end of the float as I got out of my inner tube played fresh in my mind like it wasn't years old. *Stop comparing. Aaron would* never *do that.*

"Sorry, I was only trying to lighten the mood. Everything all right?" Vicki asked with genuine apology in her voice.

"Yes." I wiped my negative thoughts away like a hand over a chalkboard, leaving the horrible memory unrecognizable. Since we arrived at this place, I'd been experiencing almost-forgotten memories and was growing weary from reliving them.

"We're going to have fun today. I'm just nervous, I guess." I felt a little guilty for not telling the whole truth.

By the look on her face, I could tell Vicki knew there was more, but she didn't prod. After letting the silence grow long enough to see if I would admit anything else, she finally spoke.

"We are. Everything is going to be amazing because we're here together and with some very hunky men. What better way to spend a summer day than floating down the river? There's nothing to be nervous about, so shake it off."

"You got it." I shook myself and laughed before grabbing the cover and slipping it over my head.

Downstairs, the guys waited on us. I was confident they'd been ready for several minutes. Good thing I shaved last night or they really would've been waiting. Guys had it so easy when it came to swimming and everything involved in getting ready.

As we exited our room headed for the stairs, I noticed the brothers had almost identical trunks. I laughed, bringing further ease to my mind.

"Ready ladies?" Michael called as we hit the first step.

"You bet," Vicki cheered, moving down the stairs faster and more confident than me. She landed on the bottom step with a bounce. Her swimsuit was a black one-piece—barely—with large cutouts and thin straps crisscrossing over her waist. She looked great, and Michael's not too subtle wide eyes confirmed it.

"Great. Let's go," Michael said, wrapping his arm around her, touching the bare skin of her waist, then nervously pulling back and moving his arm up to her shoulder.

Aaron looked at me and smiled as I came down the last few steps, but the look on my face caught his eye before my wardrobe. "You good?"

On top of everything in my head, I felt like a blimp trailing behind Vicki, so no surprise I wasn't controlling my face as well as I thought. "Mostly." I admitted, not wanting to lie.

"What is it?" His voice was full of yearning without even a hint of frustration. "Please tell me."

"I hadn't realized until we got here, but I have some bad memories from this place. And I'm—I'm just trying to forget."

The light in his eyes told me he knew what and whom I alluded to. "Well then, I'm glad we are here together to make fresh memories. Sorry, you're going through that. We can talk about it if you want to."

His words wrapped around me before his arms. I let out a sigh before admitting, "Wonderful point of view. Once again, you save my day. No need to talk about it."

He touched his forehead to mine, and I felt the heat rush to my cheeks.

"You look great," he said inches away, his turn to gain a crimson hue.

* * * *

Taking my swimsuit cover off and revealing my tankini wasn't nearly as awkward as I feared. I was pretty sure I saw a smirk grow on Aaron's face, but I wasn't going to make eye contact to confirm. He was pretty nice to look at himself without a shirt on.

Moments later, I floated down the uncrowded river in my inner tube, holding hands with Aaron. The river flowed at a leisure pace, causing our hands to gently go above and below the water hundreds of times throughout the ride. With my head tipped back on the tube, my sunglasses helped bring even more shade from the sun. The warmth of the sun soaked into every pore. It was the most relaxed I'd been in ages.

But then I gasped all the air out of my lungs when a huge splash of cold water hit my toasted body. I opened my eyes to find a guilty, but grinning Aaron. How could I get mad at that face?

"You punk!" I laughed and splashed him back, resulting in a mini water war. Aaron jumped off his tube and swam over to me, dragging the plastic donut behind him.

"I love you." He whispered in my ear as I tried to fix my hair that surely looked awful.

"I *think* I still love you too."

"Think? Are you unsure? Do I need to remind you?" He interrogated me flirtatiously before pulling himself up and resting his elbows on my tube. "Can you ever forgive me?" He gazed at me with puppy dog eyes, and his lip stuck out farther than a toddler's perfected pout.

"How could I refuse that lip?" I answered, slowly leaning in for a kiss, but pushed him into the water after a brief brush of our lips. I started laughed but fell over myself from the force of him pulling my tube with him. I scrambled back up to grab my float before it could drift too far away.

"Look at you cute little kids." Michael mocked us as they rounded the bend.

I saw Aaron's tube, but not Aaron. Suddenly, Michael flipped, and Aaron popped up underneath him, the three of us now thoroughly soaked and treading water.

"Don't even dare!" Vicki glared down at us.

Michael shook out his hair and hopped back up onto his tube. "Hilarious brother. Just wait, I'm going to get you back."

Laughing felt good. It also felt good to be in the cold river in the Texas summer heat with people I loved. I smiled as I attempted to pull myself back up onto my tube, missing the first few times and laughing harder every time I tried. I most likely looked like a fish flopping on land, which would've made me cry not too long ago, but I couldn't help but indulge in the situation now.

"Do you need help?" Aaron offered, paddling himself back toward me.

"Probably. This is ridiculous."

"And hilarious," Vicki said, confirming I wasn't the only one laughing.

"Watch it, girl, or I'll get you." I warned.

Mental Notes

Aaron grabbed my tube to stabilize it for me. "Go underneath it. It's easier to get in that way."

He was right—like always—and after only one attempt, I was safely back on my inner tube, catching my breath. Aaron continued to hold the handle while I fixed my hair into a new top knot.

"You look beautiful today. Everything about you is radiant, especially that smile. I'm glad we're here together." Aaron admitted after we began floating once more.

"Me too, but I think I lost my sunglasses." Everyone laughed.

Another twenty minutes or so later—no one had a watch on to know for sure—we came up to the last colored flag for the shuttle. I was surprised by how fast the day had gone. Vicki was the first one out, and the only one that didn't slightly resemble a wet dog. Michael followed, then Aaron after him. I was thankful to be the last one out, and even more grateful when Aaron offered me his hand to help me steady myself and not flip over.

"Thank you, sir." I grinned. He kept my hand in his, pulling me in close and wrapping his arm around my back. His closeness was intoxicating.

"You're welcome, ma'am," he said with a wink.

* * * *

We made our way back to our cabin and freshened up for lunch, but came right back to the room after eating at a local cafe. Michael looked slightly like a lobster, and we were all pretty drained from the sun. Aaron and I sat on the love seat while Michael sprawled out on the couch, laying his head on Vicki's lap, his skin glistening with aloe vera. Vicki ran her fingers through his hair, looking down at him. Her happiness was indisputable.

"Ugh!" Michael broke the silence with a pain-filled groan. "When did y'all put on sunscreen, and how did I miss it?"

"I'm sorry I didn't think to ask you, babe," Vicki said with a guilty tone.

"It isn't your fault. Michael's a grown man. Besides, he's done this since he was a kid." Aaron poked fun at his baby brother.

"Shut up. I'm hurting here. Don't you have any sympathy?" Michael threw back, their brother banter continuing to entertain. "There's no way I can get back out tonight. Can we order pizza or something?"

"Sounds good to me. I'm enjoying this lounging anyway." I agreed with Michael's request. The sun stole a good amount of my energy as well.

"Excellent. I'm going to try and nap for a bit if that's okay?" Michael tipped his head up to look at Vicki.

"That's fine. I'll do the same." Vicki leaned over and kissed Michael before helping him up and into his room. She turned to look at me before heading up the stairs, making sure I felt comfortable. I waved. "Don't let me sleep long if I even fall asleep."

"Okay. Rest well." I turned to Aaron. "Do you want to nap too?"

"Not really. This is better than sleep to me." He ran his finger up and down my arm.

"I agree." I let out all the air in my lungs and slid down farther, kicking my feet over the arm of the love seat. Aaron pulled me into his side.

"Maddison?"

"Mmhmm?"

"I'm so glad it's you. Even though it was annoying when my friends constantly tried to set me up and made comments about me needing to find someone, waiting for you was one of the best decisions I've ever made." Aaron admitted out of the blue like it was something brewing in his mind for some time.

Goosebumps grew over my arms, and I wasn't sure if it was because of what he said or the tickling sensation of him still running his hand over my arm. "I'm thrilled you think I was worth the wait. Not gonna lie though, I'm still shocked I'm the one who gets you, but pretty much elated about it."

"Tell me something that will make me smile, Maddison." I didn't have to look; I knew his phone was recording me.

"I love that you're a gentleman. You continue to amaze me. And I'm so grateful for everything in my life right now. It's like I can proudly stand on my own two feet after a few years of scraping and clawing my way above ground. I'm glad you didn't meet me then, I don't think we would've made it." I knew I went considerably deeper than the typical video clip, but it felt like a good moment to be real after he initiated the dialogue with his confession.

"I wish I would have. I could've helped you up sooner."

I leaned my head against his chest, flabbergasted, speechless, and in awe of how well he loved me. His heartbeat lulled me into a trance, and I began drifting. That was when I knew. He was the one I wanted to spend the rest of my life with. I didn't know if he knew, but I hoped he would one day. Preferably soon.

* * * *

It wouldn't officially feel like the fourth of July if we didn't see some sort of fireworks. While Michael and Vicki finished their nap, Aaron and I slipped out to grab a box of sparklers in town. We woke the sleeping beauties with pizza, and after dinner, we dragged them down to the little dock behind our cabin. Michael moved at a giant tortoise's pace, and as soon as his sparkler fizzled out, he was done. As Vicki helped him back up to the cabin, the couple gave the impression they'd aged forty years since yesterday.

Aaron looked positively amazing in the flashing glow of the sparkler he held over the water. No doubt, I was glowing too, but due to the summer sun that still warmed my skin even though it was long gone. I sat on the edge of the wooden planks and hung my feet over the side—my toes barely tickled the water. Aaron joined me shortly after I sat down, and I felt myself mold into the groove of his side like it was meant for me. I leaned my head on his shoulder as our sparklers inched their way to nothing over the river.

I love my life resounded in my head.

"Thanks for a stupendous weekend," I said just above a whisper.

"Wow! Stupendous, huh?"

"Stu-pendous," I repeated, feeling every bit of my huge grin.

"You're welcome." He kissed the top of my head. I'd never get enough of those.

~ 22 ~

Getting back into work mode after our extended weekend getaway was taxing, and it didn't help I already had this weekend's long overdue visit to see my family on my mind as well. Thankfully, Friday came quickly, and my first session of the day canceled, but the Gilmores were scheduled to arrive any minute. I pulled out their file and reviewed what we went over the last couple of visits. The Gilmore family adopted Sammy, a six-year-old boy who spent his first few years bouncing from one home of a relative to another. He landed in foster care for about a year and was officially adopted four months ago. I remembered them as soon as I saw the picture paper-clipped to the folder.

"Maddison, your eleven o'clock is here." Lisa notified me over the phone intercom.

"Thank you. You can send them back." I responded before closing the file, setting it down on my desk, and then walking out to meet them in the hallway.

Sammy was a happy boy, finally secure in a home that showed him love and consistency, but they were here today to discuss some odd habits they had a hard time breaking. Everyone took seats and got situated in my office, looking every bit a loving family.

"We find food wrappers and sometimes food under his bed," Mrs. Gilmore said when I asked how things were going. "The first couple of times, I thought maybe it was trash from his backpack, but I'm beginning to think he might be hiding food in his room." She wasn't angry, more concerned.

I had a good feeling I knew exactly what this was and asked Mr. Gilmore to step out with Sammy for a minute and wait in the lounge, not wanting to talk about Sammy like he wasn't in the room.

"This is a very common thing we see in children that have spent time fending for themselves. When children aren't provided with adequate, consistent meals, they sometimes will gather food and hide it for when they get hungry again. It's a defense mechanism to make sure they have something to eat later, after knowing sometimes they won't be fed."

"Oh my." Mrs. Gilmore lifted her hand to her chest, grieved with what her son was experiencing. "How do we help him overcome this?"

"There are several different ways, but we'll also see tendencies like these start to phase out after spending more time in your home."

We discussed techniques that could help before bringing the other family members back into the room.

"Hey, Sammy. How's everything going?" I asked with excitement and a friendly smile on my face.

"Good." His answer was short but typical of a six-year-old.

"Are you enjoying your new bedroom?"

"Yes!" He began to perk up a bit.

"What's your favorite thing in your bedroom?"

"My legos that my brother gave me." He lit up and continued to describe his legos in great detail. The Gilmores had an older biological son but decided to adopt after a couple miscarriages spanning several years.

"It sounds like you have quite the collection. That's so nice of Harrison to share his things with you. And do you like the food your mom cooks?"

"Mm-hmm." He didn't seem thrilled I changed the subject from his preferred topic. *I can relate, bud.*

"What's your *favorite* thing she makes to eat?"

"Um, probaly pasta."

"That sounds yummy." The Gilmores observed our interaction with smiles on their faces, in awe of their new son. "Did you know anytime you are hungry, you can ask your mom or dad for something to eat?"

"Yeah," he answered, looking down at his fiddling thumbs and bouncing legs.

"You don't ever have to hide from me that you're hungry, Sammy. If you're hungry, I want to make sure and fill your tummy," Mrs. Gilmore added in agreement as she poked his belly.

"Okay," Sammy replied. It wasn't an instant fix, but opening the communication would lead to less food found under his bed over the next several months.

We discussed some more things about Sammy's new year-round school and other situations that were different in his life. In all reality, everything in his life was different from a year ago. All things considered—even if they were difficult to discuss—he was fairing amazingly well. I felt like we had a very productive session.

I made lunch plans this morning with Rachel and Lisa and looked forward to getting to know them better. We planned on going to my favorite Chinese place I hadn't been to in a while, so I was also excited to indulge in some comfort food.

Over lunch, I found out Rachel was thirty-two and had been married for nine years. They had two girls, five and two, and moved out here from Alabama for this job and were loving Texas. She worked for a similar place back home—which explained her confidence in the sessions I observed. Her husband was an engineer and had some type of entry-level security clearance job, so that was all I heard about that.

Lisa was two years younger than me. She didn't finish college, and even she landed a good job before I did. Ironic. We had some things in common, and I was sure we'd get pretty close during my time at Hands of Hope. Recently single, she lived with her boyfriend for several months. Not that I thought any different of her, but that was one thing we didn't have in common.

"I don't know. It all seemed so romantic when he asked me to move in with him, but it was hard. We fought all the time, and it took away the excitement of the relationship. If that makes any sense," Lisa said after I asked her what happened.

"Oh, yes. You find out each other's flaws when you live together." Rachel reported from experience. "But you just learn to work through it when you're in it for the long haul," she added before taking the bite of sesame chicken from her fork.

Mental Notes

I tried picturing what unknown flaws Aaron had. There had to be some even though I couldn't imagine any. Everyone had flaws.

"How long have you and your boyfriend been together, Maddison? Does he do anything that crawls under your skin?" Lisa pointed the conversation back at me.

"It's been several months now, but I considered us together before it was official. I'm sure there's something that'll come up one day that irritates me, but nothing has yet."

"Oooh. You're still in the fairytale phase." Lisa teased.

"I guess, but I don't see us getting out of it." I smiled and looked down at my plate, pushing my food around so they wouldn't see my cheeks fill with color. "I think we both had things happen in our past that made us know what we wanted, and once we found it, everything just kind of clicked. True for me, at least."

"That's probably my problem. I'm not even sure what I want, really." Lisa took another bite of her egg noodles, not too moved by her revelation.

"Who does? I know for me it was always changing before I made my list." Rachel piqued our interest.

"A list?" Lisa questioned mid-chew.

"Yeah," she said matter-of-factly. "I made a list of all the qualities I wanted in a spouse. The list made it easier for me not to continue in a relationship with someone who wasn't good for me in the long run. Even if I was blinded by emotions."

"That's good," Lisa said, pointing her empty fork at Rachel. "I think your inner counselor might be coming out on our lunch break, but I'll take it."

Mental Note: *Make a list.*

In all fairness, I wasn't sure if my list would be comprised of the things I wanted in a spouse or an inventory of all of my favorite things about Aaron. It was hard to separate the two in my mind—that my future spouse and Aaron might not be the same person. Which was the case with every past boyfriend since I was twelve—at least for a week or so.

"Do you have a list?" Rachel asked, pulling me out of my thoughts.

"No. Not written out at least. I was just thinking I should make one. Technically, I've had one comprised in my mind, but it's scattered all over the place." Picturing the rainbow of sticky notes in my brain—smaller now but still a kaleidoscope of aspirations—revealed how much had transpired in my life over the last few years, molding me into the person I was today.

"I know mine will have hot, muscular, and bearded at the top." Lisa admitted unashamedly, causing us all to chuckle.

"Features change over the years. *Trust me*," Rachel said with a knowing grin, initiating another giggle session.

* * * *

I was super excited for my trip to visit family after work. My father was turning fifty-five, and my mom planned a surprise party for him. I hadn't been back to Wimberlake in probably close to three years, and I was seriously looking forward to being around my mom for some much-needed grounding after floating in La-La-Land—Population: Two—for the last few months. Not to mention trying to make up for all the visits back home I purposefully missed.

In the short drive, not even two hours, I spent my time going over the events of the last couple of months. I laughed at the silly things I'd done, cried over the beautiful ways Aaron tore down the walls I built after Garrett, belted out my favorite tunes, and did some major organizing in my brain. The feeling of being free, raw, and relaxed, with no one around me, resulted in further laughter. I could be pretty nutty sometimes when I didn't use a social filter.

I passed a sign indicating only three more exits to go when my phone rang, and I knew who it was without even looking. "He-lloooo," I answered in total flirt-mode.

"Hey you." When his low voice filled my car, I was no longer alone on this trip. "Are you there yet?"

"Almost, probably eight more minutes or so. What're you up to?"

"Just checking on you." Aaron wanted to come along or send Vicki with me. He didn't much like the idea of me going alone.

"I'm grateful for that, but I assure you I'm safe and sound. Just preparing my mind for small-town livin' again for a few days," I said, changing my accent to match my statement.

"You're too cute."

Mental Notes

"So I've heard. Don't be worried and bored all weekend, okay? Do something with Ethan. I bet he's still crying over the lack of bro-time since he missed our road trip."

"I guess I could do that. When do you come home again?"

"Sunday evening. Want to hang out when I get back?"

"Of course, do you even need to ask?"

I smiled and didn't say anything for a few seconds. "No, just like to hear your response. Here comes my exit. I should get off."

"Fine. Fair warning, I will be texting you all weekend."

"Ooh, I look forward to it."

"I love you."

"Love you too. Bye." My car fell silent again with only the hum of my tires against the road. I instantly missed him. Even the sound of his voice brought richness to my life, and the detrimental days before I knew him were a fading vapor. I couldn't help but think there was no trial I could face that his encouraging words and delicious voice couldn't help me through.

Pulling back into my hometown was like a time warp. Buildings, streets, smells, all holding more mental movies than I could quickly sort through.

The plan was to let myself in with my key and wait for my brothers and the other guests to arrive while my parents were at the movie theater.

I parked up the street and walked up to an empty house full of memories. My old bedroom hadn't changed at all. A good portion of my things remained on the bookshelf, and an old picture was still tucked into the corner of the mirror frame. I laughed as I ran my fingers over it, seeing a younger version of myself and Ethan with our high school clique. The picture revealed how much age had enhanced my friend's features. Sitting down, I fell backward and let my head hit the mattress, arms both extended out to the sides.

Oh, Teenage Maddison, you had no idea what the next few years had in store for you in the big city.

"Hey."

I jumped so hard I almost fell onto the floor. "Oh my gosh, you scared me." I touched my chest to calm my racing heart and looked at my brother, Christopher, leaning against the door frame. "I didn't even hear you come in."

"I had many years of practice sneaking into this house, undetected." He bragged. "You look good, sis."

I stood up and walked over to hug him. "As do you. When did we grow up?"

"Not sure. It happened pretty fast."

"Tell me about it. What's going on with you? Catch me up."

We walked into the living room and sat on the couch. He filled me in on his long-term relationship with Amanda—whom I'd never met—being on a "break" and not sure what the future held for them. I wished I could've had some kind of relationship advice to give him, but I *barely* felt like I was beginning to know what I was doing myself.

Before long, everyone arrived, and the big surprise went off without a hitch. My father turned beet red as he choked back tears when he saw all three of his kids huddled under the same roof again. Seeing the genuinely shocked look on his face was definitely my favorite moment of the party.

For a good portion of the night, I battled between an overwhelming feeling of joy because I finally saw my family after way too long of self-induced isolation and equally heavy guilt for putting them through my unexcused absence. Somehow every time I began to dip my toes in the sorrow pool, Aaron was true to his word and sent me a perfectly timed text, saving me yet again—I've lost count at this point. I responded to several with selfies of me with various people he'd heard stories about. He was able to get me out of my head even hundreds of miles away. I cherished him even more for it.

We spent a good hour cleaning together afterward, like our old chore chart used to dictate. I did dishes, Christopher had garbage duty, and Hank, my oldest brother, rearranged everything back to its proper location. My mom was *big* on everything having its specific place, so we all took special care in making sure to put the house back in pristine order. It felt like old times. Only we weren't much smaller than our parents anymore.

"Thank yew fer comin'. It's been a while," my mom said, coming up behind me and wrapping her arm around my waist, pulling me into a side hug.

"I know, I know. Great job on the party, Mom."

"Thanks. So how's everythin' with yew and this Aaron boy?" We hadn't had time to catch up until now with the house full of party guests.

"Fantastic. I really love him, Mom. Everything that lacked in my previous relationships seems to be there this time around." She gave me a puzzled look, which was warranted, seeing as how I'd kept her out of the loop on purpose. "For example, he always puts me first and hasn't stopped pursuing me as time has passed. He's kind, and we don't argue. Have I said he makes me laugh? And he just *gets* me—even the crazy parts. And I'm not even pretending to be someone I'm not, which hasn't seemed to scare him off. He ... grounds me, I guess. I don't know how else to explain it." I shut off the water and picked up the towel to start drying after my jumbled speech, nervous about the words that were soon to leave my mother's mouth.

"I c'n see it in yer eyes. Yew have the same look I had when I found yer father." A glow grew across her face, her eyes glistening. None of her children had married yet, and I was sure she was beginning to wonder if she'd ever be a grandparent while she still had the energy to do fun things.

"Really? Well, if I can be half as happy as you two are, I'll have a pretty great life." Her face told me a symphony of words circled in her brain, and she couldn't figure out which ones were the best to say. I knew because I didn't get that trait from my father.

"Thanks, sweetie." She was finally able to speak as she hugged me. All the thoughts spiraling in *my* mind were about Aaron, so I finished up in a hurry to go to my old bedroom and call him.

"What're you doing?" was how he answered the call.

"Laying here in my old twin-size bed staring at the ceiling and thinking about you."

"Sounds nice. How'd the party go?"

"It was awesome. So glad I came. My dad was a mushy mess. He probably thought having all of his kids under the same roof again would never happen. There were people here I hadn't seen since I left for college. Some have changed quite a bit, others not even a smidgen."

"Smidgen, huh? Sounds like you need to hurry back to me in the city."

"The accent sneaks back too easily," I said through a laugh.

"I'm glad you went. I just wish I would've gone with you."

"Stop it, you! I know you wanted to be here, but you'll meet everyone soon enough. I needed to unplug, and they needed my time. I'm coming back a better girlfriend. Promise."

"I can't argue with that now, can I? Not that I think you need improving." He sounded worried I'd take his statement the wrong way.

"Everyone can use a *smidgen* of improvement. I know what you mean." I joked to ease his worry. "What did you do tonight?"

"I played my guitar mostly, and made plans with Ethan for tomorrow —just for you." He emphasized the last portion with a bit of sarcasm.

"Oh, yeah. I have to send you this picture I found in my room. See if you can spot us." I got up to grab the photo and switched the phone over to speaker mode to snap a picture. "Okay, I sent it," I said as I returned to the bed.

A break of silence filled the call as I assumed he switched over to view the picture and analyze the faces, not sure what was going come next: laughter or a sigh.

"Oh, man. Look at little Maddison. How old are you here?" He didn't seem too interested in Ethan.

"Not sure. Probably fifteen or sixteen, but I meant for you to see Ethan." I sassed, every bit sixteen again.

"He's the goober on the end, right?"

"Yes, that's him." I laughed.

"You haven't changed much, but you've grown even more beautiful. Not that you weren't there, just—"

"I know what you mean." I interrupted, so he didn't have to try and figure out a nice way to say I too looked like a goober back in the day. A deep yawn rose from my chest. "I'm struggling to keep my eyes open, love. I think I need to call it a night." Work, the drive, the party, the cleaning, it all caught up to me in an instant.

"Okay, I guess I can let you sleep," he said with genuine reluctance, obviously missing me. "Goodnight, Maddison. I love you."

"I love you too."

~ 23 ~

That night, I dreamt about myself like I was back in high school. Same classes, same friends, same boyfriend—I hadn't even thought about him in years. JT was the boy standing between Ethan and me in the group picture, and the guy I dated a good chunk of my junior year. It must've been sleeping in this bed and seeing the picture that brought everything back to the front of my mind. Who truly understood the nighttime subconscious, anyway?

I tried to shake the dream off like the randomness it was and enjoy my day with my mom. The guys went shooting, and mom and I headed to lunch and planned on shopping—not that there were many stores to choose from. I didn't miss that aspect of this small town.

We went to the dearest little bistro that made my favorite panini sandwiches. If there was one thing small towns had on bigger cities, it was the excellent cooking and company of locally-owned restaurants.

Everything about this trip was nostalgic in a therapeutic way, erasing the couple of bad years that caused me to turn borderline recluse.

"Maddison?" A vaguely recognizable voice caused me to turn around and look for a familiar face until I found him.

It was like my dream warned me of my soon coming realities. "JT?"

"Yes. Wow, it's been what, six years or more?"

"Yeah, something like that." I stood to hug him.

"Oh, this is my wife, Stephanie."

"Nice to meet you." She looked familiar like maybe she was a couple of grades below us. "So you still live here?"

"Indeed. I was never able to escape, I guess," he said, but I wasn't sure if he was joking. He didn't look like he'd aged as well as Ethan and I had. Perhaps the weight of responsibilities that came along with marriage aged him exponentially, predominately in his face. "What are you doing here?"

"I came to visit family and head back tomorrow. Just a quick trip."

"Well, I sure am glad I ran into you. What all are ya up to these days?"

I would've been just fine not to have this reunion, personally. I wasn't sure who was more uncomfortable: me or JT's wife.

"Oh, life in the big city. I work at a counseling center for families post-adoption."

"How fantastic. You were always good at helping people back in the day, I remember. Man, I'm so thrilled to run into you. What are the odds?"

"Small-town livin' for ya. It was great to see you too, and nice meeting you, Stephanie."

"Likewise" was the only thing she said during the duration of our encounter before they left. I was somewhat weirded out that I dreamt about him last night then saw him today.

"Small world." My mom observed.

"It sure is." That's all it was—a crazy coincidence. Of course, I'd run into someone I knew if they lived in this tiny town at one of the few places to eat lunch.

The rest of our day was uneventful, which I appreciated. The Miller men had a blast and came back home reeking of gunpowder. My father loved me, but he loved having sons just a little bit more. I was okay with that, though, having a strong bond with my mother. He came by the kitchen where my mom and I were preparing dinner and kissed the crowns of our heads before heading to clean up. Before long, we all ate together at the table that didn't seem big enough to fit the five of us anymore.

"When are one of you kiddos gonna get married and help me be the world's greatest grandpa?"

"Don't look at me," Hank said right away. "I don't care if I'm the oldest, there's no way I'm ready for all of that," he paused, "responsibility." The last word came out like a profanity. Hank had always been somewhat of a free spirit. He could have any girl he wanted in high school—which he did—and perhaps that made it hard for him to ultimately settle on just one: flaws and all. From my understanding, he still rotated through girlfriends at an unhealthy pace and had no plans of changing his destructive relationship habits.

"I guess time will tell, either me or Maddy," Christopher said after I'd caught him up on all things Aaron. It'd depend on if his "break" turned out to be a period or a semicolon.

"I wouldn't mind being the first at something for once," I said before taking a bite and grinning as I chewed.

"Wa waaa." Hank wasn't impressed. "It isn't like you guys made it easy for us to settle, trying to duplicate what you two have and all." He pointed back and forth between my mom and dad with his fork in hand.

"There ain't any-thang easy about it, son. You just gotta stand by your commitment once you make it. It's mostly great, but there are hard days." Our dad confessed, looking at our mom.

"Mostly great," she reiterated, "and worth it every second."

I cherished the way they loved each other. I only recalled seeing them fight a few times growing up but wasn't sure if they did so when we couldn't see, or they truly strived not to whatsoever. Either way, I wanted what they had, and coming back home reminded me life with Aaron might not always be gumdrops and roses, but we'd have to work it through those days if we wanted something long-lasting.

Maybe we were still in the fairytale phase, but I was ready to put in the work it would take to make sure our relationship could withstand anything that came our way.

* * * *

My parents and I attended my old church the next morning. My brothers slept in and hit the road for home to whatever was more pressing than family time, but I didn't have room to talk; I'd missed my fair share in the recent past. Having my parents to myself was almost like the last few years I lived at home after my brothers had moved off.

Not wanting to give my mom a heart attack if I showed up in jeans, I made sure to pack a skirt for church. I sent a picture of myself to Aaron before we left, knowing he wouldn't get it for a while with band practice before service. When he finally responded, it was a smiley face with heart eyes. His reaction made me want to dress nicer more often, but the years of *having to* made me revere my jeans on Sundays.

Small town churches were different in more ways than I could count. Everyone knew details about your life you didn't care to share, so it didn't surprise me when everyone remembered me—and everything I'd done my entire life. I spent the whole morning feeling thirteen again, being called "Little Maddy." I also heard things like "My, how you've grown," and "Well, looky here," as I tried to refrain from my eyes rolling so far into the back of my head, they disappeared. Because nothing was as bad as my mom witnessing me lose my manners. She didn't care how old I got; she wouldn't have my bad behavior. Not to mention all her friends would think I'd gone and lost my salvation in the big city. I wouldn't do that to her.

But if I got patted on the head one more time....

My dad guided us to the same row of pews we sat in my entire life—no surprise there. Assigned seating was one of those unspoken rules in our tiny country church, and heaven forbid the Millers sit anywhere else.

The church was considerably emptier than I remembered. I leaned over and whispered to my mom, "Where is everyone?"

"This is everyone. Most people go to that new megachurch these days."

The phrase "megachurch" in this town was a joke, but I knew what she meant—the newer flashy church with a young hip pastor where attendance was so high you didn't know everyone's name. It actually made me sad. Part of me, somewhere deep down, still loved my small town roots.

I could easily see everyone in attendance as I looked around the room and knew pretty much every face I saw—including JT and his wife. They sat clear across the church and didn't seem to be in the best of moods. I caught a glare from her like she was attempting to burn holes through my soul.

Ouch. What's that about?

Needless to say, I was glad to be headed home a few hours later. I'd have enough of the small-town drama that equated to nothing and minds smaller than the town. With renewed vision, I was excited to see Aaron as soon as I rolled back into town. He wanted to cook for me again, so I drove straight to his place for dinner. After an extended time apart, it seemed like a perfect ending to my quality time weekend.

I felt the fireflies from back home spiraling in my stomach as I parked at his apartment. It made me happy they were still alive and well in there after all this time, and I couldn't get to his door fast enough. Even though I'd only been gone a couple of days, the trip down memory lane felt like ages. I knocked on the door, eager to see my man, but deflated when his roommate opened the door.

"Aaron." He called from where he stood. No hello, nothing. I could see why Aaron wasn't extra fond of the guy.

My boyfriend rushed to the door wiping his hands in a towel. "Finally! I missed you so much." He grabbed me in a grand embrace and kissed the top of my head once, twice, three times before letting go and finding my lips.

"I was only gone for two full days." I chuckled but secretly swooned inside.

"It was too long. Come in. Dinner's ready."

Roommate—I didn't even know his name—had disappeared, and I saw everything prepared in the kitchen. I hoped Roommate would stay away and not be an annoyance tonight. Aaron fixed chicken fajitas that smelled scrumptious. I wasn't really in the mood for sharing—the food or my Aaron time.

"Wow, babe. You made these?" I asked, half expecting him to admit he actually bought them from a restaurant and dumped it in the pan for the home-cooked look.

"I enjoy cooking if I have someone to cook for."

"You can cook for me anytime you want to. I'll start considering you my personal chef."

Loud music started coming from one of the bedrooms, and for the first time, I was the one who could read the emotions on *his* face. "I'm gonna get a place of my own or a new roommate soon. It's just not working with Jason anymore."

Ah, his name was Jason.

"Sorry, love. I can't even imagine."

"Let's focus on us tonight. Tell me more about your trip." He talked over the music and started to assemble our plates.

"The party was fantastic. Family time was good. Overall, a great trip. I'd kind of skipped out on a few of the last holidays, so it was the first time I was back home since I started living in my cave." *Or more than a few.*

He walked toward the table with our food and placed a plate in front of me.

"Thank you, it smells wonderful. Other than that, the weekend pretty much consisted of everyone I hadn't seen in six years or so commenting on how much I had grown or patting me on the head like I was still a kid."

He laughed at the last part. "How fun."

"Loads, but a good time to feel my roots again and make sure they were intact." I held my hands out and wiggled my fingers down like roots burrowing into the ground. When forced to reflect on the last couple of days, that was what I took away from the weekend: the importance of quality time and working on relationships. "Tell me about yours."

He started with a whine. "Ethan's still using the sympathy card after his appendectomy. I can't say our time together was fun, but it was better than being home with—" He pointed down the hall. "I basically decided I don't like spending time away from you, so no leaving again."

A smile graced my face. "Deal. I won't go again unless you are with me since you can't live without me." I teased but also loved how much he missed me. "But I'm home in one piece, safe and sound." I raised a hand to my cheek and batted my eyes as fast as I could. "So has Ethan even been back in the shop much?"

"Not really. He's *working from home* still." He used air quotes for emphasis. "It's already been a few weeks. I think he just likes the time away from Simon honestly. The shop is quieter but less entertaining." He chortled.

"This is so good. Thank you for making me dinner." I took another bite of my fajita.

"It's my pleasure." He smiled before taking a bite of his own.

* * *

I received a text on Tuesday from my mom. I would've known it was from her even if my phone didn't tell me.

HEy, I need

Mental Notes

Your address
PLease send it to me.
LUV Mom

Her over-capitalization and unnecessary line breaks brought a miniature smile to my face. Clearly, my mother was still learning how to text, so I tried not to laugh or be annoyed. I didn't put much thought into why she needed it and replied with my address. And a smiley face.

Later that week, I got an envelope in the mail filled with my mom's handwriting. Closing my community mailbox door, I headed up to my apartment, excited to open the letter. It was thicker than a standard envelope, so I suspected it to be photos from my father's party. My parents still preferred hard copies developed from their camera instead of digital pictures.

I got home and dropped everything on the coffee table, causing a loud thud to fill the air, and fell back onto my couch to open the mail. I saw more of my mom's perfect penmanship on a sticky note stuck to a second envelope.

> I got this in the mail with a note attached, asking to please mail to Maddison Miller at her current address. Not sure what it is.
>
> XOXO Mom

I flipped the second envelope over and inspected who could've sent it or what it could be. Aside from my name written in black ink, the package was completely void of any details. I opened it up to find a two-page handwritten letter.

> MADDISON,
>
> I CAN'T BEGIN TO EXPLAIN HOW AMAZING IT WAS TO SEE YOU AGAIN AFTER ALL THESE YEARS. I MUST ADMIT, I WAS HOPING THAT DAY WOULD'VE HAPPENED SOONER. IF I'M COMPLETELY HONEST, I

> NEVER STOPPED CARING FOR YOU AND HAVE ALWAYS FELT LIKE YOU WERE THE ONE WHO GOT AWAY. I DEAL WITH REGRET EVERY DAY.

What was this? I flipped to the end—my head spinning and my eyes blurring in and out of focus on the words I read—to find the letter signed by JT.

JT?

Why would he write this to me? Frustration overwhelmed my body, causing my heart to pound in my chest. I wasn't sure I wanted to finish the letter, but my brain went into shock-induced auto-pilot before registering I'd resumed reading.

> MY WIFE KNEW I NEVER GOT OVER AN OLD EX, BUT WHEN WE RAN INTO YOU AT THE DINER, SHE REALIZED IT WAS YOU. WE AREN'T REALLY TALKING RIGHT NOW. I'M NOT SURE WHERE YOU ARE IN YOUR LIFE, OR IF YOU EVEN FEEL THE SAME WAY, BUT I JUST COULDN'T GO ANOTHER DAY WITHOUT TELLING YOU. I HOPE TO HEAR BACK FROM YOU EITHER WAY.
>
> —JT

My skin felt like it was crawling all over my body. He was married and professing this to me like I'd be okay with it. Even crazier, he thought it would work. Clearly, I was never as into him as he was into me. Or perhaps he'd just been unhappy for so long he was living in this false reality where he believed there was something better in his past that he missed out on. I felt sick. I felt dirty, even though I hadn't really done anything.

What was I supposed to do about this? I tossed the letter onto the coffee table like it was as toxic to the touch as it had been to my mind. I had to get as far away from this setting as possible. I sprung from my seat, trying to leave the mental haze above my couch and briskly walked into my room, falling face-first onto my bed. "UGH!" I screamed, only it was muffled by my sheets, thus barely audible.

What bothered me the most was he thought I'd overlook the fact he was married and find his love letter as some grand, romantic gesture. Was that how people saw me? Did he—or anyone for that matter—think I was the type of person who'd entertain adultery like it was no big deal? The question circled in my mind, spiraling into a black hole that warred to suck me in.

If I took away anything from my failed relationship with Garrett, I'd never entertain cheating. Because I knew what it felt like to be cheated on.

Too embarrassed to talk to anyone about this, not yet at least, I took a hot bath. I rode a rollercoaster of emotions filled with anger, disgust, shame, and confusion until I could no longer feel the heat on my skin.

~ 24 ~

Focusing on my scheduled families the next day helped clear my head from the confusion JT's letter brought. I started a reply after my bath the night before, but I kept going back and forth on if I'd even send it, thus it was unfinished. By the time the last clients left my office on Friday afternoon, I was more focused on the positive progress I'd seen in my families, and the upcoming plans Aaron and I had for the weekend—he always cleared my head.

He was coming to pick me up this morning to go on a hike. I sported all the active gear I'd never actually been worn for athletic activities. Excited to do something new with Aaron we'd never done before, the letter was far from my mind. He knocked on the door ten minutes early, coffee in-hand as usual—I was spoiled.

"Let me go to the bathroom really quick before we leave. There probably won't be a real bathroom out there, and I'm not down with port-a-potties." I joked, walking back into my room. I began to hum as I washed my hands, eager and giddy for our time together, then checked my hair and makeup one more time to make sure it would hold up if I started sweating.

A smile marked my face as I returned. "Ready?"

But then I froze.

Standing there, wearing an expression I'd never seen, was Aaron holding the letter.

"What is this?" He looked up at me, confused.

"A letter I got in the mail. It's nothing. I can't even belie—"

"What kind of married creep sends a letter like this to someone? Why didn't you tell me about this?"

"I didn't know how to handle it yet—"

"Apparently you did. You're writing him back." He cut me off again and picked up the short reply I'd begun.

"To tell him he's a creep! That's why I was going to respond. And I hadn't even decided if I'd send it yet."

"When were you going to tell me? Or were you ever going to tell me?" He is voice grew louder and more intense.

"I hadn't made up my mind on anything." My voice escalated, matching his. He made me feel like I'd brought this on myself. How could he see it as my fault for some jerk of an ex sending me a love letter?

"I went to your ex's wedding for goodness sake. You didn't think I could handle this?" He demanded, waving the paper in the air. "Did something happen between you two while you were there?"

"No! Of course, nothing happened. I would never—"

"I'm sorry. I need to leave. I can't be here right now." He turned for the door.

"Aaron, wait. Please."

"I'll let you know when I'm ready to talk." He turned only to reveal his face was a mixture of pain and anger. Our eyes connected for the briefest of seconds before he stepped through and shut the door behind him.

It felt like my heart had been ripped out of my chest.

What just happened? He would let me know when he was ready to talk? When would that be? I couldn't believe JT had caused our first fight by sending me that stupid letter. I was so angry, the sensation to vomit curled my stomach, but before it happened, I crumpled down to the floor and started to cry.

Fairytale over.

* * * *

The hours felt like days, and the days felt like months. I wasn't sure if Aaron was waiting for me to contact him, or if that would upset him more since he told me he'd let me know when he was ready to talk, but I felt awful. Empty. At work, I put on a face and helped people deal with their issues and tried to not think of my own for the time being.

I wasn't sure who I wanted to know about this whole situation, even more so now that it involved Aaron. After a couple of days of poison eating a hole in my chest, I made lunch plans with Vicki.

I filled her in on my run-in with JT back in Wimberlake and the letter that followed. After asserting my displeasure, I told her about keeping it to myself and Aaron finding the pages at my apartment. Even though it was awkward to talk about, getting it out was helpful, as if I no longer carried the pressure alone.

She looked at me like I'd grown a third eye. "Ugh, I can't believe he did that. His poor wife." Signs of relating to JT's wife filled her face. I hadn't considered this might hit a little too close to home for her beforehand and contemplated if I'd asked the wrong person. She shook her head—no doubt to shake the memories away—and continued. "So Aaron was pretty mad?"

"He was *really* mad. I've never seen him like that, ever. Has Michael said anything to you? I don't know if Aaron talked to anyone about it."

"No, Michael hasn't said anything. How long has it been since you guys last spoke?"

"Four days. I'm not sure what to do at this point. I didn't think he'd wait this long. I thought he meant a couple of hours or something. Should I reach out to him or keep giving him space?"

"That's a tough call. Everyone's different. Some people want the other person to bring it up, and others really mean, 'I'll talk to you when I'm ready.' I'm so sorry, Maddy. This stinks."

I wiped away the tear that barely left my eye, refusing to lose my composure in public. "I don't think I can wait much longer. Maybe I'll text him tonight."

"I guess it can't hurt too much. If he isn't ready, he'll probably just say so again, but at least he knows where you're at."

"True. Thanks for hearing me out on this one. I hope it wasn't weird, you know, with everything that happened—"

"No, you're fine. I'm glad you came to me. It's been a while since we've gotten together."

I knew she wasn't trying to make me feel guilty, but I did, anyway. She was right. We hadn't seen much of each other since our road trip.

"Who else would I go to? Just because we've got men in our lives, doesn't mean we don't need our besties, right?" She grinned around a bite of her salad and nodded, letting me know we were good. "How are things going with you?" I asked before diving into my lunch, ready to change the conversation from my major dilemma.

"Good. Work is painfully slow, so kind of nice, but also boring. I did a facial party with my mom again, and that was fun. She's getting pretty good at it. And Michael's as amazing as ever. I'm so grateful you talked me into meeting him. I never thought I'd hold a cougar card, but I'm a proud member now." We laughed. I was thankful for something to lighten the mood, even momentarily. "Are you enjoying your not-so-new job?"

"Yes. I barely remember my days as an advertisement designer, honestly." I pushed my empty plate forward on the table and wiped my hands on my napkin. "My co-workers are great too. It's nice having an office full of ladies."

"Not as great as me, though, right?" She feigned concern as she gathered her trash.

"Never. I better get. I have a session in twenty minutes."

We stood, and Vicki pulled me into a hug, silently promising me she knew everything would work out. "Keep me posted on everything, okay?"

"Will do."

* * *

That night, after I ate with still no word from Aaron, I picked up my phone to text him. I started and erased a few before finally sending one.

> *I know you said you'd let me know when you were ready, but I'm seriously struggling. I miss you and love you and know I didn't handle the situation right. I hope we can talk soon.*

I set my phone down on my bed and willed it to light up with a reply, then closed my eyes and tried not to count the passing seconds. The chime made my heart leap after living dormant in my chest for days.

Are you home?

> *Yes.*

I responded immediately.
Can I come over?

Absolutely.

Finally. My heart illegally raced as I waited for him to arrive. I got up and tried to clean or do something to make the minutes go by faster. I began to wonder if I would've text him two days ago if this could've already been over but tried not to dwell on it.

Should I let him talk first? Should I start off with a rambling apology to break the tension?

My heart beat in my throat.

A near panic attack rose when he knocked. I tried to collect myself as best as possible with a few big breaths before opening the door.

"Hey." The voice I hadn't heard in far too long tickled my ears.

"Hey." I stepped aside to let him in, not sure if I should hug him and decided I better let him take the lead even though I wanted to cut the tension so badly by at least grabbing his hand.

He crossed the threshold and kissed my forehead. Dizziness spun my head. I had to close my eyes and lean against the wall.

Aaron walked down the hallway toward the couch with no further words, so I shut the door and followed him. Unsure of what was about to be said, I tried to prepare myself for any outcome. He sat angled on the couch, with one leg tucked under the other. I mirrored him in my posture and waited, hopeful all would be well again in a few short minutes.

"I've missed you." He started the heavy conversation.

"I've super missed you. I hate fighting," I said.

"It isn't my favorite thing, either. I'm pretty embarrassed by how I reacted. I guess that's part of why it's taken me so long to talk to you. I didn't know how I left you feeling."

"Not great."

He reached out and grabbed my hand, causing my head to spin again.

"Sorry. First of all, I want to say I shouldn't have allowed my anger for that scumbag to spill out on you. I think the real reason it affected me so much was you didn't tell me. It bothered me that you kept his letter a secret. I thought I'd done enough to reassure you I'm safe, and then I *blew* that safe place by overreacting. I've been dealing with shame for a few days." He ran his free hand through his hair and brought it down to draw nervous circles on my knee.

About to lose grip of the last thread I'd been holding, I didn't feel hopeless for the first time in days. I wanted to let go. His presence and gentle touch broke down barriers I took years to build.

The weighty emotions he wore on his face were as hard for me to handle as the silence from the last few days. I wanted to rub my fingers over the darkened circles under his eyes like I had the power to erase them with only my touch. But he wasn't the only one who had an apology to give.

My brain reminded me to breathe. "*I'm* sorry. I totally get where you're coming from. I don't know why I didn't say anything. JT assuming I was the type of girl to be wooed by his profession of love for me despite his being married, tortured me. Not to mention I'd actually still hold feelings for him after we ended our brief relationship ten years ago. He made me feel so gross about myself. I was trying to make sense of it all, not meaning to hide it. But I should've told you, right away."

"You never mentioned running into him, so it made me wonder if there was more I didn't know."

"Nothing really happened. My mom and I ran into him at lunch. We exchanged a few words, he introduced his wife, then they left. I saw them the next day at church, and she looked like she was murdering me in her mind. I didn't understand the glare at the time, but now it's pretty obvious. I got the letter in the mail a couple of days after I was back home."

"Did you give him your address?" he asked. Not in an angry way, more wanting to understand how everything transpired.

"Heck no! He mailed it to my mom at my old house and asked her to mail me a sealed envelope. I have no doubt she wouldn't have sent it if she knew what it was. The lamest part is I don't reciprocate the feelings, like *at all*—even if we weren't together and he wasn't married. I don't even remember being that into him or how we ended things. What I do remember is he was one of my most insignificant relationships. More me not wanting to be single, honestly. This is as shocking to me as it is to you."

"You started to reply. What were you going to say?"

"I wasn't entirely sure, that's why I hadn't finished. That he was wrong for sending it to me. That I didn't feel the same way. That he needed to apologize to his wife and not try to pin his bad marriage on the fact he married the wrong person. Something along those lines, I guess. One part of me felt like he was such a jerk he didn't deserve a response, but then the other side of me wanted to shut him down so he wouldn't live in What-If-Land anymore. I don't know." I dropped my head back onto the sofa and tried not to let my frustrated tears fall.

"I didn't realize this was such a burden. Sorry I made it worse by exploding on you."

We sat in the silence for what seemed like hours, simply looking at each other. Even his eyes uttered the apology.

"Thank you for apologizing. I think the best thing we can take from this is learning a better way to handle weird situations moving forward." I said *moving forward* like it was still the plan, but I wasn't totally sure where he was. It's what I wanted more than anything.

"Very true. I mean we're bound to have disagreements, right? Hopefully next time we'll handle it better."

Next time. My entire body released the remaining tension from the last few days. I started crying, the quiet, slow tears you can't stop. Aaron reached up and wiped my cheek with his thumb, wrapping the rest of his hand behind my neck.

"I love you, Maddison. I'm sorry I took it so personally and left you like this for days."

"Yes, days!" I chuckled, trying to keep the tears at bay. "I mean, I thought a few hours at most. That was an eternity."

"When I didn't see you at church, I feared I'd seriously screwed things up."

"I probably shouldn't have skipped, but I was a mess. A big hot mess. Plus, I was afraid you'd ignore me, and I wasn't up for that challenge." I laughed, wiping away the last few tears I couldn't hold back.

"Ugh, I'm an idiot," Aaron said, grabbing me and pulling me into his chest.

Finally!

"No, you aren't. We just learned something about our relationship that'll make us stronger. And I want it super-buff strong."

"Me too." He kissed the top of my head and squeezed me tighter. Every muscle in my body relaxed into him when he rested his cheek on the top of my head. Aaron let out his own cleansing breath. "I think you should reply to him—all the things you just said. J-Toad needs to know you don't reciprocate his feelings, and he needs to move on. Whether his wife wants him around or not." I snickered at the nickname.

"That's what you want, right?" He teased after a pause, earning himself a playful smack to the thigh.

"Whatever." I pretended to be annoyed, but I actually loved how he lightened the mood. "Do you want to read the letter before I send it?"

"No, I trust you. Sorry I made you doubt that."

"These past several days have been the roughest I've had in a long time." I admitted now that they were officially over.

"Mine too. I almost called you a few times. I just didn't know where to start and kept backing out, not ready to eat crow for my little temper tantrum. I was glad when you finally reached out."

"It's a relief to know it didn't make you more upset. I wasn't sure if it'd help or hurt. Can we sit here for hours?" I pleaded with a sigh.

"At least one, for sure."

I pulled my head away from his chest and looked up at him. He kissed me in the pure silence. As our lips touched, it was like we'd never kissed before the way my insides leaped with excitement and gasped for air all at once. Everything was right again. I couldn't control the smile, which broke my lips away from his. His eyes danced over my face as if he was committing this moment to memory. When a smile took over his face, I knew our fight was far behind us. Completely content, I laid my head back on his chest and stayed there for as long as he let me.

~ 25 ~

A normal routine resumed: work, Aaron, sleep, repeat. Consistent and predictable, and I loved it. Our first fight was a fading memory, and we were much better at conflict resolution now. I relished in the new depth our relationship reached. Nothing could shake me when it came to Aaron.

But then he invited me to meet his parents. A day I knew would come eventually—or at least hoped for—and was super excited but equally nervous. I was going to meet Aaron's parents. And Vicki was too. Good news was we'd meet them together, and all of the focus wouldn't be on me. Unlike at the river, this time, Vicki's nerves matched my own, afraid Michael's parents would feel odd about her being older. And divorced.

Vicki sent me no less than four hundred texts over the last few days, wanting to know what I was going to wear, wondering if I was bringing a gift, debating backing out. But the hour before our big meeting was about to transpire, my phone was interestingly silent.

We got this girl. The parents are gonna love us. What's not to love? ;)

I applied the pep talk/text I sent Vicki to myself while I waited for Aaron to pick me up. Saving him the trip upstairs, I told him to text me when he got close. When his text came through, I grabbed the small succulent plant I bought for his parents and bounded down the stairs to meet him. Fueled by my nervous energy, I hopped in the car.

"What is *that*?" Aaron asked.

"A gift. For your parents."

"You never bought me a plant." He attempted to pout.

"I'll buy you a plant if you want me to."

"No, you don't have to buy me a plant. And you didn't have to buy one for my parents either. You're too cute."

I'd never get tired of hearing him say that, even if he said it every day for the rest of my life.

The awkward movement of the leaves in my lap gave away the skittishness I hadn't shake completely. Aaron noticed.

"Don't be nervous. They're excited to meet you."

"Well, I am," I confessed through a laugh. "It's always awkward for me when I meet new people. I think I'll be fine once we get there and the initial introductions are out of the way. Michael's picking Vicki up, right?"

"Yeah. They just got there. My mom text me a couple minutes ago to see if we were almost there."

"Poor Vicki, she didn't want to arrive first. If you think I'm nervous."

"You girls are so silly." He grabbed and kissed the back of my hand, then laced his fingers between mine and rested our arms on the console. "Okay, a few heads up. They have a dog that barks at everything and has been known to bite. *And* my dad has a huge mole on his face, but if you stare at it, he'll automatically question your character."

"Oh my gosh! Okay, good to know."

"I'm just kidding. Well, about my dad. They do have an annoying dog, but his bite won't do much damage without most of its teeth."

"Ugh, stop it!" I squeezed his hand as he laughed.

His parents lived in the metroplex, but far enough away, he didn't make the drive very often. After forty minutes or so, we arrived, and I felt awful Vicki had been there all that time alone. Even worse, now that they've had time to get to know her, the focus would be mostly on me—something I'd hoped to avoid.

We walked up to the door of a beautiful home, much bigger than the one I grew up in. The lawn perfectly manicured, and giant porch pillars dwarfing Aaron sent an entirely new wave of anxiousness through my bones.

What was that codeword, "bananas?"

"Ready?" he asked as he reached for the doorknob. He waited for my nod before pushing the door open and stepping inside. "We're here." His voice echoed in the vaulted-ceiling entryway.

We didn't see anyone right away, not even the forewarned annoying dog. He took me by the hand and ushered me around the spectacular house.

"They must be out back."

We walked down a hall through an elegant living room with immaculate furniture toward french doors that opened to the backyard. I saw everyone outside.

"Was that a gold record framed on the wall?" I asked quietly so only Aaron would hear me.

"Yeah, no big deal. Or at least that's what my dad always says. Fair warning, if you ask, there will be hours of stories to follow." He turned to me, an embarrassed look on his face pleading not to bring up the topic. "We're here," Aaron said again as he opened the door, stepping out first and pulling me behind him.

"Hey!" His parents erupted in perfect unison, springing from their sears to greet us. As they walked toward us with arms primed for hugs, I looked over at Vicki to gauge the environment. A reassuring grin illuminated her face.

"Mom, Dad, this is Maddison."

"Maddison, it's so nice to finally meet you. I'm Marcy." His mom hugged me like we were long lost friends.

She was gorgeous. Her hair was somewhere between red and light brown, and freckles decorated her face with delicate beauty. Her eyes, much like her hair, weren't quite blue or green. Fine wrinkles around her eyes and on her forehead revealed years of laughing. And possibly worrying. I wasn't sure if any of those wrinkles bore Michael's name, but I knew Aaron's story, which also included some of his father's story. No doubt, their names were written on a few.

"Nice to meet you too."

"We've heard so much about you." She released the hug but held onto my shoulders, before hugging me one more time.

"All right, let her breathe, hon," Aaron's dad said while gently pushing her aside to introduce himself. "Hi," he greeted me through a laugh, "I'm Jack. Welcome to our home." He gave me a brief, one-armed hug. "Y'all come sit down and join us."

Jack looked exactly like a man who spent a portion of his life in a touring band. His hair was longer than most men his age, mostly black with the beginning of some gray, revealing the early stages of the salt and pepper look. His agreeable appearance gave me hope Aaron should age well.

Their backyard was just as breathtaking as the inside of their home. Everyone sat at a large glass table under an umbrella canopy. Lemonade in a glass pitcher with fresh lemon slivers floating around the top, rested on the table, beads of condensation around the outside. A rather large pool spread across the tremendous yard. They even had a pool house. I pictured this as the fun house all Aaron and Michael's friends came to hang out during their teen years.

My eyes, and jaw, finally lacked the tension they held the last hour. Aaron caught my gaze and smiled.

"You and Vicki knew each other first, is that right?" Marcy asked as she offered me a glass of lemonade.

I figured they already knew some details Vicki shared, just not sure what had been said. "Yes. We worked together. She was a lifesaver. I knew nothing about ad design, and she helped me a ton. Vicki's actually the one who invited me to the open mic night, where I met Aaron. A couple of months later, we introduced her to Michael."

Vicki smiled and held hands with their youngest son. If she was uncomfortable, she hid it rather well. Either way, I'd get the scoop later.

"We are just so thankful for both of you being in our boys' lives. A momma never stops worrying about her sons. I'm grateful they have some astounding ladies to watch over them now as well." Marcy was a dream. Everything about her was amazing from her compassionate and attentive eyes to her sweetness in hospitality. No wonder Aaron waited so long to settle down. He had his mom to compare every woman to.

Jack and Marcy shared loads of funny stories from the guys' past that had us rolling in laughter and awing over our boyfriends all afternoon. The strong sense of love in this family charmed me. It meant even more to me since Aaron had shared parts of their family history. They'd overcame great trials to get where they were today.

I pictured myself fitting into this family rather easily, never having to worry about getting along with the in-laws.

We eventually headed back inside for dinner and cool air. The parents led the way in and headed toward the kitchen. I saw Jack smack Marcy on the butt, and her face light up with excitement as she leaned her head toward him for a kiss. I didn't think anyone else noticed, but when Aaron let out a small embarrassed laugh, I knew he'd caught it.

"Y'all go sit down in the living room. We'll let you know when it's ready."

"You sure you don't need help, Mom?" Aaron offered.

"Your dad and I got it, hon. Thank you, though."

From the looks of it, Marcy previously prepared some type of casserole and only had to put it in the oven and assemble a salad.

The four of us sat down on the pristine couches and let the cold air soak into each pore, not fully realizing how hot it was outside until we entered the cooler atmosphere.

"They really like you," Michael said to Vicki, his pleased expression lighting up the whole room.

"I hope so."

"Oh, trust me. You'd know if they didn't. Especially with my mom. Right, Aaron?" Michael attempted to reassure Vicki.

"Yes. Mom's face usually gives her away, even if she's trying to be kind." Aaron confirmed Michael's statement.

Glad I'm not the only one with that problem. "I think she's wonderful." I gushed on Marcy.

"You're wonderful!" He leaned over and kissed the top of my head. "And now they know I was right about you."

"What do you mean, right about me?"

"Just all I've told them. You know." Aaron shrugged like it wasn't a big deal, but his face was chagrined.

"All right," Marcy said, rescuing Aaron from my interrogation. "There's just enough time left on the oven for me to show you ladies some pictures." She entered the other room with a massive leather photo album in her hands.

"Really, Mom?" Michael complained.

"Yes. This is the reward I get for raising you boys and everything you put me through. Now scoot." She bumped Michael out of his seat to sit between Vicki and I. The large cover flopped open onto my lap. "If you think they're cute now, wait until you see them as babies."

I looked over to Aaron on my left. He raised his eyebrows in sarcastic excitement and put his arm around my back.

"The boys have pretty much been confused for twins since they were about three and four. Sometimes I even have a hard time telling the difference myself in these old pictures. Like in this one of all four kids." She pointed to a photo where the sisters each had a brother in their lap. "I think this is Aaron, and that's Michael."

"Look at that cutie." I pointed out little Aaron. There weren't many differences in the brothers' appearance, but I'd learned the tiny details of his handsome face. They were the same on the little boy in the picture.

"That's me," Michael said, hanging over the back of the couch. We all laughed. "Just kidding, it's Aaron."

Marcy flipped through the book, highlighting different memories until the timer on the oven rang out.

"Thank God that's over." Michael griped as he hid the album under a throw pillow.

"Leave her alone. It's like a motherly right of passage," Vicki stood up and grabbed his shirt over his stomach. She'd probably been through much of this before with her ex-in-laws. I frequently forgot about her past since it was before I knew her and wasn't something that affected her much now — at least from what she communicated.

"I like it here." I leaned into Aaron's shoulder, resting my head in the void of his neck.

"I like *you* here. You fit well." I wasn't sure if Aaron meant at his parents' house or in his arms. For me, it was both.

Vicki and Michael embraced in a hug, swaying so slightly you almost didn't notice the movement. He whispered something in her ear, and an electric smile pulled her face. The thought of us being family, and not just friends, illuminated my heart.

"Y'all can come on in. It's ready." Marcy called from the kitchen.

An appealing spread filled the gorgeous, shiny dark-wood table. Jack sat at the head of the rectangular table that sat eight, leaning back in pure pleasure as he watched his sons.

I couldn't help but wonder if he ever had passing thoughts like, "I almost lost all of this," or, "I can't believe I almost threw all this away."

Honest pride took over his face as he watched his wife bring the food to the table to serve everyone. I was confident it was a fantastic feeling to have his children join him for a meal at home, serious girlfriends in tow.

Marcy lowered the casserole dish onto the table. Penne noodles rested in a light red sauce covered in cheese. Jack served some on Marcy's plate, and then his own, while she continued going back and forth from the kitchen to the table to retrieve items she'd forgotten. Jack sat the serving spoon in front of Aaron, who followed suit and served me before himself. When he scooped a healthy portion onto my plate, I saw chicken and bacon as well. Steam from my plate infused my senses with overwhelming indulgence, but I wasn't about to eat how my brain pleaded me to attack.

Aaron served himself and passed the large spoon to Michael, who wasn't going to be the odd man out and served Vicki before himself. The Walkers taught their sons not only to be gentlemen but also men who served others ahead of themselves, and I was extremely grateful.

"Sometimes I serve my wife. Sometimes she serves me." Jack joked quietly with a wink.

Michael almost sprayed me with sweet-tea and had to cough it out as Vicki rubbed his back.

"Thanks for that, Dad," Aaron said, unamused with his father's coy comment.

I let out a nervous laugh and touched Aaron's leg under the table to let him know I was fine. He offered an apologetic half-smile I wanted to kiss but thought it might be too awkward with his father sitting right next to him and all.

"Don't you scare them off, Jack. It's going so well." Marcy finally sat down to Jack's left, across from Aaron, and let out a small sigh of completion. We passed around the salad and bread bowls, serving ourselves. A loud yipping sound startled me as I reached for the salad bowl, causing me to almost drop it. I looked around and noticed the little kennel not far from the table.

"That dog of yours, Marcy. Shall we?" Jack shook his head in disapproval as he held out his hands on the edge of the table, initiating grace. Everyone joined hands, except for Vicki and I—too far away from each other across the table. "Thank you, Father, for this wonderful meal my beautiful wife made, and for the people in our home tonight. Bless these relationships. We're so grateful for all you've done in our lives to get us here today. Amen."

So he did have passing thoughts.

The sound of utensils hitting plates was all that could be heard for the next few minutes as we dug into our food.

"Mooom! I miss your cooking so much," Michael said, causing Vicki to giggle. I knew what he meant, though; this food was fantastic. I couldn't name what we were eating, but there was almost as much cheese as there was pasta. It was glorious.

"So, boys, what are your two-year plans?" Jack said in between bites, earning a backhand jab to the thigh from Marcy. She wasn't very subtle if she was trying to be. "What?" He responded, not bothered by her correction.

"Not sure if I'll still be at the guitar shop or not, but I know I hope to be married two years from now." Aaron answered first, seemingly knowing what his dad was trying to get at—how serious the guys were about us.

"I'll probably be at the same job, same field for sure, but the way my role works, you never know if you'll switch companies. I haven't put much thought that far down the road, Dad." Michael avoided the full weight of the question.

The sons communicated almost opposite facts. Aaron was thinking more about his personal life than work. Michael was more inclined to think of his future as work-related, possibly because he was younger or not as far into his relationship. Technically Aaron didn't admit to being married to *me* in two years in front of everyone, but I was hopeful that's what he meant. Vicki didn't seem bothered by Michael's answer, probably knowing his dad put him on the spot. Vicki did look down at the napkin in her lap, though.

"Two years is a long time from now. A lot can happen in that time frame. Let's just slow down, hon," Marcy said.

I quickly learned hon had two meanings, each with its own tone. Maybe, even more, depending on who said it and who earned the title. Hon was a loaded word in this house.

"I'm just glad I don't have to pay for any more weddings. Molly and Lauren almost dried me out. I'm still recovering," Jack said, wiping his brow from nonexistent sweat.

"Oh, please." Marcy laughed. "Stop being so dramatic."

Aaron didn't really talk about his sisters, but now I knew they were both married—or at least had been at some point. Which made sense seeing as how they were older than Aaron, making them most likely in their thirties.

"Have you talked to them lately, Mom?" Aaron asked. "I probably should have. I need to."

I imagined him making a mental note like I did, but I was probably the only one whose mind was so chaotically organized.

"Yes, they're doing well. Scotty's in third grade this year, and Melissa started kinder. Can you believe it?"

The conversation continued to educate me. Aaron had a niece and nephew. I wondered why I hadn't heard of them before.

Mental Note: *Ask Aaron more about his extended family.* The note was blue.

The night proceeded with questions from the parents trying to learn more about us and two decades worth of funny stories. Hours passed without anyone noticing. Aaron finally convinced me we better head out around ten o'clock since he had worship practice in the morning. Plus, we still had the long drive back to our part of town.

Marcy gave me another bearhug by the door. "I'm so glad I finally got to meet you. Hope to see you again soon."

"Likewise. Thank you for raising an amazing boy." I spoke softly as I hugged her tight.

"I sure hope he is. I tried my best." She replied with moisture in her eyes.

Vicki was a couple of steps ahead of me. I rushed toward her and grabbed the back of her arm, pulling her into a hug. "Let's talk soon," I whispered into her ear with no further need of explanation. She was my bestie, she knew.

The night sky was beautiful. The only other light came from the glow of the far-off street lights. As we got into Aaron's car, I couldn't remove the smile that took residence on my face.

"I think my mom adores you, Ms. Miller," Aaron said, reaching out for my hand. "Almost as much as I do."

Mental Notes

"You think so?" I thought it went well, but it felt good for him to confirm my suspicions.

"Absolutely. And sorry about my dad's weird antics. He can be tough to handle at times. He's probably trying to figure out if he should allow himself to get close to you or see myself bringing someone else around before long."

His words stung. "Have you brought many girls over to your parents?" I asked, unprepared for the answer.

"Not since high school. But they've met a few of Michael's exes. That question might've been slightly pointed at him. He dodged it anyway," Aaron chuckled. His response eased the knot forming in my chest. "I think they know how serious I am about you because I haven't introduced them to anyone. No doubt that's why my mom borderline smothered you." He smiled and shook his head. He appeared at ease all day as separate parts of his life finally came together.

"Just so you know, you're the one I see myself married to when I picture my life in two years. I wouldn't be stealing your time if I didn't."

His confession washed over me like a tidal wave—crashing into me and taking my breath away while simultaneously cleansing me of all my doubts.

He looked over at me, somewhat nervous when I didn't respond. "Does that scare you?"

"Nope." I wasn't sure how much I wanted to admit, still trying to slow my heart back down to a regular rhythm when he glanced over again and grinned.

"Good."

~ 26 ~

Today, I turned twenty-four. One year shy of a quarter of a century. It seemed so old when I thought of it that way. I'm also officially past the age I thought I'd be still single. Well, not married. Hopefully, I'd check the married box by my next birthday. I pretty much wanted and planned more than once to be married since I had my first boyfriend. That was normal, right? Maybe because my mom got married at twenty-three, I always assumed I would too.

I lied in bed, staring up at the ceiling, not quite ready to move in and get ready for work. Thinking back, the last handful of years was like a fading dream, leaving me unable to remember all the parts in detail anymore. Only the significant events stood out as milestone markers in my mind: leaving for college, the beginning and the end of all things Garrett, graduating, becoming a recluse, then Aaron. And from that point on, always Aaron.

My phone rang, still on the charger, different from my standard ringtone, though, the kind for a video chat. I knew who it was, and why he called this early, but I didn't know how I looked at the moment. I quickly wiped under my eyes, pinched my cheeks a couple of times, and frantically ran my hands through my hair. *Ready or not, Aaron, here I come. In all of my morning glory.* My heart accelerated as I accepted the call.

"Hello." I struggled not to grimace when I saw my reflection on the screen and tried to discreetly fix my look.

His voice was rich but slightly rougher than normal first thing in the morning. His raspy song was the best start to my birthday ever—all twenty-four of them. "…happy birthday, my love, happy birthday to you."

"Thank you, Mr. Walker."

"Did I wake you?" He was also in bed with sleepy eyes but still looked stunning to me. I felt better about my unkept appearance.

"No. I've been awake for a bit just wasn't motivated to get out of my warm bed. I kind of wish I didn't have to work so we could be together all day," I said.

"That *would* be fantastic, but I'll see you at lunch, and we have all night together too. How many sessions do you have at work today?"

"Just three, unless something changes. Thankfully it should be an easy one."

My boyfriend was so handsome, even in the morning. I focused on his face, consuming my screen instead of the tiny square of myself in the corner and tried not to dwell on my morning look filling his screen. His bedhead was actually adorable—though I wouldn't voice a word to him. He must've noticed just how entangled the long wavy portion of his hair was this morning because he ran his hand through the lovely rat's nest a couple times before giving up. And those eyes—my favorite thing about this type of phone call—they focused only on me, flaws and all. Light scruff filled his jawline, adding to my attraction. It reminded me of the night I saw him play at the coffee house months ago.

"I like your facial hair. It's kinda—" *Hot.* "I like it." A flash of crimson flooded my face.

"You do?" He rubbed his jaw, causing a faint scratching sound.

"Uh, huh." I smiled a new kind of smile he'd never seen—one I'd never seen. *Control yourself, Maddison.*

"I do believe you're equally as stunning first thing in the morning."

Initially, I wasn't sure if he genuinely meant it or if he thought I expected something in return. But we were beyond that insecure initial phase of our relationship, so I took control of my negative thought. I knew he's words were genuine.

"Oh, you mean this old look?" I messed with my already wild hair as my eyebrows climbed my forehead, giving my best flirtatious glare.

"You're my favorite. Have I told you I love you lately?" He smiled, rubbing his eyes.

"Once or twice, but you can say it again if you'd like."

"I love you. I. Love. You. *I* love *you*." He said it fast, then slow, and once more with emphasis. The combination of three simple words never meant more in all of history.

"Mmmm. I love you, Mr. Walker. What time is it?" I looked over to my nightstand to see the clock on my speaker base. "I better get ready, or I'll be late."

"Okay. Can't wait to see you."

"I can't wait to see *you*. Thanks for calling. This was the best way to start my day. See you at lunch?"

"Yes, ma'am."

"Bye."

"Bye, love."

I hopped out of bed as soon as I was sure he couldn't see me. I wouldn't have traded that call for anything, but now I seriously had to rush. Thankfully, I'd already picked out my outfit last night, which spared me some time. Since I didn't have enough time to wash, dry, and style my hair, I showered in record speed and sprayed an unhealthy amount of dry shampoo on my head. I messed with the tangle of brown strands and white powder and somehow managed to pull it into a low messy bun that rested on the nape of my neck with my bangs falling out, framing my face. I actually liked how the hairstyle looked on me, so I made a mental note to do my hair like this more often, hoping I could duplicate the look again when I wasn't in a rush. My basic makeup get up was all I had time for, but I tossed my makeup pouch in my work bag so I could embellish my appearance before seeing Aaron at lunch. Not that he cared.

Our lunch date also meant I didn't have to spend time packing a meal, making up for more lost time. I grabbed one of my instant latte packs and threw it unopened into a travel mug to make at work. They weren't as good as the real thing, but I kept packets on hand for days like this—some caffeine was better than no caffeine. Snatching a granola bar from the snack basket on my counter, I tossed it into my bag before looking through everything to make sure I didn't forget anything.

I rushed to the door, ready to bound down the stairs, but halted to a stop as soon as I opened it. A large bouquet of various wildflowers in a gorgeous purple vase sat in front of my door. I didn't have to read the card to know who they were from. I did, anyway.

Mental Notes

"Happy Birthday, my dear Maddison. I hope I can make today as outstanding as you make me feel."

I looked at my watch to check the time. When did he leave these here? I highly doubted he was able to bring them after our phone call—he was in bed too. Maybe they sat out here for a few hours. Or all night. The thought of him being so close without me knowing left a longing in me I'd never felt.

It seemed today was full of firsts.

I carefully set the flowers down the entryway just enough the door wouldn't knock them over and locked up. As soon as my phone connected to the bluetooth in my car, I commanded my virtual assistant to dial my boyfriend.

"Hello?" He answered mischievously.

"Thank you for my flowers. When exactly did you bring those?"

"I might've woken up extra early this morning, then returned home and went back to bed. I must admit it was hard not to see you when I was there, but I knew waking you up so early wasn't very considerate. That made it easier to return home instead of knocking on your door."

"This is already my favorite birthday ever, and I haven't even been awake two hours yet."

"Well, it's going to keep getting better. I have to finish getting ready for work. Love you."

"Love you."

* * * *

At work, the ladies decorated my office with streamers and balloons to surprise me. Their design made me feel special, but I had to rearrange the excess before seeing any families. I left enough of the decorations up to enjoy and also not hurt their feelings.

This birthday continues to impress.

My two morning sessions went by with ease since they were families I'd seen before, and we were mostly touching base. I was thankful nothing heavy lessened my birthday high. Finishing earlier than usual, I took the time to organize my calendar and send out some email reminders confirming upcoming appointments.

"Hey, Maddison." Lisa knocked on my open door and came in before I even responded. She walked over and leaned onto my desk with her hand centimeters from my computer. "I need to know something." She continued in a quieter voice.

"What's that?" I stopped typing to look up at her.

"Please tell me your ridiculously handsome boyfriend has a brother?"

I laughed. "He does, but he isn't single." Returning to my email, it took a second before the thought hit me; she'd never seen him before. I looked back up with a confused brow, and she explained before my brain formed a sentence.

"He's in the lobby, with flowers, and I am *extremely* jealous."

"He's here?!"

I jumped up from my desk and walked down the hallway to find him. He *was* ridiculously handsome. And he hadn't shaved. A rush of heat illuminated my face.

"Oh my goodness, what are you doing here? I thought we were meeting at the restaurant." I finally reached him and squeezed him in an embrace. "And with more flowers?" Unlike the vase at my apartment, the bouquet filled a large mason jar, packed in tight like a wedding bouquet. A small wooden circle hung from twine around the top, labeled "M & A."

"I figured you'd leave the others at home. You need flowers to brighten your office too," he said, wearing a saucy grin.

Lisa cleared her throat behind me. "Oh. Aaron, this is Lisa. Lisa, Aaron."

"Nice to meet you, Lisa."

"Likewise," she said more flirtatiously than I appreciated.

"Come on back to my office for a minute. Then we can go."

He took in the streamers and balloons, about to make a comment. But before he got a word out, I had the door closed, the jar of flowers on my desk, and my arms around his neck.

Bringing my lips to his, I kissed him. Really kissed him. Maybe my actions could communicate my appreciation for all the attention and love he'd poured into me better than any words I tried to organize. His fingers pressed into the small of my back, drawing me closer. *I probably shouldn't be doing this at work,* barely fought through my consciousness. I broke away not because I wanted to, but because I had to.

"Somehow, I don't think you'll ever stop surprising me." I whispered through a sigh, millimeters from his mouth.

"I sure hope not." I felt the pull of a smile on his lips.

I couldn't resist. He had me again—because kissing him was one of my favorite ways to spend time. The only thing stronger than the feelings exploding inside of me was the fear of someone catching us, so I finally pushed some space between us.

"I'm at work," I said for both our benefit.

"Oh, right. Sorry."

"No apology needed." I pursed my lips together to conceal my swollen smile as he slowly let me go and turned to take in the rest of the room.

"So, this is where all the Maddison Magic happens, huh?" He asked with a flirty grin as he plopped down, stretching his long—*muscular*—arms all the way across the back of the couch.

"You mean? *That* has never happened in my office before." I confessed quietly as I opened my door, hoping no one noticed it was ever shut.

"I certainly hope not," he belly laughed, "seeing as I've never been here before. Your mind magic," he pointed to his head, "those counseling skills you have."

"Right, of course." I admitted, embarrassed by my misunderstanding. "Indeed, it is." I ran my hands down my thighs and forced my brain to stop thinking about that kiss. His embrace. His—*stop!*

"Can you help me with my problems?" He continued to tease.

I doubt I'm of use to anyone right about now.

"You have problems?"

"Yeah. I. Am." *Help me, God.* "Hungry."

Phew.

"Rough life. I hear you. Let me finish this email really quick, and we can go." I sat down at my desk, utterly distracted. I felt his eyes on me as my fingers hovered over the keyboard, and I re-read what I'd typed three times. Finally, I was able to pull myself together enough to finish after multiple glances at Aaron—and the longing look he couldn't seem to shake.

"You're pretty cute when you work." He winked.

"Knock, knock."

I snapped around to Rachel in my doorway, instantaneously relieved by my decision to open the door. I was almost positive Lisa went into her office to chit-chat about Aaron, and Rachel had to come to see for herself.

"Aaron, this is Rachel. She's the other counselor here."

"Pleasure to meet you," Rachel said as she walked forward to shake his hand. A much more appropriate look filled her face than Lisa's. She was married, after all.

"Likewise, Rachel." He stood up to greet her properly then sat back down, pulling an ankle over his opposite knee. Somehow he filled the entire space a three-piece family typically occupied.

"Gorgeous flowers." Rachel pointed out, confirming her convention with Lisa. "You guys about to head out to a birthday lunch?"

"We are. I was just finishing this appointment reminder."

"Have a nice lunch, then," Rachel said, turning opposite her office, Lisa bound. Her pointless visit to my office couldn't have been more obvious.

I huffed a giggle. "Thanks." A few seconds later, I closed my laptop and grabbed my purse from under my desk. "Ready?"

"Yup." Aaron stood and reached out his hand for mine.

We had to pass the check-in counter, the only way out. I held my shoulders wide in victory—I had *the* best boyfriend. Surprise, surprise: Rachel was leaning over, talking to Lisa. They stopped abruptly and looked at us as we passed by with huge smiles on their faces.

"Bye, ladies." I laughed, knowing they talked about *my* man.

I walked back into the office alone since Aaron's lunch hour started before mine, and he had to hurry back. Lisa still sat at the front desk, eating something out of stained tupperware. She started talking as soon as I stepped through the glass door.

"Okay. He's like, I don't even know, the world's best boyfriend. He brought you flowers for your birthday *twice* and surprised you for lunch. I need one of him. How did lunch go?" She rambled so fast, I feared she might spit out some of her lunch.

"Great. Too short, but we're going out again tonight for dinner, and then he has a surprise for me." I spoke airily as if my tone could emulate how I felt—like I was floating.

"Ugh, can I be you for a day? Your love life is so much better than mine."

"That's pretty weird, Lisa." I laughed even though I was pretty sure she simply alluded my love life couldn't get any better—which was the truth.

"Fine, be that way. Your one-fifteen called and said they're running late."

"Thanks. Just send them back whenever they get here."

I headed back to my desk, although no part of me wanted to be at work. The memory of what happened earlier in my office replayed and only made the desire to spend my entire birthday with Aaron that much stronger. Especially after I caught a trace of his cologne in the air.

But I only had to make it through one more session, a few more scheduling phone calls, and next week's email reminders, and I'd be back with my favorite person.

Time to get your head in the game, Maddison.

* * * *

The knock on the door resounded into my apartment, causing my excited energy to kick up to full blast. I spent the time between work and Aaron's arrival rushing to change into a nicer outfit, redo my hair, and take my makeup game up another notch. I checked my look one more time in the full-length mirror before heading to the door.

I paired a loose-fitting, off-the-shoulder cream shirt with the word "love" consuming the entire front with my darkest skinny jeans and the highest and fanciest heels I owned. The heels were two-tone—cream with a thick gold bottom—open-toe stilettos, making me a good four inches taller. I wore them all of twice.

I grabbed my leopard print clutch and situated a large black-link watch and oversized gold chain bangle bracelet on my left wrist. Last step—as always—was a fresh coat of lip gloss before hurrying to my favorite person.

"Sorry to keep you waiting."

He stood silent for a few seconds. "Wow, Maddison! You. Are. Stunning."

I smiled as I pulled the door closed behind me. He grabbed me around the waist and closed the space between us for a kiss, faster than I could take my hand off the doorknob. Our faces were much closer to each other, thanks to my heels. We needed to start being intentional with our growing physical intensity.

He stopped with a sigh before the kiss lingered too far, and I assumed he had the same thought—or one like it. He loosened his hold on me and grabbed my hand to help me down the stairs in my stilts.

"On a scale from one to ten, how has your day ranked so far?" he asked as he opened the passenger door for me.

"I'd say ten, but there are a few hours left, so let's go with a nine. I'll leave you some room to top it off." I winked.

"Deal." After he closed my door, I leaned over and opened his for him from the inside. "Thank you."

Our hands pulled together like magnets before landing on the worn-in console. Aaron wanted to take me to a place neither one of us had been before, so after asking me a couple of questions, we decided on the Fondue Pot. It was a fancier date—and pricier—than we typically went on, but he assured me he wanted my birthday not to feel like any other date night. The restaurant was in the same shopping district as our first date and our double date with Michael and Vicki, a special place for us.

The parking lot was scarcely filled since we were earlier than the normal dinner crowd. Which was great news, seeing as how I wouldn't have to walk far in these deathtrap shoes—they sure looked great though. My ankles weren't to be trusted.

The lights inside were dim, instantly creating a romantic environment and forcing our eyes to adjust quickly. The young hostess in all black immediately greeted us. She ushered us by the bar—the only way to navigate to the seating.

"Any drinks tonight?" she asked as she motioned her hand like a pro.

"None for us, thank you." Aaron answered politely.

The hostess nodded her head gracefully with a smile, well-rehearsed. "This way." She continued through several narrow aisles before stopping at an enclosed, L-shaped booth. The small table mounted to the wall contained a round burner in the far corner by where the hostess stood.

Just when I thought I'd successfully navigated the under-lit obstacle course in stilettos, my ankle rolled as I started to sit. I ended up falling into the booth.

"You all right?" Aaron checked quietly, probably not wanting to embarrass me.

"Mmhmm. I guess I only have my trainers permit for these things. 'Additional adult supervision still needed.'"

"That's what I'm here for."

"Your server will be with you shortly," the hostess said as she placed down our menus and made her way back up front.

My eyes still hadn't fully adjusted to the lighting. I had to blink a few times while attempting to read the menu.

"Good evening, my name is Sal, and I will be your waiter tonight. Is this your first time dining with us?"

"It is," I said, still shaken from my trip.

"Fantastic."

He explained how everything worked and helped us pick out our three courses of appetizer, meats, and dessert. He returned rather quickly with the appetizer since we were the ones who cooked our own food. The kitchen only had to place our choices on a plate and send it out. I felt lost as he melted our cheese and rapidly explained how to use the cooking forks and which one not to put back where. I looked over at Aaron, who seemed to be comprehending the instructions, and let my mind drift to his good looks. His perfectly messy hair. His clear blue eyes. His lips, always those lips. And the newest feature I loved around his jawline.

"I really do like your beard," I said after Sal finally walked away.

"It isn't quite a beard yet, but thanks. I'll keep that in mind." My fingers itched to run along his jaw, but I settled for picking up a piece of bread instead.

"And I totally got lost. What are we supposed to do here?"

He recapped the protocol as we started dipping our veggies and bread into the cheese fondue appetizer. The instructions were more for the meat, not cross-contaminating the forks and exposing yourself to anything raw. *Glad I got those instructions.*

"Man, this is good," I said, chewing my bread covered in cheese and bacon.

"I'm glad you like it."

It wasn't long before another server took our empty cheese pot away, and our waiter brought out the broth pot to cook our meat. "Are you celebrating anything special tonight?" Sal asked.

"We are. It's her birthday." Aaron answered, pointing at me with a hitchhiker's thumb.

"Oh, happy birthday!" he said with an accent I couldn't quite pin.

"Thank you." I hoped he wouldn't reappear later with a horde of servers, singing some variation of the birthday song and drawing everyone's attention.

"Which is your favorite?" Aaron asked as we waited for the second round of meats to finish cooking.

"Probably the beef. Yours?"

"I like the beef too."

Eating fondue style was fun but also more of an activity than going to dinner since we cooked our own food. We enjoyed our time talking and laughing between cooking and eating. Sal came back to clear the table and deliver the dessert portion. If I was honest, I'd been waiting for this course all night. "The dessert's on us tonight. Happy birthday."

"Oh, wow. Thank you," I said.

Sal melted the chocolate in our third fondue pot and set down a plate of bite-sized brownies, cheesecake, strawberries, and marshmallows.

Aaron stabbed a strawberry and dipped it in the chocolate. He pulled it out and held it up to my mouth. I took a bite and laughed as chocolate ran down my chin, requiring me to abandon the cheesecake I put in the pot to grab my napkin.

"Thanks." I giggled as I wiped my face.

"Dang. That was more romantic in my head." We both laughed then.

The dessert was gone in minutes. Sal dropped off the check with a final salutation for the night. Aaron slid some cash into the leather folder and set it back down on the table.

"Okay, are you ready for the best part of the night?"

"I'm not sure how it can get any better than this, but bring it on." I slid out of the booth, and he grabbed my hand and led me back to his car. We didn't drive far and pulled up to a place with a glowing "Karaoke Lounge" sign.

"This last part might be selfish, but I wanted to hear you sing. Well, sing with you."

"Sounds like fun." But insecurity most likely showed on my face.

"We get our own room, though. It isn't like we'll be in front of a bunch of strangers." He quickly reassured me.

"Oh, good. Even better." I let out a sigh of relief. Aaron had already heard me, but it was still unsettling to sing in front of him since he was more of a professional in the music realm. I collected myself as he walked around to let me out. "What a fun idea, love. Thank you," I said as he helped me out of the car.

Loud music reverberated off the walls as when we entered. A registration booth stood in front of a wide hallway containing private rooms. It reminded me of the tanning salon I tried a few times during my freshman year of college, desperate to fit in with the city girls. Aaron must have made a reservation because he gave his name, and they escorted us right back.

"Have fun! Let us know if you need any help," the attendant said with an enormous smile. She must love her job.

When Aaron pulled the door to our private room open, I had to catch my breath. Flowers filled the room everywhere I looked. Tons of them. All different kinds. I turned to Aaron as tears filled my eyes.

"I wanted to make you feel the way you've made me feel for the last one hundred and sixty-seven days—one flower for every day I've known you. You make my life brighter and more fragrant. And you've made me smile, every single day. Happy birthday, beautiful. I love you."

Tears slipped down my cheeks. Thankfully they were sweet, pretty tears and not a full-on ugly-cry. At least I hoped that was the case. "I love you so much." I grabbed his face with both hands and kissed him with total abandon.

"Surprise!" The shout interrupted our kiss too soon for my liking as Michael and Vicki jumped out from the corner of the room.

"Are you serious?" I wiped the tears from my face, and walked into the room to hug Vicki, overwhelmed with the floral fragrance. "How do I keep earning these surprises?"

"Happy birthday!" She cheered as she squeezed me. "He kinda knocked it out of the park, huh?" She whispered in my ear before letting go.

"Um, yeah." I took a deep breath, and then laughed, trying to make the tears stop. I walked back over to be enveloped by Aaron. "I can't believe you. This is amazing."

"You're amazing. I hope I've been able to show you that today." Aaron wrapped his firm arms around me in a tight hug and swayed me back and forth, kissing the top of my head.

"Who's going first?" Michael asked.

~ 27 ~

Even before the sun filtered through my window and took over my bedroom, causing me to finally open my eyes for the day, a smile was glued to my face. Not only did I have the best birthday of my life, but Aaron also continued lavishing on me into the weekend in his typical "stellar boyfriend" fashion. But when he dropped me off last night, we had a hard time putting out the fire that started in my office. My lack of caution with our growing physical connection taunted me. I was nervous about his response when I finally spoke up and suggested he probably leave. Gracious as always, he apologized and reassured me his intentions were the same as mine. I was beyond thankful we were on the same page. If I made it to twenty-four still a virgin, I didn't want to sell myself short with only an abbreviated distance left in this purity race. But it wasn't exactly easy.

We made a plan not to spend as much time alone in my apartment to help keep ourselves in check. Rules could stink as much as they were good for you, even if you're the one who put them in place.

Getting ready always went by so much faster when seeing my hunk was the end result. Technically, I got ready for church, but Aaron was on his way to pick me up. I finished my makeup only a couple minutes before I got the text that he was here downstairs.

Dumb rule.

"Good morning." Aaron waited for me to descend the last few steps, leaning against his purring red Grand Prix looking way too attractive.

Good rule.

"Good morning to you, handsome." I walked a few more steps before he wrapped me in his arms.

"You look lovely today," he said, pressing his lips to mine before leading me to the passenger side of the car with his hand on my back.

"Thank you. It's probably because I slept like a baby last night, which was much needed after all the birthday fun."

Two cups of coffee rested in the cup holders of the console. Even though it was a norm, I never expected the gift and was grateful every time. I waited until he was in the car to see which was mine. He pointed to the one in the back slot like he knew my thoughts, a knowing grin on his face.

"Thanks, love." I took a sip.

"Do you have any plans for later today?"

"Not unless you've made them for me." I flirted.

"Good. Ethan invited us to his place to hang out with him and Stacy. I told him I'd see how your day looked and let him know, but we don't have to go if you'd rather not."

"Oh, fun. I haven't seen them in forever."

"Cool. I'll text him when we get to church."

"I do have something next weekend, though. My mom decided to come for a visit," I hesitated, "and wants to meet you. She called on my birthday to catch up and was pretty jealous when I told her I already met your parents." I admitted with a grimace.

"I'd love to meet your family." His response was natural and showed no signs of being nervous like I was a couple of weeks ago meeting his parents.

"Great." *I hope it goes as smoothly as when I met yours.*

We arrived at church while people still mingled in the lobby. Casey saw us and rushed across the open room with bulging eyes and a huge smile on her face. "So?"

"She loved it," Aaron said, only I wasn't exactly sure what was going on. He caught my lost look. "Casey knew my plans for your birthday. She works at the floral shop."

"Oh my gosh! Best birthday ever."

"Did you cry? I practically cried assembling everything." She admitted as she placed her hand on my shoulder.

"Of course, I did."

"I brought some extra plant food to give you today. If you trim them every couple of days, the flowers should last for a while. Although that'll take some time," she said.

No joke! There's almost two hundred of them.

"Thanks, Casey. We better get in there, the countdown has already started." Aaron interjected, leading me away.

The auditorium was pretty full, meaning we probably wouldn't get our usual seats. Aaron guided me behind him by holding my hand. Our usual seats were already filled, but the next row back and more toward the end was available, so he steered us there.

I enjoyed having Aaron next to me during worship, but I didn't think the other guitar player was as good as him. However, my opinion may be biased. I enjoyed the music at our church, regardless of who comprised the team—way better than my old church in Wimberlake. My trip back home had reinforced that fact. I for sure enjoyed the preaching here better too, probably because the pastor wasn't afraid to step on people's toes in order to say it like it was.

Aaron grabbed my hand after worship ended as we sat to watch the video announcements. The clip for the Third Annual Marriage Conference was the only portion that caught my attention. The mini-commercial appeared to be footage from the previous year's event and looked like so much fun. *I hope Aaron and I attend the fourth annual conference.*

The all too familiar futuristic relationship thought patterns grew harder to control.

Pastor Steve made his way to the podium as the lights came up, bringing me back to reality.

"Good morning, everyone. That was some great worship we had this morning." He brought his hands together in a clasp. "I'm excited about the word God gave me for today. Honestly, it's just as much for me as it is for everyone else.

"I'll tell you what, I've wasted years of my life believing the lie, '*I'm not ready.*' Ready to be a husband. Ready to be a dad. Ready to be a pastor. Whatever it was God led me to, I approached with hesitation because I didn't. Feel. Ready. On occasion, His leading even turned into dragging. You know, I've been married for twelve years now, and some days I still don't feel ready."

The congregation chuckled.

"It's also one of the most common sentences I hear while counseling people. Friends, *we will never be ready*. Jesus already knew when he came to Earth that he was going to die for us, but what happened when the time came? He prayed and asked God for the cup to pass if it was possible. We know his prayer went on with, 'but not my own will but yours be done,' but He wasn't ready. Now, do you really think that if Jesus—the perfect man, the Son of God—had a moment of not feeling ready, we won't feel that same way in our lives?"

Wow, that's good.

He continued with several realistic but powerful points on preparing yourself to be ready and another few points on what to do when you don't think you're ready for what lies ahead of you. Despite trying to take it all in personally, I couldn't help but notice and wonder what was going through Aaron's head as he took notes on his phone—because it wasn't something he typically did.

What was he ready for in his life? Or not ready for?

Was it something personal, or did it involve me?

He's seriously typing away on that phone.

Did he feel like he was ready to get married?

Did I want to know the answer to that question?

Was I ready to be married?

I knew I *wanted* to be married but was I actually *ready* to be? Being married was all I wanted for the last few years—okay, I pretty much dreamt about it my whole life. But having my trust demolished by Garrett and hearing Vicki's story placed hesitation in me. Endless questions swirled around in my mind as the service came to a close.

"I needed that. I think he was preaching at me," Aaron said as we walked back to the car, headed to lunch.

"Yeah me too. But I'm still chewing on it." Had I not been sure how to process everything for myself, his words might've been more alarming.

* * * *

Ever since Michael and Vicki started dating, we hadn't hung out with our first "friends couple" as much. It wasn't intentional. We were just naturally closer to Aaron's brother and my best friend, but I was excited to get the chance to catch up with Ethan and Stacy.

Ethan had a nice, bungalow-style house. It was actually a duplex, but that's more of a house than either Aaron's or my apartment. He opened the door in overzealous excitement and a ridiculously loud greeting.

"Heeey!" He grabbed Aaron like he hadn't seen him at work a couple days ago, and it made me laugh. He was crazy, but Ethan was one of the only friends I'd kept over the years—not including the short hiatus while I secluded myself from the world, which wasn't his fault. After Aaron walked in, Ethan hugged me in grand scale too. The embrace was nostalgic. How many times had a hug from him in the last decade brought me comfort? Too many to count.

"Hey guys." Stacy greeted us much more casually as we entered.

"Hey, Stacy. It's been too long." I hugged her, feeling guilty as I tried to remember the last time we saw them.

"Come in, come in. Sit down. Stacy made some killer chocolate chip cookies." Ethan walked over to his quaint kitchen table. "How's everything going?" He continued after barely enough time to breathe, super energetically—a little more than usual.

"Same old, same old. Nothing new," Aaron said, grabbing a cookie from the platter and popping the whole thing in his mouth.

"Ah. Well, we have something new going on. We're *getting married!*" Ethan practically yelled.

My jaw dropped as I looked over at Stacy, who held up her left hand to show her new accessory. "No way? Congratulations." I jumped up from the seat I'd just occupied to dart over and squeeze Stacy. "Let me see that ring. Wow!" The large solitaire princess cut diamond stood tall on her finger in a cathedral setting on a gold band. "Good job, Ethan. I'm impressed. Didn't know you had it in ya," I said after admiring her engagement ring from multiple angles.

I tried to mentally picture it on my hand, not sure if the style would look good on me. *What would look good on my finger?* I thought as I looked down at my bare hand.

"Yes, he did a good job." Stacy glowed. How had I not noticed moments ago?

"Congrats, bro," Aaron said, along with some other guy talk I drowned out with my own conversation with Stacy.

"I'm so happy for you. Do you already have a date set?" I asked.

"Well, I've actually been planning for a while because we already discussed getting married. I just didn't know when he'd officially ask." She glanced down and paused, hesitation in her posture. "I'm kind of a Christmas fanatic, so we're thinking probably December eighteenth. That way, we'll be back from our honeymoon by Christmas."

Perhaps her insecurity stemmed from what others would think of a festive wedding. Personally, I wouldn't want my special day close to a holiday, but I was excited for her if it meant she'd have her dream wedding. What girl didn't want that?

"Now you guys know why we asked you to come over." Ethan drew everyone's attention back to himself. "And there's just one more thing we need to know. Will you two be in our wedding?"

"Really?" I looked back at Stacy.

"Yes. Will you be one of my bridesmaids?" She pulled a cream cloth bag from underneath the table with "Bridesmaid Survival Kit" scrolled across the front in beautiful calligraphy.

Part of me wondered momentarily if she asked me simply because I was with Aaron, and he was one of Ethan's few close friends, or if she felt closer to me than I realized. I hated my cynical brain.

"I'd love to. Eek, how exciting! Let me know what you need help with. I've been a bridesmaid before. I loved helping my cousin get everything organized. You just tell me what you need, and I'll get after it. And I give you permission now to let me know if I start to steer the ship." I spit my words out so fast, the guys probably weren't able to keep up—kind of like how a dog whistle was only heard by dogs.

"For sure, man," Aaron said as he took something in a box from Ethan.

I turned back to Aaron and made my way over to him. "How fun, love. We're going to be in a wedding together!" I leaned over the back of his chair and wrapped my arms around him. A bowtie rested in the box with a card that said: "Suit Up."

Full of joy, I subconsciously grabbed a cookie and took too large of a bite. "Whoa. These are good, Stacy." Still running high on excitement, I forced myself to sit down for a minute and be quiet. It didn't work. "Ethan,

I can't believe you convinced someone to marry you." I teased my longtime friend.

"Ha ha." Ethan deadpanned, clearly not amused.

"You know I'm kidding. I'm so happy for you. Genuinely ecstatic. What's already planned?" I asked them both.

"Here we go. Aaron, let's move to the living room. It's about to get really girly up in here," Ethan said, grabbing a few cookies and walking to the couch.

Aaron grabbed another cookie and leaned over to kiss me on the head before following Ethan.

Stacy opened up her PinBoard app and started showing me the central theme she wanted to follow and some things she liked.

"How many bridesmaids and groomsmen are you going to have?"

"Just three. My sister will be the maid of honor, you, and my friend Hannah that I've known since junior high. Ethan has Billy, Aaron, and Garrett on his side."

Garrett.

Commence deflation.

I should've known he'd be one of Ethan's groomsmen. I wasn't thrilled I'd have to see him again, but it hadn't been awful at his wedding. Reminding myself I'd moved on and was no longer bitter was a must, but it was a hard root to kill. Not to mention, a constant choice.

"That'll make an attractive court. Not that I—I mean," I over-analyzed my words, "never mind. Where are you guys thinking of holding the wedding and reception?" I hadn't meant attractive the way it came out. I didn't want her to think I was still attracted to my ex, thus the rambling, but she didn't even pay it any thought.

"My uncle has several acres with a large barn type building on his property. It isn't like an animal barn. It's just that style of building; you know what I mean? We've had several family events at his place before. Plus, it's free." She laughed.

"Can't beat free. Will you invite a large number of people, or will it be a smaller event?"

"We have a one hundred person limit in the barn, but I probably won't even have that many. We both have smaller families and a solid set of close friends."

So I did make the friends list intentionally and not by default. But was I on his or her's?

Ugh, stop!

Forcing my mind to think about something else, I started imagining the scene in my mind. An intimate setting, glowing in the cold winter air. "It's going to be enchanting."

"I hope so. Planning is as stressful as it is exciting." She continued scrolling through her phone. "I'm almost positive the ladies will wear red dresses, and the groomsmen in simple black and white with an evergreen branch corsage like these."

"Oh, I love that!" The more she showed me, the more I liked the Christmas wedding theme. The soft, dark greens and bold reds gave it all an effortless elegance.

Like every other time in the history of a female looking at her PinBoard, we got lost in digital planning for longer than we intended to.

"Okay, let's go back with the guys before I eat this whole plate of cookies and require a larger wedding dress," Stacy said. I hadn't noticed her stress eating, leaving the platter almost empty.

The guys saw us coming and ceased mid-conversation. Knowing Ethan and his unpredictable conversational habits, it was probably a good thing they stopped.

"Can we crash this party?" I asked.

"Absolutely," Aaron said, scooting over to make a space for me next to him on the couch.

Stacy sat sideways on the arm of the couch and set her feet on Ethan's lap.

"Do you think you guys will live here or find something new?" I started up a group conversation.

"Probably here. At least until my lease is up. If she decides she doesn't like it, then we'll find something else," Ethan said, earning a jab to the arm from Stacy.

"You aren't suggesting I'm picky, now are you?"

"No, no. I didn't mean it in a bad way, baby. Promise." Ethan ran his hand up and down her shin while flashing his best puppy dog eyes.

"Have you thought about the honeymoon at all?" Aaron asked.

"Every day." Ethan smirked, earning an even harder jab.

Mental Notes

"I meant where you might go." Aaron clarified, laughing.

"Most likely, a cruise. I want to go somewhere warm enough to wear a swimsuit." Stacy took over answering before Ethan embarrassed her again.

"And to that, I say: yes, please." Ethan was still sidetracked, giving his bride-to-be a saucy grin.

"That will be crazy going from cold to hot and back to cold all in a week or so. Like an escape from reality," I said, liking the idea of getting to skip out on a week of winter.

"Exactly. It's going to be awesome. I hate being cold. The only thing I like about winter is Christmas, so this is kinda like I'm getting the best of both worlds." Stacy agreed.

"Oh, Aaron, I almost forgot. My dad asked if you'd go with him tomorrow to pick up some new gear he bought in Oklahoma. He's hoping to make it there and back during normal business hours. I'm still catching up on work, so I can't go." Ethan seemed perfectly fine with having too much work to allow him to have a road trip with his dad.

"Sure, no problem." Aaron looked to me, most likely since he told me I wasn't allowed to leave without him weeks ago.

"I'll pack you some snacks." I assured him.

He grinned. "In that case, we better get going, so I can run Maddison by the store."

"Sounds good. I'll let my dad know you're in."

We all stood to give hugs and say our goodbyes.

"Thanks for coming over, guys. I'll see you tomorrow, Aaron," Ethan said.

"You bet. Thank you for the cookies, Stacy. Congratulations again." Aaron, always the gentleman.

"Bye, guys. I'm sure we'll see you soon. Planning and all." I waved as we walked to Aaron's car.

As we drove away, I noticed Aaron seemed different than earlier today. Tenser maybe. "You okay?" I grabbed his hand.

"Yes. Just a lot on my mind is all. Crazy they're getting married, huh?"

"She's already put up with him this long, so I figured it would happen." I laughed, hoping he would follow suit and loosen up.

~ 28 ~

A horrible case of the Mondays brewed at work, nothing went right. My first session arrived late, causing me to have to leave my second family sitting in the waiting room for half an hour. There was no way I'd make it to lunch by noon, so I scarfed a granola bar from my drawer before bringing the next session in.

The Sanchez family was here today to discuss family rules. They adopted a thirteen-year-old girl, and she was having a tough time adjusting to the way of things in her new home. The parents couldn't understand what was so hard about a few simple rules, so I had to explain that consistency was something entirely new for their daughter.

We created a game plan to help them adjust and made sure Jenny understood the new expectations clearly. I couldn't imagine how difficult it must be going from never being a parent to parenting a teenager. And it was probably equally as hard having to learn to trust people you barely knew when the only thing you knew your whole life was let down and abuse.

My heart was heavy as they walked out of my office. We didn't see teenagers as often here, mostly because they weren't adopted as often as younger kids. All I wanted to do was get something to eat and call Aaron.

"I'm out to lunch." I told Lisa as I speed-walked by. I had to rush to get my day back on track and make sure I wasn't the reason my next session ran behind. After descending the elevator and navigating the parking lot to my car, I closed the door and held back the emotions of my day, knowing what would instantly make me feel better. I turned on my car and waited for my favorite voice to join me.

He answered after a couple of rings. "Hey you."

"Oh, how I needed to hear your voice."

"Rough day?"

"Yes. Well, just weird, but I'm trying to shake it. How's it going for you?"

"Good. We already got the gear. We're having lunch before we head back home. Want me to come over tonight?"

"Yes, please. I promise to be overly emotional and needy."

He chuckled. "Sounds perfect. I better go now. I'll see you soon."

"Okay. Love you." I knew he was trying to be considerate while he was with his boss, but I would have preferred it if our conversation had been longer.

I went to the closest place to the office and ordered a sub sandwich in the drive-thru. Not ready to be around people yet, I ate in my car and listened to music. Letting the melody of worship music float through my mind, I laid my head against the headrest as I chewed each bite and took deep, cleansing breaths. By the time my sandwich was gone, I successfully repaired enough from my Monday funk to be there for my next two sessions. I headed back up to my office to ensure I was there before my clients.

Just before the elevator doors closed the final inches, a hand slid through, startling me and causing the doors to retract open. Suzanne walked in with a smile. The pressure to perform for my boss was at an Insta-pot level—time to find out if my mood was fully repaired.

"Hey, Maddison. How's everything going?"

"Very well, thank you." Nope. I wasn't in the mood for small talk. But when was I?

"Does that mean I don't have to worry about you quitting on me and going back to advertising?"

I wasn't sure if she was joking or nonchalantly asking a tough question. Did my face still wear the strain of this morning? I laughed. "Oh, no. I love it here."

"Good to hear. I almost quit after I first started thirty years ago. I wasn't prepared for some of the heavy things I encountered."

I knew what she meant. I experienced a mini-dose this morning.

"If you ever feel like you need to talk to me to help you deal with the weight of this career, I'm here, okay? Not as your boss, just a fellow counselor, and a friend."

"Thank you, Suzanne. I will definitely take you up on that offer if needs arise."

"Good. Time to get back to it," she said as the elevator door chimed and opened on our floor.

"Back to it." I repeated like a trained parrot.

Lisa wasn't at her desk yet. I was glad to have a few more minutes without conversation before I needed to be attentive for my clients. I checked the calendar to see who'd be in my next session and was happy to discover it was the Gilmore family with little Sammy. I was genuinely excited to see how they were progressing.

A few moments later, the main door opened, followed by a little voice that didn't belong to my co-worker.

I stuck my head out of my office and called down the hall, "Hey guys, you can come on back." I watched and waited in the hallway, smiling as Sammy skipped toward me, holding some kind of Lego creation. "Hey, Sammy." I squatted down and held out my hand for a high five. He slapped my hand as his parents trailed behind at a more relaxed pace.

As everyone got situated in my office, I asked, "How is everything?" still wearing a smile. The feelings were heartfelt, and I hoped my face appeared that way as well.

"Fantastic!" Mrs. Gilmore said. "Sammy's doing really well at communicating with us and feeling like he's at home and not just visiting anymore."

"Way to go, bud! What is that you have there?" I asked, trying to engage Sammy.

"A race car. I builded it with my brother. He knows *everything* about Legos."

"Built, honey." His mother coached him.

"Mmhm. Built." He showed off by spinning the back wheels round and round as fast as he could with his little hand.

"That sounds like so much fun." I looked back up at the parents. "Any new concerns?"

"He doesn't love school. Homework is horrible." Mrs. Gilmore sighed, but she didn't laugh, so I didn't either. "He just doesn't like sitting there long enough to finish."

"First graders have homework?" I asked.

"That's what I said." Mr. Gilmore finally chimed in, giving me a reason to bring back my grin.

"Honestly, I think that sounds like an issue any six-year-old boy would deal with. I don't think this has any deeper triggers. Maybe you can set a timer and work on homework for several minutes, then take a break for a few minutes and start again. Do you think that would be better, Sammy?"

"Yeah," he answered.

"Yes, ma'am." Mrs. Gilmore continued to coach him in proper manners.

"Yes, ma'am," Sammy said, smiling, not realizing his mistake once again.

"Are you sleeping well, Sammy?" I asked, trying to keep him engaged in conversation.

"Yes, ma'am." He beamed, clearly proud of himself for getting it right on his own.

"And how about eating? Do you tell your mom or dad when you're hungry or want more?" I looked up at Mrs. Gilmore, who gave me a thumbs up.

"Yes, ma'am." He bounced his legs up and down together in his seat.

"That's great. It sounds like you're doing fantastic. Is there anything else you want to talk about?"

"One of the boys in my class asked me why I didn't look like my mom and dad. That hurt my feelings." He rubbed his forehead, which was two shades darker than his parents'.

Mrs. Gilmore's brows furrowed, apparently learning this news along with me. "When did that happen, sweetie?"

Sammy shrugged his shoulders. "I didn't know what to say. I just ran away." Sammy stared down at his car and sat perfectly still.

Mrs. Gilmore looked up at me, but I lifted my hand in motion for her to take the lead. "If that happens again, you just tell him you needed a mommy and a daddy, and your mommy and daddy needed a son."

Moved by her answer, I agreed. "That's right, buddy. You don't have to talk about anything that makes you uncomfortable. Tell them it's private, and you don't want to talk about it."

"Okay." Sammy picked up his Lego creation again, spinning the wheels as if it didn't take much to reassure him. At least I hoped that was the case. What spiraled in a six-year-old's head? No doubt, this sweet boy's mind was significantly less complicated than mine.

The session was the perfect "pick-me-up" to my afternoon. The Gilmores said they'd call to schedule if something came up, but they were adjusting better than they could've imagined.

There was an hour before my next session began, so I used the time to work on scheduling and follow up, thankful to have a slower pace and not feel rushed.

But the hour went by entirely too fast, ending as my desk phone rang with Lisa on the other end, letting me know my last session of the day was here.

A new family I hadn't seen before sat on the couch. It took us some time to get introduced and for them to share their story with me. The Pilgrims were a large family—already having four biological kids—but wanted to adopt after hearing about how many children in Texas were in the foster system. The parents were here with the baby girl they got straight from the hospital who still dealt with drug withdrawals.

"Everything is different. I have to learn to be a mother in a whole new way. I nursed my other kids, but I can't do that with her. Dealing with the emotional side of her withdrawals, knowing it was something she didn't have a choice in is brutal, I can't just make it go away," Mrs. Pilgrim said, barely holding her tears at bay.

Sometimes I knew what to say, from my schooling or past experiences, but I wondered if this veteran mother of four—now five—was going to look at me, a young, unmarried woman without kids like I was crazy for giving her advice. I hesitated to respond and sided with compassion.

"I can't even imagine what that must be like, knowing what you want to do, or used to do, but not being able to. What have you found so far that's working to help you cope?"

"Not much. She does better if she's held, but then I just hold her all day, and nothing else gets done."

"I think that's a good opportunity for others in the family to help share your workload. Or perhaps one of the older kids could help hold her when there are things you have to get done. Withdrawals are difficult to walk through, but thankfully they don't last forever." I gazed at the precious baby and wished I could will the withdrawals away myself.

"Thank you for saying that. I have to keep reminding myself this is only a season, and I can make it through it." She grinned, but it was weak.

"That's exactly right and so important to remember." My cell phone vibrated against the desk, creating a horribly loud noise. As I picked it up to decline the call, I saw it was Ethan. "Sorry about that. How are the other kids adjusting to the baby? Sometimes we see things like jealousy or acting out."

"They're doing great. My youngest has been a tad jealous, but I've dealt with that before. I just make him feel like my big helper."

Noted.

"It sounds like you're doing a wonderful job, Momma."

My phone rang again, and I declined it a second time. It rang a third time almost instantly. I was fairly sure even Ethan wouldn't be this persistent for nothing. "I'm extremely sorry, but I need to get this really quick. I'll be right back."

I stepped out of my office and into the empty client waiting room to answer the call. "Hey, Ethan, what's up? I'm with a family right now."

"Maddison, Aaron and my dad were in a bad car accident on their way back home. They're being airlifted back here to Johnson Hospital. I need you to let his family know." he spoke through an anxious tone.

I went blank.

"Maddy? Maddison, are you there?" Ethan's voice came back in but muffled like I was underwater.

"Is he okay?" I forced the words out.

"I don't know yet, but it sounds like it was a horrible accident. They were in the company van, so that's how the police were able to notify me quickly. Can you get a hold of his family, please? Tell everyone to head over to the hospital."

"Y-yeah. I can do that." I must've sat or fallen onto the couch. I stood and rushed to Suzanne's office, knocking and walking in at the same time. Thankfully she was alone. "Suzanne, Aaron was in a bad car accident and is being flown to the hospital." I repeated the words like a robot, even though they still hadn't fully registered in my mind.

"Maddison, you're pale. Sit down for a second." She jumped up from her chair to help me.

Pieces of cognitive thoughts returned to me slowly. "There's a family in my office. I stepped out when my phone wouldn't stop ringing. I have to go—" My head spun after I stood up too quickly. The whole room was rotated.

Please, God, let Aaron be okay.

"Okay. Wait here just a minute. I can move them over to the waiting room so you can go back into your office and get your things. I'll let them know you had an emergency and offer to finish their session if they'd like."

"Yes. That works. Let's do that." My brain still didn't function correctly. I'd already forgotten the plan.

"Are you going to be okay to drive, Maddison?" Suzanne asked.

She looked concerned like she wasn't going to let me leave. Blinking a couple of times and trying to shake my thoughts back together, I caught her gaze and held it. *Convince her.* "Yes, I think so. Thank you for helping."

"Keep me posted, please. Let us know if you need anything." She seemed hesitant but waited only a beat longer before turning toward the door.

"I will."

I waited for her to return and let me know I could collect my things from my office. That's when the tears hit. I tried to take slow, deep breaths to keep myself from a total breakdown, but the tears just kept coming, thicker and heavier with every breath. I remembered Ethan's request and forced myself to focus as I scrolled through my contacts. I didn't have a number for any other Walker and had to call Vicki to inform Michael. Thankfully, she answered quickly.

"Hey bestie. Sorry, I've already had lunch today."

"Vicki, Aaron was in a car accident. We need to tell his family and get them to Johnson Hospital. He's being care-flighted there right now."

"What? Are you serious? Is he okay?"

"I don't know." The words were like lead on my tongue. "I don't know. Oh my gosh, Vicki. I don't know! I just talked to him an hour ago. I'm about to leave work. Please call Michael and ask him to contact his parents immediately."

"I'm on it. It's going to be all right, Maddison, just try and stay calm. I'll try to leave too, okay? I'll see you there." Her words were positive, but I could tell she had a hard time with the news, too, by her tone.

"Yeah. Thanks." I ended the call and tried to calm down so I'd be fit to drive. I couldn't end up in a wreck myself.

Suzanne stepped back in and took one look at my tear-stained face before rubbing her hand up and down my back as I stood. "Okay, your office is clear. Please be safe on your way there."

"I will." I rummaged through my office like a thief, grabbing and yanking at my purse and shoving my laptop in my bag and practically ran out what felt like only seconds later.

"What's going on, Maddy?" Lisa asked, panicked at the sight of me sprinting toward the door.

"Ask Suzanne," I yelled, not even pausing to turn around and look at her.

* * * *

The thirty-five minutes across the metroplex to Johnson Hospital were the longest and shortest in my life. I don't even know if I followed the speed limit; my only goal was to get to the hospital as quickly as possible. I ran inside, straight to the front desk. "Aaron Walker was being airlifted here. Is he here yet? Where do I go?" My rushed words slurred together, my voice rough from all the crying. I wasn't sure she even understood me at first.

"Yes. He got here not too long ago. Are you family?"

"Y—well, no. I'm his girlfriend. Have other people arrived already?"

"Yes, ma'am. We sent them up to the waiting room on the fourth floor."

"Ok thank you." I ran to the elevator and mashed the call button repeatedly, trying to make it come faster. When it finally arrived, I hurried inside and attacked the buttons again. It stopped on the fourth floor, but the doors opened painfully slow, so I started to shove my way out sooner and walked frantically, trying to find the waiting room.

"Maddy!" I turned to find Michael.

My heart skittered to a stop at the sight of him. He looked like Aaron; only he wasn't.

My wounded heart didn't stop me from running to him and hugging him tighter than I probably should have. "Do we know anything?"

"He's in surgery. He hit his head really hard, and they're trying to control the swelling of his brain." Michael tried to sound like he was keeping himself together, but I heard the tiny quiver in his voice.

"This can't be happening. This just can't be happening."

"He's going to be fine. He is strong." Michael tried again to be tough and reassure me. "My parents are in there." He pointed to the waiting room. "I'm waiting out here for Vicki."

Despite having only met his parents once, I hurried in and embraced his mom like she was my own.

"Hey, hon," Marcy said, clearing her throat. She sat back down and tapped the seat next to her before returning her hands to her lap and fidgeting with her wedding ring.

Her eyes followed her pacing husband. One of Jack's tan hands rubbed up and down the space between his hairline and the collar of his shirt as he walked the length of the waiting room, back and forth.

"How long has he been in surgery, do we know?" I asked as I held back the urge to throw up.

"About twenty minutes now." Jack answered, looking at his watch. "They're trying to put in a shunt to relieve the swelling." He never looked at me when he spoke. His pacing seemed to be the only thing helping him function. He was minutes from rubbing his neck raw.

"We should hear something soon." Marcy attempted to comfort me—and herself.

"Hey. Any update?" Ethan barged into the room, out of breath.

"Still in surgery." Jack repeated, this time with less detail.

I looked up at Ethan, desperate for information. "What happened?"

"The officer that called me told me a dually truck towing a boat was in front of them. The boat connection came loose, and the truck slammed on his brakes, causing the boat to jackknife and come back down on its side. Dad was driving and wasn't able to get out of the way or slow down quick enough, but he swerved to try and get onto the shoulder. Aaron's side of the vehicle took the worst of the hit," Ethan said, repeating what he'd been told. I took in his appearance and realized a look of responsibility plagued his face, which made me even more nervous.

"Where's your dad?" I asked.

"Third floor. He has a broken arm and a few broken ribs, but he's stable. He hit his head too, but the driver side had an airbag."

"Aaron didn't have an airbag?" Marcy asked as silent tears streaked her makeup.

"No." Ethan dropped his head. "It was an older van. Too old for passenger bags to be a standard."

My Aaron. Marcy's Aaron. This isn't happening. Someone wake me up. Everything grew foggy. Nothing made sense.

"We just have to trust the doctors and believe God to make everything all right." Jack ordered in an authoritative voice, trying to prevent anyone from losing it—including himself.

Aaron was the one who was supposed to be sitting here comforting me, holding my hand, telling me everything was going to be okay, but I didn't even know if he was aware of what was going on.

I didn't know how long surgeries lasted. My only point of reference was movies and tv shows that solved the problem within thirty minutes or two hours max. When the fifth hour of surgery rolled around, fear seriously settled in.

Some days seemed longer than twenty-four hours, and you couldn't make them end no matter how hard you tried. Today was the longest day of my life. I just wanted to fall asleep and wake up to yesterday. Yesterday was a good day.

~ 29 ~

The doctors made us wait entirely too long before we were able to go in and see him. Aaron was moved to a private room after his seven-hour surgery, and since only two people were allowed in at once, his parents got to go in and see him first. The rest of us had to take turns one at a time because Marcy wasn't going to leave his side. I was beyond ready to see him, but Michael got to go next when Jack came back. Family first, I understood. Jack didn't say anything when he came back into the waiting room. He just sat down, placed his elbows on his knees, and buried his face in his hands.

That can't be good. But I forbid myself from asking Jack any of the dozens of unending questions in my head.

When was Michael going to come back, already? I wanted to see Aaron so bad. My anxiousness must've been evident because Vicki came to sit with me and placed her hand on my back, rubbing gentle circles over my shoulder blades. I knew the moment Michael came back, she'd be doing the same for him. Despite how much comfort it was to have her here, I felt terrible for making her split her attention between Michael and me. She must be exhausted.

I was exhausted. We'd been here for hours.

Michael finally came back into the waiting room with red-rimmed eyes. "You can go now, Maddy. Room four-twelve."

I jumped from my seat and rushed down the hall, following the signs as I passed three doors on the right, made one left turn, and halted at the second room on my left. My Aaron was in there. I entered the room to find Marcy leaning onto the left side of the bed, endlessly running her hand through his hair. Over and over. I wasn't ready to see him—like that. A massive tube came out of his mouth, attached to more beeping machines than I could decipher. My pace slowed. I had to will myself forward.

My Aaron wasn't in here.

As I got closer, I saw various scrapes and scratches on his head and arms, motionless at his sides. Tears fell from my face and hit the floor. I reached for his hand like I'd done hundreds of times, but his fingers didn't pull mine in and electrify me like they always did. Instead, his hand was heavy and limp as I lifted it to my chest.

"He's still so handsome, isn't he?" Marcy broke the silence.

"The most beautiful man I've ever seen," I said with weak, airy words, gripping his hand tighter, and praying for it to squeeze back. A tangle of cords came from under the sheets, but I couldn't tell where they were all connected to him.

"The doctor said they did all they could in surgery, and now we just have to wait and see if Aaron's brain activity resumes. I know it will."

I looked up at some of the screens above his bed and next to me. His heart was beating strong: fifty-five, fifty-seven, fifty-five, fifty-four. I closed my eyes and followed the rhythm of the monitor, drowning out all the other noises.

One of the screens had a rising and falling colored bar, and I noticed the rise on the screen moved at the same time as Aaron's chest. I deduced the monitor was attached to the tube in his mouth, breathing for him.

Time wasn't passing in minutes any longer. It passed in beats. I stood there for two hundred seventy-nine beats before anyone broke the chaotic symphony of beeping with words.

"Mrs. Walker?" the doctor said, startling me from my trance. It wasn't me he called even though that was the name I recited dozens of times in my head.

"Yes." Marcy answered.

"I understand how overwhelming and confusing this is. The nurse told me you were asking more questions than she was able to answer."

"Yes. She said you felt the surgery was a success?"

"That's correct. Aaron's main artery was impaired in multiple places, which is why it took us quite a while to locate and repair all of the damage. We were able to stop the swelling with a shunt, and we're closely monitoring his vitals to ensure swelling doesn't resume. If the shunt begins to fail for any reason, there's another option of a decompressive craniectomy where we go back into surgery and remove a portion of his skull. All that being said, we still have no way of knowing if brain activity will resume."

"All right. So all these tubes, are they what's keeping him alive right now, then?"

"In a way, yes. They're telling his organs what to do until the brain takes back over."

"And how long will it be until that happens?" she asked in a tone that communicated she expected a response in minutes rather than hours. Or days.

"That we aren't sure of, unfortunately. So far, we aren't seeing much activity. Ultimately, it will be up to you and your husband how long we keep him functioning on life support."

"I'm not sure what you mean?" Marcy's voice trembled.

"If we don't see an increase in brain activity in the next few hours, you will need to decide how long you want to keep him alive with the machines."

My knees buckled under me, and the doctor's words faded until I couldn't hear them anymore. I pressed my face up to Aaron's cheek and whispered into his ear. "I'm here, love. I need you to stay with me, okay? Please don't leave me. I haven't had enough days. I want more days."

The conversation continued behind me. Marcy asked as many questions as she could conjure up, but the look on her face told me the doctor wasn't giving any new answers. I stared at Aaron's eyelids, expecting at any second for them to pop open, for him to turn his head and look at me, and even with the tube in his throat, give me some kind of reassurance.

I waited to no avail.

* * *

Jack wanted to go back in, and one of Aaron's sisters also arrived, so I hadn't touched Aaron in over six thousand beats. Marcy still wouldn't trade with anyone and refused to leave his room for anything. I didn't blame her

—I wished I could do the same. I wasn't sure when I would break down—or lose hope—but somehow, I was still going without food or sleep for forty-five thousand two hundred sixty beats. Vicki left about two thousand seven hundred ninety-eight beats ago. She apologized for leaving me there, but she had to go home and shower for work. Ethan only stayed around two thousand five hundred beats because he left to be with his dad after he was able to see Aaron. He didn't stay in the room long, maybe ninety beats or so.

Aaron's sister came back into the waiting area when we hit fifty thousand beats. She was a younger version of her mother, gorgeous, even dressed in grief. "Hi. I'm Lauren. Aaron's told me so much about you." She spoke slowly and gently of her brother a few rooms—but an infinity—away.

That's when the dam started to crack and weaken against the pressure.

I had to swallow the lump in my throat before I could greet her. "Nice to finally meet you, Lauren. I wish we could've met under different circumstances. Any change in there?"

"No. Mom's coming to terms, I think, but Dad isn't ready. He almost tore the doctor's head off when he mentioned organ donation. They're trying to come to a common ground on how long we should wait. I should've got here sooner. I just—didn't realize the severity." Her voice cracked, and her sharp intake of breath took mine away.

The crack grew as pieces of my heart broke off at her words. I sat here with a total stranger. A woman I just met, connected only by the fact we both loved the man lying in the bed in room four-twelve.

"I didn't realize we were at that point already." Hope faded, slipping through my hands like sand.

"I think they're just trying to set up a time to gauge possible improvement. Nothing permanent has been decided yet." She reached over and squeezed my hand, reassuring me just like her brother used to, only it was nowhere near as effective.

Jack walked back in then, his face filled with grief and anger. "Maddison, you can go back now."

My feet moved double-time to the beats I still heard in my head.

Not much changed in room four-twelve. Marcy sat now, her feet probably aching, but she still perched on the left side of Aaron's bed closest to the window.

"He adored you so much," she said, acknowledging my presence without taking her eyes off of her son. "With every bit of his heart. He told me so. That night after we met. We talked on the phone for the longest time, just like we used to when he was away in recovery." She finally looked at me. "He told me he was going to marry you."

I knew. My heart knew. But hearing her words in the past tense was more than I could handle.

"I know he would've wanted you to know that, without a shadow of a doubt. And I will always consider you a part of our family."

I watched the tiny beating heart image on the monitor, searching for something to say, but no words came. Silently, I pulled the other chair over and laid my head on the side of his bed. I traced every line on his hand. Eighty-two beats later, still, no words. The room remained quiet, with only the beeping monitors filling the air as I traced and prayed. Prayed and traced.

A hand on my back woke me up. "Why don't you go home and get cleaned up, honey? Maybe grab something to eat," Marcy said in her compassionate motherly tone.

"I wasn't planning on sleeping, sorry. How long was I out?"

"It's all right, sweetie. A couple of hours. Michael left to pick up his other sister from the airport, and Jack went to clear his head and get us some food. I didn't see much of a reason to wake you up since the nurse let us break the rules."

Break the rules? But then I saw Lauren sitting in the chair her mom occupied before I drifted off.

"I don't want to sleep right now. I want to be awake for every second he's here." I spoke frantically as I stood from my chair. "You should've woken me up sooner." Her face showed me I was too harsh. "Sorry," I looked down, avoiding her eyes.

She didn't even retaliate. Marcy was even stronger than I assumed. "I understand. We're all out of sorts right now. I bet a shower would help. Why don't you go freshen up then come back after a while?"

"I don't want to leave." I looked back over at Aaron, who looked exactly the same as he did the first time I came into this room. Not even a minuscule movement had occurred. I was both oddly relieved and horrified by that observation.

"Nothing has happened, and if it does, we'll call you immediately. But I promise you, we won't do anything while you're gone." *Anything* meaning something I couldn't accept as true just yet. "There's still only supposed to be two people here at a time, although when they saw you were asleep, they didn't hold us to it as strictly. But Molly will be here soon, and you'll probably spend a good amount of time in the waiting room again. It's okay to go."

I leveled my words in my throat before they escaped, trying to ensure they didn't come out as harsh. "I hear what you are saying, Marcy, but you know I can't leave, just like you won't either."

Her stare was equally determined. Without hesitation or uncertainty, she responded, "I won't."

Lauren stood and moved so we could go back to our previous stations—Marcy on his left, me on his right. Lauren took up the recliner in the corner as we all waited until his other sister arrived, knowing two of us would lose our place. And I knew when the time came, Marcy wouldn't be in that count.

* * * *

It was miserable waiting in the lobby, but if I couldn't be in the same room as Aaron, I would at least be in the same building as him. I understood, family was family. I wasn't going to deny any of them what precious time we had left with him. No matter how badly I wanted to. I switched from pacing to sitting and back more times than I could remember. Vicki returned at some point in her work clothes and just let me cry on her shoulder. Having her there was comforting. Not that being surrounded by Aaron's family wasn't, but Vicki was the closest thing I had to my own family at the moment. Now more than ever, I was certain of how well Vicki knew me.

She sat there and let me drench her sleeve without saying anything as I attempted to process reality. She also mentioned me leaving, but didn't push the issue when I told her it wasn't happening in a tone a bit too firm. She bought me a half of a sandwich out of the cafeteria vending machine, of which I only managed to eat a few bites.

Michael returned from Aaron's room, causing Vicki to leave my side. I felt vile for her. I didn't really want to be myself right now, but I couldn't imagine being her either—trying to be there for both me and Michael. When Vicki told me she had to leave a little bit later, I assumed it must be to return to work, but I didn't even know what day it was anymore, let alone the time.

Some beats later, the nurse came into the waiting room, informing us the doctor requested all of the family members to join him in Aaron's room. I stood but couldn't move as I watched Michael and his sisters make their way back to his room. When no one looked my way to see if I was coming, it was a tough pill to swallow. All of a sudden, I was alone in a huge room full of empty seats. It was all I could do not to lie face down on the floor and release every bit of myself into the worn carpet. The rhythm of his heartbeat was the only thing with me, still pounding in my ears.

When they finally came back in after what seemed like ages, Jack was furious. Michael tried to touch his dad's shoulder and almost took an elbow to the jaw. Molly was quiet, and Lauren was crying loud enough that I heard her before she entered the room.

"Dad, you heard what they said," Michael said.

"I don't care. They are wrong. I don't see why we have to make a decision already." Jack practically yelled at Michael even though it wasn't his son he was mad at.

I stood up, waiting for someone to let me know what was going on. The fact that they seemed to have forgotten I was even in the room until I spoke up caused a sharp pain to rip through my gut. I looked down, expecting to find a knife, but of course, nothing was there. "What's going on?" I said loud enough to demand attention.

Michael looked at me with apologetic eyes and said, "You can go back now, Maddy."

I didn't hesitate. I ran to room four-twelve as fast as I could, accidentally bumping into a nurse. Only Marcy remained. This time she stood by his feet, taking in his full body. "Marcy? What's going on?" I asked, desperate to be included.

Mental Notes

"No progress has been made after surgery, and the doctor said there's no indicator it will start at this point," she said with the straightest face ever, like the only way she could communicate was by relaying the information she'd been given. "They've declared Aaron brain-dead."

"But he's still here. He isn't—" I couldn't say the word as I rushed back to his side and took his hand in my own after what seemed like an eternity of beats apart. "He's still here."

She remained quiet for a while, probably trying to give me time to process or figure out exactly how to tell me what I already knew was coming. I sat again and pressed my forehead to his hand. The three of us had been here in these positions before, but hope still been floated above us then. None was left now.

"We're going to shut off the machines, Maddison." She spoke the words I feared were true.

"I know" came out as a whisper, the sheets around my face soaked from my silent tears.

"They're going to let everyone who wants to be in here at the end stay. I'll give you a few minutes to be alone with him and decide what you want to do."

The first time Marcy left his side since she got there, it was for me. The sacrifice somehow honored the wishes her son would've had. I heard her steps behind me get quieter. Quieter.

"I love you, Aaron," I said without lifting my head, tracing his motionless hand again. "I want you to stay. I want to feel insecure and have you tell me everything will work out. I want you to show up at my door just to kiss me. I want you to surprise me a thousand more times. I want to be your bride. I want to kiss you until I'm out of breath. You're all I want. I know you are strong enough. You just have to show them that when everything shuts down."

I willed him to wake up and answer me, regardless of what the doctors said about him never recovering. Our love was strong enough, wasn't it? My last droplet of hope fell with my tears.

The melody of the monitors played between us. I sat up to look at the face that I longed to wake up next to every morning, but would never get to. I ran my fingers through his hair and down his unshaven face. For the first time since Ethan called me, a brief chuckle escaped my lips.

Regardless of the tears soaking my face and the enormity of emotions warring within me, I knew he was growing out his beard for me.

"I hope you understand I can't be here when you go. I know I'm probably a coward, and you'd tell me I could do it, but I can't—because you aren't here to encourage me. I'm not ready to hear the deafening silence. I could never be ready. Know that I'll love you even in the silence. How could I ever stop?"

Slowly, I crawled up next to him because no one was there to stop me, and I was selfish. I wanted to know what it felt like to lay in bed next to him just once, but it wasn't the same because I knew he would hold me tight.

Trace imaginary shapes on my back.

Kiss the top of my head.

Lying there was a cruel injustice.

A vain representation.

I laid my head against his chest and heard his strong heartbeat. It sounded so much lovelier than the beeping monitor.

"I will never stop loving you. I didn't get to love you long enough." I leaned up and kissed him on as much of his lips as I could.

I didn't want to get up, but I didn't want anyone to find me there either, so I carefully stood back to my feet, navigating the cords, and waited for his family to come back in.

"Thank you for loving me. I was honored to be the one you wanted," was the last thing I said to Aaron as I held his hand to my chest.

Three hundred eighty-seven beats later, Marcy touched my shoulder. Jack, Michael, Lauren, and Molly were all behind her. The doctor entered right after.

"I can't stay. Sorry if that disappoints you, but I can't hear his heart stop beating."

"I understand, sweetie." Marcy touched my cheek and ran her thumb under my eye. Her face seemed to have aged years since I met her only days ago.

I kissed Aaron's hand one more time while it was still warm, and Marcy reached out for it before I laid his deadweight limb back at his side. I started walking to the door before I didn't have enough strength to move and looked over my shoulder one more time at the love of my life, still full of color. I faintly heard the doctor start talking about what all was about to happen and how they would roll him out to the OR.

My walk turned into a run, fueled by the fear of hearing the doctor's words and not hearing the heart monitor anymore. I ran to the elevator and mashed the call button just as aggressively as when I arrived, thankful to be alone in the elevator where no one would see me, and slumped into the corner. There was no more strength—no more power to hold back. I screamed and banged the wall, my heart breaking with every last beat I knew his was taking. I had to get out of this building. Struggling to find my breath, I got back to my feet and ran for my car as soon as the door opened, catching the glances of some people in the ER but not caring.

I looked up at the fourth row of lighted windows in the brick wall as I ran out, wondering which room they were in. How was this happening? Was it already over? Was Aaron….

Hurrying into my car, I closed my eyes and dropped my head to the steering wheel, remembering the rhythm of his heart, committing it to memory. I couldn't allow myself to forget.

I can never forget.

I knew two things: I didn't want him to go, but he had to. I hoped there'd be a day I didn't have to say goodbye, only goodnight, but that was surely … never.

~ 30 ~

I didn't remember getting home. I don't know how long I slept or what time it was. My eyes were so puffy I could barely open them. I didn't know what day it was, and I didn't care to count anymore. My love was gone. There wasn't much I wanted to do, and I didn't think I could force myself to leave my apartment even if I tried. I stared at the fan above my bed, the blurry circle spinning round and round. I picked one blade and watched it until I lost track of it back into the blur. I turned over to my side and closed my eyes again. They burned. I checked my phone to see the time but still wasn't sure if it was morning or evening.

Thirteen missed notifications filled the screen, but I didn't care to look at them, let alone respond to any. Not a single one of them was from my favorite person. Everyone else could wait.

My stomach growled like a vicious animal, but I wasn't going to get up to eat. How could I eat? Nothing even sounded worth eating.

I took a deep breath, and the fragrance of flowers filled my nostrils. Aaron gave me one hundred sixty-seven flowers less than a week ago, which now took over every counter, table, and flat surface. They were the last part of him I had here. I cherished every one because I'd never get another from him.

That's when I started crying. Again.

I pulled the covers over my head and wanted to disappear into the mattress. Hoped it would swallow me whole. But it didn't. I still wasn't going to come up for air anytime soon.

My doorbell rang, and I ignored it. It rang again in a glitchy cadence. I pulled the sheets off from over my head, but I still wasn't going to answer it. My phone rang. I let it ring until it went to voicemail, but when the banging on the door began, I knew whoever it was wasn't going to leave.

I didn't even look at myself before answering the door because I didn't care. Not that it mattered anyway, because when I opened the door, it was Vicki.

"Hey, girl." She hugged me, and I let some of the weight fall onto her. I needed someone to hold me up. When I managed my own weight again, she let me go to close the door. "I needed to come make sure you were okay. I bet you still haven't eaten anything." I raised my eyebrows and nodded in agreement. Her grin was patient and understanding. "What can I make for you?"

I hadn't spoken since leaving the hospital, so I was unsure how my voice would sound. "For breakfast?" Awful. My voice sounded awful.

"If that's what you want. It's more like dinner time, but I'll start some coffee for sure." Vicki was a gem for coming to help me, but I saw the bags under her eyes. I knew this was heavy for her, too, just in a different way. Her boyfriend lost his brother. His best friend.

"How's Michael?" I still sounded like I screamed all night at a concert, so I cleared my throat.

"He's hanging in there, trying to be strong for his parents. Jack's a mess."

"Where is *he*?" I couldn't bring myself to properly form a thought or question about Aaron.

"He was transported to the funeral home, last I heard at least. I'm trying not to overwhelm Michael, so I only get information as he gives it. The family had to go pick out the casket and figure out all those details—"

"Okay. Th-that's enough." I lifted my hand in weak protest. Funeral home and casket weren't words I wanted to associate with my boyfriend, but that was my new reality. "Can you please check my phone. I don't think I can handle all of the conversations. And I need to tell my mom something, but I can't."

She scanned through the texts and missed calls. "Ethan and Suzanne called. Only Suzanne left a voicemail." She held the phone up to her ear and waited to relay the message to me. "They're rescheduling the sessions that want to see you, and she's going to take over the families that don't mind who they see." She paused again, listening some more. "She isn't expecting to see you in the office for the rest of the week and wants you to call her when you're ready to figure out when you'll be back."

"She's a fantastic boss," I said, leaning over and resting my pounding head on the edge of the bar.

"Lisa, Stacy, and Rachel sent texts saying things like they were praying and are here for you if you need anything."

"Can you send a text to my mom? If you call, she'll be persistent in talking to me. Just tell her it's you, what happened, and I'll call her when I'm ready. And not to call me until I call her. Say that part twice because I mean it. She's probably going to anyway." I lifted my heavy head and walked back to my room and got back in bed.

The bubbling sound of my coffee machine echoed as coffee blended with the floral scent filling my apartment. I felt so flat. Totally empty. Caffeine might not bring me the regular pick me up it usually did, but I hoped it'd help with the pummeling in my head. Sounds of Vicki searching my cabinets for coffee cups followed by a few sporadically spaced chimes of my phone traveled to my room, meaning my mom text back in her I-don't-really-know-what-I'm-doing way.

Vicki walked in with a mug in one hand and my phone in her other. "Your mom says she loves you and is so sorry." The phone chimed again in her hand, and she looked down to read it. "That she's praying for you and will be out here in time for the funeral."

"That's right, I forgot." My swollen eyelids fell closed. I wasn't sure how to feel about my mother visiting. She planned on coming out to meet Aaron, but now? "She's coming this weekend."

"You should probably sit up so you don't burn yourself." Vicki set my phone down on the nightstand and sat on the edge of my bed, waiting to hand me my coffee.

"Yes, I don't think I want to return to the hospital as a burn victim. I need more pain like a hole in my head."

I moved like a lazy animal, creeping up on my stomach and rolling over to lean my back against the headboard, leaving my sheets a tangled mess. "Thank you." I took a sip too soon and felt the burn on my tongue—salt on the wound.

"What do you want to eat?" In her resilience, Vicki wasn't going to leave without making sure I ate.

"A sandwich is fine. I think I have everything, but make whatever you can find. Everything's in the pantry or the fridge."

She got up and walked away. It hurt to be alone again, but it was eerily welcoming. I knew how to be alone, especially in my apartment. Her phone rang while she was in the kitchen, and from what I could hear, it sounded like she was talking to Michael. I switched my focus to the clock ticking, not wanting to listen to her side of the conversation. Her words faded out. I embraced the coffee mug with both hands and lifted my knees to rest it there. I breathed in the steam and hoped it would help me clear the fog that took up residence in my mind.

When I honed back in, the only sound coming from the kitchen was Vicki talking. She probably waited to finish her call before bringing the food to my room, for which I was thankful. Not long passed before she came back in with a plate in her hand and a fresh red hue to her eyelids.

"Was that Michael?" I asked.

"Yeah." A strained smile flashed on her face but quickly faded.

"And?" *Do I even want to know?*

"Everything's scheduled for Saturday."

"Saturday."

We should be having a date night. He should be meeting my mom. Instead, it will be the last time I'd ever see his face, as different as it might be.

At least Suzanne already cleared me from work all week, one less thing to worry about—missing ... four days of work. Or was it only two?

"Will you let my mom know?"

"Of course. This is unreal, Maddison. I'm so sorry. I don't know what else to say, but please, let me be here for you."

"Noted. Did Michael say anything about Marcy?" The image of her exhausted face came to the front of my memory.

"She's handling it better than anyone else, or so it appears. He told me she let you be alone with Aaron."

"She did." I didn't know what from my time with him I wanted to share. I wanted to keep it just between us—well, to myself. I hoped he knew, even if the monitors indicated he didn't.

"You know, I'm pretty jealous of him right now."

"Don't you dare talk like that, Maddison."

"That isn't what I mean, I promise. Here I am, probably looking worse than I ever have in my entire life, and he's looking at Jesus. Like in His eyes. I'm living the worst day of my life, and he's experiencing the best day of his. How could I want him to give that up just to be back here with me?" It was hard to admit, even harder to accept, but I was fully content with Aaron's current company.

"I bet if it were reversed, he'd be happy for you too." She smiled and laid back face-up on my bed beside me, probably the first time she stopped moving in days.

"He would, he would," I whispered.

I have to hold on to that.

"I promise to let you help me, but you have to promise me you won't let yourself fade either, dashing back and forth between me to Michael." A quiet tear fell sideways down her face and became one with my sheets. The events of the last couple of days were hitting me. Hard. But she was getting it from two sides, and that must be horrendous.

"I know. It's a conversation Michael and I had as well."

"Good." I took a bite of my sandwich. Food didn't make me feel any better, but it kept my stomach from growling at least. "Did you go to work today?"

"Yeah, for a bit. I've barely slept over the last few days. Jerry's more understanding than I expected, which is nice. He gave me some stuff to do from home," she said, taking her turn staring up at my ceiling fan. The hypnotic rhythm was transcending—even if it was brief.

Something about this conversation felt so bizarre. Vicki and I talked about Jerry like someone hit rewind, and the most wonderful days I ever lived never happened. Like I just woke up from a magnificent but cruel dream. If only I could go back to sleep.

"I don't think it's totally real yet. I still remember the warmth of his hand." The mug in my grasp was a pleasant yet torturing reminder.

"I know what you mean. I haven't processed it fully either." She wiped her face.

I couldn't stop the vicious thought we'd never be sisters anymore, only friends. It ridiculed me. But she was the friend I so desperately needed, now more than ever. I hoped it wouldn't be too painful to remain friends if she stayed with Michael—hearing all the stories of the extended family that should've been my own. I shut down the train of thought that was about to take me down a dark and twisted path. I couldn't admit to any of my disillusioned thoughts.

"Thank you for coming over. I didn't realize I needed this." I placed my empty plate next to me on the bed, took one more sip of coffee, then set my mug down on the nightstand and laid with my back to the headboard, parallel to Vicki.

We were quiet for a long time, the reticence a pleasant guest. When I opened my eyes, I discovered Vicki asleep. Even though I wanted to—begged my brain to shut down—I couldn't sleep.

After looking around my room, my eyes locked in on the flowers atop my dresser. Yellow daffodils. Red roses. Pink dahlias. White daisies. The memory of my conversation with Casey days ago—under Aaron's doting gaze, so close, forever away—about trimming the stems so the flowers would live longer came to the front of my mind.

They had to live longer.

I got up as quick as possible without waking Vicki and ran to the kitchen to retrieve a pair of scissors, my muscles in full protest after countless hours of motionlessness. I started with the vase on my bar—the purple one I found on my doorstep. I took the bouquet out, put fresh water in the vase, and added the white powdered food. I trimmed each flower—one by one. The snap of the stem was thunderous in my ears and hushed apartment. I watched as the old wilted end of the stem fell to the kitchen floor, bounced, and rolled to a stop. Again and again, the sound pierced my ears as the trimmed edges gathered around my feet. Fourteen down. One hundred fifty-three to go.

Memories flashed before me as I pressed the scissors closed over and over again. The first time I saw him. Snap. The first time he grabbed my hand. Snap. Our first kiss. Snap. Accidentally falling asleep in his arms at the river cabin. Snap.

Deafening.

I hadn't paid attention to how long tending to the flowers—and memories—took, but Vicki was still asleep, so I headed over to my couch, the grief epicenter in my world. I could barely make out the details of the paintings we made together in the dimly-lit apartment. At that moment, I was immensely grateful he took me on that date. I sat tall on my knees leaning against the back of the couch and ran my fingers over every visible stroke of his painting, closing my eyes and picturing every motion his hand made to create it. His handsome face filled my memory as he looked over at me and smiled. It was as if our date just happened. Like he was still here.

The tears came again. How were there even any left?

With my mission to trim the flowers completed, my mind sank again as I sat there with nothing to do and nowhere to go. My evil mind attacked me, scolding me for not preventing him from going on that work trip. And even worse, accusing me that if I'd never gone to that coffee shop months ago, I would've saved myself all this grief. I believed the lies, but only for a moment.

Although they were too short, the last several months were the best of my life. I wouldn't give them up, even to spare myself the heartache.

My body found the old depressing groove it made in my couch—before I knew Aaron—and slumped right back in like muscle memory. I closed my eyes and let time pass me by, tired and unmotivated, broken and hopeless. Empty. I loved him in the silence.

"Thank you for letting me sleep." Vicki broke the air with her words sometime later.

"You're welcome" came out hoarse.

She sat down next to me and leaned her head against mine. "After my divorce, my dad gave me the best advice I've ever received in my entire life. 'Sometimes, you just have to pray for God to give you grace to get you through the next five minutes. Then you start praying for God to give you grace to get through the next hour. Then you pray for God to give you grace to get through the day. And eventually, you're making it longer than you thought you could.'"

"I'm pretty sure I need it for the next five minutes."

"I remember." She let out with a sigh. "I can't tell you how many times I prayed those very words. I hope it helps you as much as it did me." She gave me time for her words to penetrate my troubled mind. "I'm going to go ahead and go, I told Michael I'd come by earlier and didn't plan on falling asleep. You better let me know if you need anything."

"Okay" escaped just above a whisper.

She gently stroked my head and fixed the ends of my messy hair with another sigh. "I mean it, Maddison. Anything."

All I wanted was an answer, a plan I could follow to get me through this. One she couldn't give, but I tried anyway. "Where do I go from here, Vicki?"

She stood and gave me another understanding grin. "I'm not sure, sweetie. But I do know you'll figure it out. Eventually."

END OF BOOK ONE

ACKNOWLEDGMENTS

If you're reading this, that means you didn't throw your book — or tablet — across the room, so thanks. Trust me, no one was as mad at me about Aaron as my husband. For days.

Josh, I super love you! Thank you for letting me read my book to you as we lied in bed at night for countless hours to make sure this little idea I had was any good. My favorite things in Aaron came from you! Being married to you since 2004 has been more than all right. You pull out some of the best parts in me and lovingly tell me when I need to chill out on some of my crazy bits. Because you've set an environment of creativity in our home, I feel empowered to try new things. Even if I doubt myself, you've always seen it in me. Thank you for all the love and lattes over the years. Oh, and for giving me four kids, because I really like being a mom.

I can't go much further into this thanks spiel without saying: Sarah, you most literally changed my adult life. I mean, if it weren't for you, I probably would've never started reading and thus never written this book (and the ones to come). The fact that we had a similar scene in our books we wrote simultaneously — my first, your eighth — without ever discussing it, leads me to believe all of our friends in our heads were in the same place at the same time in the world of our imaginations. But why wouldn't they want to hang out, they're pieces of us after all.

To all of the people who have told me, "You should write," over the years when I let out little bits and pieces of my pleasure in wordsmithing via plays, blogs, or thoughts: thank you for being the small reminder in the back of my head that I'm good enough. Because in all reality, most days I think *is anyone even going to read this?*

Back to the kids I love — which two of you aren't even old enough to read yet — thank you for giving mommy time to sit at the computer desk for hours, even if you interrupted twenty-four thousand times, because you're the best thing I ever created. Each one of you! Moriah, Judah, Elisah, and Uriah. No matter which hat I wear for the task of the day, the mom hat will always be my favorite.

Some of my best writing, in my opinion, came when a candle was lit. Once I figured that out, I went through a few fifty-hour burners and now have a staple "get in the writing zone" routine. Shout out to Pumpkin Gingerbread, Winter Moss, and #getinspired (whatever scent you may be), and once again, the amazing husband who lavished his love on me by buying said #getinspired candle—I think it worked.

A big thanks to the amazing ladies who took time out of their busy lives to help me edit my sometimes dyslexia affected writing. Or maybe it's just me Irish DNA that sometimes causes me to interchange me and my. Like I did unintentionally in that last sentence. (Not fixing it.) Sarah, Heather, Hannah, Shannon, Staci. You're all fantastic! And I just realized all your names start with S or H, so that's kinda fun.

To my readers: hopefully, you enjoyed my first novel as much as I did. I promise Maddison's story continues, and it's worth what I just put you through—at least that's my hope. Most of her story is already written. I had no idea how long this editing, multiple drafts, and nailing out the final details would take. It took me three months to write the first draft, and over a year for everything else. Crazy, right?

I'm most thankful for the one who created all things and has the biggest imagination of all time, my Heavenly Father. Seriously, just look around you. We're living in His vast vision turned reality. May I never take off the hat that worships You.

Oh, and to my mom, who tells me how awesome I am (*that's a good thing, right?*), I hope this little surprise I kept a secret from you for over a year makes you proud. Remember when you told me I should be a writer? It was pretty hard not to tell you I'd already finished my second book. Love you.

Candle count: 3.

Because Maddison loves music as much as I do, you can get more into the scene by knowing what she was listening to when....

Stacy played at the coffee shop, Ch 1, pg 16. "You Were Meant For Me" by Jewel. This song was a blast from the past, igniting memories of her teen years.

she heard Aaron sing for the first time at the coffee shop, Ch 4, pg 47. "Good Riddance" by Green Day. Aaron plays this song in reflection of his past in a slower ballad rendition of his own.

She daydreamed of her time with Aaron, Ch 4, pg 41 & Ch 10, pg 119. "I Gotta Feeling" by The Black Eyed Peas. This song becomes something of her mental theme song when she looks forward to time with Aaron.

she danced and sang with Aaron at the wedding, Ch 12, pg 147. "(I've Had) The Time Of My Life" by Billy Medley & Jennifer Warnes. They sing this song back and forth to each other as a declaration of their emotions.

she listened to her Pandora station, it is always set to Bethel Music Radio, Ch 19, pg 215 & Ch 28, pg 325. These songs always help Maddison simmer down and function better.

Have a listen. You won't regret it. Each song was picked on purpose with foreshadowing Easter eggs in the lyrics.

Keep reading for a sneak peek of the next book in the series:

mental battle

~ 1 ~

I haven't done much since my boyfriend died in a freak car accident. I've only gotten out of bed a handful of times the last few days, forcing myself to eat at least once a day. And when I have to use the restroom. I haven't showered. No doubt, my smell isn't pleasant. One perk of my nose being stopped up from all of the crying was I couldn't tell how putrid the stench actually was.

But today was his funeral, so I had to get up.

My mother planned on coming to town, but after much convincing, I was able to push her visit back to a later—undetermined—date. Maybe I needed this time to make an effort to process everything. Maybe I wanted to be alone. Unfortunately, I was really good at it. Or perhaps I didn't want anyone telling me what to do in my grieving process.

Not to mention the original reason for my mom's visit this weekend was to finally meet Aaron. Her coming to be introduced to the mere shell of him wasn't how I wanted her to know him. I wanted her to know him as the amazing man I loved—the one who still lived in my mind.

No motivation sparked when I finally attempted to get out of bed. I especially had no desire to look cute or pick out the right outfit. Perhaps wearing all black at funerals stemmed from people navigating my exact situation. No amount of makeup under the sun would cover up the damage done to my eyes this week, so I wasn't even sure if I wanted to try. I decided to wear sunglasses like a person covering up getting wasted the night before. Some might even wonder, but I didn't think anyone would judge me. Regardless, I didn't care if they did for once.

Attending the funeral of the love of my life would be the first time I left my apartment since coming back from the hospital. And Aaron's still warm touch. Life support sustained him for a couple of days with no sign of brain activity before his parents made the insurmountable decision to let him go. I wasn't able to stay for his last breath—machine induced or otherwise—and hoped one day I wouldn't regret my weakness in that decision. Would he have wanted me to stay? To be there until the end. Or would he have not wanted me to endure the pain of seeing the warmth and color slowly fade from his skin?

I'd never know.

My mind was the devil's playground.

Okay, Maddison, you better get moving before you lose control altogether.

I turned on the shower to allow the water time to heat up before grabbing my black dress from the closet and hanging it from the towel rack. My lazy form of ironing was allowing the steam from my hot shower to loosen any wrinkles in my clothes. Bare minimum efforts were happening today, not that I'd used a real iron in the last few years.

I didn't recognize myself in the mirror before getting in the shower. My eyes dark and hollow. My posture weak and slumped. I looked even worse than before I turned my life around the last time I was heartbroken. I wasn't sure I had the strength to do it again, especially since the pain was quadrupled. The steam quickly crept across my mirror. Graciously, my face was the first to distort and blur over, so I didn't have to look at myself any longer. Hopefully, the vapors were as successful overtaking my dress.

I stood in the shower motionless—leaning my head against the wall—and let the hot water sting my skin. Knowing this shower wouldn't do me any good if I didn't use soap was the only force to make me move. Although nothing inside encouraged me to proceed faster. I knew I needed to pick up my pace, but I wasn't exactly in a hurry to make it to the laying to rest of my favorite person in the world.

I never made it to the shampoo and conditioner, but at least my body was clean.

It's going to get better, I thought to myself, but not believing the lie. "It's going to get better," I said out loud, forcing myself to start agreeing. "It won't always be this hard" came out just above a whisper.

Please, Jesus, don't always let it be this hard.

I finally found the strength to slip into my semi-wrinkled dress. Afterward, I tied my hair into a knot on the top of my head—made easier by extremely dirty hair—and added a thin layer of makeup to hide my splotchy face, only to discover I had no clue where my keys were when I was ready to leave. Days had passed since I last walked into my apartment. I barely remembered anything about that night anyway—it still felt like a dream. I fell back onto my bed as I released the air in my lungs and fought with myself on even going. *It would feel so good to get back into bed.*

However, I knew I'd regret missing today. I painfully replayed the events of Aaron's last night on earth in my mind to try and remember where I left my keys.

Nothing.

The second time was exceedingly more painful than the first. Then I remembered the sounds more than the visual. I threw them on the end table in my zombie walk to my bed, but they slid off and fell under the couch. In a most unladylike way, I bent over on my hands and knees to reach for the keys, paying no mind to my dress and heels.

Leaving was torture. The sun burned my eyes even through sunglasses. I thought about staying home for the fifth time today. The stairs I eagerly bound down to meet a handsome man leaning on his red car seemed exponentially steeper today. I trudged down each step, almost hoping I'd trip for a legit excuse to stay.

I can't do this.

But somehow, I kept moving forward.

A jingle followed by a clank filled my ears. I dropped my keys fifteen feet through the open staircase.

I officially hate today. Can it please be over already?

Getting to the church took longer than it ever did when Aaron picked me up. I soaked in every minute with him, dragging it out as long as I could, staring at his perfectly handsome profile, kissing him at red lights. Each rotation of the tires was filled with dread this go-around. The thought of all the people who were going to want to talk to me was crippling. I had to fight not to pull over and slash my own tires for another reason to miss.

But then I thought of Marcy. The charming woman who raised my love, and fought through horrendously painful years to show her kids how true love persevered. Knowing I needed to be there for her was the only thing pushing my heel into the gas pedal.

The church had no physical change, but it couldn't have appeared more different to me. Familiar faces with no names greeted me. One in particular —obviously following instructions from someone—ushered me to where I needed to be. I was extremely grateful I didn't have to talk to any of the people already congregated in the lobby waiting. The middle-aged, partially balding man opened a door for me without saying a word. He simply nodded his head with a sympathetic grin of sorts. Aaron's family and Vicki were in the room. It seemed like it could be the green room the band would exit to after worship, but I wasn't sure because I had never seen it. I only knew it as the place Aaron would disappear to before joining me in my seat. Only this time, he wouldn't reappear after disappearing. He wasn't in here.

"Hey, Maddison." Marcy greeted me with a gentle hug, squeezing my arms with what little strength she had left, which was still greater than my own.

"Hey, guys." My voice was severely hoarse after days of silence, closed up in my cave. I sounded like I'd swallowed glass. It felt about as painful too.

"You look good," Vicki said, greeting me next.

"You're a liar," I replied, pulling my sunglasses off and unveiling my puffy eyes with a thin coat of mascara and nothing more.

"We'll just leave those on then." I was glad she was being honest now. "Your hair looks cute." She tried a new compliment with a mini wink. She didn't see me roll my eyes behind my glasses, and I didn't respond in any way that would cause her to find something else to compliment out of pity. I knew I looked rough in my semi-wrinkled dress, dirty hair, and underdone makeup.

I wasn't sure what was supposed to happen next, but I was glad I didn't have to do anything but hold myself together—because I was barely doing so successfully. Time moved fast and slow all at once as I stood there like a statue.

"I don't know if there's a right time or a right way to do this," Marcy said, grabbing her purse and digging through it. "We had to go through some things at his apartment, and I wanted you to have some of this. I think he would've liked for you to have it." She held a small bag out to me, her hand slightly shaking.

What the family had been doing the last few days while I was shut off from the world hadn't crossed my mind until then. I took the bag hesitantly, knowing I had small pieces of Aaron in my hand. Items he touched. I closed my eyes before gathering the strength to open it.

I saw the guitar pick key chain I gave him for his birthday on top of some other items I wasn't entirely able to decipher at a quick glance. Tears filled my eyes, still concealed by my glasses. When I purchased the present, I never expected to get it back, let alone in this manner.

"Michael has something for you too. He just forgot it. We'll get it to you later, okay?" Marcy's words regained my attention.

"Sure. Thank you," I managed to say, but only in a faint whisper as a black mascara filled tear escaped from behind my dark shades.

I stared at the bag in my hands for a few more minutes, trying to decide if I had the strength to touch Aaron's items—now mine. The thought of his family going through his silent apartment sent a chill down my spine, but the thought of his obnoxious roommate possibly going through Aaron's things chased the chill away with anger. The instant change of drastically different emotions made me dizzy, revealing I didn't have it in me to go through the bag in front of other people. I wanted to take my time, and would most likely break down, so I placed the bag in my purse, hoping not to offend anyone.

The brush of her hand against my smeared wet check brought me back into the room. "That's okay." Vicki whispered in my ear as she hugged me.

"Hey," Michael said, grabbing my arm while Vicki still embraced me. Suddenly it wasn't so cool he looked almost identical to Aaron. Not. At. All. "We're here for you."

"I know."

Everything about today lacked something. It was Aaron. He wasn't with me on the ride to the church. He didn't encourage me to walk in and face what I feared I couldn't. He didn't hug me and hold me together when the feeling of my very body breaking apart was at its greatest. Instead, I did those things alone, knowing he was better at those tasks than I was. If only he could help me now.

Of course, he couldn't because we gathered today to celebrate his life that had ended. I wanted more than anything to be celebrating with him still here, though it was impossible. I wondered when I'd finally stop feeling like he was simply missing, and the vicious truth that he'd never return would take over my predominant thoughts. It wasn't going to happen soon, I knew that much.

More people filled the room than I expected, but it didn't take long to figure out that the middle-aged man was Molly's—Aaron's oldest sister—husband and kids I only heard about a few times. I wondered how well they knew their awesome uncle. Logically, the other slender man was Lauren's husband. I didn't have a grand introduction and first impression in me, so I never attempted it, hoping someone else from the family would introduce us eventually.

Not that it mattered at this point.

The knock at the door told us it was time to begin. The family, Vicki, and I were ushered into the main auditorium. I only attended one other funeral in my life—my grandfather's—but it was when I was a kid, so I couldn't remember much about it. As the usher showed us to our reserved seats in the first row, I hoped the service wouldn't last too long, but also wasn't ready for it to be all over either. When we made it to the front of the sanctuary, I saw Aaron in the open casket. He looked similar but not the same. I couldn't take my eyes off of him.

This is unreal.

When Pastor Steve started talking, his voice finally broke my stare. "We're here today for a tragic but celebratory event, Aaron going home to his Father. If you didn't have the honor of knowing this astounding young man's whole story, let me fill you in on some of what I knew about Aaron Walker.

"Aaron grew up here in Texas with a rockstar dad and—as he would tell it—the world's most loving mom. He picked up his father's musical talent and hit the road for fame in his early twenties. When the band life chewed him up and spit him out on the wrong side of the tracks, Aaron realized more than ever his need of a Savior. He spent a year of his life detoxing the world and listening to the Heartbeat of Heaven. My life became richer when he walked through those doors." Pastor Steve pointed to the double-door entrance. "What a guy," he said a little softer, drawing from memory like it wasn't part of his prepared speech. Clearing his throat, he continued. "He was one of my favorite guitar players we ever had on our worship team. But aside from the phenomenal guitar talent he got from his father, Aaron also carried something of his mother. He loved well."

I wasn't sure if the pastor was looking at me in particular, or the whole family, but I sensed tear-filled eyes on me from all over the room.

He did love well.
He loved me so well.
Aaron loved me better than anyone ever loved me before.
I love him so much. Loved? LOVE.

My own eulogy went on in my head, and I missed the rest of the service led by Pastor Steve until Casey began singing. I was surprised she composed her emotions enough to sound so beautiful. She was a good friend to Aaron. Is? Was. He would've loved that she was singing today.

Michael took the stage as Casey's song came to an end, and Vicki reached over to grab my hand. "I want to thank everyone on behalf of my family for coming out to honor and celebrate my incredible brother Aaron." He looked down at his notes and took a deep breath before continuing. "Aaron was my favorite brother, even though he was my only brother." Light laughter filled the room.

"Our whole lives people thought we were twins. With him being older, you could tell it sometimes annoyed him, but for me, it was the best thing in the whole world. I looked up to him so much." He sniffled as if trying to hold back all the emotions banging against his insides and trying to come out. "He was more than just a brother, son, musician, boyfriend. He was one of the greatest and most genuine people I've ever known. He did love well. Thank you, Pastor, for saying that."

He shared a few stories of their boyhood adventures, which made people laugh within reason, but there was no laughter in me. It was hard to imagine there ever would be again.

This is anguishing.

I looked down at my purse, knowing it contained some of Aaron's belongings—pieces he touched that lived in his apartment. I wanted them.

But I didn't want them, because it meant he no longer owned them. What was I going to do with all of it? Lost in my thoughts again, I came to when Vicki let go of my hand to welcome Michael.

A slideshow started with pictures of Aaron throughout his life. At that moment, I knew at least one of the reasons his family went through his apartment. They must've searched on his computer in order to find some of these photos since the man didn't use social media. I recognized a few of the pictures from the early years since Marcy showed them to me a few weeks ago when I met her—how was it only weeks ago? More photos from his high school days and his rockstar days I'd never seen before filled the screen.

He looked so different back then. The shots from his teen years revealed a smaller frame paired with juvenile facial features. The photos from his band days were particularly hard for me to see. His eyes seemed hollow, and his smile like it weighed a hundred pounds. The good news was his story didn't end there.

The next picture was a selfie of us I remembered taking but never saw. Vicki grabbed my hand. The image of our ecstatic smiles was embossed in my mind even after the picture on the screen switched. I lowered my head and closed my eyes, so the picture of us remained the image I saw.

Pastor Steve wrapped everything up with a word of hope, reminding all of us even though our hearts were currently troubled, Aaron had completed his race and earned his reward. The statement was true, but his race was cut short. He should still be running. Next to me. Where we'd help each other through whatever obstacles came our way. And some children should've trailed behind us before too long. We'd eventually slow down our speed, and those grown kids would help us at a slower pace, their kids behind them. *That's* when he should've finished his race, when I finished mine too. Not now.

But the reward? I was glad he achieved it. I couldn't think of a more deserving person to celebrate and imagined all of heaven cheering him on as he arrived. Or, however all of that worked. He knew now. I still didn't.

People who wanted to offer condolences to the family and pass by the casket lined up—the part I'd been dreading. Standing with the family who'd never technically be my own while hundreds of people who packed this place out said something they thought would make us feel better, or possibly worse, nothing more to offer than eyes filled with pity, was going to be the worst part of the whole funeral. Hands down.

I had just about as much of "God needed a guitar player" and "Heaven gained an angel" as I could take for the day. Where did people come up with these things? If I wasn't so weak, I might've punched someone in the throat. Technically, I'd never, but I for sure pictured myself doing it—more than once. Grief had a way of making it harder than normal to keep my crazy side at bay.

The church shortly emptied of everyone except the family, Vicki, and me. Jack and Marcy chose to only have the family at the actual burial. For whatever reason, I didn't know. Still, a part of me was actually glad I wouldn't see my love lowered into the ground because it would be an image I'd never be able to unsee. The last few minutes I'd ever have with Aaron before the funeral home attendants came to close the casket never to be opened again ticked by fast, then slow, then started to vanish.

I will never see his face again.

Marcy stood beside the casket and ran her fingers through his hair like she did at the hospital days ago, his body just as still, only this time there was no life left in him. The final moments between mother and son were hard to watch but impossible to look away from. Jack stood behind her with his hands on her shoulders. The predominant emotion on his face was still anger. I hoped he wasn't mad at God. God didn't kill Aaron.

I wasn't sure how close I could get to him. If I closed my eyes, I could still feel my finger tracing over his hand, while fieriness still flowed through him. My heart slowed to a dangerous pace, each beat throbbing in my throat. I couldn't touch him, Marcy was the only one who did, but I had to see the beautiful features of his face one more time. Commit them to memory. I hoped they hadn't changed too much as life disappeared, and death settled in. I walked up to the closed portion of the casket, shielding him from the waist down. My eyes slowly dragged up the dark wood to his posed hands and his motionless chest.

His fawn hair, longer and kind of wavy on top. The stubble that wasn't removed in the last week of his life because I told him I liked it. Those lips that helped the world around me disappear when they collided with my own. His eyelids, forever closed, concealing the most winsome blue eyes I'd ever seen. I wanted to remember them all.

Standing there and taking him in for the last time was excruciatingly difficult, and I couldn't withstand the weight any longer. "I love you, Aaron Walker. I will miss you forever," I said in a whisper.

The last thing he said to me played again in my mind. *"Sounds perfect. I better go now. I'll see you soon."*

Only soon was now the other side of eternity, which was infinitely longer than I could handle.

If there really was only one person for everyone in the world, I'd be alone for the rest of my life. Because I found mine, and he was gone.

ABOUT THE AUTHOR

Elle (Leslie) Ann Brown is a Texas girl through and through and has lived most literally on all of the edges of the glorious state over her life but currently resides in Grand Prairie with her husband and four children. When she isn't being a mom or an author, she also co-pastors a church with her husband. She didn't pick up and read her first book for pleasure until she was thirty-two years old.

It's never too late to start.

mental notes
SERIES

www.elleannbrown.com
amazon kindle

Maddison Miller is soon to discover the best life is actually what happens after all of your plans have come crashing down. However, choosing to let go and actually doing so is the constant struggle she faces. And just when she thinks she's back on the right path to achieving her optimum goals, life comes along and scatters her Mental Notes.

Made in the USA
Coppell, TX
24 February 2023